HEART OF THE ROSE

RIKKAINE THOMPSON

ISBN: 978-0-6482970-7-9

For Kater

ACKNOWLEDGMENTS

My husband, Robert, my everlasting, for 'sponsoring' a saucier book than I suspect he knew I could write. My parents, Robyn and Neil, for constant encouragement. My amazing sister, Felicia. My brother, Daniel, who would have teased me to the ends of the Earth for writing romance, then still read it.

My three wonderful children who are growing up too fast and will *never* read this. Even if the eldest is getting ready to leave for University.

The Frakking mob, my three sisters-of-heart, who will definitely read this and start the next round of jokes.

Katie Luisier, eternal bouncing board and romance connoisseur. *Your turn!*

Elle Tharp, Sabrina Sheldon, Zhanna Postupalyo, Eden Ellis, Karyn Sands, Athiena Eades, Kym Antony, and Emily Combs for their continuing support.

CHAPTER 1

The bell above the door chimed.

The front door's fast open and close was punctuated by a blast of cold wind from outside. A crisp and clear breeze, accompanied by the noise of the morning Parisian bustle, and then it was gone and the boutique was flooded with warmth once more.

"Bonjour," Noémie chirped from the backroom where she was sorting stock to get it ready for the hanging racks. It wasn't close to Dulcie's shift start, so it had to be an early customer or a delivery. "I'll be with you in one moment." Reaching for the last of her breakfast croissant, she bit into it.

"Bonjour," a deep voice that was definitely not Dulcie said. A deep voice that sent a tingle of recognition down her spine.

Noémie tripped over a box in her haste to get out of the backroom. She stumbled, hitting her shoulder against the wall beside the change rooms and ended up sprawled on several boxes that had been tucked away in the corner.

A rush of movement as the owner of the voice hurried over to offer aid. She found herself staring at his extended hand and followed the line of his arm back up to his face.

Time had been more than generous. Once filled with boyish charm and laughter, now a carefully crafted and swoon-worthy smile that even Adonis' would pale in comparison. A face that seemed to be even kinder than the one she'd fallen for as a teen. He held out his leather-gloved hand for her, concern etched on his gorgeous features, and it was like angels had descended to offer aid.

Heir to the von Brandt fortune and face of Celestial Fashion. Sun-kissed golden hair, forest green eyes, and dazzling smile, Kian von Brandt had somehow chosen to grace her little boutique.

Her *lingerie* boutique. Chant de La Rose Lingerie. In big letters outside. The place shone feminine sexuality with its bright pink and yellow walls and its modest yet elegant rose-themed decor. Even their uniforms matched the theme, a bright yellow blouse with an intricate pink rose insignia. She specialized in women's lingerie, including adaptive and plus-size, and she didn't stock any male merchandise. So why was he here, of all the places in Paris he could be? Had the bachelor been snatched up and was buying a present for his lady love? Or was Celestial, during their expansion to Paris, looking to expand into lingerie?

Did he even remember her?

"Are you okay?"

Never in her wildest dreams would she have imagined he'd walk into her boutique. Yet, there she sprawled, frozen in shock, not at all suave and sophisticated as she would have preferred when meeting him again. Not like this, with her dark hair up in a messily braided crown held together by a pencil, nursing bruised pride, and a sore behind.

Lady luck was not smiling on her today, because between forcing down the partly-chewed bite of croissant and her battered ego trying to make her suave when she was really a mess, Noémie tried to speak and the only thing that erupted was a forlorn squeak.

A small frown marred Kian's perfect features. "Should

I call someone?" he asked in English. "Did you knock your head?"

Noémie shook her head. "Oh, don't worry, I get knocked up all the time," she replied in the same language, then her brown eyes flew wide as she realized what she'd said. "I mean—you can knock me—I knock my head all the time!" Embarrassed by her inability to hold it together, she covered her mouth with a hand. "Wow. Just wow."

Kian burst into laughter. "You haven't changed, Noémie."

He remembered her. Even after all these years, he remembered her.

She and Kian had been in the same friendship circle in England when they were thirteen. The only child of her French mother and London-born Chinese father, Noémie and her parents had moved to England when she was five so that Noémie could grow up closer to her paternal grandparents. During her primary school years, Noémie had become best friends with Zariah Talal, who, in secondary school, had fallen into a relationship with Zane Lécuyer. At the time, Zane and Kian had been best friends so the four of them had spent a lot of time together and Noémie's cute teenage crush on Kian evolved into full-blown puppy love.

Then Kian's overprotective father had shipped him back to America without a word or even a chance to say goodbye. The time differences wreaked havoc on the friendship as Zane and Kian had drifted apart. Emails and phone calls went unanswered as they threw themselves into school and then university. Noémie's crush had dwindled and disappeared as she'd met new people and had other romantic entanglements.

She'd known he'd come to Paris a year ago to help launch Celestial Paris. She'd seen him on billboards, in magazines, on television and online. She'd seen him in fashion walks, but there had never been a time to approach him to say hello and see if he remembered her from school. He was always surrounded by people and she was a small fry in a big pond.

He still had the same unbridled and carefree laughter she'd heard when they were teens. A peal of laughter that was as infectious as it was gorgeous and Noémie giggled along with him, and that same stupid crush bubbled up inside her.

For a moment, she was thirteen again, instead of twenty-four. Thirteen and in braces and braids and stuck on the thought that she knew everything there was to know about being in love when in reality she had no clue. Now, she was older. Wiser. A professional career woman, leaving her friends and family behind to attend university in Paris, then deciding to stay, now owning her own boutique, designing her own merchandise. She could talk to him like a normal person and not fumble over her words and blush at the slightest provocation. It would be nice to see if he was the same sort of person he was as a young teenager and what he'd been up to all these years.

After she found out why he was here.

"It's great to see you, Kian," Noémie said and took his hand so he could pull her to her feet. Even though Kian's French was as good as hers, she'd known him in England in her youth and because of that association, she stayed speaking English. "You look fantastic."

Fantastic and tall. Having inherited her height from her Eurasian father, Noémie was used to being shorter than her peers, but Kian towered over her. Even with her heels on, she barely came up to his shoulder.

"I think that's my line," he replied, still holding her hand. "You look *amazing*."

Noémie suppressed a flush from the touch of his gloved hand against her bare one, coupled with the appreciative look he gave her as his eyes drifted across her. Taking her hand back, she dusted down her black skirt and—with a quick glance in the mirror of one of the adjacent change rooms—fixed her appearance. "When I'm not covered in boxes."

He chuckled. "I don't know, the box look could become the new rage."

Her face burst into a smile. "If it does, let me know. I'll lead the charge."

"I'll talk to my mother," he said with a wink. "See if she'll take recommendations. Anything's better than last year's 'polka dot' craze."

Giggling, she said, "Yeah, that was really in the *spot*light."

Kian snorted. "That was a good *spot* for a pun."

"It got me out of a tight *spot*," she retorted.

He grinned widely. "Glad to see your love of puns hasn't changed. We used to have the most amazing battles! I'd almost forgotten about them."

"I'd heard you were in Paris," Noémie said, walking out of the change room alcove and led him back into the main boutique area. "What brings the great Kian von Brandt to my humble boutique?"

He smiled and averted his eyes at her proclamation of 'great'. Nodding at the display torsos by the windows, he removed his gloves as he spoke. "You know, I never picked you to work in a lingerie boutique. There are some really nice pieces here."

Noémie tilted her head at him as she took up a position behind the counter. "Did you come to check out my goods?"

The tips of Kian's ears went red, but his smile grew wider and he leaned against the other side of the counter. "Well," he said with a slow, suggestive smile. "That all depends on what you're willing to show me."

Warmth crept through her. That was a flirt! An actual flirt, not just silly or friendly banter. He never used to flirt with her. And he had definitely been checking her out. She hadn't expected him to turn on the charm. Encouraged, she kept her smile and matched his tone, "I'm sure I can find something in your size. Are you a fan of lace or mesh?"

"An immense fan of both," he drawled. Blinking, he straightened and lost the smile as he blurted, "But not on me."

"Shame," Noémie chirped. "You would look good in lace. But then, you look good in anything."

He smiled. "Thank you."

A thought occurred to her that gave her pause. Even though the media proclaimed Kian was single, that didn't mean he was. Maybe she shouldn't have gone to full-flirt-make-up-for-lost-time mode. Squaring her shoulders, she tried to be professional. "So, you're here to buy for someone special then? Do you know their size? We have lots of pieces on offer, what are you partial to on your partner? Lace, silk, satin? A combination?"

Oh, yes, Noémie. Good one. Ask about his preferences for lingerie on their first meeting since being kids.

He made a noise that sounded like a nervous twitter. "No. No special someone. My parents would never allow that."

Noémie tilted her head at that admission. It was an odd thing for him to say. She knew his father, Richard, had been overprotective and incredibly strict when Kian was younger. Richard had so many rules that Kian was required to follow, restrictions that would subsequently relax whenever Richard went away on business, which was a lot. 'I can't, my father's home' was a common reason Kian had given when he couldn't hang out. Surely now Kian was in his twenties, his father would've loosened up. "Really?"

"Yeah, I know. Pretty stupid, huh?" Kian rolled his eyes and turned so he could rest his elbow on her counter. "I'm under contract to wait for 'someone special' until I'm thirty."

Her mouth dropped open in shock. "You're shitting me." A contract? A literal contract preventing him from dating?

Kian lifted a shoulder in a shrug, like it didn't matter to

him. "It's a von Brandt family tradition. Father signed the contract and so did Grandfather. I'm supposed to focus on my studies, my career and the companies, and not romance." Dragging his gaze away from her he looked out through the windows at the front of the store. "It's not been an issue so far."

She wasn't sure how that made her feel. If it wasn't his choice as he made it seem, then he was missing out on a major part of social life. But then *why* hadn't it been an issue?

"That's *years* away," she blurted, astounded. "Are they still that overprotective? He can't expect you to blue-ball until then, can he?"

Kian laughed and winked at her. "One night stands *are* a thing, you know."

Ahh. One night stands. That explained it. "So, no one's tickled your fancy enough to make it last *more* than one night?"

"That sounds like a jab at my stamina." Though he eyed her, his smile and tone were teasing.

Noémie copied his one-shouldered shrug. "I'm just asking."

With a smile, he said, "I should've known someone who works with lingerie would leap straight into questions about sex."

She scoffed. "Lingerie isn't about sex, Kian." She put her forearms flat against the counter, clasping each elbow with her opposite hand and leaned toward him, using her upper arms to push her breasts together and provide a hint of cleavage. "It's about power."

The move produced the desired result as Kian flicked his gaze down. "I see."

Holding the pose, she elaborated, "Clothes are an integral part of personal identity. Comfort, confidence, strength, power, all these can be found in what we wear and how we wear it. A man, such as yourself, in that wonderfully tailored business suit, portrays a sense of pride and privilege. That pea coat appeals to the model in you, it cleverly shows off your figure while still keeping you warm. I bet you feel amazing wearing it. All eyes fall upon you."

Kian didn't answer, but his smile encouraged her to believe she was right.

Noémie beamed at him in return. "It's exactly the same with undergarments. If a woman finds the lingerie that she loves, makes her feel good and enjoys wearing, it's a secret confidence, worn beneath a professional appearance which will empower her."

"And the fact that lingerie can be presented during sex to tempt and tantalize is just happy coincidence, I suppose."

She smiled. "Absolutely," she assured him. "Women come in all shapes and sizes and all of them deserve to be able to slip into something that makes them feel amazing. When women feel good about themselves, their partners find that sexy." Who was this sultry vixen with the honey-coated tongue and where was she when Noémie was thirteen?

"I know I do."

Oh, the purr in his voice made her knees weak. As tempting as it was to continue to flirt with him—especially with the way he was responding to her—he was unattainable and she was working.

However, she was friends with him once, a long time ago. Could they possibly rekindle that friendship? She had missed the fun times they'd shared and wanted to know more about him as he was now.

Lifting out of her lean, she cleared her throat, brought his focus back to her face and shifted the tone of the conversation back to safer ground. "So, um, how can I help you? I'm fairly certain you didn't come for a lesson on women's sexuality and if you're not looking to buy something for a partner, then I'm at a loss at what I can do for you."

The suaveness was lost as Kian gripped the back of his neck with one hand and turned uncertain. "I came to see y—ahh"—he blinked and rushed—"I mean, um, I'm trying to get in touch with Zane. We lost contact after I left for America. He's not answered his Instagram or his YouTube messages; not that that's surprising. You're Zariah's best friend, so I figured you'd be able to tell me. I know he's coming to Paris soon and I was really hoping to reconnect with him."

"A reasonable assumption, although I'm a little disappointed you didn't come to see me," she said with a playful pout. "We were friends, too."

"I absolutely would've come and seen you, had I known you were still here," he assured her. "I thought you planned to move to Milan."

She pressed a hand to her chest and pretended to be in pain. "Ouch. That hurts. Milan? My plan was always to come here."

"Oh." That seemed to make him sheepish as he laughed at himself. "Right. Sorry."

"You're assuming that I'm still in contact with Zariah."

Kian appeared surprised at that. "You're not? But her Instagram has pictures of both of you."

Raising her eyebrows, Noémie asked, "You follow Zariah's Instagram, but you can't get a message through to her?"

He turned sulky. "I guess she's a famous travel blogger now and keeping up with her inbox is hard."

"That and she's Zane's long-time girlfriend and is sick of fans harassing her about him. If you put his name in the message, she probably ignored it on principle not realizing it was you."

Kian's eyes flared wide. "I didn't even think of that."

"It's the same reason mine's on private now."

"Ahh," he breathed with a nod. "That explains why I couldn't find yours."

Smiling, she said, "As much as I'd like to help, I don't

give out their details. If you give me yours, I can get it to him though."

Kian nodded. "He's absolutely huge now. He got to live his dream. What an amazing achievement."

"Massive." Noémie was so proud of Zane and all he'd accomplished. After building a thriving YouTube channel dedicated to his music, he was now living his dreams composing, as well as singing on stage. Along with Zariah's success as a travel blogger, they still found time to be deliriously in love. Everything was working out for them. It was hard not to be envious.

"I can't wheedle it out of you?" Kian asked in a cute tone and battered his eyelashes at her.

Thirteen-year-old Noémie would've been in a dead faint by now from the sheer fact he was flirting with her. Twenty-four-year-old Noémie squashed the urge to drag him into the backroom and see how well he could wheedle. Smiling, she shook her head and reached under the counter for her phone and scrolled through until she found what she was looking for.

Playing the message on the speaker, she rested her phone on the counter between them.

Zane's voice echoed through the speaker, with music from his hit single playing in the background. *"I don't care who it is. If the King of France asks for my number, Noémie, you have my permission to tell him to eff off."*

Zariah's long-suffering sigh sounded. *"Zane, darling, there is no King of France."*

"I rest my case. Zane out."

"So," Noémie said and shut off her phone. "Eff off, your majesty."

Kian burst into rambunctious laughter. "He hasn't changed either."

"My hands are tied," she replied with a shrug. "As I said, I can pass on your number."

After pulling his phone out of his jacket's breast pocket, he scrolled through the screen. Peeking up at her and wriggling his eyebrows, he said, "And keep it for yourself too, I hope."

She giggled at him. "I was already planning on sending you memes at two in the morning."

He laughed. "Excellent. Can't wait for that pleasure."

She flicked her gaze to him, startled by the way he said that word. It was both odd and satisfying hearing him flirt with her.

Kian held her gaze. "I fell out of touch with a lot of people. I would absolutely love a chance to catch up. May I take you out for coffee?"

Hope filled her at this chance to reconnect with him. And maybe flirt with him some more, but if he thought he could add her to his list of one night stands, he'd have to think again. "Is that before or after I give Zane your number?"

He handed her his phone, open in his contacts with his number on display. "Regardless of whether you pass on my number, I'd like to see you again."

"Coffee can be hard," she replied truthfully. She added his number to her phone and fired off a quick message to him so that he had her number. "I don't have a lot of free time during the day, but let me check my sche—"

"Dinner then," Kian responded and Noémie's spirits were uplifted by how eager he sounded for that. Accepting his phone back, he rushed, "Tomorrow night. I'll text you the details."

"I would love to," she replied.

He broke out into a grin. "Excellent." Reaching out, he plucked her hand off the counter and lifted it to his mouth, kissing the air above her knuckles and allowing his breath puff against her skin. "Tomorrow," Kian replied with a decisive and not-as-confident-as-he-probably-wanted nod.

And with that, he strode toward the door, not quite a run, but not the swagger he'd had when he walked in.

Wasn't that interesting?

As the door chimed shut, Noémie slumped against the counter and fanned herself. Fumbling for her phone, she hit Zariah's number, desperate to talk to her best friend. "You are not going to believe who just waltzed into my boutique."

CHAPTER 2

"And then Zane gets down on one knee and begs Mrs. Watson to marry him."

"While *wearing* the tutu?" Kian asked, his green eyes twinkling with laughter. "Tell me you have pictures?!"

"Absolutely!" Noémie chirped. "Zariah and I are standing there, completely dumbfounded by this point."

Kian laughed and leaned toward her, completely engaged with her story. "What did Mrs. Watson say?"

"She's not impressed in the slightest, and doing the over-the-top-of-her-glasses stern look as she gears up for a lecture." Noémie mimicked the look as best she could. "I'm sure you remember that look."

"She haunted my dreams for many years," he agreed. "It was the 'Mister von Brandt' tone she used with it. It still sends shivers down my spine."

"Mine too. But Zane, he's ready for it. He starts singing. Loudly. And off-key. He's in the middle of serenading her with 'Bicycle Built for Two'." She tilted her head. "We had to do it for the school play, were you there for that?"

"I remember," Kian said, with a nod and a smile of encouragement to continue.

"So, the whole class is basically wetting themselves with laughter and the Headmaster storms around the corner, all fire and brimstone, and Zane books it. As he's running down the hallway, the tutu falls down and he ends up with it around his ankles and does this silly shuffle-walk into the boys' bathroom to hide."

Kian guffawed. "Oh, man, I wish I'd seen it!"

Soft candlelight, a cozy corner, a nice meal, and a string quartet were all the ingredients required for an evening of reminiscing. Kian had specifically asked for a table where they could sit side by side instead of opposite each other, even requesting that the waiter rearrange the table. While she didn't object, Noémie wondered at that since they were supposed to be meeting as friends.

The waiter arrived with the bottle of wine Kian ordered and conversation dimmed while the waiter poured a glass. While Kian tasted the wine and approved it with a nod to the waiter, Noémie had an overlapping image appear in her head, one of thirteen-year-old Kian pretending to do something similar, and she had to smother a giggle and hide her smile.

"What's humorous?" he asked after the waiter had poured Noémie's glass and left.

Smiling, Noémie answered, "Do you remember that café the four of us used to go to after school sometimes? When we were supposed to be at the library. You and Zane would do this ridiculous wine tasting impression while pretending your milkshake was wine. The face you made then reminded me of it."

Kian's face lit up in memory and he grinned. "Elderberries and stinky toes!"

Pleased that he remembered, she laughed. "Exactly!"

His eyes glazed in memory and his smile warm, he said, "Man, I hadn't thought of that in years! We used to go off on huge descriptive tirades. Fun times."

She giggled. "Absolutely was."

Kian lifted his glass and held it out toward her so she

could clink her glass with his. "What do you make of this one?"

"For real, or fun?"

"For fun," he said, giving her a smile that made her heart skip.

She swirled her wine and evaded. "I was never very good at that, unless you wanted a pun in there. The fake wines were your and Zane's thing."

"Fair point," he said. "Enough about Zane, let's talk about you. You received a degree from ESMOD, but you work in a lingerie boutique. Did you give up on the dream of being a designer?"

Noémie lifted her head in surprise. "Who said I gave up? I own Chant de La Rose. All of the lingerie I have in stock are my designs, or purchased with my approval."

Startled, he rocked back on his seat. "You *own* it?"

Noémie's laughter was light and airy. "Yes. Really, I did think you, of all people, would figure out the name. Chant de La Rose. Think about it."

His eyes widened and he snapped his fingers. "Belrose-Song," he said and wilted. "I can't believe I missed that."

She giggled as he remembered her last name. "Your pun game is off."

"Atrocious," Kian said in a dramatic voice, putting the back of his hand against his forehead. "I'll never live it down."

"Lack of practice, we'll whip you back into shape."

"I deserve a good tongue-lashing. If it's not too rude of me to ask, how did you come to own Chant de La Rose?"

"Oh yes," she teased and gave him a playfully stern glare. "Very rude. How dare you." Giggling, she lifted her wine glass and took a sip. "My grandmother's grandfather built his legacy and handed it down, with the understanding that each generation would take what they need to be happy and add back into it for the next. It's not much, and certainly not von Brandt caliber, but it's enough to get us all started on the path to our dreams."

He nodded his approval. "Prudent."

"Maman used her portion to put herself through culinary school and now she and Papa own and operate one of the best chocolatiers in London and have opened a second store here. My cousin used his to beef up a down payment on land in the Bordeaux."

"Ooh, wine growers," Kian asked, intrigued. "What's the cellar name?"

Noémie shook her head. "Not wines, truffles! Although my great, great grandfather was a wine grower, which is where the legacy came from to begin with. When I graduated, Mamie's present was to front me the start-up costs for the boutique itself, since we'd been talking about it and planning it for years. I had already been selling my designs online since I was about twenty and everything grew from there."

With a puppy-like tilt of his head, he asked, "You didn't want the glitz and glamour of a job at one of the larger fashion houses in Paris? Like Chanel?"

"Glitz and glamour might make some happy, but I never wanted to be global," she said with a small shrug. "I have simple needs. I wanted to keep control over my designs and do things the way I wanted to and I have that. Besides, I don't do well in the rat race. I became a designer to help people. I love being able to design an adaptive piece of lingerie and seeing my client's face light up when they realize they have something they love they can actually wear, it really is the best thing. I love that interaction and I don't want to lose it and I'm very lucky my family was able to provide me with the opportunity."

"Adaptive lingerie?"

He was so attentive and engaged and it was wonderful. "Lingerie for people with limited mobility or special needs," Noémie explained. "There are some women who can't put their hands behind their back to unhook bras, or have difficulties removing underwear, so I modify my designs to have hooks at the front, or zippers, or buttons and stud presses. Whatever people prefer."

"Ahh. I'm impressed," Kian replied.

"Magnets are pretty popular as well, and that can be a hit for women without mobility issues too. Imagine being able to have that feeling of being able to *rip* lingerie off your partner, without damaging it."

Kian's eyes widened and his jaw made an impressive drop. "That would be so sexy!"

"That's what my customers think too." She giggled behind the wine glass and nudged his foot with hers. "Guess you didn't do your research before you came knocking at my door."

With a sheepish smile, he said, "No. Not so much. I was more after Zane's number."

"Did he call?" she asked, curious, and placed her glass back on the table. Zane had been delighted to hear Kian was looking for him but that didn't mean he'd had time to call.

"He did, thanks to you. Blasted my eardrums about losing his number, without any consideration to the fact that he lost mine too, and they invited me for dinner Friday. He has a concert Thursday, right?"

She beamed at him, glad he received an invitation too. That meant she'd see him again. "Yeah, I'll be at that dinner too, along with several other old school friends who now live in France."

His smile and eagerness felt genuine. "I'll look forward to it."

"What about you?" she asked, directing the conversation back to what they had been discussing. "Are you following your dreams?"

He pulled a face and shrugged, flopping back on the chair as he considered her question. "I enjoy what I do, but I always wanted to do more. Make an impact. Make my own choices, but somehow I'm still stuck with doing my parents bidding. I'm still a model, I thought I would've been allowed to give that up by this age."

"You don't enjoy modeling?"

"I don't like that it's the only thing people remember about me. I have a Bachelor's degree in Business and my Master's in Finance. I *run* Celestial Paris and yet people only see the model. And if they're not remembering me for that, they're patting me on the head for being my father's son. I don't like the attention it gets; it's hard to tell when someone is being genuine. I've done everything he's asked, but despite what my father wants, I don't see myself taking over."

She nodded and hoped that didn't apply to her. "Well, I always remember you as the dork who failed at pun battles and had to eat a tub of ice cream as punishment."

"I'd forgotten about that!" Kian blurted with a laugh.

Curious, she asked, "What do you see yourself doing?"

He looked away from her for the first time. "I don't know."

The sudden disengage was concerning and Noémie studied him. "You did all those extra classes in school and nothing interested you?" She frowned and tapped her chin. "I seem to remember you getting incredibly excited about a photography course … and then how sad you were when your father said no."

He snapped his gaze to her. "You remember that?"

"I remember a lot of things, especially about my friends." And especially the very few she had crushes on and awkwardly tried to find out everything she could about them.

"I have an Instagram," Kian said slowly, as though he was voicing it for the first time. "For photography. People, places, especially when I'm traveling for shoots. Never selfies, so people don't know it's me. It's got a decent following and I've had a lot of comments." He looked away again and said, "It's just a hobby."

"So?"

"So, I could never actually do anything with it, not publically. I wouldn't be allowed."

Her heart went out to him and Noémie touched the back of his hands with the tips of her fingers. "At some point, they have to let you live your life, not the one they have planned for you."

Kian shrugged. He flexed his fingers, then rested his other hand over the top of hers. "I don't see that happening any time soon."

She hadn't meant to hold his hand like this, just show support. The warmth of his touch against her skin was wonderful and the way his thumb stroked against the back of her hand made her keenly aware of him. She wasn't going to take her hand away until he wanted to let it go. "I'm sorry. If it helps, I think you'd be an amazing photographer."

He brightened. "Really?"

"Judging from your model portfolio, you know all about angles and how to make good use of lighting."

"On myself, yes. Sometimes it's hard to transfer that to other objects, but I'm working on it. You follow my model portfolio?"

"And your public Instagram."

His knee bumped into hers as he shifted in his seat. "Really?"

"Well, I do like to keep up with fashion trends but"—she lowered her eyes demurely and rubbed her thumb against his hand—"I would love to look at the photos that actually matter to you, if you would allow me to."

The flirt seemed to work as he smiled at her. "Only if you allow me to follow yours back."

Reaching for her purse with her free hand, she pulled out her phone. "Expect creepy stalker likes from way back at the beginning of history."

With a light laugh, he said, "Only if you do the same. Why did you never send me a message?"

"I wasn't sure you would remember me," she replied. "We were only friends for a year and I am an awkward bean."

"Are you kidding me?" he blurted, squeezing her hand then releasing it to reach for his phone. "I would've been thrilled if you had messaged me. I was always fond of you."

Noémie beamed at him. "Likewise."

Exchanging details, they spent a few minutes glancing through each other's Instagram's. "These are really good," Noémie said as she skimmed through his photos. "I'm impressed. Wow, the colors of that sunset, it's inspiring. Do you use filters?"

"Hmm?" he asked, leaning toward her. His shoulder pressed up against hers as he looked at the photo in question. "Not on that one."

"Where is it?" she asked, acutely aware of his closeness as well as how comfortable he seemed to be.

"In Nice. I was there for a photoshoot and took that when we were done."

"It's absolutely gorgeous."

He turned his head to look at her and the intensity in his forest green eyes sharpened for a moment. "Thank you." Clearing his throat, he moved away from her and swiped his phone. "You have a budgie!" he blurted. "Does she talk? What's her name?"

Noémie laughed. "His name is His Royal Highness, Majesty of all that is and ever will be, King Floof."

Kian burst into rambunctious laughter. "He sounds like a character. Why that name?"

"He loves water," she replied, giggling. "And when he goes for baths, he shakes afterward and just becomes this little floofy ball of feathers. He doesn't talk, but we're working on it."

"Delightful," he said. Thumbing his phone, he turned the screen around to show her. "I have a cat. I call her Purrfect."

Noémie reared her head back in surprise. 'Purrfect', the black and pink hairless cat looked more like a goblin than a cat.

Kian turned the phone back and his smile turned fond as he looked at his cat. "She's a Sphynx cat." With his chest puffed in pride, he said, "She's the ugliest thing I've ever seen and even though I've only had her six months, I can't imagine living without her."

"She looks like she'd be cold this time of year," Noémie noted. "Do you have little outfits for her?"

"I do. She's the best-dressed kitty in Paris." Kian laughed, and his smile invited her to join in.

Noémie rested the elbow closest to him on the table and placed her chin on her palm as she smiled at him. "We descended to the pet comparisons pretty quick."

"Needed to see if we were pet compatible," Kian replied. "Seems that we are."

"You know, cats like to nom on cute defenseless birds."

"Not Purrfect," he replied primly. "She's too spoiled for that. Besides, pets are a safe topic. But! Here's a decidedly unsafe question for you." Touching her arm, he leaned toward her and lowered his voice. "Have you ever caught anyone in a compromising position in your change rooms?"

Noémie laughed at his eagerness. "There's a sign that says 'One per stall' for a reason."

He grinned. "Sounds like a story," he purred. "Do share."

She shrugged. "Let's just say an older gentleman was thoroughly surprised by his lady's unmentionables and was overcome with the urge to make a closer examination of the stitching."

Kian snickered.

"We're always attentive when couples come in together. For a French woman, a beautiful set of underwear is part of her personality. We wear lingerie because we want to feel gorgeous and sexy every day and women often bring their partners in so they can choose what they like too. It's all part of the process, so men in my boutique isn't uncommon."

"As long as they take their examination of stitching elsewhere and not your boutique."

"Exactly. So we're extra helpful so they know they have an audience. The girls and I sometimes have bets on which partners are more likely to accompany the woman into the change room to 'sample'."

With a wiggle of his eyebrows, he asked, "Have you ever snuck off to the change rooms?"

She laughed. "And who would I sneak off with? I'm *working*. I've never had the incentive to risk my business." She peeked at him through her eyelashes. "I suppose that could change. They would have to be an *exceptional* specimen."

Kian grinned at her, the soft lighting from the restaurant accenting his handsome face and giving him an ethereal glow. That look of soft desire in his eyes, a silent invitation for *more* especially when directed at her, made her breath catch in her throat. It could've been the romantic atmosphere, it could have been the copious amounts of laughter they'd shared, or even perhaps the wine she'd drunk, but she was almost overwhelmed with the sudden impulsive urge to lean over and kiss him. It was way too early in the evening for that, especially since she didn't want to be added to his list of one night stands.

To distract herself, Noémie reached for her wine glass and took another sip. "What about you? Any antics backstage?"

Kian pulled a face. "Not backstage. We're usually rushed off our feet. Worried about clothing changes and concentrating on our walk."

"Models get naked back there," she pointed out.

"Who has time to notice that?" he asked. "We're surrounded by dressers and other models similarly compromised. It's polite not to mention anything. You're a designer. You must have seen copious amounts of naked chests when fitting people. It gets old after a while."

Noémie nodded in agreement. "There's a mindset that forms."

"Indeed. Product over person."

With a frown, Noémie said, "I wouldn't have been that extreme. People matter."

"In some of the fast-paced fashion houses, it's definitely that mindset," he mentioned, sounding sour about it. "You have to be the first. Be the one who sets a trend rather than follow one. Even at the photoshoots, everything is so rushed. Deadlines and designers." He smiled and winked at her. "So, the antics come at the after-parties."

Her lips swept upward as she caught his meaning. "When no one's looking."

Kian nodded. "Mostly girls flaunting or guys trying to be impressive. Prank wars and strut-offs. People slipping off together, or not bothering to slip off." He sat back and averted his gaze. "It's not happened to me."

"Shame," she said.

"Not really." He studied her and seemed to decide something. "Models and designers … are really only interested in me for one reason. To get ahead. What I can do for their brand or their careers. They don't care about me as a person. It's tiresome."

The romantic mood was fast dissipating, but that was okay. Now was a time to comfort instead of flirt. Noémie touched his wrist with two fingers. "Kian, I'm sorry. That's a horrible way to live."

With his other hand, he took her hand and placed it firmly against his wrist, leaving his hand there to hold it in place. "You're not like other girls I've had dinner with."

She didn't want to ask how many girls that was. "If you're talking about comparing me to French girls, then I would agree. I fall on the more English side of the dating scale."

"The dating customs here are so unique!" Kian declared, leaning toward her in his enthusiasm. "There's all these little rituals and nuances. I've traveled and lived all over the world and I tell you, keeping up with dating customs in each country is hard. I have to be very careful whose gaze I meet across a crowded room now, less it be confused as an invitation."

Noémie laughed, knowing exactly what he meant. "They don't 'date' here, not in the way you or I would. You can flirt as much as you like, with anyone and everyone, but if you participate in that first kiss, then you're in a relationship." She sighed and let her voice croon. "Ahh, that art of seduction though. It's something to be marveled at."

"You speak from experience?" Kian probed.

"I've lived here long enough to appreciate the techniques used," she replied. "A French man will enjoy the view and ask for nothing more. They see elegance and beauty everywhere and aren't afraid to express it. It can make a girl feel wonderful and the constant compliments certainly boost the ego." She lost her smile for a moment as an old hurt panged. "For the most part."

Kian pouted. "And here, I thought I was doing a good job."

Heart pounding in her chest in hope and anticipation, she tried to make light of it. "Depends. Are you trying to seduce me?"

"I would never presume to compare to the French," Kian replied, his hand on his chest. "But it does beg the question, why haven't you been snatched up?"

She stalled by taking a sip of wine while she considered an answer that might both satisfy and encourage him. "I'm not looking for a short-term liaison."

His smile grew wider. "I see."

"I was ultra-focused on my business for a long time," she continued. "But since I now have the income to be able to hire staff to take some of the workload, I have more spare time. So, you never know, there could be one in my future." Wondering whether that was too subtle, she asked, "I could ask the same for you."

"Well, I have a good reason," he replied.

She saw an opening and took it. "Haven't you ever been tempted to break this contract?"

The light in his eyes dulled for a brief moment and he looked away. "No."

He lied. She was sure of that, but she didn't know why. A broken heart, perhaps? And if he lied about it that meant the contract was real. She felt horrible for questioning and wanted to make amends. "Kian—"

He looked back and changed the subject. "Your mother's French, right? And you were born here?"

Noémie nodded and went along with it. "She and Papa met when he was visiting from London, and he moved here to be with her. He was an Interpreter at the time, so the move was pretty easy. We moved to England when I was five so I could grow up closer to my paternal grandparents, since my maternal ones live in Calais, it's just across the water anyway. Even though I'd come back to France a lot, coming back permanently was still a bit of a culture shock for me. I think not having an obvious accent when I speak French makes it worse, because I forget words, or never learned them, and then I get judging looks. It's tiring to say"—she switched to French to say—"'I was born here and moved away young, so I have no accent yet am still learning French'."

He laughed and pointed at her like he understood completely. "Same! That disapproval. If you get something wrong and you don't have an accent, they look at you like you're a complete dumbass! Glad I'm not alone in that. Sometimes I have to American-up my French when I forget words and my mother *hates* it."

"It's so weird!" she agreed.

He nodded. "That's why she pushed so hard to open Celestial Paris here. It gave her an excuse to come back and throw me into her culture, so I don't American it up too much."

"It was only a matter of time Celestial came here," she said. "Since you're doing incredibly well in the other fashion capitals. After New York, London, Tokyo, and Milan, I'm surprised you waited this long to open one here."

He shrugged as though it didn't matter. "My father likes to … well … monopolize as much as he can. Earn as much money as possible. Open a new location every few years."

"There's such a thing as too much money."

He grinned. "Don't tell him that."

She giggled and then asked, "Dating woes aside, are you enjoying Paris?"

"I am," Kian replied and sat back in his chair, glancing around the restaurant. "It's nice to settle down somewhere and think about some long-term goals. I bought an apartment. I have a pet and that's a first for me."

She smiled, happy for him. "So you'll be here a while?"

He pursed his lips as he nodded. "I hope so. Father is using Celestial Paris as a proving ground for me. I'm doing all of the business and finance sides of management while Mom focuses on the designs."

"And still modeling on top of that?"

Kian inclined his head.

That surprised her. He must be working so hard, managing and modeling. How would he have time for anything else? "You must be incredibly busy."

He shrugged, then his eyes focused on something beyond her. He retreated from her as he sat back with a smile. "Here we go."

Seeing their dinner approaching, she retreated as well to give the waiter more space to place the food, switching to French to thank him and offer compliments about the plating.

"This place is famous for its duck," Kian said as his meal was placed in front of him. "I've not had the opportunity to try but it looks delicious."

Distracted by their meals, chatter returned to more neutral topics such as the winter celebrations, politics, and pet antics.

Kian was easy to talk to and his laughter made her heart pound. It was surprising how much they'd had in common too. A love for cosplay for example. A passion for the cliché sunset walks. Followed the same YouTubers. Enjoyed the same genre of movies.

Conversation flowed from one topic to the next with ease, and they never ran out of things to say. They talked about her business and his modeling. They talked about charities they helped, Kian expressing eager interest in the special needs and adaptive wear charities that Noémie participated in, and Noémie listened with rapt attention as Kian explained the amazing things the charities he donated to had managed to accomplish to aid the homeless or send kids to school. They talked about his overprotective parents and discussed her parents and their chocolate shops. They talked about Zane and Zariah and the possibility of wedding bells in the pair's future.

They talked about the other friends they'd made in school and it seemed that Kian was lacking in that department. The only name that popped up with any regularity was someone called Charlie, someone he'd met in high school in America and still had regular contact with. He talked about acquaintances, not friends. That made her sad, especially when he mentioned he'd never stayed in one place long enough to form lasting relationships. His parents were always moving to their next business endeavor and dragging him with them or shipping him away to school.

By the end of the night, her cheeks hurt from smiling so much, her side hurt from the laughter they'd shared, and she was sure it wouldn't take much to fall in love with him properly this time.

While the flirty, lustful side of her was deep in desire and denial, the more rational and mature side pondered whether it was possible he only wanted one thing from her, that maybe he had changed that much and saw her as a conquest. There were other friends she'd grown up with who had gone playboy in their later years, breaking a string of hearts. It wasn't a stretch to think he might have changed too.

She didn't want to be one among many in an apparently long list of one night stands. She wanted to be special, to feel special. She wanted romance, love, and long-term. She could see that with Kian and if she ruined it now with a one night only clause, she mightn't get another chance.

His touch, so warm and tender, made her feel wonderful and he'd done no more than touch her wrist and her arm, and one brush against the small of her back as they'd left the restaurant and bid each other goodbye.

The way Kian responded to her and the way she responded to him made her wonder if this contract even existed. Through the flirting, the smiles, the coy looks, and the tender touches, there was also genuine laughter. True joy and companionship and a rekindled friendship. A connection she couldn't explain. They were testing the waters to see which way they fell. Right now, she didn't mind which way they fell as long as they fell somewhere.

She could flirt and tease and see if there was anything in his feelings that they could build from. See how rigidly he followed his family's contract if there was one at all. She wouldn't coerce him into breaking it, but she wouldn't sit idly on her intentions either.

If she had to wait until he was thirty before anything began, so be it, but he would know she was waiting this time instead of living with a crush she'd kept secret and losing the opportunity. She wouldn't let that happen this time.

Paris was the city of love, after all. Perhaps it could work its magic on them.

CHAPTER 3

"Really?" Zariah asked, her English accent echoing through the speaker of Noémie's phone. The pair were catching a few minutes of chat time through the messaging application Discord while Noémie worked on her mannequin torsos and Zariah baked. Finding time for them to talk instead of sending memes and messages was hard, but they always managed to find a few snatches every couple of days. "Another one tonight?"

Noémie removed the pencil from her mouth and put it back in the holder on the table. "Yes."

"Wow. He's moving quick."

Noémie rolled her eyes. Prying off a piece of invisible tape, she used it to secure the strap to the display torso she was preparing. "We're *friends*, Zaz."

"Uh-huh. What five-star restaurant did he take you to Saturday night? And where's he taking you tonight?"

She was never going to hear the end of it, but it was nice being able to gossip about romantic entanglements with Zariah about something related to herself instead of Zane. "I told you, there's some sort of no-dating contract. He can't and you know I don't like one night stands."

"Maybe you should start. And then keep going."

Noémie laughed.

"I mean, he was *responding* to you flirting, wasn't he? And doing a healthy amount of his own."

"Well … yes." Heat rose to her face. "He was … he was *excellent* at it."

"Girl, you got it bad already. You practically breathed that word. '*Excellent*'," she puffed out, copying Noémie's wistful tone. "Wow."

Embarrassed, Noémie muttered, "Shuddup."

"Besides," Zariah said with a little huff. "I personally think that contract is bollocks."

"Rich people all have their crazy traditions."

"Bol-locks," Zariah sang.

"Even if he considers this a date, it's only the second and you know that whole third date clause Americans have."

"Yes, but you could snog."

"Stop it," Noémie said, exasperated. Another piece of tape secured to the inside of the cup of the bra to keep it in position and she pressed her hands against the front of it to make sure both cups were level.

"He looks like he'd be a good snogger. C'mon, Noémie, you need to get back in the dating game."

She wasn't sure about it. Kian, yes, but the contract gave her pause. "I … I don't know."

"It's been years. Time to open yourself up to the possibility of being loved again. You've probably got cobwebs."

Noémie threw a glare at the phone even though Zariah couldn't see. "Hey!"

"So, what are you wearing to this second 'not-date'?"

Noémie rolled her eyes and scooted her stool around to the back of the torso to make sure the panties were secure. "I thought I'd start with clothes and go from there."

"Oh, that sass is so snazzy. You know I'm talking about your underthings."

"Zaz!"

"It could happen! You need to be prepared."

"You are incorrigible."

"Looking out for you, that's all. Oh, come on, Miemie, he's gorgeous. Your crush on him was huge and you were so cut up when he left. You already know each other pretty well and—"

"I knew him then. This Kian is all new and I'm enjoying learning about him. Besides, I'm not looking for a relationship—"

"*Liiiiies.*"

Noémie finished that torso and scooted to the next one. Picking up a lacy teddy she'd chosen to be in the window for the next few days, she set to the task of dressing the torso. "I'm not looking for a relationship with someone who only wants one night. Or can't date."

"That's better. He could always be lying about the contract to save face."

Tired of the interrogation, Noémie changed the subject. "What time does your flight get here tomorrow?"

"Oh. Nice redirect. We're talking about you and your underthings. I'm onto you." Zariah sighed and Noémie heard the clatter of a spoon and then paper flipping. "Okay. So. Flight's in at two and it's Wednesday now, not tomorrow."

"Aww, what?" Noémie whined. "What happened? I was looking forward to seeing you!"

"'Scummanager' booked Zane into a last-minute recording session, so now instead of being completely rested for the rehearsal, he's cramming."

"Argh!" she complained, feeling Zariah's indignity as her own.

"Tell me about it. I'm so pissed that he keeps doing this. We've told him under no circumstances is he to book anything on Friday night or Saturday morning, leaving us free for Friday's dinner. I'm looking forward to seeing Kian."

"Ouch," Noémie teased, glancing at her phone.

"Betrayed by my best friend. Woe is me, however will I go on? Here I thought you were coming to see me."

"Dude," Zariah deadpanned. "Who was it that pushed you to enter this year? Don't give me that. I'm *only* coming because of you. Oh, that reminds me! Are you doing anything Sunday?"

Noémie frowned. "Yes. *Recovering*. We're having a girl's night Saturday, remember? Dinner and dancing. You wanted to try the clubbing scene. I plan on getting very drunk and then never waking up Sunday."

"I caaan't," Zariah whined. "Sunday I have to take a trip out to … ahh, I forget the name. A winery for a fluff piece they commissioned, but they only speak French and mine's so rusty it is non-existent. Google translate only goes so far. Dinner, dancing, drinking responsibly and then I take you to a winery Sunday? Please?"

Noémie pretended to consider. "Gee, I don't know. I'm pretty booked solid. So much stuff to prepare. Sleeping to do. And my best friend's coming to town and needs my attention."

"Exactly!"

"Who said I was talking about you?"

Zariah laughed. "You can't tell, but I'm fluttering my eyelashes like mad at you."

Laughing, Noémie agreed. "Sounds like fun."

"Excellent. Now," Zariah continued, her voice returning to the happy chirp of someone who wanted gossip. "Can we get back to what underwear you're wearing tonight?"

Noémie rolled her eyes and sighed. "I'll finish dressing these then I'll send you a picture."

"So you *have* chosen a set to wear tonight! I expect deets. Complete and in triplicate!"

"Down girl. All you'll get is mannequin pictures."

"I'll take it."

Signing off, Noémie finished the dressing duties, before she pushed each torso in front of a blue cloth backdrop and took photos so she could update Chant de La Rose's Instagram page and website.

As she was uploading them, her phone buzzed.

Kian

> How does Epicure sound? Say Eight?

Noémie's eyes widened at his suggestion, then she bit her lip to consider her answer. Three Michelin stars, Epicure was one of the best restaurants in Paris and had a price tag to match. She'd always wanted to go but could never justify the cost.

Noémie

> While I appreciate the enthusiasm, that is out of my price range. Don't you need to book months in advance?

Kian

> My treat.

Noémie

> Well then, who am I to refuse? I'll just have to order the most expensive meal on the menu, and wine. Lots and lots of wine.

Kian

> If that makes you happy, then by all means. Your smile alone is worth a fortune.

Noémie

> You flirt. Do it more.
>
> But I get to take you out next time.

Kian

> That's fair.

Noémie

> I know a really good baguette place where you can get two baguette sandwiches for the price of one. winkyface.emoji

Kian

> Lol okay

Noémie

> I'm teasing. There are a few really nice places I've been dying to try. I'm gradually working my

way through the cafes and restaurants, but there's just so many.

Kian

So, the way to a girl's heart is through her stomach?

Noémie

Technically, the way to my heart is through my breasts.

Kian

omgcat.jpeg

Noémie

Oh please. I'm sure both of us have seen enough breasts to last a lifetime. I'll see you tonight.

Zariah

DID YOU FORGET MY PICTURES? Answer, woman!

With a light laugh, Noémie lifted her camera and snapped a shot of the bra and panty set she had set up. Switching back into her messages, she hit the newest message and inserted the picture.

Veroniqué, Noémie's youngest staff member who was working her way through her fashion degree, wheeled herself up to the sewing room doorway. She'd come in for an adaptive wear fitting six months ago and ended up meshing so well with Noémie and Dulcie, Noémie offered her a part-time job while she finished university. Since she was working on a degree, Noémie often had her help out with the seamstress side of this job as well and the option to take her on as a junior designer when she finished was floating around in Noémie's head. "Dulcie's back from her break," she said, brushing her blonde bangs away from her face before resting her hands on her lap. "All today's shipping orders are finalized and ready for tomorrow's post."

Tapping send, Noémie lifted her head and beamed. "Excellent. Classes tonight?"

"Yeah. We're doing presentations, so I'm a little

nervous."

"You'll do great," Noémie said.

"They look amazing," Veroniqué said, nodding at the display. "Do you want me to ask Dulcie to bring any of those out?"

"No. It's only a couple of changes today, I'll do them after we close," Noémie replied. "Good luck with your presentation."

Veroniqué smiled at her and turned her wheelchair to wheel away. "Bye!"

Smiling, Noémie looked down at her phone and gasped. Kian's messages glared back up at her.

Kian

> I'm looking forward to it

Noémie

> <image1175.jpeg> sent.

She'd sent the picture of the bra and pantie set to Kian, not Zariah. Worse was the dotted line that worked to show Kian was replying. Thumbing the phone, she sent a panicked message to Zariah.

Noémie

> I sent the picture of my bra to Kian instead of you!

Zariah

> ahsdjahsd while you were wearing it?

Noémie

> It was lingerie for the window! And we were just sort of flirting and omg. What do I do?

Zariah

> OWN IT!

Holding her breath, she switched back over to Kian's messages to see what he'd replied.

Kian

> Breathtaking. I'm certain it looks better on you.

Noémie made a noise rather like a tea-kettle boiling. She squeezed shut her eyes and scrunched up her face, then switched to Zariah's number.

Noémie

He's gonna think I'm coming onto him!

Zariah

You are!

Noémie

Not this strong! It's all harmless fun atm.

Zariah

Use it as a talking point tonight. He's been flirting up a storm, that has to mean something right? Now the ice is broken, see how he really feels.

By the time she arrived at Epicure, Noémie was a nervous wreck. The place was exquisite and she'd never dined anywhere like it before, not even when she'd lived in London. It was fine to splurge and treat oneself to these sorts of places but Noémie wasn't sure she was the type of person to be comfortable dining like this every night. If this was the sort of place Kian liked to frequent, if this was where he felt at home, she was severely under classed and out of her comfort zone. But she couldn't be sure he wasn't showing off and throwing a bit of wealth around to impress.

She'd taken extra care to dress elegantly for tonight. She'd tangled her dark hair up in a classic twist, accented by a delicate flower and pearl comb, applied a light bronze eyeshadow above her brown eyes, and pinked her lips. Because it was winter, she'd opted for a long sleeve dress over short, but the sky blue dress was a snug fit on her torso and flared at the skirt.

Kian was already at the table when she arrived and he rose out of his chair as she approached, escorted by the Host for the evening. The chairs and cutlery were positioned on opposite sides of the table, instead of side by side as they'd had on Saturday night.

"You look enchanting," he said, holding the back of

the chair to help her sit.

With the chair between them, there was no option to kiss his cheek in greeting. "Thank you," she replied and left her small clutch on the table beside her as she took her place.

The Host handed them over to their waiter for the evening, who graciously suggested several wines and presented them with their menus.

"This place is amazing," she said looking around after the waiter had given them some space to decide what they wanted to order and fetch the champagne Kian had asked for.

"The food is absolutely divine," Kian said.

Not sure what she wanted to do with them, she clasped her hands on her lap. "Do you come here often?"

He nodded. "With Mom. She loves the food and she loves dragging me out to places like this, then never allows me to order what I want to eat. So I sneak back when she's not in town to try the food out."

Noémie's eyes widened and her stomach dropped.

Spotting her expression, Kian assured her, "She's in London."

Noémie puffed out a breath. "She's …"

"Mom can be scary. I'm aware. I remember the ice cream debacle."

Noémie cringed. "I don't think I've ever been yelled at so much in all my life."

Lips pressed together, Kian nodded. "You and me both, especially because we got so sick over her nice shoes in the middle of her rant."

"Do you think she's forgiven me?"

"I don't think she remembers."

Noémie allowed herself a small sag. "That's a relief." Smiling, she asked, "If she never lets you order what you want, what are you going to sample today?"

He held her gaze for a long moment before he dropped it to the menu. "We'll have to see what the chef's suggestions are."

Noémie worried her bottom lip with her teeth, then looked down at her menu. Last dinner, he would've been laughing with her, tonight, he seemed to look straight through her.

The atmosphere was awkward. Different from the cozy dinner they'd shared on Saturday night. It was bright and the waiters were attentive and eager to charm and serve. It didn't help that Kian seemed to know all the waiters by name and they all looked upon her with curiosity before inquiring after his mother. And it certainly didn't help that she expected Celeste von Brandt to appear at any time and question what Noémie was doing with her son.

Noémie didn't know if it was the elegant atmosphere or the way Kian seemed to be evaluating her every move, but she was uncomfortable and out of her element.

After the waiters had supplied them with champagne, Noémie tried to find something to say. "So … um … How was your day?"

"Routine, I guess," Kian replied. "It's always pretty tough to balance a large company like Celestial. So many different personality types all meshed together and I have to manage them to get them to work toward a singular goal. I don't suppose you'd have that problem."

Noémie was taken aback at the sudden rudeness in his attitude when she compared it to Saturday. He was blasé, bland. "No. I guess not. I saw Celestial in the lineup for next week's walk. Will you be walking?"

"If my mother gets her way," Kian said in a tone that suggested he wasn't interested, but she didn't know if it was the conversation that bored him, or his mother making him walk. "And she usually does. We still have a few days before final decisions on models are made, so I'm hopeful I'll be able to get out of it."

"What about the outfit selection?" she asked, genuinely interested. "I always loved Celestial's clothes for men, they're so stylish. You always look gorgeous."

"Again, that's my mother's department. I just manage the people and make sure everything's ready for her to do her job."

"Oh. I see." Noémie waited, expecting that he'd ask if she'd be attending. Or if she'd be entering her brand in the lingerie walk that was coming up in two weeks. She and Zariah had worked hard to get their exhibit organized and while she was excited about it, it would be her first one and she was nervous too.

Kian said nothing as he studied his champagne glass.

Noémie, not sure what else to do, picked up her glass and gulped a generous mouthful without really tasting. Putting it back down, she ventured, "Is something wrong?"

Kian sighed and shuffled in his chair. "Bad day."

"I'm sorry," she said, wanting to reach out and take his hand but unable to because neither of them were on the table. "We don't have to have dinner if you're not feeling up to it."

He waved his hand. "No. No," he said and gifted her with a dazzling smile. "I'm fine. I should leave work at the door and focus on spending time with you, right?"

The smile didn't feel real. It didn't sit on his face right and alarm bells went off in Noémie's head. "I … I think maybe I should … um …"

Kian's expression slid into a knowing smirk. "Change your mind, did you?"

"I beg your pardon?"

"I've gotten texts like that before."

Noémie's heart sank. So, his abrupt change in attitude was about the picture. She should've cleared the air straight away, instead of leaving it hanging between them. "I'd like to explain—"

"Granted, it's normally a real person flaunting lingerie and not a mannequin. They flirt and tease, trying to get themselves into my bed. They're very over the top. Lots of touching and 'totally accidental' slippage to show me what they're wearing and invite me to see more. After that picture … Well, you're just the same, aren't you?"

Noémie drew back at the hostility in his voice. "You said you liked it."

"I thought you were different. I thought that sweet girl I knew would never change. You just couldn't help yourself, could you? One meal together and you show your true colors. You're like all the rest, after my body, my money, or Celestial. It's never about me."

Where was the cute and funny guy she knew? Where was the dork who filled his pockets with stones and frog spawn with Zane on a sunny afternoon? Where was the gangly-legged kid dancing at the arcade as they spent all their pocket money on Dance Dance Revolution? Where was the boy who lost a pun battle and had to eat so much ice cream that he puked all over his mother's shoes?

Was he really gone? Had he changed that much?

Lifting her chin, Noémie snapped, "The picture was an accident." She lifted her napkin off her lap and dropped it onto the table. "It wasn't meant for you. It was meant for Zariah. I was chatting to her at the same time and wasn't watching who I sent it to. She convinced me that all your flirting meant something and to leave it."

"A likely story," Kian scoffed.

Noémie snapped open her clutch, yanked out her phone, and opened up Zariah's last message, shoving the screen toward him. His head reared back in surprise as he focused on the words and she watched realization, then horror dawn on his face. "I thought having dinner would be my chance to see if *you'd* changed from when we were kids. To see if we could build something, even if that was just rekindling our friendship. To see if that same funny, cute, dorky guy still existed." Shoving away from the table, she stood. "I can't believe I ever thought we had potential."

Noémie spun on her heel and stalked toward the door.

She'd badly misjudged the entire situation. Part of it

had been her fault by not coming clean about the picture, but he didn't have to be so harsh about it all. He didn't have to accuse her of things she didn't intend when in all likelihood, he'd accepted offers like that before.

She wasn't going to cry. Not now. Not over this. The tears pricking at the corners of her eyes could just wait. She wasn't going to acknowledge them.

"Noémie, wait—"

"Rather not," she said, shoving the main entrance open without even putting her coat on first.

She didn't make it far, not with the weather being so crisp and cold. She couldn't afford to get sick, she had so much prep work she had to do. Falling ill right now would put her back so far. But her winter coat didn't want to slide on and it tangled as she wrestled with it.

"Noémie, let me help—"

She jerked away from him. "Don't touch me!"

Kian's hands flopped to his sides. In his hurry, his gray winter coat was thrown over his shoulder and left to hang. "I'm sorry."

"I can't believe I *ever* had a crush on you," Noémie whined, still wrestling with the coat. "Why couldn't you have stayed in my past where I could remember you fondly? Why'd you have to come back now? "

"I'm sorry," he said again, his voice ringing with regret. "You were supposed to be the highlight of an incredibly shitty day. And I fucked it. "

"Damn right you did." She sniffled, finally getting her arms through her coat. Doing up the buttons, she said, "You've probably gotten that message hundreds of times. You've probably followed it through just as many. Why do I have to be the one who gets yelled at for it?"

"I have *never* had a one night stand," he insisted. "I need an emotional connection before I'll sleep with someone. Which makes it incredibly difficult considering I'm not allowed to get emotionally involved with anyone. I'm sorry, please give me a chance to explain."

"You didn't give me one," she muttered.

"I know. You don't owe me anything. If you walked away now, I'd never bother you again. Just know I'm really sorry."

Reaching into her pocket for her gloves, she wondered why she was still standing there. But she was. And she was listening because she wanted an explanation. "Talk," she muttered.

He puffed out a breath, then rushed, "There have been so many people throwing themselves at me, models and staff at Celestial, and daughters of my parent's friends—and—it's … so hard to know who to trust. No one in Paris knows me as Kian and not the supermodel face of Celestial. No one except you. I was so excited when I found out you were here. I thought, maybe I'd have a chance, a real chance at something more. Something special."

Noémie frowned at the ground. "So asking for Zane's number was a ploy."

"An excuse," he admitted. "I could have gotten it other ways but I wanted to see you. Asking for Zane's number … was a back up in case you were …"

He *had* come to see her. "In case I was what?" she prompted.

"Dating someone else," he mumbled. "Or married. Or … I didn't know what to expect. I couldn't bring myself to look you up … and then you responded to me in ways I always dreamed you would and it made me so … I was *happy*."

She flicked her eyes up to him. "Dreamed?"

He gave her an unhappy smile. "I had the hugest crush on you when we were kids. But … I knew we were only in London for as long as it took to get Celestial London up and running and … I didn't want to hurt you. Or myself."

She didn't know what to do with that information. Ten minutes ago, it would've made her happy. Now, it made her sad. "You put me on a pedestal, and then got angry when I supposedly betrayed an imagined expectation. You don't even know me."

"I know some parts of you," he replied softly. "I know you're very driven and passionate about your designs and you love what you do. I know you're thankful for Veroniqué and Dulcie and how well they work with you. I know you have a precious bird you love dearly and your face lights up when you talk about him. I know that when you laugh, really laugh, you throw yourself into it and it's absolutely stunning. You're right, there's so much I don't know anymore, but I *want* to. I want to know you."

Staring at him, she had no response to that.

He took a tiny step toward her. "I'm so sorry. I know it doesn't excuse anything, but I really am."

His words were enough that she was willing to listen. With a nod, she said, "Go on."

With a ragged sigh, he continued, "I ... I tried to break the contract before. And it went bad. It went so *bad*. It almost ruined me. I thought ... if you and I took things slow. If we learned about each other, if we made sure we were still the sort of people who could fit together, I could be more confident about it all. But, I should've talked to you. I should've made my intentions clear."

She nodded. "You should've." She pushed her hands into her gloves, then had to take them off again to get her fingers in the right slots. "It went bad?"

Kian gulped. "Can ... can we go back inside for this conversation? Where it's warm? Please, there's more to explain."

Noémie shook her head. "But I'll give you a chance to put your coat on before I start walking toward the metro."

He fumbled for his coat, shoving his arms through the holes before he fell into step beside her while doing the buttons up. "I have my car. I can drive you."

And lock her in a moving vehicle with no chance of escape? "No," she replied, her tone just shy of a snap. "The metro station is two streets that way. I suggest you talk fast."

"I … okay, fair enough." He cleared his throat and shuffled. "When I was nineteen I fell in love. Or in lust, I can't really tell anymore. She was a budding designer and she was everything I thought I wanted. She was—I defied my father and declared I was ending the contract to formally date her and … well, he kicked me out. Cut me off completely."

Noémie raised her head and glanced at him. "Wow."

"It wasn't … it wasn't bad, at first. I had some money. My father couldn't take what I earned myself. All that modeling I was doing, I had some income. But, I mean, living at home was all I'd ever known, so I turned to her, expecting that because she said she loved me, she'd understand and be supportive." His voice got quiet and sad. Hunched shoulders to make himself smaller, he seemed to shrivel as he spoke. "Because I no longer had the money to wine and dine her like she expected, because my family's wealth was cut off, she didn't want to have anything to do with me. It'd been a ploy and since I didn't have what she wanted, she dumped me faster than you could snap your fingers. I found out later she'd won a job at Celestial. So … she got what she wanted."

"Bitch," she ground out. What a horrible thing to have to deal with and the wave of dislike for this person who hurt Kian was intense. But it could also be a ploy to make him seem sympathetic, and she had to keep that in mind, even though she suspected it wasn't the case. The emotion in his voice, his body language, it all indicated a deep hurt.

Kian's puff of breath was humorless. "My father had warned me that there would be a lot of young women out there who saw me as a cash cow, and that's what the contract was designed to prevent. I didn't listen. Thought I knew better." Defeated and sad, he shoved his hands deep into his coat pockets. "I tried to hold it together, tried to continue living the only life I knew, but I was bleeding money and living beyond my means and … then modeling work dried up. I think because Mom … so I had a partial degree, no job, and no savings. I was in New York and I was too well known. People didn't believe I was willing to work in a coffee shop or a store … I'm a von Brandt, no one wanted to risk hiring me, so …" he shrugged. "I eventually found a job at a youth center. It wasn't much, but it was enough to survive on and honestly, it was the best six months of my life. It opened my eyes to how many people struggle daily, so I vowed to make a difference. Mom found out and declared that 'menial work' was unbecoming of a von Brandt and talked to him on my behalf and … next time, he said he wouldn't take me back."

Noémie nodded in understanding. "That's why you're so proud of the charities you donate to."

He lit up for a moment at the mention of his charities. A good memory among the dark and his reaction felt true. He was proud of them. "They mean the world to me. Being able to help those who opened their arms and welcomed me was the first thing I did after having money again. I would be a very different person if it wasn't for them." Studying her for a second, Kian pressed on, "Now, I'm living on my own. I have my degrees, I have my partnership at Celestial. I own my apartment. I have Purrfect. I have prospects and I'm able to help a lot of people. He doesn't have a name here, but I do. Defying the contract again won't be an issue. It's more a matter of motivation."

Bitterness filled her and she hugged her arms to herself. "If the person was worth it. And because of that picture, I wasn't."

"No. No. Noémie." He reached for her arm and stopped shy of touching her. "You *are* worth it. I'm an ass. It … it's been an incredibly bad day and I reacted badly. It's been … my father … he wants to pull me from Celestial Paris, claiming I'm not ready for an executive role but I'm fighting tooth and nail to stay here."

"I can see why that would put you on edge." Kian had thrown himself into Celestial Paris, she'd heard the way he'd talked about it. To lose that … She frowned. "If your father would disown you for dating, aren't you already risking your position at Celestial?"

Kian gave her a sad smile. "He can disown me for falling in love," he explained patiently. "He can't fire me for it. My position is under contract and I have a partnership. The most he can do is transfer me. I've already checked, so I'm not worried about that."

"Oh. Right. Okay." That made sense, and she really should've realized that. It sounded like his parents were using this contract as a way to control him, but she didn't think she should mention that. He probably realized that himself. It might have been prudent to have something like that when he was younger and impulsive, in a skewed sort of way, if he was the type of person to be frivolous with who he loved, but to keep it until he was thirty would be torture.

Why break it at all? Why go to all this trouble? She flicked her eyes to him. Head down, hands in pockets, shoulders slumped as he trudged by her side. He wanted to make this up to her, but why? Why her? Was he lonely? He said it was hard for people to see past the money. He was looking for someone who saw him.

"I shouldn't have reacted the way I did," Kian mumbled. "It's not your fault. I thought I was in a better place mentally and—and ready for—I'm sor—"

She nodded again. "No more sorrys, Kian," she said. "I get it."

They stopped at a street corner and waited for a car to turn before they crossed the road. The metro entrance was getting closer, and Kian slowed down, trying to delay. "Noémie?" he prompted, sounding rushed. "Please, can I try again? Can we—I'd like to try. I can make this up to you. I promise I can."

Noémie lifted her head and looked up into the inky

black sky, peering at the tiny stars, dimmed by the surrounding Parisian glow. While he reacted badly, there were certain things he'd done right. He'd come after her straight away and explained himself. He apologized, more than once. He followed her directives on what she would allow, wasn't forcing her into anything or demanding. He offered her a lift in his car which, in hindsight, came from a place of generosity rather than trying to trap her; didn't press when she said no, walking with her while he explained. He was asking for another chance. He'd never once called her derogatory names, or swore. That set him apart. Did his explanation change things? Maybe. She didn't know. But it deserved some reciprocation on her part.

"I dated in university," she said. "A fellow fashion designer. Had myself someone I thought I could spend the rest of my life with. He was cute and funny, and very popular. Always surrounded by friends and I was drawn to that."

"What happened?" he asked, his voice soft and gentle.

"We were together for a year. I thought we were exclusive right up until I found him in bed with someone else." Her voice turned sour as the memory filled her mind. "He laughed at how upset I got and told me that we weren't even dating, that he considered me a friend with benefits, and I was stupid for putting a label on something. He even tried to blame it on the French way of life, you know? That whole idea of a mistress around every corner. City of love, why not share it around? But he was a dick. The French pride themselves on being discreet, if they choose to have one. There's a culture and a courtesy surrounding it. He wasn't discreet and he wasn't French and he was in *my* bed."

He reached for her to offer comfort, then let his hand fall back into his pocket as he murmured, "I'm so sorry that happened to you. That's horrible."

Acknowledging that with a nod, she stared straight

ahead. "Everyone has a sob story, Kian. Everyone has their own demons to fight. You're not the only one who was hurt in the past. I prefer clear and open communication. I have been down that road of secrets and lies before and it's not pretty. I don't want to do it again. I need you to be able to give me the benefit of doubt without jumping to conclusions like that. If something bothers you, talk."

"I can. I will."

Noémie stopped at the entrance of the metro and gazed down the stairs. "And it's not all on you. I need to prove that I can be trusted too. I should've told you the picture was an accident straight away and I didn't. If I had, none of this would've happened. I'm sorry for that."

Kian dropped his head so low his chin was almost on his chest. "We're both damaged."

"No," Noémie said and turned to face him. "We're both cautious, and that's okay. We can learn from the past and make this one a better experience."

Lifting his head to look in her eyes, he seemed to approve of that sentiment.

"Relationships are a two-way street and … if there's to be one, then we're already off to a rocky start." Taking a deep breath, she released it in a gentle puff. "I was honestly ready to be all-in and see where the flirting took us and now I'm not. I need to think. I need a chance to talk this through with Zariah. And she's probably going to want to kick your ass."

Kian's shoulders hunched as he curled in on himself. "I deserve that."

She smiled. "Maybe." Taking her hand out of her pocket, she held it out to him as an invitation to take it in a way that was more familiar than a handshake.

Kian shook his hand loose from his coat and rested it in hers.

"I'll see you at Zane's dinner on Friday," she said, squeezing his hand. "We can talk about this then."

CHAPTER 4

Noémie pressed her finger to the buzzer of the townhouse Zane and Zariah had rented for the duration of their stay in Paris and heard thumping feet in response.

"Noémie," Zariah announced, thrusting open the door. Born in Egypt, Zariah Talal had moved to England at age two when her mother, who Noémie knew affectionately as Mama Talal, married an Englishman. With her always-gorgeous mess of brown curls, tawny skin, and dark honey-colored eyes, Zariah always looked like she'd walked straight out of a movie set. Even now, looking harried and rushed, with her cheek smudged with flour and her apron covered in splotches, Zariah was beautiful as she blurted, "*Help,*" then rushed off back inside.

Noémie shrugged out of her yellow coat and left it on a hook at the door, carrying the basket she'd brought with her farther into the apartment. "What's wrong?"

"Everything!" Zariah called. "It's a mess and I haven't had a shower yet! Zane was supposed to be the one cooking, not me, and that stupid manager of his pulled him out. This is a two-chef menu!"

"Why didn't you call me earlier?" Noémie called, making her way through the apartment. "I would've come to help."

Zariah appeared out of a room and shoved an apron around Noémie's neck, then hurried away as she vented, "The prick *promised* me Zane would be back by now! We deserve to have a life beyond singing and music and concerts!"

"Absolutely, you do. What do you want me to do?"

"You know how to make a ..." Zariah cleared her throat. "Okay, I'm gonna butcher this." She pronounced the words slowly and with great care. "Boeuf bourguignon?"

"Close," Noémie replied as she tied the apron at the back and glanced around the apartment. Separate dining and living spaces. Beyond the lounge set that surrounded a lit fireplace, she could see a small closed-off balcony. "But yes, I know."

"Please, can you start?" Zariah called from the kitchen. "We can let that simmer through starters and seconds, right? The recipe said three hours simmer time."

Noémie followed her voice. Spotting the table, she placed her box of goodies her parents had sent in the middle of it. "Yes, there'll be enough time."

"I need some wonderful French person to set the table and do a cheese platter."

Noémie snorted as she saw the hurricane in the kitchen. It was small and had a tiny alcove attached which joined the dining and living areas. Tucking her basket against the wall in the alcove, she said, "Why are we having a traditional French dinner? Everyone coming is English or American!"

"*You're* French!"

"Only half! I appreciate the English dinner too!"

"Don't question!" Zariah blurted, brushing a lock of hair away from her face and flailed her hands toward the beef. "Cook!"

For the next few minutes, Noémie and Zariah danced around each other, chatting and laughing as they chopped and cooked. Zariah had most things cut and prepared, it was a matter of getting it cooking. With Noémie's assistance, it didn't take them long to get dinner simmering on the stove or cooking away in the oven.

"I still think you should've boned him. One night stand. All that pent-up sexual energy you've stored over the years, he wouldn't have been able to resist."

"Zaz!" Noémie scolded.

"You should try it! You might like it."

"You never have!"

Zariah tossed her head. "I'm one of the lucky ones, I found Zane early."

"If you're that desperate for me to get laid," Noémie muttered. "Let me borrow him."

She laughed. "Zane would blow your mind, then I'd never get you back." She lost the light tone to mutter, "At this rate, I'm not getting him back either. Fucking manager."

"Tell him we're running off into the sunset together, and see how fast that gets him home."

"He'd probably wish us luck."

"And ask for pictures. And then ask when he can join in."

Zariah snickered. "That too. How's the … stew? It smells delicious."

"Simmering beautifully," Noémie replied. "I still don't know why you thought you'd try it. You're a meat and two veg girl."

"It was Zane's idea, hence why he was supposed to cook it," Zariah muttered. "He was supposed to do all of this. If I had my way, we'd be out to dinner, then clubbing all night. But *noooo*, he wants to do some fancy, five-hour dinner thing, with a stupid amount of courses, then bails."

Noémie nodded. Zariah loved clubbing and the two of them would be going out together while she was in Paris, but Zane didn't like that scene, especially when his songs appeared in the DJ list, so they tended to compromise, and

Zariah would reserve all her party-girl antics for when she and Noémie got together.

Zariah sighed. "He's lucky I love him so much. What are you going to do about Kian?"

"Talk to him," Noémie replied. "Proper relationship conversation. Expectations and reality."

"Horror of horrors."

"I knoooow."

"And then what?"

"We make an informed decision. Together. Give it a go … or don't."

"Are you sure about this?" Zariah asked. "An argument like that isn't the best start, especially on the second date. What if it happens again?"

"Hmmm … true. But the anger in him felt like I'd scraped against an old hurt, like mine. He was trying to protect himself. He didn't swear or resort to name calling and he came after me straight away to clear the air and apologize. Everyone makes mistakes in the heat of the moment, it's what you do after that matters."

"Look at my girl," Zariah declared proudly. "All grown up."

"Oh, shut it."

As the time for the dinner party approached, and still no sign of Zane, Noémie sent Zariah off to shower and dress while she cleaned the kitchen and did last-minute preparations for the first two courses.

Hearing the doorbell ring, Noémie wiped her hands on her apron and walked to the door. It was too early for guests so she expected that Zane, king of the perpetual lost things, had forgotten his key again. She fixed a bright smile on her face and opened the door, ready to tease.

Kian stared at her from the small stoop in front of the apartment. Windswept blond hair, designer clothing, he was dazzling and looked like he'd stepped from a magazine into her life. In his hands he held a bouquet of pink roses and a bottle of wine. "Hi."

She'd expected that he'd be here, was even prepared for it. She'd envisioned being deep in conversation with Zariah, wine glass in hand, and able to be pristine and gorgeous at his arrival and pretend to be aloof and in control upon their meeting, not standing there wearing a stained apron and a stunned expression. "Kian," she breathed. "You're early."

Taken aback, Kian blurted, "Ahh … sorry? Zane told me to come early. He had things he wanted to show me."

Noémie huffed out a breath. "That would be right," she said and stepped away from the entrance so Kian could enter. "Unfortunately, Zane had something urgent come up and we're still waiting for him to return."

"Oh, really?" Kian said, stepping inside the small foyer and moving so Noémie could close the door. "Damn, I was looking forward to it."

"We're told he'll be back soon."

Kian placed the bottle of wine and roses on the small cupboard beneath the coat pegs so he could remove his coat. "These are for Zariah," he said. "Although, knowing Zane, he's probably already brought several cases of wine."

Noémie picked up the bottle to study it. "More wine, the merrier, that's what Zane says. And, *wow*," she breathed as she read the label. Expensive but not over the top, she'd heard this one was delicious, but never had the money to lay a couple hundred Euro down on a wine. "I've heard wonderful things about this one, you have good taste."

"Something my mother drummed into me was good wine."

She smiled at him. "You'll have to excuse me. Zariah's getting ready and I'm supervising the food."

"Okay. Um … forgive me, but"—he reached for her and dusted her cheek with his finger—"some sort of sauce?"

Heat flooded her face. "Thank you," she said as she moved down the hallway toward the kitchen, making sure to check the mirror on the wall on the way. "Would you like something to drink while you wait? Zariah has a chardonnay open—"

Kian touched the tips of his fingers to the inside of her wrist, a gentle request for her to stop. "Noémie, can we—"

"Is that Zane?" Zariah bellowed from the beyond the closed door to the bedroom. "Trust you, darling! Waiting 'til I'm naked to—"

"Kian's here!" Noémie bellowed to prevent Zariah from embarrassing herself.

Zariah yelped. "Ahh … I'll be out soon! You good?"

"We're fine," she called back, smiling to herself from Zariah's concern. "Don't rush!" With a soft squeeze, Noémie smiled and disengaged her hand from his. "We'll talk. Just not when I'm burning dinner."

"May I help?" he asked, following her like a lost puppy.

"I'm really just supervising what's cooking." Reentering the kitchen, she checked on the pots simmering on the stove.

"It smells delicious," Kian said as he leaned against the door frame.

Concentrating on cooking, she watched him in her peripherals, amused as he adjusted his position several times against the kitchen door frame before settling on having his shoulder against it, his hands clasped ahead of him and one ankle hooked over the other.

Smiling to herself that the model would be so nervous he'd have trouble posing, Noémie leaned down to peer through the oven window and check the food.

"You look gorgeous."

Noémie snorted. "And you're a flirt."

"Only with you. And only as long as it's welcome."

She straightened from her lean. "It is."

"Really?" Kian blurted.

Turning to wash her hands in the sink, Noémie said, "Flirting is fine."

"But not anything else?" The caution in his voice was evident and she found that refreshing.

Drying her hands on a towel, Noémie turned around to face him and used her hands to cushion her lean against the counter. "We need to have a serious conversation about expectations. In more ways than one."

"Yes. We do."

"Like that contract of yours. The last thing I would want to do is put you in a position where your family would disown you."

"Financially stable big boy now," he told her. "I'm not worried. I'm sick of being controlled to this degree. If he disowns me, then he does. It won't be because of you."

The contract was a crutch that he didn't want to remove unless he had an incentive. While it wasn't healthy, she could understand why he did it. If he broke it on his own, while he might be free, he'd have no one. Why not wait it out until thirty? She considered him and said gently, "I'm more worried about you losing contact with your family. You love them."

"Oh. Well." He rolled his shoulder and pulled a face. "I mean, Father can't stay angry forever and Mom's usually on my side. So, we'd eventually fix it. Probably. It's possible if he sees me happy with someone, he'll let it go."

Noémie nodded, although she didn't agree with that assessment. After all, Kian was probably happy with his last girlfriend, and breaking the contract didn't work then. Still, he was older and wiser now, so there was hope.

If he was this blasé about breaking the contract, why bother mentioning it to her at all? Transparency. Honesty. Good foundations for a relationship. The contract was there. It was a big deal. It was an obstacle. They both needed to be aware of it. But it wasn't something that should stop them from seeking happiness.

Watching her, Kian asked, "So, does this mean …?"

Noémie dropped her eyes and crossed her arms over her stomach, cupping her elbows. "To clarify: You want to get to know me better. So we can learn to trust each other and we can both determine if we want to take the risk, or remain friends."

"Yes," he replied, the huskiness in his voice producing a tingle down her spine.

"And whatever we do, we need to take things slow. Take the time to learn about each other as friends, before we try for anything else."

"Yes, I think you're right about that."

Chewing on her lip, she frowned in thought, then looked at him, "Can I ask you something?"

"You can ask me anything."

Noémie swallowed her nervousness. "Initially, you responded positively when I sent that lingerie shot. Was that an act?"

"Ahh," Kian breathed and then gulped. "No. That was truthful. I … was going to ask you about it when I got a chance. Tease and flirt and see if you were wearing it."

"What happened? Was it your father? You said he called you."

He pushed up out of his lean in the door frame so he could use both hands to grip the back of his neck. "Yeah. He got in my head."

"If he hadn't, what would you have done?"

"Oh." He shuffled awkwardly and tilted his head back so he could look up at the ceiling. "No clue, honestly. I've …" He swallowed, dropped his hands from his neck, and squared his shoulders. "I was sorely tempted."

Noémie tilted her head at him. "But you said you need an emotional connection."

He ducked his head in a nod. "I do but I think we have one. There's a history here. We were friends, even if we've changed, we still … we knew how to be friends then, we can do it now."

Noémie nodded.

"So … best-case scenario …" He cleared his throat. "I guess … if he hadn't gotten into my head, I think I would've kissed you and … seen where it took us from there. See if there was enough of a connection to, um, continue."

Noémie hummed and slipped into silence, trying to figure out what she wanted to say next. Did this information influence her decision in any way? She didn't think so.

He regarded her. "What do you want to do, Noémie? Do you want to give us a shot? Or try to remember how we were as friends? Or do you want me to walk out the door and never talk to you again?"

She pulled a face. "That's a bit extreme. I certainly don't want that."

"I don't want that either."

Noémie lifted her head and smiled. "Maybe we could take a page out of the French way. Lots of rendezvous. Lots of talking and chatting and learning about each other. Lots of flirting."

"And more lingerie shots?" he asked, hopeful.

Noémie laughed. "If you like. It won't be on me, though. You have to earn that."

He smiled at her. "I can live with that."

"We could give it … a month? Maybe two? And then, if we both feel the same way about each other, we can share a kiss and go from there."

Kian's eyes widened and the sad puppy look returned. "So … I can't kiss you otherwise?"

"No," she said and pretended to consider. Offering him her hand, she chirped, "But I'll let you hold my hand."

Kian moved across the room and took her hand. Smiling, he bowed, lifting her hand at the same time so he could float his lips over the top of her knuckles and dust her skin with his breath in a way that made her heartbeat race. "You drive a hard bargain, but I'm in. May I take you to dinner tomorrow and we can discuss expectations in greater detail?"

"Zariah and I are going clubbing tomorrow night. How about lunch instead? We could get pastries and hot chocolate and walk and talk."

He beamed at her, his entire face lighting up. "Absolutely."

"Are you all done?" Zariah asked, poking her head around the corner of the lounge room then she walked toward the kitchen. She grinned at Noémie and Noémie could guess she'd eavesdropped for most of the conversation. "Cause Kian and I need to have a little chat."

Kian squawked and ducked behind Noémie to use her as a shield against Zariah, which was hilarious since he was so much taller than she was.

"That won't save you," Zariah said.

"Zaz," Kian said. His hands curled around Noémie's shoulders to keep her between Zariah and him. "You look amazing, it's great to see you again. I brought you flowers, they're … ahh … by the door."

"Your feeble flirting attempts won't work on me," Zariah said. One hand on her hip, she wagged a finger at him. "You hurt my girl. You need to pay for that."

"Zaz," Noémie said, smiling. "Have you seen what's on the dining table yet?"

Zariah frowned and, with her finger still pointed at Kian, took a step back so she could peer into the dining room. Spotting it, she threw an eager look at Noémie. "Is that what I think it is?"

"Absolutely."

"What is it?" Kian asked in a hushed whisper.

"Are you attempting to bribe me?" Zariah accused.

"I would never," Noémie teased, hand on her chest to show her sincerity. "I can always take them back to Maman if you don't want them."

Zariah took a large side step toward the dining room. "Nope. No. Mine."

"They need a taste test," Noémie added. "Quality control."

Talk with Kian abandoned, Zariah vanished.

Giggling, Noémie turned to Kian. "Remember when I

said my parents opened a chocolatier here?"

"Oh my god," Zariah moaned from the other room. "My fave! If your mother wasn't already married, I'd marry her in a heartbeat."

Kian perked up. "Your mother's chocolate?"

Noémie nodded.

Bursting into a grin that reminded Noémie of when he was thirteen and experiencing her mother's chocolate for the first time, Kian called, "Zariah! You have to share!"

"No, I don't!" she called back. "Sweet, sweet ambrosia, it's all mine!"

With a lightness in his step that further reminded her of that boy, Kian darted out of the kitchen and into the dining room. "I want some too!"

Noémie laughed. "Save some for Zane," she called as she turned back to the stove and grabbed the closest wooden spoon to use to stir.

"Nope. It's his fault if he missed out!" Zariah called back. "Hey! Mine! Give it back."

Laughing, Kian darted back into the kitchen, holding two pieces of stolen chocolate. Offering one to Noémie, he popped the other piece in his mouth and closed his eyes to enjoy it.

The front door banged, followed by, "Honey, I'm home!"

Zariah rushed back into the kitchen and hid the chocolate box in the cupboard. "Shh," she said with a conspiring look at the two of them. Satisfied they would keep her secret, she called, "We're in the kitchen!"

"Something smells amazing," Zane called as he moved through the apartment. "How dead, am I?"

"Very, very dead," Zariah said. "You are lucky my girl loves me."

"Hi, Zane!" Noémie called and put her wooden spoon on the counter. Wiping her hands on her apron again, she took a step away from Kian and toward the middle of the room.

"Noémie!" Zane called back and they could all hear his hurried footsteps.

Dark hair that flopped over his eyes yet was short at the back, dark brown skin with smoky gray eyes and a smile all the teen girls fell in love with, Zane rushed into the room, headed straight for Noémie and swept her up into a hug. Lifting her, he spun her in a circle. "Hey you!"

Laughing, Noémie hugged him back. "You saw me Wednesday."

"I didn't get my Nomnom hug though," he replied and plopped her back on the ground, then rubbed his stubbly chin against her cheek to make her squeal and shy away from him. Spotting Kian, Zane grinned. "Dude. Great to see you again." Kian held out his hand to Zane to shake, and Zane, with his eyes twinkling, ignored it to pull him in for a hug.

Clapping Kian on the back heartedly as he pulled away, Zane said, "We have so much catching up to do."

"We do."

"But not now," Zariah said. "Noémie and I are going to sit down and have a drink"—she gestured to the kitchen—"and you get to finish up this."

His sheepish smile lit up Zane's dark face as he turned to face his girlfriend. "Sorry, babe, you know I wanted to be as quick as I could, but—"

"Don't you sorry me, Zane Lécuyer," Zariah told him. "You're in the doghouse."

Reaching behind her, Noémie undid her apron, unhooked it, and shoved the strap over Zane's neck. "It's all nearly done," she said, joining Zariah. "Finishing touches. Kian can help you."

Kian's brow rose. "What?"

"You did offer," Noémie said. "And it'll give you both a chance to chat before the others arrive." Turning to Zariah, she asked, "Wine?"

"Love some," Zariah said as she and Noémie linked elbows to head into the living area.

CHAPTER 5

Hurrying down the street, Noémie wove her way through the crowd of people. She'd been caught up at work which made her late to the metro by a matter of seconds and she'd missed her train. Not a very good start to any rendezvous.

When Angelina's came into view, she was relieved to see Kian's head above the crowd as he waited outside. He hadn't seen her and was looking in the opposite direction she was coming from, so she reached into her coat pocket, retrieved her phone and sent him the message she'd prepared of the lingerie she was wearing today, on a torso rather than on her. Light blue, lacy, functional over sexy but still containing that hint of playfulness she liked to have in her designs.

Since she was close, she got to see first-hand his reaction to the picture. Eyes flaring wide, head coming up as he started looking for her in earnest, and the bright smile that made her happy when he spotted her.

"Noémie," he said. "You look amazing."

Hardly, she was still in her work clothes, hidden beneath her winter jacket, but she appreciated the sentiment. "I'm so sorry I'm late," she rushed, flustered. "I missed the metro. I hope you weren't waiting long."

"Not long. I could've picked you up," he offered.

"It's fine, but thank you for the offer. So," she said, looking at Angelina's. "This place is famous for its hot chocolate and baked goods. I'm sure you've at least heard of it if you haven't had any."

"I have. Never had a chance to try it though."

"It's absolutely divine on a cold winter's day like today. I thought we could take a walk through Tuileries Garden while we talk."

He grinned at her. "You're cheating on your parents, I see."

Noémie laughed. "It's called 'sampling the competition'," she retorted with a lofty tone. "Perfectly reasonable thing to do. Besides"—she rose up on her tiptoes, cupped her hand around her mouth so she could whisper this secret to him—"it's Papa and my cheat spot."

He chuckled in response. "Of course. I should've known." He turned toward the storefront to regard it. "Been drooling from the smell just standing outside." Looking back at her, his hair caught in a gust of winter breeze that ruffled it up. "Are you sure you don't want to dine in?"

"I'd rather walk and talk," she said, stepping closer to avoid being buffeted by a crowd of people walking by. Reaching out her hand, she pinched the sleeve of his winter jacket to keep them together. Kian was tall, people gave him a wide berth naturally and she wanted to use him as a buffer. "It's a heart-to-heart talk. We might need space from each other to collect our thoughts. Hard to do if we're at a table."

He frowned in concern. "You suspect that might happen?"

"I'm being cautious," she said. "That's all." Offering him a bright smile, she continued, "Shall we?"

Upon seeing the assortment of pastries in the delicatessen, Kian turned into a kid at a candy store, wanting to try absolutely everything. Making a mental note to bring him back here so he could, Noémie ordered two hot chocolates and an assortment of pastries to try. Treats in hand, they walked across to the Tuileries Garden. So hyped about the treats, Kian had practically inhaled all his by the time they walked across the road to the entrance and made all the appropriate noises to show he enjoyed it.

"We definitely need to go back," Noémie said as she offered him the bag of her pastries.

He tried to contain his glee as he eyed the paper bag. "You don't mind?"

"I saw how you were in there," she teased. "Just like Papa. He gets the same look as you did. So, I bought extra, just in case."

"Glad to know I amuse you," he said, dipping into her bag of goodies. "Thank you."

It had snowed over the weekend, leaving the ground muddied and the hibernating trees laden with snow-covered branches. The contrasting dark branches with the white snow resulted in a rather picturesque walk as she and Kian ambled below them.

Kian walked in a slow circle as he looked upward as he studied the branches above them. "This is so pretty. Would you mind if I took some shots for Instagram?"

"Go for it," Noémie said, holding out her hand to accept his hot chocolate to hold. "Do you take photos often? Or just when you're on photoshoots?"

"All the time," he said and dug his hand into his pocket and pulled out his phone. "I love it. Photography is pretty amazing, and Instagram is a great platform to share that," he continued while lining up a shot between the branches and into the gray sky. "You can experience the world through someone else's eyes. See what they find worth recording. Viewpoints and angles, the same place through a thousand different eyes." He took a large step to the side. "One step and the world changes. Instagram lets us visit exotic places through photos. Meet animals we'd never get to see. Watch a couple fall in love."

So poetic of him, he almost sounded like a travel brochure and it amused her. "Or fall apart."

"That too," he said, wandering around as he snapped a few pictures. He took his time, lining up each shot so it was perfect. "But I prefer to be optimistic about that sort of thing."

Tilting her head at him, she asked, "A romantic at heart?"

He shrugged sheepishly. "I don't know about that."

She looked upward at the trees and wondered. His phone was probably top of the line, but, "Ever think about getting a professional rig?"

"Got one," he said. "But it's bulky to cart around and I wanted to concentrate on us."

That was sweet. "And yet, you still can't resist," she teased.

"It's all a ploy," he said, grinning at her. "May I get one of you?"

Noémie laughed and hid her face behind the two takeaway cups. "No. Not yet."

"Not for Instagram," he promised, resting his hand over his heart. "No people in mine, just landscapes and scenes."

"Still, no. We're not there yet."

He pouted at her. "Not even a selfie together? Document the first not-date?"

She laughed at both the expression on his face and the offer of documentation. He seemed pretty cute like that. Plus, she could get a natural photo of him too as she had no recent ones. "Okay, fine. But I get a copy."

"Yes!" he crowed and bounced over to her. Tucking an arm across her back, he curled in close to her face and lined up a shot.

He had no right to be that handsome. She could feel the warmth between them swelling against the icy wind of winter. She could lose herself in his arms and she wouldn't have cared in the slightest. Distracted by the smell of his cologne and the closeness of his body, she had trouble smiling for the camera.

This was going to be tricky, but at least she knew she was attracted to him.

As they viewed the photo he took, she had to admit, they did look nice together. A cute couple, enjoying a winter's day. Once that was done, he retrieved his hot chocolate from her and tucked his phone back inside his winter jacket. "Really is death by chocolate, isn't it?"

"Hmm, yup. Paris likes things sweet."

He fell into step beside her as they ambled along the path between the trees. "So. Heart-to-heart time."

Noémie nodded.

Kian cleared his throat. "Okay. So. Um. We're doing like a trial run. To see if we're romantically compatible, or if we'd be better suited to being friends."

Noémie nodded again. "If it's deeper than surface lust."

Kian raised an eyebrow at that.

"Well, you want to break this contract," she explained. "That's an end goal. So we need to know that we're going to be a strong couple who could weather something like that, because it sounds like it'll be a battle. There's no point getting all cozy if we get cold feet in the end."

He considered that with pursed lips, like he'd eaten something sour. "True."

"So, it's important to recognize that, yes, while we do both want to become a couple, that could change at any moment. Maybe we're not romantically cut out for being a couple and we'll be better suited as friends." She bit her lip and said, "Maybe we'd rather be friends with benefits."

Kian frowned. "Is that actually on the table?" he blurted, like he couldn't believe she even mentioned that. "I don't want that, Noémie, and I'm pretty sure you don't either. Not after your last boyfriend."

She puffed out a relieved breath. "No, you're right, I don't want that. I just … felt it should be mentioned."

He inclined his head. "Mentioned, and dismissed."

Thank goodness for that. She'd been hesitant in mentioning it, and it appeared that thought hadn't even occurred to him, which made her feel more confident. "When our feelings do change, we need to make sure we talk about it. We need to listen to each other's concerns or worries."

"When?" he questioned.

She clarified, "When we decide if we want to make a go at this or not. There'll be a point where that happens, and we need to make sure we talk."

Kian transferred his cup to his other hand, then gently touched his fingertips to the side of her hand. "May I?"

Heartbeat picking up a notch, she considered.

"You did say we could," he reminded her. "The French way, the first kiss is important, it sparks the beginning of a relationship. Once a couple share that, they're all in."

She raised her eyebrows at him.

He grinned. "You were so adamant, I looked it up why a first kiss was so important. I get it. I want that." He laughed at himself. "Mom never ... I mean, I'm too American and she complains about it, but I didn't get to see much French culture. This ... I like it. I like the idea behind it."

She nodded. "I only realized it myself after living here. Had a few close calls."

Chortling, he said, "I can imagine. Looking back, I think I have too."

"We'll have to exchange stories."

"Sounds fun." Lightening his tone, he chirped, "So, no kissing until we're absolutely sure, but hand holding should be okay."

Nodding, she spread her fingers so they could intertwine their hands. Not skin-to-skin contact, since they both wore gloves, but it was still intimate. More than friends.

His thumb stroked against hers. "Communication is

important and friendship is also an end goal."

She snorted out a laugh. "He says after asking to hold my hand."

"We have to trial some romantic things, right?" he countered. "No kissing, but hand holding allowed." He lit up and chirped, "It's a rule."

"We're making rules now?"

"Seems like the best way to go about this. Clear boundaries and expectations. Don't you think?"

She nodded, seeing the logic. A set of boundaries they both agreed on would be a good start to this.

"So. Rule one. No kissing, but hand holding is allowed. What do you think rule two should be?"

She bit her lip as she considered how to approach this aspect. She'd rehearsed what she wanted to say, but now the moment was here, she didn't know how he was going to react. Her hand, tucked inside a glove, still felt clammy and she could feel a heat rising through her neck. How he reacted to this would determine how comfortable she was with all of this. "There's a large disparity between our incomes."

"There is," he acknowledged.

"I don't want or need a sugar daddy and you don't want to be one."

He blinked at her. "Wow. Dive right in."

Noémie lifted an eyebrow at him. "If you wanted to be one, you wouldn't have yelled at me over wanting your money over you."

With a woeful expression, he said, "Can I apologize again for that?"

She giggled and bumped into him with her shoulder. "It's fine. I understand where you were coming from. I forgive you."

He puffed out a breath. "Thank you."

Swinging their hands, she said, "I have a … fairly strict budget. It's starting to loosen up now, but there are things I can't do. I can't jettison off for an exotic holiday just because you feel like it—" she paused, thought, then skipped sideways to face him. "Is that something that you actually do?"

He laughed and it was warm like their hot chocolates. "Me personally? No. Not really. I travel enough as it is. For me, a holiday is being able to sleep in my own bed without getting up until midday."

She brightened at that because that sounded amazing. "Ooooh, I like that. You have good taste."

He grinned at her.

"So, in terms of these rendezvous, we need to find a happy medium. I want to go stag as much as we can. Or take turns paying for dates." She turned from her side skip to settle into a walk again. "Can I be honest with you for a sec?"

"Absolutely. That's why we're here."

"Epicure was … incredible but it made me nervous. It's outside my comfort zone. I'm still not sure—is that a place you like to frequent?"

He nodded. "Mom loves Epicure."

Which didn't answer whether or not he liked the place. "Okay. With the knowledge that I cannot afford a place like that on my own, and have never … um … how do I put this? … I'm not used to it. I don't know how to act or how to dress for a place like that. I have a total of three fancy dresses in my closet and you already saw one… look, I know that … it's probably standard for you and something I'll need to get used to and I'll definitely need advice. Is it something we can build up to? Rather than starting there?"

He'd been nodding through her rambling and when she took a breath, he said, "I'm sorry I made you uncomfortable."

"You didn't, just the situation did. You were trying to impress me and that's okay. But … I'd feel terrible if you constantly took me to places like that and I couldn't reciprocate. And"—she slowed her walk—"I feel bad about walking out. I mean, I had to, but I also left you with the wine bill and you didn't even get to eat and—"

Kian squeezed her hand. "Noémie, don't worry about that. It's really fine and I deserved it." He put his other hand, still holding his cup, on his chest. "We can take turns organizing dates and I promise not to go overboard with mine."

"That would be appreciated."

They resumed their amble, passing from one row of trees to wander down the next. "So," Kian said. "Rule one. Hand holding is all the rage. Rule two, try to keep things equal in terms of dates."

"You can splash out a bit," Noémie conceded. "I mean, obviously, it's something you do a lot and you shouldn't have to, um, bring it down to my level all the time." She bit her bottom lip. "I don't know how to explain what I'm feeling without sounding … It's your money and you absolutely should decide what you want to do with it but—"

He smiled and squeezed her hand again. "Basically, I'm extremely extra and can I tone it down?"

"Except, what about your comfort level?" she fretted. "I mean … can you be happy on walks in the park and baguettes? Or hitting up a different café every date just to see what they have? I don't want you to feel uncomfortable with my ideals either."

"I'm happy simply spending time with you," he promised. "I'm not exactly comfortable in high-end luxury places either."

That surprised her. "You're not?"

"I used to be," he acknowledged. "Before I was disowned, you would never find me doing something like this. I would've thought it was beneath me."

That was disappointing because this was her ideal date. Walking, talking, flirting. "Oh."

"Now, I miss being able to order a pizza on a Saturday night. I miss ducking into the closest supermarket and grabbing a bunch of hotdogs, popcorn, and beers for an impromptu movie night. I miss having friends and not worrying about whether they were using me for my money or not. I lost so many people I thought were my friends, only Charlie stuck around."

Her heart went out to him. "He didn't help you?"

"No, he did. But he was having issues at the time and I really didn't feel good imposing on him. I want to enjoy life, Noémie. Live in the moment. See beauty in a snowflake on a tree branch. I wasn't seeing it before, all I saw was luxury and wealth and people being shallow. I want to see it now. This is… this is what I want." He gestured downward. "Walking in a park, having proper conversations, holding hands with a gorgeous girl, and drinking hot chocolates."

Seeing that he understood her concerns and was on the same wavelength she was, she relaxed.

"So, I tone down the extra-ness, and we don't go to any luxury restaurants until we're both sure we want to do this. When we are sure, I'll introduce you slowly and give you time to become acquainted before we throw you into my parent's world."

She would need to know how to act in high society, and his way would make it easier. "That would be appreciated."

He considered, then his eyes widened. "Except Le Jules Verne. I really want to take you, Zariah, and Zane there. Zane and I have been making plans and it was supposed to be a surprise. Please?"

Le Jules Verne was the restaurant located on the Eiffel Tower itself and Noémie's breath hitched in excitement at the thought of going. "Oh, I'm sorry I ruined the surprise then! Cause I really want to go there, too. I've wanted to go there since moving here!"

He grinned. "Excellent."

"Wow, I'm fickle," she said and laughed at herself. "Breaking a rule just after it was made."

"To be fair, I booked before you made the rule. So, technically, it doesn't count."

"I like your reasoning," she said, winking at him.

"Don't tell Zariah, okay?"

She mimed her lips being zipped, then rushed, "Is Zane proposing?"

Kian blinked. Pulled his head back in confusion. "I don't think so?" he said, the answer sounding more like a question. "It was my idea to go, we're just organizing it together."

Noémie huffed. He was taking forever to propose, but she was probably more upset about that than Zariah was.

He eyed her. "Do you think he will?"

"No idea," Noémie replied. "I can remain hopeful."

"Should I warn him Zariah is expecting one?" Kian asked, cautiously.

"No," she replied. "Because Zaz isn't expecting one. She knows he will when he's ready. I just… I want to be close, you know? I've watched their relationship grow from the beginning and … I want to be close enough that I can hug the living daylights out of them when it happens and not with them in England and me here and …" She sighed and chided herself, "That's probably selfish of me. Sorry. I'll be glad when it happens, that's all."

"Oh. Okay. Um …"

"Rule three," she prompted, changing the subject.

"Right. Rule three," he said, going back to their earlier conversation. "If anyone asks, my mom or the press or something, we're just friends and there's no hurt feelings to call each other that."

"It's not a lie to say we're friends," she said and opened and closed her fingers around his hand. "Hand holding friends."

Kian's smile turned playful. "Hand holding, flirting friends."

"But… exclusive friends, if you get my meaning."

With a hand squeeze, he replied, "I wouldn't have it

any other way."

She flashed him a smile that soon faded. "It feels weird to be this skeptical about a hypothetical relationship."

"Yeah. A bit," he conceded as he nodded. "But … I mean, it's a tricky relationship too, with my contract in play. So I think it's good that we're being this cautious about it and making joint decisions. Rule four?"

She knew what she wanted this one to be. "Chant de La Rose is off-limits."

Kian tilted his head as if to ask for elaboration.

"I'm proud of my business," she explained. "I don't … I don't want to be seen as using you to get ahead. You're a powerful person in the fashion world and I want to make it on my own. So … don't feel obliged to help me out in any way, or offer advice, things like that. I'm not going to ask either."

"Oh." He puffed out a breath of laughter. "I thought you meant like, 'Don't ever visit you at work'."

She giggled. "No, no, you can do that! I don't mind."

"Okay, good." He took a sip from his drink. "It's fair to keep business separate from pleasure. It's a good rule."

He just had to purr out the word 'pleasure' and it did delightful things to her.

"Rule five," Noémie said, fighting the flush. "No judgment. If either of us needs to back out of this, or need space, that should be okay to do so. We communicate our needs and act accordingly. I've already experienced how your father can affect you."

The smile on his face dimmed. "I'm sorry."

She poked him. "Stop," she whined. "I think we need some sort of signal for when we're feeling emotional and need some space, that's all. That way we can be considerate."

He seemed to accept that. "Agreed. That should be where the communication comes in. If he calls, I'll just tell you, how's that?"

Noémie nodded. "And if you need to talk about it, you

can, but you don't have to. I'll understand."

"Thank you. Anything else?"

She considered. "I don't think our rendezvous should include going to each other's places yet, but it's not a hard and fast rule."

"Alright," he agreed easily. "Are pick-ups and drop-offs okay? Depending on the rendezvous, I guess. I have a car, it would be a shame not to use it and will give us more time together."

"Sure. Did you have anything else? Other concerns or rules?"

He pressed his lips together. "Tabloids. Don't listen to them."

"That was a given," she replied with a light laugh. "How many people do they have you dating?"

He laughed with her. "Apparently I have two secret girlfriends back in New York, pining away for me. Not to mention all the models or secretaries I'm having secret affairs with here."

She nodded woefully. "Poor them. How could you be so cruel?"

Seeing she was joking, he flashed her a grin. "All while simultaneously being reported as an eligible bachelor."

"You're a wanted man."

"So it seems." He sighed. "I don't like that kind of attention."

She leaned into his arm and rested her head on his upper arm briefly. "I'm sorry."

He hummed, leaning back into her. "I like your attention. Don't take that away."

She giggled. "I got that but thanks for clarifying."

"What about you?" he asked. "Any other concerns?"

"I think we covered everything," she said. There were other concerns, like how they were going to break this contract, what would happen when they did, how his father would react, could she cope with it all, but those concerns could wait until she was sure a relationship with

Kian was what she wanted. That this feeling between them was genuine and not infatuation. "For the moment."

Kian seemed to echo her thoughts as he said, "I expect more will arise as we get to know each other better. Does any of what was said change anything for you?"

She considered that with the same seriousness he had when asking the question. "If anything, I'm more confident about pursuing a relationship with you now."

"So, you'd still like to try?" he asked, sounding nervous. "I haven't scared you off?"

She gave him a woeful expression. "You stole all my treats and I'm still here."

He grinned. "Good point." Glancing over his shoulder, he said, "We could go buy more."

"Maybe later," she replied, tightening her grip on him so he didn't bounce away. "Greedy."

"They were yummy!" he protested and continued to playfully try and get away from her. "It's just there! I can still see it."

She giggled and refused to let go of his hand. "You're so silly."

Dragging his eyes away from Angelina's, he fixed them securely on her. "But you like me that way."

A nervous tickle in her belly soon spread through her body. "You're going to be a handful, aren't you?"

Lifting their joined hands, he pressed his lips to the back of her hand. "Even more now," he practically purred. "Are you up for the challenge?"

Heart thudding, Noémie smiled and returned the flirting volley. "I think I can handle you."

Kian's smile lit up his entire face. "I look forward to that."

CHAPTER 6

Noémie stared at the row of torso mannequins ahead of her and then stepped back until she was beside Zariah so she could take them all in. Seven pieces of lingerie, representing a range of different types. A teddy, a baby doll, a chemise, lingerie sets featuring both a bra and a bralette, a sports bra, and even a corset. The best of her designs, chosen to represent her brand. Ranging from demure to playful, her items were designed for comfort as well as practicality and while only the teddy was chosen to be modeled plus-size in the walk, Noémie had each design represented with its plus-sized variant for the exhibit itself, as well as two adaptive pieces.

"I think you've done it," Zariah said, nodding in approval. "These are your best ones."

Noémie worried her thumbnail as she looked them over. "The pink. Maybe I should go for the blue set, there's that shine on it that—"

"The pink is perfect. It draws in the eye and the lace holds it. Which one are you going to send to Kian?"

Noémie raised her eyebrows at Zariah, aware that Zariah wanted her to be risqué.

"Do the corset," Zariah prompted. "And then box me

one up. I want to take it home."

"I am not wearing a corset today," Noémie replied, rolling her eyes at Zariah.

"Well, which styles have you sent him so far?"

"They've been pretty tame," Noémie replied. "I kept them neutral. Nice pieces, but everyday wear."

"Maybe you should spice it up today."

"I thought I'd build up to it."

After they discussed the rules, they'd decided to go to a movie together and Kian had clutched her hand because he couldn't handle zombies. Their next rendezvous had been a sunset dinner with Zane and Zariah up the Eiffel Tower, which she'd absolutely loved to bits. Watching the sun sink slowly through the sky, eating divine food, and chatting to her best friends, all the while Kian had flirted with his feet beneath the table had been an amazing experience.

The two lingerie shots she'd sent so far had been a bra and pantie matched set. Little bit of lace, a hint of temptation, but ultimately safe.

Giggling, Zariah patted her on the head. "You're too cute for your own good. Go stand in front of them and pretend you're doing the dressy thing. I wanna get a photo."

Resisting the urge to roll her eyes at the 'dressy thing' comment, Noémie nodded. "Which one?"

"Any of them. Pick your fave."

"Just don't put it on Instagram," Noémie said as she headed for the baby doll. "We're not supposed to reveal our entries."

"Have no fear," Zariah replied loftily, brandishing her phone as she pretended to be a professional photographer.

Noémie lifted her hands to the lacy cleavage of the red baby doll and posed, appearing like she was adjusting it.

"Perfect," Zariah said as she took several photos.

Dropping her hands, Noémie looked at her displays and said, "Now all I have to do is pin the numbers on and box them and we're all set for Thursday."

"This is so exciting," Zariah said. "I'm so proud of you." Tucking the phone into the pocket of her jeans, she said, "We'll be late for brunch if we don't leave soon. Pick your poison for today."

"I've already done it," Noémie said. Lifting her phone, she skipped through her photos until she came to the mannequin wearing the set she wore.

Zariah rolled her eyes. "So vanilla. Good thing I sent him one of you with the baby doll."

Noémie's eyes widened. "You what?"

Zariah shrugged. "You'll thank me later."

"Zaz!" Noémie scolded. "The idea is to wear the lingerie I send."

"You didn't send it. I did. A little bit of a sneak peek at possibilities." Her phone binged and Zariah grinned. "Shall we see what he said?"

"You are completely incorrigible," Noémie said.

"And you love it," Zariah replied, checking the message. "Ooh. He loves it too."

Noémie hurried over to grab Zariah's phone and check what Kian had sent. A little emoji heart with the text *'She's gorgeous, thank you for sharing.'*

As she watched, Kian texted again, *'She does know you sent me that, right?'*

Scowling playfully at Zariah, Noémie handed Zariah her phone back and used her own to text.

> **Noémie**
>
> She does now. Please don't show anyone. That's an entry piece.

> **Kian**
>
> Busted. Have no fear, this beauty is mine and mine alone… and I wasn't just talking about the baby doll *winkyface*

Shaking her head in amusement, Noémie reached for her coat and bag. "We should go."

"What about my corset?" Zariah complained, looking

over her shoulder longingly at it.

"You really want to carry it around all day? We can come back and get it this afternoon if you like."

"I thought I'd wear it out of here."

Noémie frog-marched Zariah to the front door of Chant de La Rose and unlocked it so they could exit. "Not without washing it, you heathen! We don't have time to prepare it today, you'll have to wait."

Zariah laughed. "You're such a stickler for proper lingerie etiquette!"

Giggling, Noémie locked up behind them.

When they arrived at the cafe they'd decided to have Sunday brunch at, Zane and Kian were already seated and chatting over a hot drink. By the look of the empty glass teapot beside Zane, and the coffee cup Kian nursed, they'd been there for a while, but neither of them complained about having to wait.

"Tell me they have baked beans on the menu," Zariah asked Zane after greeting him with a smacking kiss.

"Alas," Zane replied with an almost-woeful look. "But they have bacon and eggs and tea."

Zariah huffed and flopped on her chair. "That'll do. Noémie, your next mission is to find me somewhere that does a proper English breakfast."

"What if I don't choose to accept it?" Noémie asked, smiling her thanks at Kian as he pushed the chair in behind her, then sat back down beside her.

"Then I will bring it from home and I will gross out your delicate French sensibilities by opening a can and bloody drinking it in front of you."

Hands to her mouth, Noémie mock gasped. "They will banish you from France. You'll never be able to return."

With a lofty air, Zariah said, "I'd like to see them try."

"That's just gross, even for you," Zane told Zariah, pulling a face at her. "Drinking it? Ew."

Zariah glared at her boyfriend. "Who's the one who said if they could intravenous tea straight into their veins, they would?"

Noémie placed her hand over Kian's wrist and leaned in close to whisper in French, "This is the point of the conversation where we back away slowly and run for the hills."

"She wouldn't really drink it from the can, would she?" he asked, replying in the same language.

Wrinkling her nose, she considered that. "Doubt it, but you never know."

Kian moved his hand so it covered hers and leaned close. "Do we even have a chance to escape?"

Feeling as cheeky as he was, Noémie murmured, "As long as Zane keeps her attention, we should be able to make a break for it."

Zane turned his head to look at them. "I heard my name."

Distracted from her argument with Zane, Zariah whipped her head toward them and glared. "Hey! No French!"

"Oops, caught," Noémie said, before switching back to English for the benefit of their friends. "I was complimenting Zane's shirt. I like the design."

"It suits you," Kian said, helping cover for her.

Zariah narrowed her eyes at the pair. "I'm onto you."

"Ahh, give it to them," Zane said and waggled his eyebrows at her. "French sounds sexy. Say something sexy in French, Nomnom."

Noémie smiled at him. Resting her elbow on the table, she cupped her chin with her hand and crooned in French, "I could say anything I like and he'd believe it. I could even say that new haircut looked like he lost a fight with a hedgehog and he'd think it was sensual. He's such a silly man, but I love him."

"What'd you say?" Zariah asked, frowning at her as she tried to translate it for herself. "Something about ... hair, fighting and silly? And I heard a 'love' in there."

"She said Zane's socks are stinky and he looks like he

rolled in a pile of dog shit," Kian said in English.

Noémie laughed and smacked Kian's upper arm with the back of her hand. "I did not!"

Zane cackled and smacked his hand on his knee. "Doesn't matter what she said, it sounded awesome."

"She also said that your hair was *sharp*," Kian continued.

"Totally on *point*," Noémie agreed.

Kian's eyes twinkled in delight as he turned toward her and leaned in closer. "*Cutting* edge humor, right there."

"Zane," Zariah complained, tucking a stray curl of hair away from her face. "They're doing the thing."

Zane grinned, leaning forward eagerly. "Been a long time since we've seen a pun battle."

The four of them laughed and chatted while enjoying a slow brunch. Several cups of tea and coffees later, and a hearty meal of bacon and eggs, then the four of them strolled through the streets of Paris toward their next destination.

Zane and Zariah, their arms wrapped around each other, laughed and talked loudly, even sharing the odd kiss while they walked ahead. Noémie, her hand snuggled and warm in Kian's, smiled to herself as she watched her friends.

Squeezing her hand, Kian asked, "Are you all ready for the walk?"

"As ready as I'll ever be," she said, trying to squash the sudden burst of nerves. "Everything is prepared. I have to pick up my business cards from the printer tomorrow and spend Thursday morning setting up."

"I wish I could be there to support you," he lamented.

"That wouldn't be appropriate," Noémie said, wishing he could be there as well. "Zariah and I have got this. Dulcie and Veroniqué will help so I can move around as I need."

"You'll be fantastic," he said, sounding proud. "I look forward to hearing all about it afterward."

"If I don't burst first," she admitted. "I'm somewhat terrified."

"First show can be nerve-wracking," Kian said and squeezed her hand. "But if that baby doll is anything to go by, you're going to take them by storm."

That made her feel better. "I hope so."

"You'll be fine," he soothed. "It'll start and you'll throw yourself into it and forget you were ever nervous."

She rested her head against his arm for a second. "Thanks. That helps. So!" she chirped, changing the subject. "What were you and Zane doing before we arrived?"

"Were your ears burning?" Kian asked with a mischievous grin.

Noémie was surprised. "You were talking about us?"

"You specifically," he said.

That made sense. Zane had always been like a protective older brother to her. "'Treat her right or I will end you?'" she asked with a light laugh.

Kian chuckled at her impression of Zane. "In a nutshell."

She nodded in approval. "He's never been able to give that speech before and I'm surprised he waited this long."

With a shrug, he said, "I think he wanted to get me alone."

"That's a possibility. Did Zane do well?"

In a lofty tone, Kian announced, "I am suitably quelled and reminded of my civic duties."

"Wow," she said, feigning offense. "That makes me sound like a chore."

Kian smiled at her and dropped his head so his mouth was beside her ear, "It would be my pleasure to treat you the way you deserve."

Her heart skipped a beat then picked up at a faster pace as Kian lifted their joined hands and pressed his lips to the back of hers.

Zariah looked over her shoulder as she and Zane

reached a crossroads, and Noémie pointed a direction for her to walk.

"So, where are we going?" Kian asked, curious. "Zane wouldn't tell me his plans."

"Didn't he? Well, even though Zariah's going to be here for a while, Zane's only here until Friday, so he wanted to do something cliché."

"Cliché? In Paris? There are only a few things that are cliché. The Eiffel Tower is the other direction—Oh." Kian missed a step and stumbled. "Oh no."

"It's okay," she assured him. "If you get scared, you can hold my hand and I promise there won't be any zombies."

"Cliché is the Eiffel Tower, Arc de Triomphe, the Louve or Pont des Arts. Not the *catacombs*."

Noémie tilted her head up at the sudden strain in his voice. "Are you okay?"

Kian swallowed. "I … um … would you … would you think less of me if I said I, er, do not do well in enclosed spaces."

Reaching over with her other hand, she clasped his arm above his elbow. "Of course not," she soothed, relieved. "Let's drop those two off and do something else. I wasn't looking forward to it either."

Kian puffed out a relieved breath. "Thank you."

She smiled at him and gave his arm a quick, reassuring squeeze. "Is there something cliché you would like to do?"

He hummed as he considered. "We could go ice skating. I saw an ad for it at dinner the other night and thought it looked like something we could do that was fun. I haven't been in a while. Doesn't Paris do those pop-up rinks in winter?"

"Most of those finish after New Year's. There's the one at the Tower," Noémie replied, pulling out her phone so she could check. "And I think the one at Hôtel de Ville is still running." Noémie smiled as she confirmed it. "We could catch the metro over. What do you think?"

Kian returned her smile. "I like that plan."

After dropping Zane and Zariah off at the touring entrance to the catacombs—Kian made several jokes about not wanting to see Zane's 'boner' fetish—and promising to return before the tour finished, Noémie and Kian made their way across to Hôtel de Ville and hired some ice skates.

She didn't think she'd seen anything more adorable than Kian von Brandt, model extraordinaire, with his natural grace and charming charisma, clad in his high-fashion tailored suit and gray winter coat, wobbling around on the ice as he tried to remember how to skate. Noémie giggled behind her hand, gliding just out of reach of those flailing arms.

"You could help," he scolded, bent in half, with his skates pointed in different directions as he tried to keep his balance. "How are you making this look easy?"

"One of Papa's many talents was as an ice skating instructor," she replied, skating up to him. Holding out her arms, she clasped his at the elbow and aligned her forearms with his to help support him. "We go skating every year and he moonlights teaching kids."

"And here I was thinking I could impress you."

"You do impress me," she replied. "But maybe next time you should pick something you know you can do."

Kian laughed. "Point taken."

As slow as she could, Noémie skated backward, pulling Kian along with her. "Do you want an actual lesson? Or a cheat's way that will get you through today."

His smile grew. "Cheat's way."

Smiling in return, she asked, "Do you know how to ride a scooter?"

He laughed. "Mom would never let me. Scooters and rollerblades lead to bloody knees and noses. I can snowboard and ski though, mainly because everything can be covered for that. Less risk of damaging my pretty face."

"Lucky you," she replied. "But you know the theory

behind scootering, right? Pretend one foot is the scooter, and use the other to push forward."

Kian looked at his feet. "Can you do any tricks? Jumps and such."

"Mmm-hmm. I'm not the best, but I can." She smiled and encouraged. "That's it. Glide your feet instead of stamping and shoving. Good."

"Can you show me?"

She lifted her head from studying his feet to meet his eyes. "I could, but that would mean I'd have to let go of you."

He seemed more interested in her than watching his feet. "I'd love to see."

She laughed. "Okay, but let's at least get you skating on your own first."

They glided around the edge rink, with the side rail within grabbing distance. Noémie skated backward, half pulling, half encouraging Kian as he gained confidence. By the end of two laps, he was barely using her as support. Releasing his arms, she held his hand and matched his pace as they skated around the rink.

Noémie nudged him with her hip. "I think you got it."

"This is fun," Kian told her, gleeful now he was getting the hang of it. "Can you teach me to skate backward?"

Noémie laughed. "Concentrate on going forward first. Will you be alright on your own for a moment?"

He beamed at her in excitement. "Absolutely. Show me what you got."

She laughed. Lifting their joined hands, she pecked the back of his before she released.

With this many people around, there was no way she was going to be risky and do anything more than a single jump, but she could do some spins and twirls. Most people used the outer rim to skate at their own paces, the middle of the rink was open for more experienced skaters. Tucking her scarf into her yellow coat so it wouldn't tangle, she used a lap to pick up speed, then turned into a backward glide. Lifting one foot from the ice, she used it to point in the direction she was traveling.

Judging her path free of obstacles, she lifted off the ice to do a single toe loop. A smooth landing and she picked up a little more speed so she could twirl into a scratch spin, holding her arms across her chest to give her more spin. She lifted her hands above her head to spin faster before flowing out of the spin into a one-footed glide. Eyes skimming over the ice skaters, she offered a sheepish smile and wave toward the scattered applause from skaters watching while she looked for Kian.

Both hands clutching the railing for support, and looking like he'd barely made it to the edge, Kian watched her with an awed expression. "Wow," he breathed as she joined him.

She flushed. "That's about all I can do. I used to be able to pull off a double jump, but I haven't practiced in a while."

"That was *amazing.*"

There was this smitten expression on his face. Green eyes, soft and gentle as they held her gaze, an equally soft smile gracing his lips. Kian reached for her hip to tug her toward him and she let the skates glide her closer.

Stopping before she bumped into him and the toes of her skates almost touching his, she waited to see what he'd do. With her heart pounding and extra adrenaline from the jump, she was of two minds about the situation. One part of her wanted to steamroll ahead, the other was filled with trepidation.

She wanted ...

New beginnings, a fresh start. Their ancient friendship renewed into something more. Had there been enough time to fully decide how they felt? Not really and they'd agreed to take things slow. She shouldn't let this happen. So why wasn't she moving away?

The hand on her hip flexed and it seemed that Kian was following through the same line of thoughts she was, except she didn't know which side he'd land on. She didn't know which side she would either if he decided to go for it.

With aching slowness, he dipped his head down toward hers and pressed a tender kiss to her forehead. Noémie exhaled in a slow breath, then leaned into his lips to show she approved of the gesture. Romantic in nature, but not breaking any of the rules they'd both created. Close though. Close enough to bend them. Close enough to make her heartbeat race and wish he'd push a little further, but also be thankful he wasn't trying for an early decision.

Pulling back, he locked eyes with hers. "Noémie," he murmured. "I'm really glad—"

A phone shrilled. The noise startled Kian and his skate slipped. The sudden grab and clutch at her for balance made her squeak and brace to keep from falling. They floundered, his feet going in different directions. One hit the wall, the other knocked her foot out from beneath her and they both tumbled onto the ice.

Noémie laughed and Kian joined in. With his phone still shrilling, Noémie untangled from him and picked herself up off the cold ice, offering her hand to aid his rise.

Only once he was braced against the wall, his skates planted on the ice, did he reach for the phone. Frowning at the screen, he said, "It's my mother."

Noémie's eyes widened and she resisted the urge to look around, certain Celeste had somehow spotted them and they were incurring her wrath.

With an apologetic look, Kian answered. "Hi Mom, I'm in the middle of—" He winced and pulled the phone away from his ear. "Calm down."

Even at this distance, Noémie could hear Celeste's shrill tone through the phone, even if she couldn't make out what she was saying.

"It's *Sunday*, Mom. The banks won't be open until … yeah, I am aware of the situation. I've been watching for a while … Because it's my job to be aware of these sorts of

things! ... No, Mom, I can do that from home and ..."
Kian's shoulders slumped. "No, don't call Father. You're
right ... yes, send the car. I'm around the corner from
Hôtel de Ville, he can pick me up from there."

Noémie dropped her eyes and pressed her lips together
as he hung up. "Is everything okay?"

"One day I'll be allowed to have Sundays off," he
muttered and tucked his phone back into his pocket. "I'm
so sorry. There's a ... duty calls. I need to go."

That saddened her, but she nodded. "That's okay."

He touched her elbow, as he moved by her to skate for
the exit. "Can I drop you anywhere?"

She smiled at him, pushing off the wall to accompany
him. "No. It's fine. I'll hang out here for a while and head
back to Zane and Zariah."

"I would've liked to have stayed longer. I had an
awesome time."

"Me too. Um ... I'll be pretty busy this week as we
prepare for the exhibit."

"I know." Stepping from the rink, he turned around
and smiled at her. "I'll call you tonight."

"I look forward to it."

Sitting in the back row, in a darkened corner, Noémie twisted her fingers and jiggled her leg. Streams of conversation rumbled through the room as people chatted with each other while waiting for the show to begin, but all Noémie could feel was the incredible anxiety buried deep in her belly and the urge to run screaming. She'd taken care to dress appropriately for tonight, dark pants and blue blouse, and let a little bit of her personality shine through with the bright yellow clip against the twist in her hair, and yet she felt like people were staring at her.

Of course, they could be staring at Zariah and her gorgeous, cleavage heightening red dress, as the woman in question reached over and slipped her hand into Noémie's. "Breathe, Miemie. You've gone pale."

"I shouldn't be here," Noémie said, swinging her head from side to side. "I shouldn't be sitting here. I should be out the back, making sure everything's going smoothly. Or helping Dulcie and Veroniqué. Or …"

"That's what you hired a dresser for," Zariah reminded her. "And your girls are amazing. Let them do their thing."

So many worst-case scenarios were firing off in her head. "What if the dresser mixes up the pieces? What if something breaks? The pink one was always flimsy, maybe I should go and check and oh my god, what if the model falls over or it doesn't fit or—why the hell did I let you talk me into this?"

Zariah rolled her eyes. "Because a year ago, you promised yourself that you'd enter this year and you made me promise to help you, and six months ago we both sat down and went through the entry form and you've spent the last six months perfecting these designs. Breathe. It's your *best* stuff."

"I should've stayed out with the exhibit."

Zariah, with her eternal patience, said, "If you did, you wouldn't be able to see everything everyone else entered. You stock lingerie too, remember?"

Noémie allowed herself a deep breath in, letting it out slowly. "Okay. You're right. I know you're right. You know you're right. We know you're—"

"Noémie," Zariah said, squeezing her hand. "Calm."

"Okay." Noémie took a shuddering breath. "But what if—"

"The models are fine," Zariah soothed. "The dresser is fine. Dulcie and Veroniqué have your exhibit covered. Your designs are brilliant. You got this."

Closing her eyes, Noémie concentrated on her breathing and the feeling of Zariah's hand clasping hers. "Thank God you're here. I wouldn't survive without you."

Zariah bumped her shoulder against Noémie's. "There is nowhere else I'd rather be."

Music swelled, the lights dimmed and the show started.

There were simple designs and outrageous designs. Designs with feathers or sequins. Designs that were practical and some that were not. Sports bras, swimwear, sleepwear, lingerie sets, baby dolls and teddies galore, no undergarment was unrepresented.

Noémie bit her tongue, clutching at Zariah when her first piece walked onto the stage. Diverting her eyes, she swept her eyes across the audience, trying to gauge reactions. Interest was politely excited, nods of approval, or tilting heads to get a better look. Some even seemed to be taking notes.

"It looks amazing!" Zariah proclaimed, bouncing up and down in her seat.

Noémie breathed out and allowed herself an excited smile.

The longer the catwalk went on, the more Noémie relaxed. Her mind started wandering as she studied the products of her fellow designers, analyzing the designs, and making notes of what she might do differently to represent her brand. Now and then, Zariah would nudge her and whisper appreciation for something she saw up on stage and Noémie would make mental notes. Some of the designs would fit right in with hers, so she wrote down those numbers so she could speak to their designers after.

Because she specialized in feminine attire, she hadn't been paying attention to the male models and spent her time idly watching and admiring both physique and lingerie. Right up until she recognized a swagger.

Noémie clapped her hand down on Zariah's arm and hung on for dear life.

Zariah winced in pain. "Noémie, wha—?"

"It's *Kian*."

Hair slicked back on his head, makeup stark and striking, skin glittering, he looked like he'd been etched from starlight. Straight-faced and stiff back and *oh my*, his perfect body. She'd seen him model swimming trunks and a t-shirt, but the water-slicked cloth had nothing on bare skin and briefs.

"Oh. *Fuck me*," she breathed in awe.

"Noémie," Zariah said, similarly star-struck. "You totally need to expand your stock."

"Do I ever." Was she drooling? Did she care?

He looked nothing like his natural self. No happy-go-lucky smile and wink. He looked … bored. Sad. Tired. Going through the motions.

Or maybe she was overanalyzing. Maybe this was his model face. Professional, aloof. Untouchable.

She hadn't even thought to look for him. He hadn't mentioned attending at all. Celestial wasn't part of the show, they didn't even have a lingerie line, so why was he here?

Blank eyes swept across the sea of people as he rounded the corner of the U-shaped platform and walked in her direction. She saw the exact moment he spotted her in the crowd. How, she didn't know, since she was sitting in a darkened corner, but he found her.

His lips parted, he broke stride for a microsecond and his eyes seemed to ignite. He locked his gaze on her and held.

Everyone around her seemed to disappear. Shrouded in fog and film, all she could see was the shining light ahead of her. Even his movement seemed to slow. The swagger, the sway of his hips, the muscles on his legs, the way the glitter on his sparkling chest seemed to direct eyes downward, except she couldn't look because she was lost in the forest green gaze which was utterly devoted to her.

Her heart pounded in her chest so hard she was sure it was going to burst out of her and throw itself at him. Her eyes, while focused on his, took in everything, storing away his image to be conjured up at a more appropriate time.

"Gurl, you got it bad," Zariah giggled.

Pinned, like a butterfly to a wall, she could do nothing but flutter madly and surrender to him completely, if he would but ask. "Uh-huh."

Heart hammering, thighs chafing as she squirmed in her seat as Kian walked, all while Zariah looked on in amusement. The spell broke as he turned the corner and left the platform, allowing her to take a complete breath and calm her heart while still leaving her on the edge of her seat, yearning for his return.

He walked on stage twice more, and each time Noémie melted into a puddle under the intensity of his gaze.

Distracted from the other lingerie on display, even hers, she could see nothing else when Kian was present.

Once the walk was over, Noémie sagged sideways into Zariah. Heart pounding, head whirling, a craving inside, she felt overwhelmed by his presence. Overwhelmed in a good way. A fantastic way.

What would she give to have him walk like that again, just for her? To be able to touch and tease. To be able to taste—

Grinning, Zariah pulled Noémie to her feet. "C'mon. We need to find a bottle of water to cool down that thirst of yours."

No. She was resigned to be goo for the rest of her life. "Shuddup."

"The exhibits await," Zariah replied, tugging Noémie into a walk. "You still have an afternoon of merchandising before you can jump his bones tonight."

"Why was he even here?" Noémie asked and looped her arm through Zariah's. "He didn't tell me he was walking."

"Maybe it was supposed to be a surprise," Zariah replied, with a shrug. "I mean, that jaw drop was impressive."

They wove their way through the crowd of people, back through the hall to where Dulcie and Veroniqué were manning their exhibit. Zariah's role, beyond that of keeping Noémie calm at the walk, was drawing to an end. Since she knew little about the business and the products, she would be available to help out where she could and run errands while Dulcie and Veroniqué helped clients and explained lingerie. Dulcie, who could speak English and would act as Zariah's translator if needed, came over to them while Veroniqué, who could not, called out a greeting and then continued to help her prospective client.

"How'd it go?" Dulcie asked in English, her brown eyes shining with interest and delight.

"It was divine," Zariah replied. "The pieces really

shone and Noémie fell in lust with one of the models."

Eeping, Noémie shoved Zariah lightly. "Zaz!"

Dulcie looked gleeful. "Kian modeled? Tell me *everything.*"

"Two words," Zariah said, her eyes gleaming and lifted her hand so she could count them down. "Glitter. Trail."

Noémie rolled her eyes and looked beyond Dulcie at Veroniqué, who was making signs that she needed Noémie's attention. "I'll leave you two to gossip."

"Noémie," Veroniqué said and swept her hand out to indicate a blonde woman also in a wheelchair. "This is Ava. We're having a little trouble communicating but she's excited about the adaptive pieces." She held out the woman's card. "She gave me this."

While Veroniqué was speaking, the woman was typing furiously into her phone into what looked like Google translate. Noting the English prominent on the card, Noémie said in English, "Hi, my name is Noémie Belrose-Song, how may I help you?"

"Oh thank goodness," the woman replied, looking relieved. "I have been fumbling with this app for ages, I probably sounded ridiculous. Can you tell her I'm sorry if I was rude in any way?"

"Of course."

Ava straightened and wheeled her chair to face Noémie more, then offered out her hand to shake. "My name is Ava Jacobs, I'm an event organizer from the London Adaptive Clothing Exhibition. I don't know if you've heard of us."

Noémie nodded. "I have, I've been to one of them while I lived in London."

"Excellent. We're liaising with Paris Fashion groups to organize a similar event here in Paris. I'm very interested in offering you an exhibition spot. Veronica—" she cringed, "No, sorry. Veroniqué, I'm fumbling, I'm just so excited. Veroniqué was showing me some of your pieces and I must say they're fantastic. I would love to discuss them further in-depth with you."

Noémie smiled, a sense of excitement filling her as well. "I would be delighted."

The afternoon went fast. All her pieces drew interest, and as she and her staff worked the exhibit with them on display, she had had a steady stream of visitors. There had been a lot of specific questions about her plus-sized designs, and a few about her adaptive pieces, which thrilled her to no end. Her stack of business cards had run so low, Sofia, her casual staff member, had come to her rescue, closing the boutique to bring some more.

She'd fired off several introductory emails as requested by some of the fashion houses who had approached her and she was feeling great about the interest in her lingerie.

Now, as the event dwindled to a close, she had a chance to relax. Zariah had wandered off to look at the other designer booths and steal a plate of nibbles from the buffet. Dulcie was having a break and Veroniqué was talking to a client about an adaptive bra and pantie set.

Noémie had spotted Kian among the crowd a few times. Longing glances, secret smiles, and special waves, she knew he wouldn't be able to approach her. There were too many people here in the fashion industry, including the Celestial representatives. Too many that knew him and could, potentially, report to his parents. He wouldn't risk it.

She didn't mind. She'd been incredibly busy as it was. But it would've been nice to say hello.

Noémie sighed in contented exhaustion. Her feet hurt, her face was sore from smiling and greeting people, her voice was beginning to become raspy. She was glad for the moment of peace and was considering wandering around so she could visit more exhibits. And maybe catch a moment with Kian.

"Bonsoir."

Turning to greet the new arrival, Noémie's heart leaped to her throat in shock.

Celeste von Brandt smiled. "Well, if it isn't little Noémie Belrose-Song. I did wonder if that was you."

So distracted watching for Kian, she hadn't seen Celeste von Brandt approaching. Not much she could do about that now. "Bonsoir, Madame von Brandt," she said and greeted her with cheek kisses. "I'm surprised you remember me."

It was easy to see who had bestowed Kian with his looks. Styled golden hair, the same forest green eyes set in the face of an angel, her clothes screamed aristocracy of the fashion world. "Look at you," Celeste said, sweeping her eyes over Noémie. "I remember you all tiny with braces and covered in ice cream stickiness. You grew up well. How are your parents?"

"They are well," Noémie replied.

"I haven't had a chance to visit their chocolate shop in London in ages. Such beautiful treats, I really should make the time."

"They've opened one here in Paris," Noémie told her, proud of her parents. "Just before Christmas."

Celeste brightened. "I'll have to pay them a visit." Scanning the area, her eyes landed on the name in bright letters on the back wall. "Song of the rose," she mused and gave a delighted gasp. "These are *your* designs."

"They are."

Choosing the closest mannequin, which happened to be the corset, Celeste strode over to inspect it. "Well," she said, sweeping her hands over the red silk. "You haven't lost any of that fierceness."

Noémie lifted her chest in pride.

Celeste moved onto the next one, a pink bralette and panties. "These are wonderful and alluring. Exquisite craftsmanship. You bloomed into quite the designer." The third one Celeste studied had its adaptive counterpart beside it. "Impressive. That's very clever, almost invisible," Celeste said, studying the front clips, and flicked a glance over to Veroniqué. "You've made a lot of effort to be inclusive."

"Every woman deserves to feel good about herself," Noémie said.

"Absolutely," Celeste replied and smiled at Noémie. "I need to appropriate the name of your lace supplier." She moved onto the next one and ran her fingers along the straps. "Ooh, is that a magnetic latch?"

"Yes."

"You've got it in a little hidden compartment."

"It's easier to remove for washing or replace with different magnet strength."

"Very clever. Quite a unique style you have, Noémie, and it seems you are just bursting with ingenious ideas. It would be a shame to waste them all on lingerie. Mathilde!"

Celeste's ever-present assistant, who had been standing off to the side, stepped forward. Brown hair tied in a bun and round glasses, she had a few more worry lines around her eyes than the last time Noémie had seen her. "Yes, Madame?"

Celeste switched to an accented English. "Ensure Noémie has my details. Noémie, if you send me your introductory information, I'll see what Celestial can do for you."

As Mathilda extended her hand, offering Noémie a business card, Noémie voiced, "I didn't think Celestial was interested in lingerie."

"We're always interested in *talent*." Celeste waved her hand and went back to inspecting the mannequins. "Richard and I have been discussing expanding our available stock in stores to include accessories and Kian suggested we partner with some of the smaller designers." Celeste gave Noémie a sharp look. "You remember my son?"

"Of course," Noémie replied and allowed a bit of cheek to creep into her voice. "I have a clear memory of being called a 'bad influence' on him."

Celeste laughed. "Ahh, yes. I remember that. You had

that unfortunate accident on my carpet." She smiled and shook her head. "You were such an impudent child. You and that Zane, always dragging him off for adventures." Celeste rested her hands on the mannequin's shoulders as she studied the baby doll. "Kian lives here in Paris now. I should tell him to seek you out, he's rather lacking in the social circles as of late. Always working, just like his father."

Hope blossomed in her chest. If she could get approval from Kian's mother, it might make breaking his contract easier on him. "That would be wonderful."

"He's toddling around here somewhere," Celeste said and turned around to regard the decreasing crowd of people attending the event. "Mathilda, when's my next free brunch?"

"Not for another month," Mathilda replied, brusque as she checked the schedule. "And even then, your timetable is full, I'm uncertain whether or not you could keep an appointment."

Celeste dragged out a sigh. "Very well. When's my next brunch with Kian? Noémie can join us." Turning away, she strode back to Noémie to kiss her cheeks. "Mathilda will contact you for confirmation closer to the time. Lovely to see you."

"Wonderful to see you, too," Noémie replied, beaming. She waited until Celeste had disappeared into the next exhibit before she pressed a hand to her chest and exhaled a long breath.

Veroniqué wheeled over. "Was that Celeste?" she blurted. "*The* Celeste?"

Noémie nodded. "It was indeed." She looked down at the card she clutched, then waved it around. "And I have her number!"

Veroniqué squealed right along with Noémie. "That's so amazing!"

"This has been incredible for Chant de La Rose," Noémie said. "All those people asking about my designs. If even a tenth of them sign a supply contract, all this would be worth it."

"We should celebrate tonight," Veroniqué said.

"Excellent idea," Noémie replied and glanced around. The crowds were dwindling, and there was only half an hour left before the formal end of the event. "I'd like to take another look around. Message Dulcie so she can help out until the end and take a break yourself too."

Veroniqué nodded. "I'll be quick."

"Thank you," Noémie said, smiling as Veroniqué wheeled away. With no potential clients in her booth at present, Noémie went for her phone to make sure she copied Celeste's contact details straight into her address book.

"Well, well. What a *pleasant* surprise."

Noémie froze, holding onto her phone. The way 'pleasant' was said sent a chill down her spine. She hadn't expected to see him here. Not now. Not ever. Just when her life was starting to look up. Past experiences with this man warned her to be extra vigilant and careful. It took barely a second to hit the record in her camera.

Etching her face into a stony expression, she turned. "Jacquez."

Folding her arms on her chest, she tried to make the position of her phone look as natural as she could. Professional. She could be professional. She didn't like him. She didn't like the way his eyes slid all over her. She didn't like the smile, something she used to find so charming. It was funny how fast her feelings had turned from admiration to repulsion, but then, his actions had deserved her ire.

She had to hide her reaction. There were still representatives around. And if *he* was one of the representatives, undoubtedly he was going to milk it for all he was worth.

Jacquez sneered, "I'd heard you went into lingerie but I never expected to see you at one of these. I didn't think you had the drive. Or the skill."

"There's a lot you never bothered to learn about me."

Eyebrow raised, he glanced over to her display pieces. "Quaint, but not at all risky. Just like in university. You've not grown at all. And plus-sized? Tsh."

She bit back a retort by grinding her teeth and tried to maintain civility. It wouldn't be good if she punched him in the nose. Even if it would make her feel better. "Are you representing anyone?"

The stupid smirk widened. "Celestial."

He was lying. He had to be. Celeste von Brandt had already been here *and* left her number, so there was no way he could work for them. That made her wonder what game Jacquez was playing. If he was preying on young designers by pretending to represent Celestial, she'd need to catch him in a lie so she could report him to the organizers.

"The representative group is slowly making their way here and I'm their frontman," he informed her with that insufferable drawl of his. "This can go one of two ways. One, I can hurry them passed and say you're not worth their time. Or," he winked at her. "I can put in a good word—if you can make it worth my while."

Noémie felt a surge of anger and her hand clenched around her phone.

His eyes stroked her again, with an added suggestive look.

She wondered if that was enough. Or if he was that stupid he'd incriminate himself further. "Not happening."

"We used to be so good together, Noémie. All those nights, and days and—"

"You disgust me."

He shrugged. "Fine. Give me one of your designs, with your fancy hidden rose removed this time, and I'll make sure Monsieur von Brandt stops at your exhibit personally."

Noémie narrowed her eyes. "You're still stealing

designs? You were expelled for that."

Jacquez scoffed. "Be real, Noémie," he said and had the gall to try to touch her hair. "We're friends, aren't we? This is how the business works, you know that."

"We were never friends, Jacquez," Noémie snarled. "You stole my designs and then you used me and I was stupid enough to think—" she huffed out a breath. "I'll take my chances."

He raised his hands and gave her an 'I tried to warn you' gesture.

She gritted her teeth. She had to warn Kian about this guy, especially if he was using Celestial as a cover. She'd have to admit there was a lot more to the story than what she'd told him, but she could handle that. She would've told him eventually. And she'd have to do it without alerting others that she and Kian were close.

"You're making a mistake," Jacquez said, his expression brightening as he looked beyond Noémie. "Last chance."

"No." She refused to be mollified by Jacquez. And she would never stay silent about his antics. Had he forgotten that? It didn't work last time, it wouldn't work now.

"Ahh. Monsieur von Brandt!" he chirped and moved away. "I was just coming to find you. I have some delightful designers for you to meet. This way."

Noémie turned in time to see Jacquez throw an arm around Kian's shoulder and turn him away from her exhibit, and spot Kian's frown in response.

Her heart sank. That familiarity meant that Jacquez did work for Celestial, but not enough so that he was allowed to be on first name basis with Kian.

She had to warn Kian about Jacquez as soon as she could. She didn't hear what Jacquez said next, but Kian's expression flat lined.

She mightn't be able to alert anyone they were close. But she could say they went to school together. That was public record. Celeste remembered her. What did they have to lose? "Salut, Kian," she called, using informal

French and his name to illustrate she was on friendly terms with Kian. "Are you that run off your feet you don't even have time to say hello to an old friend?"

Kian lifted his head and beamed, and the asshole beside him stiffened. "Noémie, you know how it is." Shaking himself free from Jacquez, he approached her with a smile. "You look wonderful."

She held out her hand for him to shake, only to have him take it and pull her in for the customary cheek kiss greeting.

"You know her?" Jacquez said, with a hint of fear in his voice.

"Absolutely," Kian said, keeping her hand and clasping it with both of his. "We're old friends."

Oh, the look on Jacquez's face was satisfying.

Kian cast a look at her booth. "So it *was* your designs," he said, playing the part. "I thought I recognized them backstage. They're amazing." His eyes landed on the baby doll and Noémie watched with glee as he tried to contain himself. With a will of steel, he kept a straight face as he said, "That one is my favorite, I think."

"Mine too. It feels *divine* when you wear it," Noémie replied, watching as the slight pinking of his ears betrayed him.

Rattled, Jacquez tried to interrupt. "Monsieur von Brandt, we have designers we need to meet."

"I know, and I'm meeting one," Kian said, his hands still clasping Noémie's as he turned his gaze to Jacquez. "Which reminds me, why did you say Noémie wasn't worth my time?"

Jacquez blanched. "You misheard me."

"Jacquez and I have a *history*," Noémie said, meeting Kian's eyes and hoping he'd get the message. He wouldn't get all the message, but enough to know there was bad blood between them.

Kian's hands tightened around hers and the smile dimmed.

"*You*!" Zariah roared.

Jacquez's head snapped in the direction of the roar, and, as he saw who it was, raised his hands to ward her away. While they'd only met once or twice, Zariah was quite unforgettable. "Oh shit."

The firestorm approached, blazing red dress and a stormy expression, Zariah looked set to gut him. As she stalked toward him, she pulled off her stiletto shoes and clutched them as weapons.

Noémie used that distraction to tell Kian, "You need to check *all* of his designs for plagiarism. And check with every designer he spoke alone with tonight. He just tried to coerce me."

Jacquez skittered backward away from the oncoming terror and began searching for a place to hide. "What does she want?" he asked, deliberately speaking French instead of English, something Noémie knew would anger Zariah further, since she knew Jacquez could speak English.

Kian studied her. "Noémie," he said in a low voice.

Lifting her phone, she showed him she was recording. "I have proof."

French privacy laws prohibited the use of unconsented recordings as evidence, even though they were currently in a public space, she could land herself in legal trouble. However, she knew Jacquez wasn't adept at hiding his tracks, and it would give Kian a place to start. "I'll email you the video," she said and swallowed. "I'm sorry. You … you won't like what he says."

"No, don't—"

Zariah's expression wasn't the only one that reached epic hurricane proportions. "I always hoped I'd get this chance," she spat. "You're going to regret what you did."

Realizing that Zariah was one step away from braining Jacquez with her shoe, Noémie released Kian's hand and stepped between Jacquez and Zariah. "Zaz," she murmured in a quiet, controlled voice. "Not here."

Zariah tried to get around Noémie. "I don't care—"

"What is she saying?" Jacquez asked, still speaking French and obvious in his attempt to pretend he didn't know Zariah.

"What the fuck is he saying?" Zariah snarled, too angry to translate with her limited French. "I know you can speak English!"

Noémie clasped Zariah's upper arms to stop her. "Time and place," she told her and threw a pointed look around. They were drawing attention and this was her reputation on the line.

Zariah focused on Noémie, before her attention was back on Jacquez. "You and me. Outside. Let's go. I have *words* saved up for you. Lots of big words that need to be delivered with force."

"Who is this woman? Why is she so angry?"

"You know why," Noémie told him, then addressed Zariah. "He's trying to pretend he's never met you."

"You lying two-faced bastard. I can announce it to the *entire* world, if you like," Zariah threatened.

Kian stepped between Zariah and Noémie, and Jacquez. "Enough," he said in a low tone.

Zariah growled, angry at being interrupted. "Kian—"

"Zaz," Noémie hissed in warning.

Extending his hands to Noémie, Kian cupped them both around her hand. "I appreciate you bringing this to my attention," he said in a professional tone, to contrast the completely unprofessional way he held her hand. "May I call you later?"

Holding her tongue, her other hand on Zariah, Noémie nodded.

As Kian turned his back on Jacquez, Jacquez had issued Zariah and Noémie a look of triumph, which quickly turned sour as Kian turned to him. Voice as cold as ice, Kian said to Jacquez, "Come with me."

CHAPTER 8

When the dust had settled, everything was packed away and the event was over, Noémie cuddled on her sofa with Zariah. Seeing Jacquez again had brought bad memories to the forefront of her mind. Had she been prepared to see him, she would have been fine, but being blindsided like that upset her equilibrium and it had all come crashing down as she and Zariah had packed up.

Zariah had called Zane, who'd gone on an ice cream run and delivered Zariah a change of clothes and her pajamas, before retreating to the rented apartment to allow the girls to talk it out.

"You should've let me brain him," Zariah muttered. She sat with her back wedged between the armrest and the back of the sofa and allowed Noémie to cuddle between her legs, with the ice cream tub on Noémie's lap. "I've been itching to for years."

"I know," Noémie said and licked her spoon. "Would've liked to have seen it too, but there were too many people around."

Zariah dropped her spoon down to scoop out some more ice cream. "I suppose I could've taken him out the back and brained him there, but I was just so angry when I saw him. This prick ruined your life. How dare he come back now when things are looking up?" She made angry noises as she gulped down her spoonful of ice cream.

"He can't hurt me anymore," Noémie said, smiling as Floof, her budgie, flew across the room and landed on the ice cream container to chirp at her.

"Damn right, he can't," Zariah said, sour. "If he tries, I will punch his lights out."

Noémie scooped Floof up and tucked him against her chest for scratches. "Thanks for being here, Zaz."

Zariah closed her arms around Noémie to squeeze her. "You know my biggest regret is Zane and I were in London for that mess. I'm glad I was here this time." Still stuck on the appearance of Jacquez, Zariah lamented, "I can't believe he works for Kian. How the hell did a scumbag like him land a job at Celestial?"

"No idea," Noémie muttered, concentrating on a spot on Floof's neck he absolutely adored getting scratched. "I suppose Kian might tell me when he calls, but he might not. Depends on what he finds."

"There's no way he's not doing something sketchy. Once a scumbag, always a scumbag," Zariah preached. "I hope he gets fired."

A knock on the door caused Floof to startle, chirping and bouncing around.

"Did Zane forget his key?" Noémie asked, kicking the rainbow patchwork blanket off their legs.

"Probably," Zariah replied. "But I didn't think he was coming back."

Passing the tub of ice cream to Zariah, Noémie hauled herself up, clutching Floof to her chest as she went to answer the door.

Kian stood at the other side, still dressed in the suit he wore to the gala. He looked exhausted and harried, and yet there he was, standing at her door. "Noémie, I was—" he blurted, then cringed as he took in the fact that she was in her oversized flannel pajamas. He dug a finger under the sleeve of his coat to check his watch. "I apologize for the late hour. Were you asleep?"

"No," Noémie replied as Floof climbed from her chest to her shoulder. "No, it's fine. I just didn't expect you. I thought you were going to call."

"I wanted to see you," he admitted softly. His eyes fell on her little yellow budgie and he smiled. "Is this Floof?"

"This is him," Noémie replied, turning her head to kiss him as Floof responded to his name with a cheep.

Kian offered Floof a finger and made a scratching motion in the air to see how he'd be responded to, which Floof squawked at him over and darted up to the top of Noémie's head to scold the man who dared enter his domain. "He's adorable. And loud."

"He'll get used to you," Noémie replied and stepped away from the door to give Kian access to her home. "Do you want to come in?"

"Please," Kian said with an incline of his head and followed her inside.

Noémie helped him out of his coat and hung it on the rack beside hers while Kian wandered down Noémie's small hallway into a small one-bedroom apartment. Since she and Floof lived alone, Noémie didn't need a large apartment. One decent-sized living space, which doubled as a sewing room, a small kitchen and bathroom, and her bedroom. All her sewing equipment was packed neatly away in the cabinet in the corner, ready to be brought out at a moment's notice. Beside her cabinet was an artist's desk and bench. A single three-seater sofa in front of her TV and a small coffee table. The feature wall in her apartment had been painted a royal purple, matching the walls of her bedroom, and her kitchen cupboards had been painted yellow with lilac flowers to continue the theme through the rest of the apartment.

"I'd give you the tour," Noémie said and gestured the room, "but this is pretty much it. I don't need much to survive."

"It's cozy," Kian said, smiling as he looked around. "Very colorful. It suits you."

"Thank you."

Upon spotting him, Zariah hauled herself from the sofa and grabbed the melting ice cream container. "Hey, Kian."

Kian greeted her with a warm smile. "Hi, Zaz." Glancing back at Noémie, he asked, "Am I interrupting something?"

Noémie gathered up Floof, returning him to his cage by the TV, much to Floof's disgust. "Just a pity party."

"It was supposed to be a celebration," Zariah said from the kitchen where she was putting away the ice cream. "But some prick decided to ruin it. I hope you fired him. Tell me you fired him. For that matter, how did someone like him get a job at Celestial in the first place?!"

Kian looked awkward and evaded Zariah's question. "I can't answer that one, but yes. He's been fired. And reported to the police."

Zariah punched the air with a whooping, "Yes!" followed by a happy dance.

"Really?" Noémie asked, astounded.

Kian nodded, then asked tentatively, "That was the ex? The one who …"

Noémie dropped her eyes, both embarrassed and ashamed. "In a manner of speaking."

"That," Zariah announced, still in the throes of her happy dance, "was a lying scumbag who deserves to have his balls ripped off and stuffed up his nose, just so he can smell how horrible he is. And then—"

"Zaz, can we have a minute?" Noémie asked as Kian turned an alarming shade of green.

With a huffy noise, Zariah swept her phone off the bench. "Yeah. Sure. I need to call Zane," she muttered and headed for Noémie's bedroom for some privacy.

"She's really intense," Kian murmured as Zariah closed the door behind her.

"Yeah," she replied with a nod. "Never give her a

reason to go for yours."

"So kind of you to warn me. There's an image I didn't want."

Noémie turned to Kian. "I didn't know you were going to be there tonight," she said, deciding to talk about the easiest thing first.

"Last minute switch," Kian told her. "An acquaintance got sick and called in a favor. There wasn't time to tell you." Stepping toward her, he asked, "Would you tell me about Jacquez?"

"You really fired him?" At Kian's nod, Noémie flopped down on her sofa. Grabbing one of the cushions, she hugged it to her chest. "What a mess. This is not how I wanted you to find out."

Kian sat on her coffee table before her, knees on either side of hers, and reached out to coax one of her hands away from the cushion so he could cradle it. "He stole from you," he said, matter of fact. "That's why you warned me about plagiarism."

Noémie dropped her eyes since it was easier to talk to him when she couldn't gauge his reactions. "He … yes … the … um …" She puffed out a hard breath and tried to form her thoughts into words while Kian waited patiently. "We worked together on projects before. I was so desperate to prove myself that I carried him and did all the work."

Kian's thumbs stroked against her hands, a soothing gesture which encouraged her to speak more.

"After I found him in bed with … um … the … the break up was messy and … things went missing. Among them were my sketchbooks. Turns out, he …" she cringed, then rushed, "He submitted almost all of my designs as part of his portfolio at the end of the semester."

"Oh no."

She raised her head and met his compassionate eyes. "I reported him. He said I was just bitter and sore about the breakup and it was my word against his. We had to go to the University disciplinary board and he's proclaimed his innocence and said I was out to get him because I was jealous. Until I pointed out *my* signature in every single design he'd submitted. As far as I knew, he'd been expelled."

Kian released one of her hands to touch her cheek, then her shoulder to offer comfort. "He's been under investigation for fraud," he explained. "I've been concerned about a few things with him, including a large sum of money misappropriated. That's why I disappeared on Sunday, Mom found out and wanted to know what I was doing about it. He's been vocal about Celestial getting into lingerie so it was decided I would use the exhibit as an excuse to monitor his movements. After we spoke to you, I went around to all the designers he'd spoken to and I had two reports tonight of him trying to coerce … sex or designs and using my company to do that."

Noémie squeezed shut her eyes. "Oh, Kian, I'm so sorry. That's horrible."

"We filed a police report for sexual harassment tonight," he said. "The fraud one is coming."

"Do you need anything from me? A statement of what happened tonight?"

"A statement would help." Kian leaned forward, bringing their foreheads together briefly. "But, please, delete the video. We don't need it to convict him and I don't want you getting into trouble."

She nodded. "I will," she promised. "Whatever you need. He has to pay for this."

He exhaled slowly. "I never expected it ran this deep. I mean, he seemed like a nice guy. Friendly and polite, little too open with his sexual prowess, but all around, he seemed okay … if I'd known how far he'd go, I would've found a way to warn you."

"Sounds like he's stepped up his game. He was never that blatant before." She sighed. "Or maybe he was and I never saw it, I don't know."

Kian pursed his lips. "It's possible he knew I was investigating him."

She shook her head. "It's far more likely he got comfortable and confident he wasn't going to get caught. He really seemed to believe he had you in his pocket." She dropped her eyes. "I'm sorry I didn't tell you about him."

"You probably never expected to see him again. Like you said, he was expelled. No reason to think he'd still be in the industry."

"True," she mumbled.

"Besides," he said, and squeezed her hand. "You were very quick to warn me once you knew he worked for me. Thank you."

She lifted her gaze to meet his eyes as she said, "I couldn't let him steal from you, too."

Kian's voice was husky and low. "Noémie ... can I ask ... I mean, tell me if I'm out of line, but ...what—why did you date him?"

Noémie sighed. "No judgment?"

He unclasped one hand from hers to press it to his chest to show sincerity. "No judgment."

"I was young," she explained, hugging the cushion tighter. "New to the country and lonely. Still becoming confident in a language I'd really only spoken with family. Trying to fit in. I met him within a few days of the start of classes and he was so charming. Lavished attention on me, showed me Paris. Laughed at all my language mistakes and made it seem like he was teasing out of the goodness of his heart, but he never corrected me, or gave me the right words to use. Seemed to encourage mistakes."

Kian nodded to show he understood.

"In class ... he told me he had nearly finished his degree, but was doing some basic stuff again so he could branch out. Seemed legit. He gave me advice, little niggles, things that sounded right, but felt that little bit off and I wasn't confident in my ability back then. Small red flags that I didn't see because I was new to the whole love thing, and he was older and had been in the industry longer than me."

"And probably having a bit of culture shock, too. I know I did."

She nodded. "I'm sure that played a part," she agreed, then sighed. "He started directing the way I dressed, how I did my hair, everything, telling me he was helping me fit in. Before I knew it, I was under his thumb and *allowing* him to copy designs off me and … Starstruck by my first grown-up romance and it made me stupid."

"I'm so sorry that happened to you. Sounds like a terrible experience."

She shrugged. "I got over it. He was a long time ago and I have definitely moved past him. I'm confident in my designs and my skill. He took me by surprise today and while I might be moping now, I'm okay. I promise."

He nodded. "Okay."

Deciding they needed a change of topic, she giggled and pushed forward to nudge him and tease. "And I have a very nice image in my head of you. *Mmm.*"

Although Kian laughed, his cheeks went red. "Liked that, did you?"

"Very much. It was impressive." She allowed a deliberate croon to seep into her voice. "Very impressive."

"Glad to be of service."

"You're going to be finding glitter in … um … various places for weeks."

Kian laughed. "I think having glitter in my unmentionables is worth it, especially when I can put *that* look on your face."

"Monsieur von Brandt," she teased. "Are you trying to seduce me?"

"It depends," he purred. "Is it working?"

"Perhaps."

His voice took on a softer tone. "I'm relieved you're alright. I was so worried."

Noémie closed her eyes. He was almost too good to be

true. He'd come here, in the dead of night, after dealing with that to see if *she* was okay. "Kian?"

"Yes?"

"May I hug you?"

Instead of responding, Kian pushed away from the coffee table. Kneeling in front of her, he wrapped his arms around her torso and pulled her to the edge of the seat and she ended up with her legs on either side of him.

He touched her arms, coaxing hers up and over his shoulders, allowing her to bury her face in his neck while hugging his head tightly. His hunched over position, along with his broad shoulders and tight embrace, meant that she was surrounded, swallowed up by his body, safe and warm.

With his cheek against hers and his arms around her, she was squished against him and this was the closest she'd ever been to him. It was different and comforting and absolutely wonderful too. Something more than all the hand holding and gentle touches.

Noémie closed her eyes and hung on. Hands stroked her back, little comforting movements designed to soothe. She never wanted to let go.

He smelled amazing and she breathed him in. Cologne mixed with hair gel and some sort of coconut scent. A hint of natural musk lurking beneath, he hadn't had a chance to shower. Slight tang of peppermint on his breath.

Kian made a small noise at the back of his throat that reminded Noémie of a cat's purr and before she could comment on it, his lips were against the side of her neck. Soft and gentle, trapped in a moment between a linger and a peck, before his chin was on her shoulder again and his arms were tightening his embrace around her.

She didn't know what to make of the kiss. So much more personal and intimate than a forehead or cheek kiss, and she wasn't sure how to react. He'd made no move beyond that and was instead content to cuddle her.

Was he waiting for a reaction from her? He didn't seem to be. Had he even realized he'd done that? Probably not, if she thought about it. Not if the way it felt like he was settling in for a longer, comforting cuddle was anything to go by. They'd both had a horrific end to what was an otherwise wonderful day. Him: having to fire an employee and charging someone with fraud, sexual harassment, and theft. Her: having to confront a past she thought was behind her. He needed a hug as much as she did, which is why he'd bashfully admitted he'd come to see her.

She could be there for him as much as he could be here for her and perhaps make the ending of today better for both of them.

Sighing, Noémie snuggled in close and held on tight.

CHAPTER 9

"This was a great idea," Kian chirped, holding the door open. "Indoor swimming at the heated pool in the middle of winter. Delightful."

Zariah cast Noémie a significant look, completed by an eyebrow waggle. "You realize, he's only come along to see you in your swimsuit."

"And then be disappointed it's not a bikini," Noémie quipped with a smile and a bounce in her stride. "I am well aware." Stepping up to the counter, she showed the assistant her membership card and handed over some Euros to pay for her friends to use the pool.

"I will never be disappointed in whatever Noémie chooses to wear," Kian said and with an air of grandeur, pressed his hand to his chest and bowed slightly to show his sincerity. "And I assumed that, since you said you wanted to do laps, a bikini was out of the question."

"Well, I can be disappointed," Zane said, looping his arm around Kian's shoulders. "Noémie looks hot in a bikini."

"Ahem," Zariah said, glaring at Zane.

"Well, now I'm jealous," Kian said, folding his arms on his chest. "Unfair."

"Don't be," Noémie told him, patting his arm. "At least you have a minute chance of seeing me in lingerie. Zane will never get that option."

"Woe is me," Zane said with a roll of his eyes.

Kian gave her a dopey looking smile. "Intriguing. Tell me more."

Heat flooded her face from his expression and she lost her nerve to flirt more.

"The promise of bikinis is what got me out of bed this early in the morning," Zane lamented, draping dramatically around Kian's neck. "I feel lied to."

"Again, you didn't have to come," Zariah said. "We were fine with meeting you both for breakfast before Noémie has to open her boutique. No need to wake up this early at all."

"Nuh-ah. We need to protect your virtue!" Zane declared.

Noémie lifted her eyebrow at Zane. "From whom? All the hot guys here are more concerned with doing laps."

"Am I not hot, Nomnom?" Zane asked, fluttering his eyelashes at her. "I don't want to do laps."

Scoffing, Noémie pointed toward the change rooms. "Go get changed. Before Zariah murder-death-kill glares at you. We'll see you in the pool."

It didn't take Zariah and Noémie long to store their gear in the lockers in the women's change rooms, don their caps and take to the water. Both girls had worn their swimsuits under their clothes to make life a bit easier. Noémie tried to swim twice a week and use the gym at least once. While she and Zariah often exercised together, she hadn't expected Kian and Zane to want to come as well.

Taking a place in the lanes, Noémie stretched her arms to warm them up.

Kian coming, she could understand. She had been upset about Jacquez last night, making the most of the permission to hug him to the point where she'd fallen asleep on his chest. After waking her up, he and Zariah had helped her to bed, and he'd offered to take them out to breakfast and she'd been almost asleep as she replied she was going swimming first thing.

So he invited himself along. Then Zane had turned up too.

Zane, Noémie supposed, had wanted to spend as much time with them before starting his next round of concerts. Zariah would remain in Paris for a few more weeks working on a Paris series for her travel blog while Zane was on the road again.

Seeing Kian first thing in the morning had been thrilling. Her heart had skipped a beat when she and Zariah had arrived and Kian and Zane were chatting out the front waiting for them. It felt like a double date since they were going to breakfast afterward, something she'd always missed out on when going places with Zane and Zariah.

Seeing Kian waltz out of the change rooms wearing designer cat print swim jammers was another kind of thrilling. One that settled straight between her thighs.

"Whoa," Zariah said as she spotted the men. "He doesn't like to leave much to the imagination, does he?"

It was obvious she was talking about Kian since Zane wore a beater with trunks. "It's the model in him, I guess," Noémie said, stuck in a pretend pose of stretching her arm when she was really staring at Kian.

"I think he may be trying to seduce you," Zariah said. "That's two days in a row he's down to the bare minimum."

Noémie chewed on her bottom lip. "I think he might be too." If it was only seduce, she might let him, just so she could run her hands over that chest. But both of them wanted more, and that was worth waiting to see if it would work.

"Better here than while he's up on stage," Zariah crooned, winking. "You can get up close and personal."

"Yup."

"Pick your jaw off the ground before he sees. You're playing hard to get. Not 'oh my god, do me now'."

Noémie snorted and cast Zariah a quirked eyebrow. "You should probably stop looking too, you're giving Zane a complex."

Zariah flopped her hand at Noémie. "I can appreciate excellently crafted male physique if I want to. Did you not just hear Zane saying he wanted to gawk at you in a bikini?"

"True."

"Swim first, gawk later," Zariah said and fixed her goggles over her eyes.

Noémie followed Zariah into a dive position and the two of them dove into the pool. She went slowly at first, warming up her muscles as she set into a freestyle rhythm. Nice and easy. Stroke and breathe and stroke again, gliding through the water. Keeping her eye on the clock, she kept it easy for ten minutes, then for the next two laps went as hard as she could.

Swimming always made her feel better. The water washed away hurt and pain, replacing it with clarity and calm. She worked her body and her mind as she sorted through her feelings. The pain that came from Jacquez and his actions were replaced with Kian's kindness, caring, and thoughtfulness. He didn't have to come to check up on her last night, but he had. He didn't have to follow through the next morning, but he did.

Their short time getting to know each other confirmed what she knew about him already. He was funny. Silly. Sweet and kind. He was caring and considerate and wonderful to be around and when he smiled at her, she was all bubbly and flustered.

It would be very easy to love Kian. And that thought was both amazing and scary to her.

Switching it up, she fell into an easy breaststroke so she could relax, catch her breath, and have a look around to see what her friends were up to.

Zariah backstroked past her in the lane next to her. Zane, on the other side of Zariah, who much preferred gym workouts, had commandeered a kickboard and was lazily kicking up and down the lane.

Kian was in the lane on the other side of Noémie and he'd paused down the end. Standing in the shallow end to stretch his arms, he'd drawn the attention of another swimmer. In the lane next on the other side of him, the woman was right up against the lane dividers as she talked to him and by her posture—the way she was practically thrusting her chest at him—she was flirting with him.

Even though it wasn't unusual and expected for women to harmlessly flirt in Paris, Noémie felt a flare of jealousy. While Kian's body language didn't suggest he was flirting back and he was as far away from her as he could get without appearing rude, all Noémie wanted to do was swim over there and mark her territory.

That thought embarrassed her.

Kian wasn't hers. He wasn't her territory. They were, until they both agreed otherwise, friends.

Handholding friends.

Handholding flirting friends.

Exclusive handholding flirting friends.

He looked down the lanes to spot her approaching. His face lit up in a smile and he waved at her. A rush of endorphins surged through her and she was soaring, followed by heat flooding her cheeks. She ducked her head down into the water under the pretense of swimming when she was really hiding.

How could a simple smile from him undo her as much as this? It seemed impossible, and yet, it happened.

"Your technique is exquisite, Noémie," Kian exclaimed, speaking French, an oddity because they used English unless in the company of others since that was the language they met each other with.

Touching her fingers to the edge of the pool, she stood

so she could stretch out her muscles. She flicked her eyes over to the woman in the opposite lane, then fixed her smile on Kian. "Thank you," she replied in the same language. "Are you finished? I seem to recall you mentioning you had pretty good stamina."

"Taking a stretch break," he said and he turned so he was looking straight at her, excluding the other woman from the conversation. He stepped closer to the lane barrier between them. "I'm with Zane. Gym workouts are preferred. The chlorine in the pool tends to mess with my hair regime."

"You could get a cap you know. Protect that pretty, pretty hair of yours."

He perked up. "You think it's pretty?"

Noémie laughed at him and didn't answer. The now-sour woman who'd been talking to Kian got the hint and returned to her swim.

Kian relaxed the moment he heard water move behind him.

"You attract a lot of people," Noémie noted, watching as the woman swam away.

"Most of the time I can ignore it and pretend that I'm a bumbling American who doesn't speak French," he said with a light shrug. "And that's mostly a turn-off, no matter how pretty my hair is. But she opened with heavily accented, halting French and a 'nice abs' comment before she'd even asked my name, so I pretended I couldn't speak English and used elaborate wording. I'm not interested in being picked up while working out, unless it's by you."

Flushing, Noémie tried to ignore how happy that made her. "I've done that language thing before. It's an easy way to ward off unwanted attention. And to be fair," she said, and allowed her eyes to drop as she inspected him. "They are pretty spectacular abs."

He grinned at her. "Glad you approve. How are you today?"

Dragging her attention away from said abs, she said,

"I'm fine."

"Well rested?"

"Well … Zariah snores. So I'm rested, but not necessarily 'well'."

Kian laughed and rested his hands on the lane barrier.

Flicking her eyes along the lanes, she saw that Zariah and Zane were busy flirting with each other up the other side of the pool, so that gave her and Kian some time alone. "Um … Thank you for last night."

"You don't need to thank me for that."

"I do," she said, and placed her hand over the top of his. "I … the whole situation was sprung on you and you were very sweet about it all."

"I want to be a part of your life, Noémie. Friend or otherwise, and that means supporting you through the bad and sharing the good. Besides, it wasn't without its perks for me too, you know."

"Oh?"

He smiled at her. Lifting his hand a little, he spread his fingers, inviting her to intertwine their hands, an invitation she took. "I got a taste of what it was like to cuddle you. That's not something I'm likely to forget." His voice dropped to a purr. "You are very nice to cuddle."

How could a simple thing as a purr in his voice make her feel so wonderful? "So are you."

Kian smiled. "Plus, I like knowing our lives would have intersected even if I hadn't come to Chant de La Rose."

Noémie nodded. Kian would've still investigated Jacquez. Noémie still would've recorded their conversation. They both would've been at the exhibit last night and seen each other. But they might not have become reacquainted like they were now, and their meeting would've been hampered by Jacquez. "Personally, I'm glad you walked into Chant de La Rose. I much prefer a flirtatious, teasing reintroduction over one that would have always reminded me of Jacquez."

"Me too." He was obvious about his eye drop and it

gave Noémie a boost of confidence. "I bet you look just as amazing in gym gear as you do in a swimsuit." A grin burst onto Kian's face. "How about a race? I win, and you show me your gym getup."

Noémie raised her eyebrows at him. "Really?"

"Really," he drawled and took another step toward her. "So, what do you want if you win? Name your prize, Noémie."

She paused in thought and settled on something she'd been meaning to ask him anyway. "You're in Milan this week, right?"

"Yeah." He tilted his head at her and squeezed her fingers. "Why? Are you going to miss me? Or you want me to bring you back a souvenir?"

"I might miss the free dinners," she retorted which made him laugh. "You're back on Saturday?"

"Yes."

Nodding, she said, "There's a food market next Sunday I've been dying to go to, but I have to pick and choose what I buy carefully because it's hard to carry food on the metro. If I win, you drive me there and you carry all the food I buy."

Kian lifted his eyebrows at her. "Really?"

With her free hand, she tapped her lip in consideration. "Maybe, if you're a good pack mule, I'll let you come over for dinner that night to share."

He drifted through the water even closer, so he was pressed against the barrier between them, "You know, if you wanted to go, all you had to do was ask. A food market sounds like a wonderful date and I'd be happy to take you regardless of who wins."

She gave him a dazzling smile. "If you wanted to see me in gym gear, all you had to do was ask. But now, you have to win a race for it."

"A day with you, or seeing you in gym gear," he pondered. "I think that's more than enough incentive for me to lose this race."

Noémie laughed. "Okay, how's this? We'll go to the food market and you come to dinner after. You win, and I'll *cook* in my gym gear."

He grinned. "You have a deal."

"You don't even know if my gym gear is a baggy sweater or not and you're still willing to deal?"

"You would look amazing in anything," he said.

"You're a dork."

"Absolutely."

Flexing his hand, he then lifted their intertwined hands to his lips to ghost a kiss against the back of her fingers. With deliberate care, he turned her hand over and then placed a delicate kiss on the inside of her wrist. Then, with a sly smile he rushed, "Three-two-one-go!" and dove into the water.

Noémie stared for a moment, her wrist tingling, before yelping and diving in after him.

CHAPTER 10

"You're ridiculous."

"*I'm* ridiculous? I'm not the one pining over someone who I'm not even official with yet."

"I'm not pining!" Noémie complained, her voice rising in indignation.

"You've mentioned four times in the last five minutes that he's late and you're worried. Totally pining."

"Well, he *is* late, and I *am* worried and I haven't seen him all week."

Zariah gave her a bland look through the video screen. "Zane has been AWOL all week too, you know. And I'm not mentioning him every few minutes like some lovesick schoolgirl. Face it, Miemie, whatever you have between you, it's shifted."

Noémie pressed her lips together, then chewed on the bottom one as nerves got the better of her. "You think? I'm … I don't know. It doesn't feel like it's shifted. It hasn't been enough time. Has it?"

"Trust me on this. Love hides, until it's ready to smash you over the head so you can't ignore it anymore." Zariah leaned toward the screen. "Bae, it's okay. Opening your heart up again is a scary thing, but if you aren't willing to let yourself take the opportunity, there's no telling how long it will wait. It's adulting at its finest."

Noémie sighed. "True."

"Although, personally, you should keep playing hard to get and let him seduce you with glitter and jammers. If you ever manage to get him to do both at once, I want pictures."

Noémie snorted. "Yeah. Sure."

"That's my girl."

"Am I really pining?" she asked, sounding like a petulant child.

Zariah cupped her face with her hand and smiled. "How many times yesterday did you check your phone to see if his plane had landed?"

She wasn't going to admit the high number. "Um …"

"And how late do you stay up talking to him at night?"

Last night it had been one in the morning because he'd gotten back. During the week they'd been good, however, and only talked until ten. Certainly a lot longer than she spent talking to Zariah. "Er …"

"Who was the first to like or comment on the Instagram pictures he put up?"

While Kian had been in Milan, he'd taken her on a mini-tour of some of the touristy spots by snapping pictures of places he knew she'd like and posting them on Instagram. It'd been fun to follow him through Milan and chat with him over Discord at the same time. They'd swapped roles too, she'd taken heaps of photos for Chinese New Year and shared the celebration with him. "To be fair, no one else knows that's him."

"I know. He knows. I'm pretty sure he noticed you were the first to comment. Last question to ponder. How distracted were you yesterday that you didn't even notice I was in the store because we were supposed to go to lunch together?" Zariah said, smug, and then her voice became a sing-song tease. "You're pining."

All those moments were adding up to make Zariah's

pining claim somewhat viable. "Welp," she said and popped the 'p'. "Shit."

"Yup," Zariah said with a similar pop. "You got it bad."

A knock on the door and Noémie snapped her head toward it, then broke into a grin as Kian announced it was him. "He's here!"

Zariah laughed. "Definitely got it bad. Have fun!"

"Gotta go," Noémie rushed as she signed off. "Love you! Bye!"

Snatching her bag from the sofa, she grabbed her coat and scarf on the way past the rack and then the handle of her shopping trolley bag. Bouncing to the door to answer it, she chirped, "Hi!"

Kian's grin was as wide as hers. "Hi! Sorry, I'm late, I overslept. A certain someone kept me up late last night."

"That's okay. I wasn't worried," Noémie said, the happiness at seeing him bubbling up inside her. "Let's go!"

One of the best things about food markets was the smell. Fresh fruits and vegetables. An assortment of cheese and meats. Loaves of bread and various pastries. Herbs and spices. An intermingling of different smells and colors.

With Kian's car and his willingness to help, she didn't have to consider her meals for the next day or two. She could get enough fruit so she could make her breakfast salad last for a couple of days. Vegetables for dinner tonight, and enough that she could make soup and a stew to freeze for when she didn't feel like cooking or going out to dinner. She could take her time considering her cheeses and talking to people. She could pack the heavy stuff in her trolley, then carry the more delicate fruits and bread and still have a hand free to hold Kian's hand.

He didn't let her get two steps from the car before he took her hand. Smiling at her, his gloved thumb slid across hers. "I've never actually been to one of these markets," he said, looking out onto the jigsaw of market stalls and alleyways. Bright rainbows of color and warmth against the winter morning. It had warmed and the sun had peeked out from behind the clouds, which made it a wonderful time to be outside.

Pulling her trolley behind her, they moved into the lanes between stalls. "This will be a unique experience for you. How to be an adult and go food shopping."

With a flat stare, he said, "I know how to food shop. I can even cook!"

She smiled at him and pretended she didn't believe him. "But are you any good?"

Kian mock glared at her. "I think I need to have you over for dinner soon."

"Don't worry," she chirped, feeling mischievous. "I'll teach you how to squeeze cantaloupes to check for ripeness."

"Now, that sounds *juicy*," Kian crooned at her.

She'd expected that he'd take that opportunity to flirt and be suggestive about her 'melons', and instead, he went for puns. She loved that about him. Grinning at him, she responded, "I can make you lose your *rind*."

"Wow, that was *seedy*."

"Don't be *melon*-dramatic," she replied.

"*Water* do you take me for?" he returned.

Smirking at him, she quipped, "*Honeydew* you want me to answer that?"

Kian opened his mouth to respond, frowned, and then pouted. "You are so quick on the draw for puns. I have much to learn."

Noémie giggled. "Indeed, you do."

He nudged her with his elbow and shook her hand to get her attention. "Can we go back to the squeezing melons comment?"

"Nope. Too late. You should've seized the opportunity, instead, you chose to pun."

Kian stared at her for a moment, then belly laughed. "Seizing the opportunity! You're just *ripe* with innuendo today. I love it."

"Me too."

Smacking a kiss on her head, he said, "So, where to first, Mademoiselle Belrose-Song?"

"We scout the fruits," she said with a nod, her plan set in her mind. "I have a tight budget and sometimes stalls are open to haggling. I want to price check first, then figure out what I want to buy. I like having fruit salads in the morning, but depending on the season, it can be expensive."

"I'm more than happy to purchase—"

"This is my date," she told him, batting at his upper arm playfully. "I pay. You're here for the good company and spectacular muscles for carrying purchases."

Kian snorted. "And my car."

"Yup," she chirped.

He sighed. "You're really hard to spoil, you know that, right?"

"You spoil me enough when it's your turn to pay for dates, Kian. I don't let Zariah stock up my fridge unless she's staying with me, and therefore directly benefits from it, so I'm not about to let you. Unless you have some sort of massively expensive exotic fruit in mind to try, I'm buying." She paused and pretended to consider, then made a dramatic show of being charitable. "Except for strawberries. You can buy me strawberries."

Kian laughed. "Strawberries it is. Wait, wait," he said. "I have an idea." Pulling them both to the side, he tucked the trolley in behind them. Releasing her hand, he fiddled with his phone for a moment, then looped his arm around her shoulder and held the phone up. "Selfie."

Noémie laughed at his eagerness and smiled for the camera.

It was so wonderful not to be worried about the weight that Noémie may have gone overboard with her vegetable purchases. She packed the potatoes, pumpkin, and carrots down the bottom of the trolley and put all the leafy vegetables and squishy tomatoes on top.

She bought a nice piece of meat to carve up for a stew, then dragged Kian back toward the fruits, since they'd seen all the stalls and prices and she'd decided what kind of fruit salad she wanted to make.

"Are you having a banquet?" Kian asked, nonplussed. "This is a lot of food and you're so tiny, it's hard to imagine you'd be able to eat this all."

Noémie laughed and moved the bok choy she was going to use in their dinner tonight so she could put some apples lower in the bag. "There's this thing called a 'freezer', Kian," she teased. "I'll spend an hour or two when I get home sorting and cooking food to freeze. Some days, when I know I have a lot of orders to do, I take a packed lunch, and a soup or a stew is always nice to have tucked away for emergencies."

"Ahh. I see." He nodded. "We should make this a regular date destination then. Once a month? Or every two weeks? How often do you like to come here?"

Noémie looked at him in surprise. She hadn't even thought this could be a regular thing for them to do, and the possibilities were already piling up in her head.

"You don't want to?" he asked, judging her expression. "You look like you're enjoying yourself, and I'm having a lot of fun and I'm insanely curious what you're going to cook with most of these ingredients. Why wouldn't we want to come back?"

"Well, it's rather mundane in terms of dates, don't you think?"

Smiling at her in a way that made her insides melt, he lifted their joined hands to kiss the back. "Mundane with you still sounds incredible."

It did. It really did.

She should tell him what Zariah said. She'd have to admit she had been pining while he was gone, but that wouldn't be so bad, would it? If things were, in fact, shifting between them, he'd want to know, wouldn't he? Maybe he could shed some light on how he was feeling about them as a couple too. "Kian, I wanted to ask you—"

"Noémie?"

Noémie's eyes widened at the call of her name and she beamed with happiness as she spun. "Maman!"

"I thought that was you!" Roxanne Belrose smiled as she walked toward them. With fiery red hair and warm brown eyes, it was sometimes hard to imagine that she and Noémie were related since Noémie took after her Eurasian father more than her French mother. Roxanne was a full head taller than Noémie, but even then Roxanne only came up to Kian's nose. It wasn't easy being a foot shorter than Kian, and Noémie wished she inherited some of her mother's height.

Stretching up on her toes to greet her mother with a kiss, she blurted, "What are you doing here?"

"Food market," Roxanne said as though it explained everything. Which, in essence, it did, since Roxanne was a trained chef as well as a chocolatier and Noémie had many fond memories of traipsing through the London markets with her mother. Pointing down the way she'd come, she said, "They have strawberries down that way, turn left."

Noémie bounced at that news. "Ooh, excellent. I was looking for them."

"Salut, Kian, it's lovely to see you again," Roxanne said, smiling at the man.

"Madame Belrose," he replied. "It's wonderful to see you again, too."

Roxanne dropped her eyes to their clasped hands. "I see this 'not dating' thing is going well. You're progressing to domestic tasks."

"Kian has a car, Maman," Noémie explained. "I'm just borrowing it so I don't have to carry things on the metro."

"And him too it seems."

Noémie smiled at Kian and teased, "He's like a lost puppy. Follows me everywhere."

Roxanne laughed. "It seems he hasn't grown out of that."

"I feel like I should take offense to that," Kian said, smiling.

Roxanne checked her watch. "I need to dash. I have a metro to catch and you know your father will worry if I'm late," she explained and shook her finger at the two of them. "Dinner. Saturday night. I expect to see both of you."

Taken aback by the demand, Noémie answered, "Yes, Maman."

"I can give you a ride home, if you like," Kian offered. "We're nearly finished here. I think." He frowned and addressed Noémie, "Are we nearly finished?"

"After strawberries."

"Strawberries. You mustn't forget those. What a kind offer," Roxanne said and bounced forward to kiss Noémie's cheeks. "But, alas, I have to decline. I don't want to get between Noémie and strawberries." Reaching up, she tugged Kian down so she could kiss his cheeks too. "Plus, there's a few stops along the way I need to make. I'll see you on Saturday."

With that, the whirlwind that was her mother departed and Noémie was left blinking up at Kian.

"She's just like I remember her." He grinned and laughed. "But shorter."

Noémie huffed. "It's not our fault you turned into a giant. How tall are you? And not the sneaky magazine tall where they embellish."

"Six-three."

She gaped. "Gigantic. You're a beast."

"All the better to reach the top shelf, my dear," he teased. Glancing the way her mother left, Kian said, "I guess she knows."

With a nod, Noémie explained, "I spoke to Maman after you walked into my store. And then again after that first disaster. She knows everything."

"Ahh."

Worried, Noémie studied his expression. "Is that okay?

I didn't think it would be a secret from Zariah or Maman. I tell them everything. Did I overstep?"

Smiling in response, he shook his head. "It's fine. I just didn't realize. I suppose they think my family has some weird traditions."

"All families have weird traditions. Yours likes contracts. Mine is infatuated with food. Case in point"—tugging on his hand to make him walk faster, Noémie growled out the word, "*Strawberries.*"

Kian laughed as she dragged him behind her. "Strawberries beware. Nomnom's on the hunt."

Noémie wrinkled her nose. "No. That's Zane's nickname. I'm sure you can be more original."

Kian put on a sad face. "I kind of liked Nomnom. It was a nummy nickname and now you're putting me on the spot." He considered. "What about mon canard?" he said, using the French endearment 'my duck'. Seeing the look of judgment on her face, he offered up, "Mon chou? Mon ange?" using 'my sweet' and 'my angel'.

"Please don't," she said with a playful cringe. "It won't work. No ducks or gazelle or fleas."

"You sound like they've all been used on you, ma rose."

She laughed at 'my rose'. "You *would* make an endearment like that."

Grinning, he asked, "Would you prefer an American one? Babe? Sexy? Smol one?"

She wagged her finger at him. "Don't you dare. I *like* my name, Kian. You don't have to give me a nickname. It's not like 'Kian' can be shortened." She tapped her chin and then teased. "After all, you don't look like an 'An'."

Kian's quick smile held fondness. "Charlie used to call me Vonny, or Von-Bee or other variant. Sometimes even Vee-Bee," he said, mentioning his American friend from high school.

Noémie giggled in delight. "I like it. Makes you sound like a Pokémon. If I give you enough affection, will you evolve into Key-vee-on?"

Kian laughed at her quip. "We can certainly try."

Tearing her gaze away from him, she concentrated on weaving through the market patrons. "I'd like to meet Charlie one day. He sounds like he has a great sense of humor."

"Oh, he'd definitely want to meet you."

Noémie spotted her prey. "Oh, strawberries!"

Laughing, he continued to allow her to drag him through the crowd. "Ma petit fraise it is," he said, calling her 'my little strawberry.'

"You'd better not," she warned. "I've been here longer than you, I know all the disgustingly sweet names to call someone and I'm more than prepared to use them on you, ma crotte."

Kian's eyes widened at the name that was an endearment in French, but toilet humor in English and then nodded. "Point taken, Noémie."

Smiling, Noémie looked out over her bounty of food as it was spread out over her kitchen counter. "I may have gone overboard."

The smile Kian had worn all day grew wider as he laughed. "Maybe. But it was fun. Are you going to cook all this?"

"Most of it. Some will last a few weeks in the cupboard, but this is the reason I opted for a larger freezer and less fridge." Bending down, she opened the cupboard beside the oven and got her two large stock pots out, one for the vegetable soup and one for the beef stew. Then, in the cupboard beside that one, she fetched her large fruit bowl.

She took a minute to sort out what vegetables and fruits were going where, putting them in their corresponding pot or bowl.

Leaning against the bench by the fridge, Kian watched her sort. "So ... soups, stews, and fruit salad?"

"Yup."

Kian grinned at her and suggestively wiggled his eyebrows. "In your gym clothes, right?"

Noémie quirked an eyebrow at him. "The gym clothes were supposed to be while cooking dinner and I won't be doing that for hours. Plus, I maintain you cheated."

"It was supposed to be while cooking, and stew and soups are cooking too. And I didn't cheat. You had a slow start."

She rolled her eyes and shook her head at him. It wasn't her fault he'd stunned her by kissing the inside of her wrist. "Are you really planning on hanging around while I cook all this?"

"Are you trying to get rid of me?" he asked, giving her the most woeful puppy eyes she'd ever seen. He dropped the act the moment he saw her soften her expression. "I don't have anywhere else to be and it seems a waste to leave and come back for dinner. I know how to cut things up and I promise I won't get in your way."

Feeling cheeky, she mock whined, "But I gotta cook in my gym gear."

"You made the deal."

Noémie sighed. "Okay." Heading for her drawers, she pulled out a potato peeler and a knife. Grabbing the chopping board, she placed it on the bench in front of him. "Fine, I'll put you to work. Everything in both these stock pots need to be washed, peeled and diced, and"—ducking down, she grabbed two large plastic bowls—"put in here. You do know how to do that, don't you?"

He gave her a deadpan look. "I took the same cooking class as you did in school."

She eyed his suit. "First, take the jacket off and roll your sleeves up. No need to be so prim and pretty all the time. Forearms are just as sexy as a suit."

Kian laughed and went to do as he was told. "Starting to think I should invest in some t-shirts and jeans if we keep dating."

"Now, there's an idea!" she chirped, thoroughly pleased

with that idea. Kian in tight jeans. Kian's butt in tight jeans. "Something with a bit of color too. Not everything is black and white and gray."

He gave her a decisive nod. "Yes, Ma'am."

"A hoodie too. So I can steal it. Nothing better than wearing an oversized hoodie and yours would be the *best*."

He laughed. "I'd better get one then! I do miss wearing them," he replied with a small smile.

She glanced at him. "Why don't you have any?"

With a wrinkled nose, he concentrated on what he was doing. "Mom got rid of everything from before. And I was trying to be a good boy and fit into their ideals."

"No hoodies and jeans?" she asked, a little saddened by that.

"Or black t-shirts. Nothing."

"We need to fix that. It could be a date. 'Help Kian slum it' intervention. I need to buy you one of Zane's band shirts."

Grinning at her, he said, "Sounds awesome."

Floof sang to her as she walked past his cage to go to the bedroom. "Not while I'm cooking, Floof," she said, knowing his singing and fluttering was due to him wanting to come out. "We don't want bird soup."

She changed into her gym gear as fast as she could and shrugged into the gray sweater she always wore exercising. Tying her hair up in a ponytail, she forewent the shoes in favor of wearing bright pink woolen socks. He could deal with it.

Grabbing her small Bluetooth speaker from beside the bed, she synced it to her phone so she could play music through it and walked back out to the kitchen.

Kian had started on the vegetables but there was a small bowl of cut up strawberries waiting for her. Not all of the strawberries, but enough that she could snack on them now. "Aww," she announced, pouncing on him to give his back a quick hug before she scooped up the bowl and picked a larger one to try. "You do love me."

Kian laughed as she popped it into her mouth. "Yup."

She'd meant it as a joke, but the casual and somewhat playful way he agreed made her heart sing. He held her gaze, then dropped his eyes down to what he was chopping. Chewing, she carted the bowl to Floof's cage and slid a slice of strawberry through the bars for him. "Here you go. Nom on that."

"It occurs to me that he could have some of the scraps, but I don't know what they're allowed to have and what they're not."

"Keep the carrot peel separate," she responded, popping another strawberry into her mouth. "He loves those."

"Gotcha." He placed the knife down on the chopping board so he could check her out. "So this is the infamous gym gear."

"Yup." She twirled for him so he could get a good look. "Sexy, huh?"

"Very," he agreed, his eyes sweeping over her and lingering on the hem of her sweater.

She poked him in the nose as she walked into the kitchen. "I did warn you I wore an old sweater."

"You did. I'm not complaining."

Noémie moved past him to the stove and set one of the stock pots on the heat. Grabbing her meat chopping board, she made short work of one of the chunks of beef and set it cooking.

"You know, I've never made stew before," Kian said. "Soup, yes, but not stew."

"The difference is in the flour." Cleaning off the chopping board, she returned it to the cupboard and got out a small cheese board. It would do for vegetables so she could help Kian. "I don't suppose there'd be much call for you to make your own meals."

"I do try," he said. "But it's often just easier to eat out, or to have someone deliver it."

Picking up a potato off the pile, she peeled it with her

knife. "To cook, you'd have to go shopping too."

He laughed. "I'm finding a lot more merit in that."

"I have extra containers. You're welcome to take some home."

"Or I could invite myself over here for dinner for the next week," he said, nudging her with his hip. "You've only just started and it smells divine already."

Noémie laughed as she deftly cubed the potato and reached for another one. "Just wait until we're finished with all this, it'll be even better."

Kian watched her peel. "Have you ever done that trick where you peel a potato in one long strand and throw it over your shoulder, and whatever letter shape it lands in, that's the starting letter of the person you're meant to be with?"

Noémie squinted at him. "Are you asking me if it came out a K?"

He evaded. "Maybe."

She finished that potato and started on the next. "Zariah and I did once. Apparently, we'll both be marrying squiggles."

Kian laughed at that. "Zane must be very disappointed."

"And you're not?"

"I can impersonate a squiggle very well."

Noémie giggled.

They worked side by side, so close that their arms brushed against each other when they moved and they made no effort to move away. Noémie moved around him to take the browned meat from the heat and start cooking onion, then returned to her original position without breaking the conversation. They diced and laughed and fed each other bits of chopped up carrots or strawberries.

The bare forearms on him were exceptionally nice, especially with rolled-up white sleeves beneath the suit vest he still wore, and Noémie found herself often touching his wrists as they talked. Little brushes, tender touches, and bodies that kept moving closer the longer they worked. Small side glances at each other, followed by ducked heads and blushy smiles.

She had it bad. She really did. She could see that now. And it wasn't as scary as she thought it might've been. But she didn't want to broach the subject in case it ruined the wonderful atmosphere they had going.

She would tell him. And soon. But for now, some payback was in order.

They finished dicing the vegetables and Noémie floured the beef so the stew would thicken, she added stock to both pots, set them to simmer and covered them.

"Okay. I admit. It smells even better now."

"Fruit salad next," Noémie said and hooked her fingers underneath the hem of the sweater she was wearing and dragged it over her head.

The spoon Kian held clattered to the ground.

Nonchalant, Noémie folded her sweater and left it on the corner of the kitchen counter.

Kian gurgled. "Um …"

Noémie laughed. "Well, you didn't expect me to stay in a sweater, did you? Once I warm up, it usually comes off." Leaving her in a stripy blue sports bra and matching exercise pants. While she usually did wear a top over the bra, he deserved to be teased too. After all, she'd seen glitter-Kian, and jammers-Kian, he could have a little bit of sportswear-Noémie.

"I … um …" He coughed and cleared his throat. "I have a private gym if you ever want to work out together."

Of course, he did. Amused, she threw him a smile. "Why? Jealous of all the other men who might want to look?"

His eyes were fixed on her face, but Noémie got the distinct impression his peripherals were concentrating elsewhere. "Can I say 'yes' without getting in trouble?"

That pleased her. "I might go to an all-girls gym, you know."

"Offer still stands."

She'd meant what she said to him, way back when he'd appeared in her store. When women felt good about themselves, their partners found that sexy. Right now, she was *powerful* beneath his gaze. "What's the matter, Monsieur von Brandt," she said and stroked her hand over her side until she could rest it on her cocked hip. "See something you like?"

His eyes blew wide, his pupil's dilating as they followed her hand, but he remained where he was. "Very much."

His restraint was admirable and she wondered at that. There were consequences of a kiss. By the look on his face, he wanted to. If he'd been a different sort of person, if there wasn't so much riding on that first kiss, she was sure he'd be over here taking what she playfully offered.

Was he holding himself back because he wanted her to be sure? Or was he refraining because he wasn't ready?

Maybe she shouldn't be teasing so blatantly.

"Good," she told him and lost a bit of the playful flirty attitude. She took her hand off her hip and straightened her back to be less tempting. "I figured you deserved some payback from that glitter walk you did."

With a breathy chuckle, Kian leaned back against the kitchen counter. "I think you're right there."

She couldn't resist one last jab. "If seeing me in sportswear makes you this breathless, what are you going to be like when I wear one of the lingerie pieces I've been sending you?"

"I might just implode." Kian swallowed hard to clear the squeak out of his voice. "You're a tease."

"Only with you." Coming to stand beside him, she picked up her knife in one hand and an apple in the other. "But I can stop if it's too much."

He moved. A hand slid across her stomach and his chest pressed against her shoulder as he kissed the shell of her ear. "Don't you dare. I love it."

Dropping what she held in her hands back on the

board, she touched the back of his hand before he could retreat. "Kian?"

He halted, his face still close to hers. "Yes?"

Rubbing the back of his hand from the wrist down to his fingers, she slid her hand back up until their fingers were interlaced, then she turned her face toward him. Heart in her throat, she fixed her eyes on his. "I was wondering—"

The intensity of his gaze froze the breath in her chest. She lost her train of thought as it raced away down a different track. She wanted to be pressed against the bench and kissed for all she was worth. She wanted to be carried to the bedroom and made love to for hours on end. She wanted—

He spoke her name with a huskiness that sent a shiver of delight shooting down her spine. He was so close they could share one breath. Time stretched as he lifted a hand to her cheek, his eyes dropping to her lips then back to her eyes.

His phone shrilled its piercing song and sliced up the mood.

The look of desire in his eyes melted into an aggravated expression. With a growl, Kian retreated. "I'm going to start turning that blasted thing off," he muttered as he headed for his jacket to retrieve it.

As aggravated and frustrated as he was, Noémie leaned against the bench to try and catch her breath. "That seems like a good idea."

"Great," he muttered, seeing the name on the screen. "Excuse me."

One hand on her chest, feeling the frantic beating of her heart begin to slow, Noémie nodded. "Take your time."

"Thanks," he said and answered. "Hi Mom, I'm a little busy—" He paused and tilted his head, moving toward her living room. "It's Sunday. You know. The day I *don't* work ... What do you mean 'what about Jacquez'? I've been in

Milan all week. You *insisted*, and now you're asking …" He made a frustrated noise. "My lawyer is running point. Everything is with the police, and I assume they're running their own investigation …"

Noémie had turned to look at him when Kian had mentioned Jacquez, and now she frowned at the sharpness in his tone.

"No, I do not need to inform Father. Mom, you wanted me to run Celestial Paris, let me run Celestial Paris. Everything's already been sorted, we're waiting on …" He listened for a moment, then paled and twisted to face her with a panicked expression. "Noémie Belrose-Song? Yes, she … oh."

Noémie's eyes flared, her entire body tensing.

Kian dropped his eyes. "Right. Yes, okay. No, you're absolutely right … no, I can do that … well, she's an old friend and we didn't get a chance to catch up. I'd love to. What time? Okay … Sure … Bye Mom."

It took her a moment to find her voice. "Everything okay?"

Kian nodded. Squaring his shoulders, he looked up at her. "Noémie, you've been formally invited to brunch with my mother on Saturday."

CHAPTER 11

Noémie's boots clipped along the sidewalk.

She wasn't ready. She so wasn't ready. Not for this.

Brunch with Celeste and Kian? While Noémie and Kian were trying to hide a friendship that was a breath away from slipping into a budding relationship? Even after preparing with Kian for the last week before this brunch, she still didn't feel ready.

Impossible.

She was going to walk into that brunch with his mother and have to *pretend*. Pretend she didn't know him. Pretend she hadn't been seeing him on secret dates. Pretend she didn't spend hours every night flirting with him over text. Pretend she hadn't been teasing him with shots of her store mannequins in lingerie and then worn the piece herself.

How was she going to survive?

Noémie paused at the edge of a street and waited for a car to turn before she crossed over. She could do this. She could smile and talk with Celeste and pretend that she and Kian had only just rekindled a friendship, rather than it burning for a while.

She hoped.

Taking a deep, calming breath, she put her hand on the door to the restaurant Celeste had chosen and opened it. She'd thought Kian had expensive taste until she learned about the places Celeste visited when she was, as Kian said, 'slumming it'. This place was immaculate, golds and white, with a spectacular view of the Seine and the Eiffel tower. That same nervous, out-of-place feeling she'd had in Epicure swelled in her chest.

After hearing her name, the Host took her coat from her and then escorted her through the restaurant to Celeste's table. Tucked away in the corner, where it could have two windows to view from and ample space and privacy, it was obvious it one of the best seats in the house. The table had a small circular bowl of fresh white roses in the middle of it.

Kian rose from his chair as she approached. He flicked his eyes down at her appearance and a frown marred his face before he grinned broadly. "Noémie. You look amazing."

"Thank you," she began, wondering what was wrong with her beige dress. It was an elegant v neck pencil dress with a gold belt. Not the sort of thing she normally wore, but she was trying to look the part. Professional. Not flirty or fun. Something that would appease Celeste, as it was, it was incredibly similar to the blue dress Celeste currently wore.

It didn't impress Kian, it seemed.

She squeaked in surprise as she was drawn in for a hug.

"Kian, you are decidedly American," Celeste said with a long-suffering sigh. "Cheek kiss in greeting, not a hug. You startled Noémie. Petit lapin, you've been here long enough to know." Although she spoke in accented English, she slipped into French to use 'little rabbit'.

"Sorry, Mom," he chirped in reply. Releasing Noémie, he winked at her and she realized he'd deliberately done that as he leaned in to kiss both her cheeks, and actually kissed them instead of floating above the skin and kissing the air as would be the protocol if they'd just met. "Forgive me, Noémie," he said as he moved back.

"It's okay," Noémie said, trying not to draw attention to the way Kian's hands lingered on her shoulders as he helped seat her. "I don't mind."

"Noémie, thank you for joining us," Celeste said conversationally as she leaned back on her chair and lifted her coffee to her lips. "I'm so glad I discovered your exhibit, you have remarkable talent. It's so nice to see the young children I knew growing up discover their passions."

"Thank you, Madame von Brandt."

Celeste smiled. "Celeste, please, we're all friends here. It was a shame to hear your night was marred toward the end. I understand you had an altercation with Jacquez and that he tried to coerce you."

Noémie flicked a glance at Kian and said, "Yes. It didn't work though. I … um … I went to school with him and something similar happened. I know how much he twists the truth. Honestly, seeing him there was a shock. As far as I was aware, he was expelled for rather grievous plagiarism. I was so surprised to find out he was working for you."

Kian nodded and put on his best woeful-yet-earnest face. "I do apologize for you enduring that. We … well … 'acquired' Jacquez when we opened Celestial Paris. The way my father likes to open a new Celestial is to buyout several smaller businesses or designers for their staff or talent and put them to work while bringing in more experienced staff who are willing to relocate. Jacquez came highly recommended from one of the smaller businesses, which, after checking their performance ratios, wasn't actually a good buy. It's only benefit was the location it came with, allowing us to buy out the whole building instead of just the upper floors. We refurbished the whole thing for our design headquarters and expanded their old store to have our own."

"It's not your fault, Kian," Celeste said and waved her hand at him. "Your father's need to open Celestial Paris quickly didn't allow for proper vetting procedures."

Kian scoffed. "I wasn't blaming myself. Father probably thought the office building that came with it was worth the risk." Kian softened his voice as he addressed Noémie. "He's been charged and detained by the police for fraud and embezzlement, as well as several counts of sexual harassment."

Noémie puffed out a breath and smiled as she pretended she hadn't known that. "That's good." Her hand curled, preventing her from reaching for him. His eyes flicking down, it appeared he'd noticed, so Noémie tucked her hands together on her lap.

Kian's smile told her he understood and was probably feeling the same way. "I'll keep you updated on the case. There's a chance you might be called as a witness."

"I'll help in any way I can." She beamed at him. "Thank you. I really hope he gets what's coming to him."

Winking, he returned her smile with a bright one of his own. "Definitely going to make sure of it."

"Noémie," Celeste said, taking control of the conversation. "Why don't you regale us with what you've done? I think it—it must be ten years since we've seen you."

She nibbled on her bottom lip for a second before she said, "I stayed in England until I finished secondary school, then returned to France when I was eighteen to attend ESMOD to get my undergraduate degree as well as cramming as many business management and lingerie courses as I could."

"ESMOD? Excellent school," Celeste crooned with a nod of approval. "I went there as well. Had I known you wanted to follow in my footsteps, I would have kept a closer eye on you. Please continue."

"I started Chant de La Rose when I was twenty, selling my lingerie online while I worked in a café. It wasn't much but I got by. Two years ago, my online business was doing so well, I opened the store and then this year was the first time I entered a walk."

"Why lingerie?" Celeste asked, intrigued. "It feels like an odd choice for you. I remember you asking me all sorts of questions about women's clothing. Jackets and scarves, if memory serves."

She could feel Kian's gaze on her, burning into her, and every time she glanced his way, his smile softened even more. He wasn't doing a good job of portraying friendship at all. But neither was she as she'd caught herself more than once smiling back.

"Um … well, two people in my life steered me this way. The first was Mama Talal. She's Zariah—my best friend's mother. I don't know if you ever met her," Noémie said and cast a glance at Kian. "She's well-endowed and Zariah and I heard her complaining that she could never find anything pretty to wear. That lingerie in her size either cost a small fortune or was limited to black, bone, or white. I wanted to create plus-size lingerie that was elegant and pretty."

Celeste nodded regally. "Very true."

"The second person was someone Zariah and I became friends with during our last year of secondary. Lexi has mobility issues and clasping a bra at the back or lifting her arms over her head was very difficult for her. She found out I wanted to be a designer and we spent about two weeks designing and creating a set of underwear she could put on by herself. Just seeing the expression on her face at the end made the effort all worth it and I knew I wanted to do something that would make a difference in people's lives. Everyone deserves to feel good about themselves. Lexi and Mama Talal are my biggest cheerleaders."

Celeste smiled. "Sometimes dreams that are close to the heart are easier to come true and more fulfilling in the long run. And business is good?"

"It's growing steadily," Noémie told her with pride.

"The exhibit really spread the brand. I've had three supply contracts from that so far. I'm really happy with its progress."

"That's great," Kian said, excited.

"Why your own brand? Why not work in a larger house for a few years and get a name for yourself?" Celeste asked in what seemed like genuine curiosity.

"She's a lot like you, Mom," Kian said, keeping his eyes on Noémie as he spoke. "Noémie wants to keep control over her designs and the best way to do that is to have your own company." Noémie's brown eyes flared in warning and Kian echoed her look, throwing a startled glance at his mother as he covered, "I mean, that's what I assume."

"Yes," Noémie hurried to back up his opinion and divert suspicion. "That's exactly why. I get to control every element of my designs, where it goes, who stocks it. I don't have to answer to anyone."

"Prudent," Celeste said, narrowing her eyes at Kian. "That was the same reason I started Celestial so long ago. Once you've taken Paris by storm, where to next? London? New York?"

"Just Paris," Noémie said with a small shrug. "Internet trading is booming, so I don't need to open up more than Chant de La Rose and I really don't want to be global."

Celeste raised an eyebrow at her as if she didn't believe that.

Self-assured, Noémie smiled. "Right now, Chant de La Rose earns enough to support two and a half extra staff and earn a tidy profit, which I'm saving in the hopes of expanding my design workshop. I don't believe I have the right temperament to be a global house. That exhibit, while a lot of fun, was also incredibly stressful and took us so much time to prepare for. I can't imagine doing that all the time."

"That's what you get a manager for, Noémie," Kian said. "Someone to take the organizational edge off so you can concentrate on the design aspects."

Noémie gave him a look of surprise.

"I agree," Celeste said. "Good managers are vital for the operation of any business. I was fortunate Kian's father took an interest in me. He had ideas for Celestial that I never would have dreamed of, and it would never have grown so huge if it wasn't for his input."

Noémie's eyes widened and she cast a wary glance at Kian who was busy frowning at his mother.

"You make that sound like Father was only interested in helping your business, Mom," he scolded.

Celeste laughed and stretched out to pat his hand. "My darling, you are exceptional, but you still have a lot to learn about life."

"What does that mean?" Kian questioned.

Ignoring that, Celeste addressed Noémie. "With your business going well, how is your love life? I'm sure you have plenty of suitors with that pretty face of yours, yes?"

Noémie swallowed and dropped her eyes to the fresh flowers that adorned the table to keep herself from looking at Kian. "I've been too devoted to my work."

Celeste laughed, delighted. "Just like Kian."

Kian frowned, then pulled a face. "Mom, that's not fair."

She gave him an amused look. "The French have perfected the art of being discreet, Kian. Embrace that."

"Father would never approve," Kian told her, his mood turning sour.

"He's in New York. Not here." She waved her hand at him to dismiss his concerns. "You remain overly concerned about what he thinks of you."

"That's not what you said last time," Kian muttered.

Noémie, desperate to help Kian out and steer the conversation away from love, asked, "So, Kian, did you know Zane's now pretty famous for his music? He's touring through Europe and even had a concert here last month."

Squinting at his mother one last time, Kian turned toward Noémie. "I saw that."

"I'll have to give you his number," Noémie said, knowing that Kian hadn't told his mother about meeting up with them as well. To admit that would be to admit meeting Noémie before this. "That way you can catch up with him, too. He and Zariah come to visit me a lot and the four of us could catch up."

Fighting the urge to cringe at how fake the conversation sounded, Noémie was relieved when the waiter arrived to take their orders. The whole situation was awkward and she didn't know what to say or how to act. This was Kian's mother, and she needed to make a good impression if there was any chance of a relationship being accepted in the future. And Kian wasn't helping with the doe eyes he kept throwing her way. Or the fact that his foot was against hers beneath the table.

"Celestial's doing very well in Paris," Noémie noted, having spent the ordering interruption to think of a topic. If she could get Celeste talking about her business, the focus would be off Kian.

"Yes," Celeste replied, beaming. "Kian's done wonders in bringing Celestial Paris into the limelight. It's the triumphant return I always dreamed of."

With an amused snort, Kian leaned over to talk to Noémie behind his hand while looking at his mother. "Mom started in Paris before she met Father. The way he tells it, her first brand failed dramatically and she ran away to America and into his arms."

Celeste laughed. "Don't forget the horrid pouting and weeping."

"I didn't know that," Noémie said. "The history of Celestial I studied at ESMOD doesn't mention anything like that."

Celeste waved her hand dramatically, an action she seemed fond of doing. "The magic of money and von Brandt backing. Richard reinvented everything, from the ground up. The amount of money he threw at my business was quite appalling, but we put it to good use to build Celestial into the mighty house it is today." Celeste laughed lightly. "Although my first brand was Celeste's Shoes, so you can see why that would fail. Turns out my talent lies in clothing and not shoes."

Noémie fidgeted with her fingers, her hands hidden on her lap. Something in Celeste's speech rubbed her the wrong way. "Oh."

Celeste patted Kian's hand lovingly. "His father is an extraordinary man. When he sets his sights on something, he never lets it go. Kian inherited that."

Money really did buy everything and Noémie never realized how much Kian would inherit. It was no wonder he was careful about who he would share that wealth with and it sounded like his mother's success owed a great deal to his father and the money.

They lived in different worlds and that had never weighed more heavily on Noémie. Celeste talked so candidly about money and funds and how proud she was of Kian being able to manage the multi-million dollar Celeste Paris project. Kian never threw money around like Celeste seemed to. While there might've been a few dates to expensive restaurants, Kian had never been over the top about it and he was just as happy to go on a date to a swimming pool and a movie or having a baguette in the park as he was going to an expensive restaurant.

She had asked him to do that though. Go stag and not go overboard. And she'd thought he would be satisfied living a simple life in Paris with her, because he'd told her he would be, but what if that wasn't true? What if he got bored? He'd lived all over the world and she was happy in Paris. What if he found someone whose ambitions and drive matched his?

Kian's brow furrowed at her and she gave him a smile that turned out a lot unhappier than she intended because he grew more concerned. His leg moved until their knees bumped together and he left it so they were touching.

"Tell me about your parent's chocolate shop," Celeste said. "You said they opened one in Paris?"

Noémie snapped her attention back to Celeste. "Oh. Yes, they opened before Christmas. Maman is very excited about Valentine's Day, it will be her first in Paris and she's expecting huge sales. We're—I'm going there for dinner tonight."

"Are they making it into an event?" Celeste asked, leaning forward on her chair as she waited for the answer.

"Of course." Her mother always made Valentine's Day a grand event and had been working hard on a chocolate sculpture for it since Christmas.

Celeste's hand fluttered against Kian's arm. "Kian, we should go. Roxanne's chocolate is divine, do you remember it? Such a rare treat and—"

"Of course," Kian said, smiling at Noémie. "We used to spend every second Saturday helping out Roxanne in exchange for a box."

"Oh, did you now?" Celeste asked. Elbows on the table, she rested her chin on the back of her hands. "Petit lapin, you're caught."

Noémie tensed and Kian made an odd squeak.

"I always wondered why your diet was so ruined on Saturdays," Celeste said. "Now I know."

Kian puffed out a laugh. "Oh. Right."

Celeste burst into laughter. "My darling," she crooned and reached over to pat his cheek. "You are the absolute worst actor in the world. You're lucky your father isn't here."

"What?" Kian squeaked, his head rearing back.

Celeste crooned, her voice silky and smooth. "It's obvious you've reconnected with Noémie before this morning, and in more ways than one." She waved her hand. "You know I don't care who you seduce as long as you're discreet."

Wide-eyed and desperate not to draw attention to

herself, Noémie swallowed hard and looked to Kian.

With a sheepish smile, Kian's hands closed over the top of Noémie's. He tugged it out from beneath the table and placed it on top so he could hold her hand. "Busted."

Noémie's heart sank. He didn't correct his mother's assumption. Intellectually, she knew why. Neither of them was ready to go public, or even admit to each other how they felt. They'd talked about it. Kian had a contract with his father. He couldn't contradict that to his mother.

She was a side piece. A mistress. That's all she could be in the eyes of his parents.

It hurt.

She knew she shouldn't let it. It was a rule. It wasn't supposed to hurt if they called each other friend in front of others. They knew the truth and that should be enough.

That didn't stop the barb lashing at her heart.

Celeste nodded, pleased with her assessment, however wrong it was. "You know the rules, Kian. I trust you'll keep them."

"I know, Mom."

"And you, Noémie?" Celeste asked, pinning her with a stare that withered roses. "I trust you'll keep to the rules as well."

Looking to Kian, Noémie sought clarification. Were the rules the same as the contract? Why was his hand suddenly so clammy?

"Body," Kian said, staring down at the table. "Not heart."

Such a clinical look at love and sex. "Oh."

"Know your place, Noémie," Celeste said and the kind tone of her voice didn't match her words. "Sex is fine, but don't tangle your heart with a von Brandt. It won't end well if you do. Enjoy it while it lasts, but Kian won't choose you over family."

Kian made an angry noise in protest. "Mom, that's not fair."

Noémie dropped her eyes. It was becoming more and

more clear that she didn't fit into his world. It was a good thing she hadn't given in to desire and kissed him. "I know."

As though he were afraid she'd retract her hand, and her feelings, Kian's hand tightened around hers until his grip was almost painful.

Unaware of the turmoil her words had caused, Celeste beamed. "Right, now that that's out of the way, shall we enjoy our brunch?"

CHAPTER 12

A soft knock at the front door of her apartment interrupted Noémie's train of thought and she looked up from her designs. "Shit," she blurted, spotting the time. She tangled in the chair, almost falling in her scurry to get the door. Opening it and seeing Kian, she rushed, "I'm sorry! I forgot the time. I'll be five minutes."

"That's okay," he said, smiling.

Noémie rushed away from the door and back over to her designs. "Come in. Make yourself at home. I just need to pack this stuff up and"—she rolled over her foot with her chair as she pushed it aside to get to her desk easier—"*ow*—and find my shoes, then we can go." Leaning over her laptop, she made sure she saved what she was working on, then started securing the paper patterns she'd been preparing for a new bra design.

"Noémie? Can we talk?"

Noémie froze. It sounded serious. She wasn't ready for a serious conversation. Not after brunch. She peeked at him, unwilling to engage.

He'd removed his coat, hanging it beside hers in the small hallway and, as usual, he looked amazing in his tailored black suit with a blue shirt. There was a small zing in her heart as she noticed the color. He hadn't worn it this morning. "About what Mom said," he mumbled, sounding guilty about the interaction.

"You don't have to explain," she responded and continued putting her patterns away at a less hurried pace. "I get it. You and I live in very different worlds."

He tilted his head at her. "What do you mean?"

Noémie sighed and watched him out of the corner of her eye. "We're having fun, aren't we? Why ruin that when we both know it can't go anywhere."

Kian lost the expression on his face. "No," he blurted. "No. Noémie, *please* don't." He walked toward her, stopping at the sofa and held out his hand to her. "Let's talk about this. Sit with me?"

Noémie looked down at the stack of wax paper in her hands and didn't move.

"I know you're trying to protect yourself by saying that. I'd probably say the same thing if this was reversed. I can't …" He sighed sadly. "About what Mom said … the whole 'me choosing you over family', um … I can't—"

Tears stung her eyes and she was miserable. "They'd really ask you to choose?"

"They would," he told her. "They *have*. And, given Mom's reaction today … That demand is coming again, I can feel it—"

She lifted her head and fixed her eyes on the photograph of her parents on the wall. "It's not fair." She dropped the fragile paper so she wouldn't scrunch it and destroy her work. "I'd never ask you to make that choice."

"I wish you would."

She jerked her head toward him. "What?"

Kian's smile was reassuring, if a little sad. "I wish you'd make some demands of me. I feel like … I'm flying blind sometimes. I don't know for sure how you feel about me and … I don't know if I'm ready to know how you feel. Like … I *want* you, Noémie. So much it feels like I'm burning. You're beautiful and fun and sexy, and it's so hard to hold myself in check sometimes."

She blinked owlishly at him. Rooted to the spot, frozen in time, she clutched at the table so her jelly legs wouldn't send her sprawling onto the ground. Or bouncing across the room into his arms.

He dragged a hand through his hair. "Sometimes I wonder what it would be like to just let go. Allow myself to taste and touch and—but I remember why we're doing it like this, and what a dumbass I was and … I don't want … I don't want the 'side piece' my mother made you feel you were. And don't tell me she didn't, I saw your face."

She pressed her lips together, watched him rant, and tried to quiet the frantic beating of her heart.

He seemed harried, rushed, and desperate to talk. "I don't want to give in, even though I know it'll be exquisite. If I give in, I know it'll only be once and—and—that's not what I want. Plus, it's exquisite not to give in," he breathed. "To linger and hope and want—and … what I want most of all is your heart, Noémie. A proper relationship. For that, we need time. So much is riding on that first kiss and … It's a big decision, one we shouldn't take lightly. Once we take that step, there's no going back. When I try to break this contract, either he accepts it, or I leave and I want us to both be certain. I mean, I'd choose you over this stupid contract, and if that is seen as choosing you over my family, so be it."

When. He *was* waiting for her, giving her the time she needed to make an informed decision. But her heart wouldn't slow its speed and she pressed a hand to her chest. "You certainly know how to take a girl's breath away," she exhaled.

"That wasn't my intent," he said, then hesitated and admitted. "Well, maybe a little. But it's not my intent to rush you into a decision." He laughed mirthlessly. "It's probably not hard to see how much I desire you. Mom picked up on it right away."

She nodded.

"You're worth waiting for, Noémie."

If it was just her body, she'd be all over him too. Drunk on sexual gratification and lust. But her heart?

Her heart was scared. Bruised. She'd thought she was ready, but after this morning she was filled with doubt. If he'd kissed her before the meeting with his mother, would things have gone different? Would she have let Celeste trounce all over her feelings like that? Would she have been more confident in their relationship? Would he have reacted differently?

Noémie didn't know. She needed to tell him that. Open and honest. "I'm worried," she admitted. Sniffling, she left the stack of patterns and took his hand.

He drew her in, coaxing her to sit on the sofa beside him. They sat side by side, their legs angled toward each other so their knees were touching. "What about?"

"Don't tell me you don't see the similarities between me and your mother. Your father poured his money into her business and made her an international success, and that's within his right to do. But that's not me."

Hurt splashed on his face. "I haven't offered you—"

She lightly pressed her finger to his lips. "I know. All your offering is yourself," she said and dropped her hand to her lap. Kian moved so he cupped her hand with both of his. "But I'm worried whether *I'd* be enough for you. You live in such a magical world, a world I've only seen glimpses of. I don't fit in there. You have ambitions and money and power. You're going places with your life. I'm … I'm happy where I am. I have no desire to move from Paris. I like my boutique and my designs. This is where I want to be."

"That's one of the things I like about you," Kian assured her. "Everything is magical with you. From wining and dining you at an expensive restaurant, to something as simple as walking in the park. There's wonder in the little things." He lifted his hand and cupped her cheek. "You are very special to me and your world is just as magical as mine. Even more so. You're more than enough for me." His thumb stroked against her cheek and he dropped his eyes to her mouth, then back up again and he removed his hand. "I understand why you're worried. That's why I want us both to be sure."

Noémie nodded.

"Don't let Mom walk all over you," Kian said. "I'm surprised you didn't throw something at her and storm out."

"Thought about it," Noémie muttered sourly, scowling at the floor. "But then I thought getting her on our side would be better and if I threw something at her, she might forbid you from seeing me again."

Kian laughed. "She won't be able to stop me." He glanced across at the clock on the wall. Patting his knees, he made to stand. "We should go. We'll be late to meet your parents."

She stalled his rise with a touch to the wrist. "Maman's French. Being late is expected. Besides, I … I need to ask you something."

"Okay. What's up?"

Resting her hands on her lap, she tapped her thumbs together. "Hypothetically, when we start something, what would happen after? What would we do with your father and … and the contract. I mean … you said you wanted to break this contract, but what do you think will happen when we try?"

"Oh. Oh." Hunching his shoulders, Kian deflated. "I see."

Noémie reasoned, "It's the whole reason we wanted to be sure. I feel … it should be discussed and given consideration before … you know. We need to be on the same page."

He held her gaze a moment longer then looked away with a sigh. "Okay. Well …" He huffed out a larger sigh. "Hypothetically … I wouldn't tell Father straight away. He didn't find out for almost six months last time. We have time, especially since we're here. I have a public relations advisor here who I'll take you to see, he'll be able to teach you how to talk to the media. How to act in front of a camera, how to commercial smile. There's definitely going to be interest in you for a while, both from people here and in America and, if you're certain, I'd help you get prepared for it."

Noémie nodded. "That makes sense."

"I want all my affairs in order too, so if he does disown me, I'll be ready for it." Kian stared at the floor in defeat. "I want a plan in place in case he lashes out at you."

That shocked her, snatching her breath away. Fear burst into her chest. "You think he will?" she blurted.

"I have no idea," he said, dejected. "I doubt it, because he didn't lash out at her, but maybe because he knew she was a gold digger and would leave …" He pulled a face and continued, "I'm just trying to see all possibilities. Plan for everything. I need to be a step ahead of him. I didn't want to do too much, or think too much in case … and … um …" he cleared his throat. "We'd start with my mother. She already thinks she knows about you. If we can get her on our side, it'll go better with Father."

"Okay."

Nodding from her agreement, he continued, "We should tell Father together. We'd have to fly to America. There are expectations of how we'd have to live and act while there, expensive hotels and cars and parties, that sort of thing, so I'd pay for everything and that's non-negotiable."

Noémie hummed and raised a finger to interrupt him. "While that's understandable since we'd have to keep up appearances, can I buy the hotdogs? I really want to try an American hotdog. I've heard good things about them."

Kian snorted and smiled mirthlessly. "Okay, you can buy the hotdogs."

"Thanks."

"I'd teach you how to deal with paparazzi. They're not

invasive here because of the privacy laws, but I think America will shock you."

She'd dealt with British paparazzi before when she'd gone to visit her parents after Zane's career had taken off, but American paparazzi was notorious for invading privacy and she was relieved he had a plan for that.

"And … you'd have to play and look the part, so …" He pulled away from her then, elbows on his knees to support his hanging head. "Luxury designer clothes, shoes, even jewelry … that sort of thing … God … I'd have to change you to fit his perceptions and I … I don't want to do that. I want everyone to see how amazing you are."

Noémie didn't know what to say to that. She'd known there would be a price to pay to be with Kian, and she appreciated how cut up he felt about that.

"There's a lot I'd have to ask you to do or … change when in his presence," he said. "It's not without its compensations, of course, but … I mean, ultimately, I would want you to be able to be yourself, but the initial meeting …" Kian turned his head away and his voice cracked as he spoke. "I don't want to be Jacquez. I don't want to make you into someone you're not, just to please my father. That's not fair on you. I hated seeing you in beige to please my mother. You belong in the light and the sun, bright and colorful, not muted. And there's … you could lose so much. A relationship with me may not be worth the trouble."

Noémie stood and moved so she was in front of Kian, and touched his cheek lightly. Dusting her fingers down to his jaw, she stroked a single finger along the line until she reached his chin. Thumb on his chin, finger curled under, she tilted his head up toward her and held him still as she bent at the waist.

Kian's breathing ceased and his eyes flared wide.

Keeping her eyes on his until he went out of focus, Noémie pressed her lips against the corner of his mouth. Holding the kiss, she breathed out before she moved back and released his chin.

It must have taken a lot of restraint for him to remain still while she did that and she could see his hands clutching the fabric of the sofa. Especially after his admission, hindsight told her it might not be wise to tease him like this.

"Noémie," he said and his voice cracked for a different reason.

Keeping it light, she booped him on the nose. "Don't be silly. I understand about your father, Kian. You dance to his tune to keep the peace, I know there will be times I will do the same. I've thought about what a relationship with you might be like with all the extra pressures you had. Yes, your mother put doubts in my mind. I worry whether I'm capable enough to be part of your world, I know I couldn't afford the cost of appearing the part and, and I definitely don't want to embarrass you—" he looked set to argue at that so she took his hand and stroked her thumb against his—"which is why I'm really glad you have a plan to help. We're talking about this and working through it all."

He lifted their joined hands and kissed the back of hers.

Smiling fondly, she continued, "I also know there's certain aspects of your life I might never find comfortable. The glitz and glamor for example."

"I'm not comfortable there either. It's stifling. So I understand your hesitation."

"I am comfortable and happy with you and if you're beside me, I know we can do it. Together."

"You think?"

"Yes. You're kind and sweet and gentle. So silly and funny." She booped his nose again. "Being pretty to look at is a bonus."

Kian snorted and his lips quirked up.

"You brighten my day in so many ways and I really enjoy spending time with you. I like your smile and I love your hugs and I want more of both. And, if we're going to admit it, I want you too."

He looked relieved at that. "Good."

"All that other stuff? It might be a part of your life and important to consider, but it's not who you are. It won't be like that all the time. There'll be quiet moments and times where we can be together. Fun times, flowers and photos and making soup together. Watching movies and walking in the park. Moments where we can just be. Those are the parts worth it."

He stood, keeping his eyes locked on hers the whole way up. He made a soft, delighted sound and enveloped her in his arms. "Thank you."

Snuggling deeper, she promised, "I'll be ready soon."

Noémie's parents had rented two floors of a building for their chocolate shop. The entire bottom had been newly refurbished for their shop and connected kitchen, with a small outside patio area for those who liked to drink their hot chocolates in-house, and the second floor, directly above the shop, was living space.

In London, they'd lived in a house away from their shop and close to her grandparents, but in Paris, it was cheaper for them to live in the smaller apartment above. All five levels of the building were accessed by a tenant door behind the shop that opened into a stairwell.

Jin, her cuddly teddy bear of a father who was not much taller than her, met her at the tenant entrance where he scooped Noémie up without a care in the world. "Here's my girl," he said, jovial.

Used to her father's overexcited greetings, Noémie hung on tight as she was twirled in the air, catching sight of Kian's startled face on the way around.

Jin dropped Noémie back on the ground, leaning in to nuzzle her cheek.

"Papa," Noémie complained, feeling the tickle of his mustache. Stepping back, she said, "Papa, you remember Kian."

With puppy-like eagerness, Jin held out his hand. "Of course. How could we not? Little blond boy who followed you everywhere on a Saturday, looking for treats."

Kian laughed nervously as he shook hands with Jin. "Nice to see you again, sir."

"Jin," he corrected and, clasping Kian's hand with both of his, he winked. "'Sir' is reserved for Roxanne's father."

Kian smiled. "I'll remember that."

"Maman's upstairs," Jin told Noémie, gesturing with his thumb. "She's jamming. You know the rules."

Indeed she did. Never interrupt her mother during a jamming session. "The shop's looking amazing," Noémie said, peeking around her father to look in. "You're all the rage, it's great. How are the Valentine's preparations going?"

Jin made an over-exaggerated sidestep so he blocked the door. "Ah-ah," he scolded. "Off with you."

"I can't even sneak a look?" Noémie asked and gave him her best pout. "But, Papa, aren't I your little girl?"

Unperturbed by her put on cuteness, he wagged a finger at her. "Don't try it. I'm making our dessert in there."

"Oooh," Noémie purred, trying to move by her father to see what he was preparing, but Jin scooted so he was blocking her. "Aww, I wanna see."

"Good children wait until after dinner."

"Good thing I'm so naughty," Noémie replied, ducking under her father's arm, only to be caught by the waist and spun so she was heading back toward the stairs.

"You haven't got by me yet," Jin laughed. "Don't think you can start now."

"One of these days," Noémie warned him.

"Be off with you!" he scolded.

Noémie bounced up the stairs. "Come on, Kian," she said and glanced over her shoulder in time to see Kian get caught trying to sneak a peek too.

"You need to get up early to get around me," Jin said,

laughing harder as he made shooing motions with his hands. "You might be tall, but I am faster. Glad you tried," he continued with a wink. "Means you have good taste."

Kian shuffled up the stairs after her, looking like a cat that had its cream stolen.

"Did you see?" Noémie asked, curious, as she climbed up the stairs toward her parent's apartment.

"No," Kian grumbled, then brightened. "But it's chocolate, whatever it is. There was a pot of it on the table."

"Well, of course, it's chocolate," Noémie said and sniffed the air. "But … it smells … like pastry." She licked her lips. "Papa, are you making eclairs?"

Jin mock scowled at her from the bottom of the stairs. "Go, Noémie."

Noémie pretended to huff and rounded the top of the staircase. She peered down the gap in the banisters. "Profiteroles?"

"You'll find out," Jin called and closed the door so she couldn't call after him again.

"He bakes?" Kian asked.

"He took a pastry course. They don't sell them, but his pastries, smothered in Maman's chocolate"—she kissed her fingers—"divine."

"Sounds amazing," Kian said. He glanced down between the banisters. "I'm jealous. I'd kill for a hug from my father. He'd *never* give me one like that."

While the thought Kian couldn't get affection from his father made Noémie sad, she tried to keep the mood light. "I'm sure Papa would give you one if you asked him nicely."

Kian laughed at that and held up his palms. "No. I'm good."

"I could do it if you want," she said and did a bodybuilder pose for him. "I'm sure I could pick you up and spin you around."

He grinned widely and winked at her. "I'd like to see

you try."

Noémie looped her hands around Kian's waist and heaved. Kian, suddenly subjected to a grievous case of gravity, flopped against her. Giggling, Noémie staggered under his size and bulk. "You're cheating."

Planting his feet back on the ground, he hugged her and pecked her forehead. "I would never."

Holding hands, they walked into Noémie's parents' apartment to find Roxanne in the kitchen, belting out the words to Bohemian Rhapsody. Something delicious simmered on the stove behind her, completely ignored as the music reached the iconic head-bashing moment and Roxanne went all out. Long red hair twirled through the air as Roxanne jumped and head bashed in time with the music.

Noémie giggled at the sheer astonishment on Kian's face. "Maman was full rocker in her younger years," she said, unbuttoning her coat. "It still comes out sometimes."

In an action intrinsic to his nature, he helped her out of her coat while staring at Roxanne. "Wow. That's impressive."

"Maman and Papa met at a Led Zeppelin reunion concert," Noémie told him happily.

Kian tore his gaze away from the rocking Roxanne. "I see."

"I grew up knowing all the words to every Queen, Mick Jagger, David Bowie, and Led Zeppelin song. Which was very handy when we moved to London."

"I bet it would've been. And it explains why you and Zane get on so well."

Spotting them, Roxanne picked up the music remote from the kitchen and lowered the volume. "Noémie, ma fée," 'my fairy' "I'm so happy you're here."

"Salut, Maman. Still got those moves."

Roxanne playfully squinted at Noémie, before coming over to greet them both with cheek kisses. "Salut, Kian. It's great to see you again." Hands on his upper arms, she looked Kian up and down. "I didn't get to mention it last time, but you've grown up so well. Such a handsome face, but I still see the chocolate covered young boy."

"Thank you, Madame Belrose," he said, bowing a little.

"Still overly polite I see," she said with a smile and a wink at Noémie. "We'll knock that out of you. And please, call me Roxanne."

Noémie wandered farther into the room, allowing her mother to pepper Kian with questions. Spotting the bottle of white on the counter, she headed for the glass cabinet and set out four glasses on the bench.

To distract her mother from Kian, Noémie lifted the lid of the pot on the stove. "What's for dinner? It smells amazing."

True to form, Roxanne was instantly across the room and shooing Noémie out of the kitchen. "We have a jumble. Dumplings, bisque, red snapper, and your father's secret desserts."

With a grin at Kian, she pressed, "Dumplings! My fave. Can I help? I can—"

Roxanne fussed, taking control of her kitchen. "No, ma fée. I'm fine."

Noémie was shooed by little pokes and prods until she stood beside Kian. "Can I cut up anything? Bread? What about what's in the oven?"

"Got it covered," Roxanne replied with a lofty air.

Noémie allowed a little whine to creep into her voice, specifically designed to annoy her mother. "Are you sure I can't do anything?"

Conceding, Roxanne pointed to the bottle. "You can share a glass of wine with Kian. Papa will be up in a little while."

Once the initial meet and greet was over, and all ice was broken, Noémie was unsurprised with how well Kian got on with her parents. The four of them sat around the benched table, sharing wine and bread and as many stories as they could think of. Conversation slipped from the recent Chinese New Year celebrations which Kian was in Milan for, to Kian's job, to Noémie's boutique, and even the Valentine's preparations for the chocolate shop, meandering like an easy river, natural and slow while still allowing a bit of winding.

It was nothing like the brunch she'd shared with Kian this morning, awkward and unsure and answering whatever questions Celeste posed. No one person ran the conversation, instead they shared.

Of course, it had to be Jin who asked, not that Noémie expected anything else.

"So, Kian," he said, with all the subtle parental air he could muster. "What are your intentions toward my daughter?"

Noémie let her spoon clatter against her bowl. "Papa!" she scolded.

"It's a simple question, Noémie," Roxanne told her. "He's allowed to ask."

"We talked about this," she said, making an effort to keep the whine out of her voice. "Kian's my friend."

"A friend who wants to be more than a friend," Jin replied with an all-too-knowing smile. "Or do you not have your knees pressed together beneath the table."

To move her leg away from Kian's now would be a definite sign her father was right. "But—"

Kian placed his hand over Noémie's wrist, stalling any more complaining from her. "My intention," Kian said, fixing his steady gaze on Jin to respond, "is to love and cherish her. It's her choice as to whether that's as a friend or a romantic partner and we're taking the time necessary to decide which that will be."

Noémie blinked at him. Heat flooded her cheeks and she ducked her head in embarrassment.

Jin nodded in approval. "Good answer," he said to Roxanne.

It was a good answer. It was a wonderful answer. Kian stroked his finger along her wrist before he removed his hand and all Noémie wanted to do was keep it in hers.

"Better than the one you gave my parents," Roxanne replied with a cheeky toss of her head.

Jin looked at his wife, affronted. "They loved 'to rock with you forever'!" he protested.

"They didn't, really," Roxanne teased and patted his hand. "But they love you and that's what matters."

With a dramatic sigh, Jin lamented, "I suppose."

After dinner, Roxanne and Noémie cleared the table while the men chatted in the kitchen as they filled the dishwasher.

Roxanne wrapped her arms around Noémie in a hug. "I like him."

"I like him too," Noémie replied, smiling as she watched Kian joke with Jin.

"It's been a while since I saw the smile of passion grace your lips. You're falling for him, aren't you?"

Noémie pressed her lips together and dropped her eyes to her clasped hands. "Yes. I think I am."

Roxanne touched Noémie's cheek, sweeping her fingers across it to tuck a strand of hair behind her ear. "I can see you have reservations about it. You have so much love to give, ma fée. Don't let one past mistake ruin a chance for you to be happy."

"There's a lot to consider," Noémie said. "We're from very different worlds."

Roxanne pursed her lips as she considered Kian, then sipped at her wine. "It seems he fits into yours well," she commented.

"But I don't fit into his and I need to take that into consideration."

"You don't know until you try. His lifestyle is something you can learn." Roxanne tapped Noémie's chin. "Take your best pieces of lingerie and don't give him a chance to turn you down. Valentine's Day is coming, you could—"

"Maman!" Noémie scolded and covered her ears with

her hands like she used to do as a child when she didn't want to be told it was bedtime.

"Oh please," Roxanne scoffed, ignoring the mini tantrum. "It's obvious. Even if I didn't take into account what he said tonight, the expression on his face when he thinks you're not looking, everyone can tell he adores you. Put yourself out there."

"It's not a question of that," Noémie said. "We talked about this; there's a contract we have to deal with too. I … the fight that's coming when he tries to break that … we need to know we're strong as a couple so we can face it head on together … and, Maman, there's still doubt. I— The fact that someone could bind someone's ability to love behind a contract and no one bats an eye at it? The fact that Kian accepted it? That *scares* me."

What else would Kian accept? What else would he sign? Granted, he was probably blindsided and forced to sign a contract or be cut off early, but everything about it troubled her.

Roxanne lost her playful mood. "That's just wrong. How can his father possibly ask that of him?"

"His mother is so certain I am a passing fling," she lamented. "What if his father decides I'm not worthy?"

"Do you think that he might levy his power against your business if he disapproves?"

She'd thought about that possibility. Thought a lot about it. And she was glad Kian was thinking about it too, and making plans to prevent that.

"Chant de La Rose should be fine," she said. "It's lingerie. Celeste Fashion doesn't have a lingerie branch." But what if they were looking to acquire one? The thought troubled her and she needed to ask Kian about that. Perhaps that was what he meant by her losing so much?

Her thoughts turned heartbreaking.

If she had to choose between Kian and her business…

Roxanne wrapped her arms around Noémie. "Love is never easy. Petit a petit, l'oiseau fait son nid." Little by little, the bird makes its nest. "Time and patience. You have an amazing soul, ma fée. The future is always uncertain. Maybe they will love you. Maybe they will see how ridiculous this contract is. Who knows? The real question is, do you think he's worth it?"

Noémie lifted her eyes to watch at Kian and her expression softened. "Yes. He absolutely is."

CHAPTER 13

In front of the Saint-Michel Fountain, Noémie loitered by the large potted tree closest to the metro station exit. Nursing two take-away coffees, she watched the tourists study the architecture of the fountain, taking photos, posing and laughing. Nearby, a woman with a basket full of single roses offered them to couples to purchase for each other.

Valentine's Day had been two days ago and there were still trinkets and flowers being sold. As it was one of the most important sales week for Chant de La Rose, Noémie and Kian had agreed to celebrate after the purchasing rush was over, and after the rush to return 'unused' items was also dealt with.

Because of her plans for the afternoon, she'd worn her walking boots, but also tried to keep the theme. Thick gray stockings beneath a floral fit and flare dress—rose prints of all things—and a pink winter coat. She'd braided her hair into a half-crown and she was especially pleased with her appearance today and hoped Kian appreciated it. She knew he appreciated the picture of the cotton candy pink lingerie she'd picked out to wear.

Taking a sip of her coffee, she glanced at the sky. While

overcast, it was still a pleasant day to be outside. Not too cold and no chill to the wind. Perfect for a romantic walk through Paris.

Kian bounced out of the metro, his smile broadening into a grin as he saw her. "Hi!" he chirped as he reached her, leaning over to kiss her cheeks. He'd gone for a more casual approach today. While he still wore a suit beneath his gray pea coat, the shirt was bright red and he lacked a tie, leaving the first button open and exposing a tantalizing view of his throat.

Her smile as bright as his, she handed over his cup of coffee. "Happy Valentine's Day!"

"Wow," he teased as he rotated it around in his hands so he could take a sip. "A cup of coffee. I shall treasure it forever."

"You better," she responded, laughing. She touched her chest to indicate his shirt. "Red. Love it. Very handsome."

"Well, love is in the air," he replied. Reaching inside his pea coat, he pulled out a long single-stemmed red rose which he offered to Noémie. "A rose for ma rose."

Delighted, she took the rose from him and lifted it to her nose to take in its sweet aroma. "You're really going with ma rose?"

"Absolutely," he replied. "It suits you."

"And only a single rose?" she teased.

"I contained my enthusiasm," he said, primly. "The rest are *absolutely* not going to be delivered to your apartment later."

She laughed in delight. "Of course not."

With a mischievous smile, he said, "Plus, I might have a box of strawberries in my pocket for a certain someone special."

Her eyes widened. "Which pocket?" she asked, eagerly. The pea coat had so many, her precious strawberries could be anywhere.

He winked at her. "That's for me to know and you to

find out."

"I *will* search your pockets, you know," she threatened playfully. "You cannot keep me and strawberries apart."

He laughed and she loved the sound of his laughter. "I'm counting on that."

She wagged her finger at him. "If you pull that 'little to the left' trick, I will end you."

He laughed and twisted, offering her a hip. "That one. Enjoy." He glanced around as she gleefully rummaged through his pocket for her precious strawberries and his eyes landed on the fountain. "Oh! I've been here before. I knew the name was familiar when you asked me to meet you here."

"It's a pretty popular stop," she said, glancing over. "The metro station makes it a good landmark and meeting place. Ha!" she crowed, pulling out the box of strawberries. Selecting one of the bigger ones, she took great delight in sampling her present. "Delicious. Thank you, Kian!"

"You're welcome. I guess I can see why you didn't want me to bring my car. Not many bays around here. What are we doing?"

"You'll find out." Placing her almost empty coffee cup on the rim of the potted plant she stood beside, she bent and picked up the backpack at her feet. She slung the strap over one shoulder and moved the bag part to the front so she could open it. As she tucked her flower into the side where it wouldn't get squashed and made sure her strawberries were secure, she said, "Your Valentine's Day present is an activity I thought we'd both enjoy. There's a tour that runs from here, but I thought we'd get more out of the experience doing it ourselves. I borrowed this from Papa for the day," she finished and pulled out a Polaroid camera to hand it to him. "I thought we could scooter around Paris and take silly snapshots at some of the landmarks."

"Is this?" He turned it over in his hands as he

examined the camera. "Oh wow! I've never used one of these before! I always wanted to try but my father—Wait, did you say scooter?"

Biting her bottom lip to try to contain her smile, she nodded.

"Like the kid's toy? Two wheels and a handlebar?" he asked, miming the handlebars.

Noémie giggled and pointed to the row of electric scooters for hire down the street. Commonplace around the center of Paris, they were one of the easiest ways to get around and even had dedicated lanes in some parts. "Scooter."

Kian's eyes widened in childlike delight as he saw the scooters. "Fuck yeah," he drawled, sounding decidedly American at that moment. "I've never done that either!" Eyes still on the line of rental scooters, he bent down and smooched her cheek. "You're the best."

"I have a loop planned along the Seine, or we can just scooter around and stop where we want to," she said, pleased with his reaction.

"Will those scooters be tall enough for me?" he asked.

She understood his concern. "There's a Rent&Go close. We can go hire one from there if those don't work. Do you want me to show you how to work the camera?"

Kian laughed. "No, I got this," he said and lifted the camera to his eye so he could snap a picture of her.

"It takes fifteen minutes to process," she said as the camera ejected the photo. "And needs the dark to do it."

"Pocket pictures," Kian said and slipped the picture into his pocket so it could develop. "Gotcha."

"I have five reloads left," she explained. "Eight per pack, so don't go overboard."

"Yes ma'am," he chirped, checking out the features of the camera.

"Not too lame?" she asked, nervous. He seemed excited about it but she had to make sure. When planning this, she'd worried he'd find it too silly.

Grinning at her, he said, "This is going to be an *awesome* experience, Noémie, thank you. I feel like my gift for you pales in comparison."

"Nonsense," she said. "I adore roses, you bought me strawberries. We get to spend the afternoon together *and* I can teach you to ride a scooter. That alone is priceless."

Looking toward the fountain, he reached out and grabbed her hand. "Let's take a picture together by the fountain."

They took a few photos together at the Saint-Michel Fountain, both with the Polaroid camera and Kian's phone. Then they hired two electric scooters, and, after a quick lesson, they set out, motoring through the streets along the Seine.

The first stop was the Pont Alexandre III, to view its exuberant Art Nouveau lamps, nymphs, cherubs, winged horses, and other architectural wonders. An everyday wonder for the residents of Paris, now new and exciting with a Polaroid camera. Kian spent ages studying lighting and angles, and explaining what he was looking for to Noémie, before he took his retro photos.

Dedicated to each picture, and honoring her request not to go crazy, he tested the composition of each picture with his phone before taking a Polaroid. He took Instagram shots to post on his page, landscape shots without either of them in the picture, as well as taking couples shots.

Noémie became his model for the day, it seemed, as he instructed her to sit on the staircase leading up to the bridge, while he lay on a lower step so he could get one of the cherub vases in the picture behind her and she couldn't resist poking him in the stomach with her foot to make him laugh.

Her modeling continued at Champ de Mars and the Eiffel Tower. Shots from beneath the Eiffel Tower, looking up at its majesty or upside down with her leaning over him as he lay on the ground. They swapped places so that Noémie could take photos of Kian, following his wishes for the photos exactly.

They wandered over to Trocadéro Gardens so they could include the entire Eiffel Tower in the background, lining up the photos to incorporate silliness, like Noémie holding the tower in the palm of her hand, or Kian pretending to hide from the tower like it was a dinosaur. They dipped their hands into fountains or copied the poses of the various statues in the garden, and poked playful fun at the naked ones.

From there, they went to Place de la Concorde and the Obelisk of Luxor for more candid or silly shots. Like using perspective to make it seem like Kian was pinching the top of the Obelisk and holding it in place.

Nipping here and there on the scooters was such fun. The ability to dash between spots, to ride beside each other and talk as they navigated the streets and stop whenever they felt inclined, to feel the cool winter wind in their faces. Kian looked flushed with happiness and Noémie couldn't stop smiling.

Stopping in a café for a warm drink and a snack, they perused the photos they'd taken already, excited over how they'd developed. Kian was incredibly creative with his photos. Noémie was a point-and-click photographer, but Kian was thoughtful and careful. His eyes shined with boyish charm at every new location and he burst with ideas of what he could shoot. Even now, sitting across the small table from him, he was wriggling with excitement.

"These are incredible, Kian," Noémie said as she studied the table of photos. She picked one up to study the colors. She'd never be able to take a shot like this, especially not the very first time she was using a specific type of camera. "I think you missed your calling."

"The Polaroid adds a depth I never expected!" he gushed. "I need to purchase one of my own. Practice. Think of the shots I could do if I knew what I was doing. I bet there's even a way to do a double negative on this!"

Noémie took a sip of her coffee. "We can do this again sometime."

If it were possible, Kian perked up even more. "I would *love* that. We could go outside Paris too! I really want to go down to Loire Valley, so many different wineries and, oh the *castles*, Noémie."

She blinked owlishly at his enthusiasm and didn't bother hiding her smile.

He picked up one of the shots he'd taken of her to admire it. "You are so beautiful," he crooned. "And these photos are just breathtaking. I wish I'd known this is what we were doing, I would've brought my kit with me. I'd love to see the photos I could get of you with a professional camera."

Her heart picked up its beat and she hid her embarrassment at how warm and fuzzy that made her feel behind sass. "If that's a pickup line for a lingerie photoshoot, you need to do a lot more work."

Kian's grin morphed from boyish charm to a sensual smile that reached his eyes and made her inner thighs tingle. "It wasn't, but now I'm intrigued."

The urge to grab him by the lapels and lay one on him was strong and by the soft expression on his face, he felt it too. Wanted it as much as she did. Yearned and craved. This is what they had been steadily moving toward.

His hand rested over the top of hers, then slid up over her wrist to her upper arm in a subtle request for her to move closer.

Zariah had warned her of this, the temptation and allure of the Valentine's Day's spell. They were so close to starting something, everything was falling into place and her feelings for him were true and right. But they were in the middle of a crowded café, people talking and laughing, plates clattering, mish-mashed music and the sound of traffic outside.

She wanted privacy. Time and space to explore and enjoy, not a quick display of public affection, however tempting that may be.

Swallowing, she forced herself to pick up her coffee instead and hide behind the cup. Delay the moment. Find it again when it was more appropriate.

The mood snapped, spilling into disappointment and hurt. Sitting back on his chair, Kian's expression betrayed his emotions before he concealed it behind an easy smile.

Noémie regretted withdrawing immediately and hastened to explain. "Kian—"

He dropped his hand from her arm to take her hand. Lifting it, he pressed his lips to her knuckles and said, "I'll just have to work harder then."

"You could come back to my place," she said, heat flooding her cheeks at the brazen invitation.

His eyes widened and his lips parted to gape. He was so impossibly handsome. If she had the ability to rewind time, she'd go back thirty seconds and take the opportunity to kiss him.

Losing her nerve, she spluttered, "I mean, after. Unless you need to go back to work? I could make us dinner and we could watch a movie. If you want. It's just … It's been an amazing afternoon and I'm not ready for it to finish and—"

"I'd love to," he said.

She puffed out a breath. "Oh. Okay. Good."

He smiled in a way that made her heart dance. "I'm not ready for the day to end either and I don't need to go back to work. Do you?"

"Dulcie and Sofia are closing tonight," she replied, shaking her head. "Dulcie's teaching her the ropes."

"Ahh, the elusive Sofia. I've yet to meet her. Where to next?"

"Pyramid de Louvre," she replied. "Last stop for the day and we've almost done a complete loop back to the scooter drop zone."

"It's perfect. Would you—" he hesitated, touched the breast pocket of his jacket with a slight frown, and then smiled at her. "Would you like another coffee?"

"Is everything alright?" she asked, nodding at his pocket where she suspected his phone was. "That's the third time you've done that."

"I'm trying to ignore it," he muttered. "Seems every time I'm with you, Mom finds a reason to call me. I told her I was leaving for the day. She's got no reason to call."

A small bolt of fear and concern shot through her. "Perhaps it's an emergency?"

"It's always an emergency," Kian muttered. He sighed and reached into his pocket. "She's not going to stop. I'm sorry, Noémie," he began and glanced at the screen of his phone. An eyebrow lifted in surprise. A couple of taps with his thumb and he lifted the phone to his ear. "I'll be one sec."

"Take your time."

He smiled, then looked away from her as whoever he was calling answered. "Milo," he said and switched to French. "I said I was off for the day. There are no scheduled meetings, why are ... so sign it ... I never needed to before ... is she being pedantic again?" He heaved in a sigh. "Can it wait? I can come by at four and ... Milo, you were supposed to be gone an hour ago. You're *my* assistant. She has Mathilda for this sort of thing, not you." He pulled a disgruntled face. "Yes. I understand your hesitance. I'll come now. Please send a car to ... um ..." He glanced around, then shook his head. "Saint-Michel Fountain. I'll wait there." Bidding Milo goodbye, he hung up, sighed again, then gave Noémie a woeful look.

She gave him a sad but understanding smile. "Duty calls."

"Some sort of documentation that needs an original signature and not an electronic one. Mom's being noisy about it and"—he sat up straight and grabbed her hand. "Come with me."

Noémie rocked back in surprise. "What?"

"You haven't seen my work yet," he blurted, excited

about the idea. "Come with me. I'll sign it and we can leave. That way I can't be roped into staying and working."

So many things could go wrong with it. "But … um … if your father—if he found out before we're ready—"

"You're my *friend*," he said, stressing the word. "Zane's been to my work. Why can't you? Mom keeps complaining I don't have a social life, even though she monopolizes my time. With you there, I can show her I do, and she's interfering. Please, Noémie?"

Against her better judgment, she agreed with a nod. "Okay."

Kian beamed. "Wonderful."

CHAPTER 14

Milo was a tall, thin, handsome young man. Light brown hair which he'd spiked, blue eyes and clean-shaven. He met them both, tablet in hand, at the elevator as they arrived. Not as pretty as Kian—and Kian was unfairly gorgeous—but he would draw the attention of a lot of people.

"Kian, she's been calling once every ten minutes, asking whether I got hold of you," he informed Kian in French. "I explained we always electronically signed that document, but she's insisting your father needs your proper signature this time. A print is on your desk and I've labeled where to sign."

Holding onto the strap of her backpack, Noémie looked around. The elevator had opened into a small reception area, where a woman manned the desk. Dark wood walled the hallway and a sign behind the woman proudly declared Celestial and then listed the services available here. Financial, HR, Marketing as well as Kian's name in gold on the wall.

"Of course she insists," Kian replied and held out his hand to show Noémie they were going to be walking toward the glass door at the end of the hallway. "What a waste of paper. Anything else? Wait—" he turned and addressed the woman at the desk. "Yvette, this is Noémie Belrose-Song. She's with me."

Noémie offered Yvette her best smile as Kian said her name.

Yvette's eyes scoped out Noémie in almost a predatory fashion, narrowing at the sight of the rose on Noémie's backpack before she beamed at Kian. "Yes, of course, Monsieur von Brandt."

She'd never seen a cleaner 'back off' look than that. Noémie flashed Kian a look to see if he'd noticed Yvette's glare, but his attention was on her, not the receptionist. He smiled as he touched Noémie on the elbow. "This way."

"Not if your mother finds out you're here," Milo muttered, rushing ahead to use a keycard on his belt to hold the door open for them. He inclined his head at Noémie as she entered. "Nice to meet you, Mademoiselle Belrose-Song."

"Better that she doesn't then, isn't it," Kian replied with an arching eyebrow. "Anything else?"

Milo closed the door behind them. "Monsieur Sterling left a message for you to call him, he said he couldn't get hold of you. The financial reports for the week have been compiled and are in your emails, but nothing is marked as urgent and can wait until Monday."

"Good. Thank you."

Feeling out of place in such a grand office, and completely underdressed, Noémie followed Kian through the door and into the main area. A long, rectangular space, with offices lining the windows and two conference rooms tucked against the back wall. The space in the middle was sectioned into cubicles.

About ten people were in the office, but there were desks for so many more. It was late in the afternoon, so Noémie guessed most of them had gone home for the day. Several people looked up as they walked in, two of them completely stopped what they were doing to stare.

Kian led her to the corner office beside the conference room, with Milo taking a seat at the desk situated directly in front of it. "Milo," Kian said as he opened his door to usher Noémie inside. "Get Monsieur Sterling on the phone, please."

Kian's office was larger than her whole design workshop, storage room, and teeny staff room altogether. A large mahogany desk facing two comfortable chairs. A large bookshelf filled with matching books, which might have been ornamental but Noémie doubted it. One wall had a TV mounted on it and below it were several armchairs and a coffee table. Exotic plants Noémie couldn't identify adorned the corners and an expensive painting that seemed vaguely familiar was behind Kian's desk. There was even a painted portrait of him and his parents.

"Have a seat," Kian said after he'd helped Noémie out of her coat and hung it, and his, on a coat rack in the corner behind the door. "Do you want a coffee?"

She sat in the armchair furthest away from the door, and the closest to Kian's desk and rested her backpack by her knees. "I'm fine," she replied. Aware that there were eyes on her, she tried to behave as prim and proper as she knew, hooking one ankle over the other and pressing her knees together while resting her hands on her lap. "Any more and I won't sleep tonight."

Kian noted her position as he closed the door. "Relax, ma rose. We'll be out of here soon."

She relaxed the tiniest amount. "I feel like they're all watching me."

"They are," he replied as he crossed the room to his desk. "Office gossip, you know how it is. They were watching Zane too, and he was especially loud and obnoxious about it. Ignore it. Milo's out there glaring everyone into submission." He slid his chair back and flopped down in it. Sliding the document he was meant to be signing toward him, he picked up a pen. "Okay.

Speedrun."

Having nothing better to do, she reached into her bag and pulled out her phone to check her messages. The sound of scribbling and paper turning filled the room.

A beep, and then Milo's voice echoed through, "Monsieur Sterling for you."

"Thank you, Milo," Kian said as he pressed a button and switched to English. "Charlie, you're on speaker."

Noémie's ears perked and she looked over at Kian with interest. Charlie. Kian's friend from America.

"Vonny-B," a crisp, American accent said merrily. "You are a hard man to pin."

"Been busy," Kian responded, his voice rising happily. "You know how it is. What's so important that you needed to call me at work?"

"Busy, huh," Charlie drawled and Noémie could practically hear the air quotes around that. "Hopefully it's your love life that's keeping you busy and not your mother. How's the courting of your little French munchkin going?"

"My little French munchkin is sitting right there," Kian said, glancing up at her to wink. "And I'm pretty sure you didn't call me to talk about her."

A warmth filled her. He talked about her. He talked about her to his friend even though he was in America.

"Ahh," Charlie said, taken aback. "She can't understand me, right?"

Noémie pressed her lips together to keep from laughing, then had to raise her hand up to her mouth to muffle the giggle that escaped.

"She was raised in England, Charlie. Keep digging, she's finding it hilarious."

Deciding that since Kian was including her and joking about it, it was okay to talk, she piped up, "Hello, Charlie. It's nice to speak with you."

"Oh heavens," Charlie muttered, then his voice grew stronger and more apologetic. "Little French munchkin, I'm sorry, I'm going to pronounce your name wrong if I try and I seem to have made a terrible first impression."

"Noémie," she said, slowing down so he could hear her better. "Noémie Belrose-Song."

"Delighted to make your acquaintance," Charlie said, sounding posh. "I'm Charles the dumbass. Now, excuse me while I go find some quiet ditch to die in."

Now she did laugh and Kian chuckled along with her.

Taking control over the conversation, Kian said, "So, Charles the dumbass, what's up? I'm hoping to escape here before Mom figures out we're in the office. She chucked a fit that I wasn't available to sign a document she urgently needs."

"Oh joy," Charlie deadpanned.

"Tell me about it."

"I'll make it quick. Did you take a look at the latest foundation report?"

Kian flipped to the next signing page, his eyes darting across the page as he read it. "Yup. Saw the new project options, too."

"And?"

"The numbers look good, but I worry they're trying to expand too fast. Not that I blame them, there's so much more good they can do. Is Simon hounding you?"

"No. Quinn is. There's a certain project in there that will tie into something he's hoping to do, and it's more economical and beneficial for the youth center to do it at the same time."

Kian laughed. "Nepotism it is. I'll have another look at them tonight, see what I can do. You'll have a recommendation by noon tomorrow … your time, not mine."

"Thanks, man. I appreciate it. I'll leave you to it. Noémie," Charlie said, sounding it out carefully. "It was a pleasure to talk to you. I hope we can talk again and I promise my second impression is better than my first."

"Absolutely," Noémie called.

Kian leaned close to the speaker as he moved to switch

it off. "Bye, Charlie."

"He sounds nice," Noémie commented once Kian had hung up.

"He's a dumbass, by his own admission," Kian said, a smile in his voice. He glanced over at her. "Charlie co-partners with me for a couple of my charities," he explained. "I fund, he's the face as I prefer to stay anonymous."

She nodded. "Why stay anonymous?"

"Remember when I said I got a job at a Youth Group." At her nod, he said, "Same group. So I prefer to be remembered as Kian Brant who worked there, not some rich benefactor."

He'd changed his name, because no one wanted to hire a von Brandt. "I see."

He shrugged. "I just prefer not to have that sort of attention on me. I can do better for them if I'm in the shadows. Charlie and I fund them under the name VB and Stirling. Also," he continued and gave his pen a nervous tap against the document he was signing. "Um, I should tell you that Charlie and I used to—"

A knock on the door sounded loud enough to make Noémie jump.

"Well, it's not Mom," Kian muttered with a heavy sigh. "She never knocks. Sorry, Noémie."

"It's okay," she replied, trying to reassure him. "Would you like me to leave?"

"It's not," he replied and shook his head. "Stay. Please." Seeing her nod, Kian raised his voice to call, "Come."

A short portly man entered the room, leaving the door open behind him. He cast a look over at Noémie and puffed out his chest. "Kian, I need your approval on the marketing budget for Thursday's photoshoot."

"I'm not here, Pierre," Kian replied, his attention back on reviewing the document. "It can wait until Monday."

"I need approval for it today."

Pressing his lips together, Kian picked up his phone and checked something. "Then it should have been emailed before I left for the day. Everyone was given adequate warning I was only available for a half-day. As it is, I see it was emailed barely an hour ago."

"Marking is waiting for the go-ahead. They need time to order—"

"That budget was due Wednesday," Kian said, a little bit of anger creeping into his voice. "It's Saturday. This is not the first time you've been late. I am not approving anything else until Monday."

Noémie pressed her lips into a thin line as the man looked toward her again. Did he think her presence meant he couldn't be held accountable for not doing his job? Whispering at the door drew Noémie's attention as Pierre began to whine at Kian and make excuses. In the room beyond, Milo and Yvette spoke in hushed tones to each other. By the way Yvette was gesturing at Kian's door, he was hot topic. Office gossip perhaps? Or something more? Was Yvette one of the office workers supposedly in a romance with Kian? Or one of the ones who threw themselves at him?

"Your father would never have treated me this way!"

"My father would never have tolerated one missed deadline," Kian replied, nonchalant. "But *do* take it up with him, I'd love to know what he thinks. Milo!"

Milo bounced out of his chair and walked for Kian's door, Yvette rushing around Milo's desk to follow. "Yes, Kian?" Milo said, blocking the doorway to prevent Yvette from entering.

"Pierre needs an appointment with me," Kian said nonchalantly. "And if, and only if, he leaves now without uttering another word, he can have the first available on Monday, otherwise—"

Without saying anything further, Pierre turned toward the door. Milo stepped aside to allow him through.

Dropping his pen in the holder, Kian pushed away

from his desk and stood. "Milo, once you'd dealt with him, this is finished." Looking at Noémie and seeing her watching, he indicated their coats with his eyes. "Was there anything else that required my attention?"

Taking the hint, Noémie rose, bringing her backpack with her and moved to where their coats were hanging. Draping them both over her arm, she waited and ignored the pointed stare from Yvette.

"No," Milo replied. "Have a nice evening."

Kian reached Noémie and divested her of both the coats, then looked at his assistant. "Milo, finish up and go *home*. Claim your overtime and come in late Monday."

Milo grinned at him. "Thank you."

"I'll have words with my mother," he said, then, with a smile, he offered Noémie his elbow. "Let's get out of here."

She wove her arm through his and rested her other hand on the crook of his elbow and resisted the urge to childishly poke her tongue at Yvette. It was best not to engage in a power play—especially because Noémie would win—and instead get out of there before someone stopped them.

Kian shut his office door behind them and led her through the building toward the exit. Noémie didn't need to look over her shoulder to feel that Yvette was trailing behind, or that most people had their eyes on them. "I'm just glad I left my car here instead of at home," Kian muttered.

"Had a feeling she'd call you in?" Noémie asked, following suit and keeping her voice low.

"You could say that. She seems to be more attentive lately and it's tiresome."

She hugged his arm, wishing she could give him more comfort than that.

Yvette sat huffily at her desk while Kian called the elevator.

Standing back from the door, he leaned down to speak

to Noémie in hushed tones. "Is the offer to come to dinner still valid?" he asked. "Or would you like to come back to my place for dinner instead? I'd love you to meet Purrfect."

She smiled. "I'd like that."

The elevator dinged open and Noémie's heart dropped into her toes.

Celeste stood there in a white and gold-trimmed business suit and she broke into a smile as she saw them. "There you are, petit lapin," she cooed, speaking French.

Noémie's hands slithered away from Kian's arm. Behind Celeste was a blond man in a dark gray business suit. For a moment Noémie thought it was Richard before she realized he was too young for that.

"You look lovely today, Mom," Kian said, his voice dripping with sweetness as he stepped forward to greet his mother with kisses on her cheeks.

"Thank you," Celeste chirped happily, flopping her hand at him. Her eyes flicked to Noémie and her gaze became calculated. "Noémie! Ma chérie, what a delightful surprise."

"Salut, Celeste," Noémie replied, opting for more informal language, especially since she had permission. Regretfully, the elevator closed behind Celeste and the man, taking any chance of escape with it.

"I'm glad I caught you," Celeste replied and switched to English. "You remember Mr. Thornton from Pineford Silks. He's here to discuss our upcoming silk tender."

"Yes, of course," Kian replied, following his mother's language switch and held out his hand in greeting. "Mr. Thornton, a pleasure to see you again."

"Likewise, and please, call me Colin," Colin said. "You look a lot like your father. Good man."

"I look more like my mother," Kian responded curtly. "Please excuse us, I have a—"

"Mr. Thornton was hoping to have a word with you before our dinner tonight," Celeste chirped.

Dinner? Noémie's heart sank as her excitement flat-lined. It was clear that this was being thrust on him last minute or Kian would never have suggested she come home with him.

Kian flicked a glance at Noémie. "I have a prior engagement and—"

"Kian," Celeste crooned and Noémie saw the tense in his spine. "You were on your way down to have Noémie select a dress for tonight, yes? I can help Noémie and surprise you."

Noémie's lungs locked and she threw Kian a look of distress. Celeste wanted *her* to come to dinner as well? Where was the sense in that? The way it was worded, there was no way to object. Anxiety filled her from head to toe. She hated things being thrust upon her like this. Manipulated into doing something she didn't want to.

How did Kian keep such a straight face? "Of course." Kian glanced behind him. "Yvette, can you show Mr. Thornton to my office please, I need a word with my mother. We'll be one moment."

Yvette stood and gestured, and, as she walked, she offered Colin a coffee.

"Mom," Kian hissed as soon as the door to the office closed behind Yvette and Colin. "There is no upcoming silk tender, let alone a discussion. There was nothing in the schedule."

"Because it's a dinner discussion," Celeste replied as though it was the easiest thing in the world.

Kian narrowed his eyes. "There's still no tender, and that contract doesn't run out for years."

"You have a lot to learn about business," Celeste responded, flopping her hand at him.

Frowning, Kian explained, "It would be good business practice if we were entertaining the idea of switching. The silk tender is *Father's* contract to play with, not ours."

"I'm simply following your father's instructions. We're to allow Mr. Thornton to woo us, and report back to him our opinions."

"Then there's no need to include Noémie in your ploy. Father would never approve."

"Au contraire," Celeste replied and flopped her hand, again, and added a huffy sigh. "We just won't tell him. It's not like Mr. Thornton will get a meeting with your father to betray your little secret rendezvous. Besides, Mr. Thornton is such a bore, whereas Noémie is so entertaining. At least with her there, we'll have some fun." Flicking her eyes to Noémie, Celeste said, "You want to come to dinner, yes?"

She knew a trap when she heard it. Caught and caged, there was no way out of this. Switching her startled gaze from Celeste to Kian, she could see the reluctance and resignation in his eyes. He couldn't fight this, not without unleashing a war he wasn't ready for.

So Noémie gave him an encouraging smile and said, "I would love to."

Celeste laughed. "Good. Now shoo, petit lapin. Let us girls shop."

CHAPTER 15

Shopping with Celeste was like nothing Noémie had ever expected. By the end of the session, she felt an odd kinship with a doll, having dressed up in so many of Celeste's 'suggestions' and nothing that matched with her own opinion and style. When Celeste started bringing out the designer cheongsams, Noémie had to put her foot down. She wasn't going to be wearing Celeste's version, not when she had her own.

Finally, after several subtle hints, and one not-so-subtle one that involved Noémie picking the dress from the rack, waving it around and saying, "How about this one?" Celeste allowed Noémie to try on her choice of dress.

A knee-length, A line, off-the-shoulder pink cocktail dress. Satin, the dress hugged her in all the right places, gave a delicious view of her shoulders but not much else. Plus, she had a pair of pale pink shoes that would go with them. Noémie didn't feel the dress would be too tempting for Kian. Alluring and beautiful, since she was the jewel he was going to show off, but she knew he would enjoy a little bare shoulder action more than the sequined, backless, transparent, or thigh-split-up-to-her-neck dresses Celeste kept demanding she tried on.

Although she was sure he'd enjoy those dresses thoroughly if they were alone as some of them rivaled lingerie, she didn't want to unnecessarily torture him.

Well, maybe a little.

As the dress was being 'put on Kian's account', the man himself arrived, harried and exhausted. Barely speaking a sentence to Celeste, except to ask the where and when's of dinner tonight, he bundled Noémie out of the building and into his car.

Sliding into the driver's seat, he gripped the steering wheel with both hands, and then rested his head on it.

Noémie adjusted her grip on her dress bag, then turned to spread it out on the back seat of the car. There was just enough time to get it washed and pressed for tonight, if she was quick. "Kian?" she asked, focusing her attention on him and touched his shoulder lightly.

"I'm so sorry you got dragged into this," he said, morose, his voice muffled by his defeated posture.

"I'm not," Noémie said. "It could be a good opportunity."

He sat back to look at her in disbelief.

"We knew we'd have to introduce me into your world at some stage," she explained gently, trying to see the other side of things. "This is part of what being with you will be like and I accept that. It seems to me that a small, intimate business dinner would be a good start. I get to be there and support you in what Celeste made sound like a very boring dinner and I get to learn about what you have to deal with every day. And, if your father complains"—she made her voice cheeky—"it was all your mother's idea."

He laughed and his shoulders relaxed. "Good point."

Pleased he was laughing, she said, "It had to happen sometime."

"Maybe," he admitted. "But I wanted more time to help you prepare. This is being thrust on you and … I—I just want you to feel ready."

"Poor Kian," Noémie soothed, stroking his arm. "Do

you want a hug?"

He flashed her a smile. "Raincheck," he said and started the car. "I need to get us out of here before we get roped into anything else."

Noémie nodded. "So what's the plan?"

"I take you home so you can prepare," he said, pulling out of the parking bay. "I go home, scream into a pillow, shower and get ready, come back and try and give you a crash course about what to expect tonight. Then we make the best of it. Did you get a dress you liked?"

"It's pretty," she said, glancing over her shoulder. "I felt it suited me better than what your mother wanted to dress me in. Lace and sheer and … well … one of them looked like it was made out of bubbles and nothing else." She looked back at him. "It was like she's trying to torture you. Picking the sexiest things she could find."

Grunting, he turned the corner and headed the direction of her apartment. "Probably."

"This one, I could wear again," she said, being practical about the situation. "I'm pretty sure you'll *love* the lingerie picture."

"Oh?" he asked, intrigued.

Feeling sly, she beamed at him and crooned, "It'll be just my knickers."

Kian jerked his head toward her to see if she was joking, but Noémie gave him an oh-so-innocent smile. Groaning, he said, "You're gonna be the death of me."

"But it'll be a good death," she promised.

"Totally worth it," he replied, reaching over to squeeze her knee.

Tucked up snuggly in her winter coat, Noémie didn't allow Kian to see her dress until they reached the restaurant. He caught snatches of the pretty pink color of the flared skirt peeking out from beneath her white coat, but not the style of dress.

Noémie didn't know why she delayed his viewing in

preference of the dramatic reveal. Maybe it was to bring some of that spark back into his eyes rather than resignation. Maybe it was because she wanted to see the jaw drop up close. Maybe it was more fun that way.

She wasn't disappointed by his expression. Carefully schooled to be neutral, professional, aloof, and yet his eyes took their time as they stroked her body, lingering on the bare shoulders and the hint of cleavage, leaving her with a wonderful ego boost and flutters in her stomach.

He swallowed. Hard. Twice. "Gorgeous. Simply stunning, ma rose. I am not worthy."

Her heart sang and her ego preened at the compliment. "Thank you."

They followed the Host through the restaurant to their table and as they approached the table, Noémie realized this was a much bigger affair than she thought it was going to be.

Celeste sat at the head of the table, basking in the attention of three men in suits—one of them Mr. Thornton—seated around her. Elegant and regal as always, she looked beautiful in the low-cut silk dress. The chair beside her was left free, obviously for Kian, and the only other free seat was down the other end of the table, seated alongside several women.

"Bonsoir," Celeste announced as she saw them coming. She rose regally out of her chair and sauntered around the table to them. In French, she said, "Petit lapin, this is already going poorly." Leaning in, she received her kisses in greeting. "The epitome of rude foreigners."

Unimpressed, Kian responded in the same language. "I thought Noémie and I would be sitting together."

"And I would have," Celeste replied, looking at Noémie, "Except that, given the state of things, I need Noémie to do something for me." Without letting Noémie know what that was, Celeste turned to the group sitting at the table and switched to English. "I'm sure you all know my son, Kian. This is his *friend*," she stressed the word oddly, "Little Noémie, unfortunately, doesn't speak English, but I do hope you'll make her welcome."

It took everything in Noémie's power not to react to that.

As the group called out greetings or waved at her, Celeste turned back to Noémie and said in French, "I need to know what the wives are gossiping about. There is something … wrong … with Richard's request I entertain this debacle. I need to know what he's planning."

This was why she'd invited Noémie. For her to spy on Celeste's guests. That didn't sit right with her at all, but she was trapped. If she complained or refused, what would happen? She glanced at Kian to see what he thought.

"Mom," he said in French, with a perfectly cheerful smile on his face that hid the bite in his tone. "If you told us this was your plan, we wouldn't have come."

"Which is why I didn't," Celeste told him with her classic hand flop and the sweet smile never leaving her face.

"She's not ready for something like this."

"Nonsense," Celeste said. "Don't embarrass me. Sit. Eat. Listen."

A feeling of dislike for the woman settled down in Noémie. Celeste was a viper, hiding beneath charm and smiles. She was poised and ready to strike and if Noémie wasn't careful, Kian would be the one bitten and would suffer for her disobedience.

Was Celeste trying to scare Noémie off? Or was she simply using everything at her disposal to learn whatever the game was? Regardless, Noémie needed to show she wasn't going to be intimidated by her again.

Noémie stretched out her hand and stroked her fingers across Kian's chest, over his heart. "It's okay," she told him in French.

Celeste's eyes narrowed at the physical contact. "See, she doesn't mind," she announced and flounced back to her seat. "Come, Kian. Our guests await."

"I'm sorry," he implored unhappily and led Noémie to her chair so he could help her sit. "I didn't know."

"It's okay," she lied. They weren't even officially in a relationship and she was dancing to Celeste's tune. What was it going to be like when they were official? She could do this. They weren't ready to break his contract yet, so she had to play her part, just as much as he did.

He slid his fingers across the back of her neck in a way that made her skin tingle as he moved away. "It's not."

Her eyes followed him as he moved up to the head of the table with Celeste, reaching across to shake the hands of the three men. At least, if she was in a relationship with him, she could reap the benefits of that. To kiss him and hold him at night? To truly feel him? That would be worth enduring Celeste's requests. Wouldn't it?

Turning her head to the women who watched her curiously, she opted for the greeting they would be sure to know. "Bonjour." Touching her hand to her chest, she repeated her name.

The ladies around her introduced themselves, speaking their names with a tone as if they were speaking to a two-year-old. Renee, Clair, and Scarlet.

Scarlet even made a great show about pulling out her phone and translating a sentence from English to French so she could 'compliment' Noémie's dress, then proceeded to butcher the language by reading from the phone and pronouncing it all phonetically. The attempt was considerate, the grandeur of the gesture was misplaced, and it left Noémie feeling insulted, especially since she could tell the woman was mocking the language.

If she embarrassed Celeste now, by having perfect English when answering, she might never get another chance to prove herself. It would hurt Kian. She didn't want that. Lying through her teeth, Noémie made a show of answering them in the same way, plugging what she wanted to say into Google and answering with the worst French accent she had. To seal the deal, she even translated several words wrong.

They asked her several questions, mostly about Kian and how she knew him, all the while speaking amongst themselves about how handsome he was, and how if they were younger they'd … well, they were explicit about what they wanted to do to him. They gossiped about what they thought 'friend' meant, and if that was French for 'mistress', all the while being nice to Noémie.

Vipers. All of them. Such confident vipers.

It was torture listening to them and not being able to correct them or berate them for being horrible.

The whole group seemed loud and obnoxious and knew nothing about dining in France. They ordered the most expensive wines on the menu, without care of what they would be eating. One of them ordered a well-done steak. Another tried to substitute a sauce from a different dish to theirs. Another one asked if they could have the salad as a main. All horrible faux-pas in France. They were foreigners, their ignorance was understandable and usually ignored, but their attitude made Noémie's skin crawl.

Was this what the rich were like? Or was it restricted to this particular group of people? She hoped for the latter because if the former was true, she'd never be able to endure it.

Celeste hid her face behind her wine glass, possibly feeling a similar sort of shame Noémie did. Kian looked apologetically in her direction. She was horrified for the poor waiter, but he took it in his stride, answering in flawless English.

After the initial attempt to use a phone to translate was deemed too time-consuming for the woman, they resorted to speaking among each other. Catty woman who even insulted Noémie's English sensibilities. Every sentence they said was laced with innuendo or bitchiness as they gossiped about someone behind their back.

They had comments on everything, from the food to the atmosphere, even the men in the room—which the trio spent some time 'grading' on looks and twittering to each other about the 'art of French seduction' and whether or not they would witness it while they were here. Partaking in the 'French way' and that suggestion was met with mock gasps and intrigue.

It made Noémie wonder what they would've been like had she been allowed to speak English. Would this dinner have gone differently if she wasn't the silent participant? Was this what Celeste wanted? To know the true nature of the women at the table? Or to show Noémie what this life was like and scare her away?

The trio only made an effort to include Noémie in any conversation when Kian looked their way. Which, granted, was a lot. He would catch Noémie's eye and hold her gaze. A soft smile would play on his face, a smile just for her, and for a moment no one else would exist. The room would empty and they'd be at a table for two, flirting with each other through the windows of their soul, conducting whole conversations with their eyes. The intensity in his eyes would sharpen, then he would release her to join in on the conversation again.

It was the highlight of her night. Those little moments where the room ceased to be and it was their eyes meeting across a crowded room.

With the free-flowing wine being consumed too rapidly to be considered polite, the conversation inevitably turned to why the group were in Paris. The silk avenue was a sham and the woman knew it and were quite happy to discuss it in hushed whispers, confident that Celeste couldn't hear them.

Their husbands were here at the behest of someone called 'Randall', who, according to Clair, was looking for chinks in the von Brandt armor. Renee swore that wasn't the case as there was an amalgamation coming soon. Scarlet remarked how it was unfortunate that Noémie couldn't speak English because she'd certainly have dirt on Celeste they could give back to Randall.

Oh, the scandal. There was something they weren't saying, due to the looks they were giving Celeste, but Noémie could tell there was something they were itching to talk about. Or someone.

Then, with the influence of more wine, they were back at dissecting the men around the room with their eyes and saying derogatory things about Kian and …

Unable to bear it anymore, Noémie dropped her napkin on the table beside her empty plate and stood. "Excusez moi s'il vous plait."

Taking her clutch, she strode away from the table and headed toward the back of the restaurant. Directed to the unmarked bathroom door by a waiter, she was glad to find the room empty of other patrons and she hurried into a stall both to use it and to hide.

When she was done, she rested her clutch on the vanity, washed her hands, then braced them on either side of the bowl and hung her head. She needed a moment. A single moment of silence. A hundred moments. She wasn't running away. She wasn't hiding. She was taking a much-needed breather.

She was absolutely hiding. Coward.

Looking at her clutch, she considered texting Kian and asking him to come and give her a hug and some comfort and let him know what was going on, but she knew that would be misinterpreted by the vipers waiting outside.

Voices beyond the door, a loud American voice asking for directions to the bathroom and Noémie straightened. While she still struggled to regain her equilibrium, she did at least appear to be put together in the mirror. The door opened and one of the men who had been sitting up the other end of the table with Kian stood there. He checked his stride, checked the blank face of the door, looked over his shoulder, back at her, and then entered.

In France, there were many bathrooms, especially in restaurants and cafes, which were gender-neutral, and most of them were unmarked for politeness. Still, when he closed the door behind him and brushed his hand against the handle—as if to look for a lock—Noémie felt a chill.

The man inspected her, his eyes lingering too long around her throat, then walked toward her in a mock swagger, the wine he'd had clearly affecting him. "You're very beautiful," he said. "How about you give us one of them French kisses I heard about?"

Pretending she didn't understand him, Noémie picked up her clutch and stepped around him.

"Hey, now, don't save it all for the pretty boy." He made a clumsy grab for her elbow and managed to graze his fingers across the small of her back.

Noémie tensed, all thoughts of playing Celeste's game vanished. She had to get out of here. She was done with all of it. She battered the man's hand away from her and darted to the door of the bathroom. Once there, she strode through and stormed back toward the table.

Kian saw her first, the smile of greeting dropping from his face as he saw her expression. He was halfway out of his chair by the time she got there.

Noémie barely managed to remember to use French. "I'm going home."

"What happened?" Kian blurted, at a complete stand now. His eyes flicked from her, toward the bathroom and back again.

Unable to voice it, she switched her gaze to Celeste. "Someone sent them here, someone called Randall. There's a last name but I don't—" There was a flare of recognition in Celeste's eyes so Noémie guessed it didn't matter that she didn't remember his last name. She didn't want to look at Kian to see if he knew. "They don't know why—they're very fond of gossiping and imagining slights and I have *never* felt so insulted in all my life—they're looking for dirt on you. Secrets and lies and—the silk avenue is a ploy to get a seat at your table. Which is good, because I found the quality of their silk to be poor, overly fragile when sewing and tends to unravel." Flicking her eyes to Kian, she wrestled with the tears of frustration that were forming and said, "I cannot do this anymore. I'm sorry."

Celeste regally rose out of her chair, clasping her hands in front of her but Noémie couldn't wait around to see what was going to happen. She didn't want to see the disappointment on Kian's face. She dropped her eyes, closed up her heart, and walked away.

It was horrible to walk away from him. She'd failed. She'd tried, really she had, but she couldn't cut it in his world. She wasn't built to smile and insult someone at the same time. The first real test and she'd let him down. Her feet were like lead, her stomach churned in protest, and her heart was breaking but she pushed it all down. She could deal with it when she was outside.

Her voice didn't betray her as she asked the attendant for her coat back.

"Mine as well, please," Kian said.

Noémie froze, unwilling to believe he followed her.

Placing his hand on her opposite hip, he tugged her toward him. She went limp, allowing him to pull her until her shoulder was pressed into his chest. His lips lingered on her head. "I got you."

Curling into him so she could hide against his chest, she gripped the lapel of his dinner jacket. "I'm sorry. I couldn't …"

"It's okay," Kian replied.

"They were *horrible*," she said. "Said such nasty things. Rude and racist and … I couldn't say anything to stop them! If I could have talked … there's only so much I can take."

"In the bathroom," Kian said in a soft, yet urgent, voice. "Did he touch you? Did he hurt you?"

She whimpered. "He … implied I shouldn't save it all for the 'pretty boy'."

There was anger in him now. She could feel it radiating through him. But he draped her jacket around her shoulders and held her close. "Noémie, I'm so sorry. Let's get you out of here."

By the time they reached his car, the tears were falling and she didn't want to let him go. So he stood there, leaning his back against the door of the car, his legs on either side of her, in the cold and the dark, and held her.

"I'm so sorry I put you through that," he whispered, stroking his hand up and down her back, while also trying to coax her to slip her jacket on to keep her warm. "I could see you wilting from the other end of the table and I wanted … The whole thing was unfair."

"I agreed," she mumbled, the cold wind toying with her skirt. "I thought I could handle it."

"And you could have, had this been a normal dinner. And it wasn't. The second Mom made it so you couldn't speak to them, I should've done something to stop this. I should've said no. Right from the beginning."

"You were trapped, too." She raised her head from his chest. Stroking her fingers on his ruined shirt, she murmured, "I'm sorry, I let you down and I couldn't—"

"You didn't," he insisted, using the cuff of his jacket to dab tears from her cheeks. "Not ever. You did your absolute best. You were put in a terrible situation and I feel awful about it."

"It's not all going to be like this, is it?" she asked, feeling pathetic and needing reassurance.

"No," he promised. "No, it's not. This was an extreme example and—I mean, of course, there are people like that, there are always people like that—but there are some really good people you'll get to meet, too. Positive experiences you'll have. Like Charlie. Noémie, you're going to love him, I promise. He's one of the kindest, most considerate men I know."

Kian was the kindest, most considerate man she knew. Standing in the cold consoling her. Doing everything he could to make her feel better, even walking out of a situation that could potentially become a bad move for his career. Slow and gentle with every step of this, never pushing, always her choice.

She loved him so much.

"Thank you for coming tonight," he whispered, his face framed by twinkling stars set against an inky sky. "Despite everything—"

Noémie stretched up on her toes and pressed her lips to his. A soft kiss. Sweet and full of love, all she wanted to do was show him what he meant to her because she couldn't find the words. He was warm and he was safe and he made her feel loved and it *mattered*.

He was still for several heartbeats. While her kiss was welcomed, accepted, his return felt restrained. Carefully contained in its reciprocation, enough not to be outright rejection. It certainly didn't contain the unbridled passion she'd suspected would emerge during their first kiss.

A soft noise at the back of his throat, a tone of regret. Kian lifted a hand to her face and gently disengaged. He stroked her cheek with his thumb and looked into her eyes. "Noémie, ma belle rose, you fill my heart with joy. You don't have to do this."

Fresh tears stung her eyes. He didn't understand. Didn't see what she offered. "No, Kian, I want—"

"I know," he soothed. "But you're not ready." Leaning sideways, he opened the passenger door for her. "Let's get you home."

CHAPTER 16

Zane and Zariah had always been avid thrill-seekers and adventurers, hiking and traveling as Zane sang his way across Europe and Zariah wrote her travel blogs. They hit all the thrill spots, often sending Noémie photos from activities from bungee jumping off the Verzasca Dam in Switzerland, kite surfing at Tarif in Spain, to skydiving in Italy.

So it came as no surprise when Zariah rushed into Chant de La Rose to purchase lingerie for a surprise extended weekend away skiing in the French Alps. Zane and his band had finished a mini-tour around Italy while Zariah finished all her commissioned travel pieces around Paris. Overworked, Zane declared a week break for everyone and was taking Zariah away and Noémie was more than happy to open her stock to her best friend to ensure she had the best time.

Halfway through Zariah's frantic rush to pick the perfect lingerie, Veroniqué, beckoned her to the phone. "Sorry to interrupt," she said, "but Kian said it was urgent."

A burst of panic. Urgent? He never called her boutique. *Urgent?* Was it his father? Was he coming to Paris? Was there another dinner Celeste insisted she attend? Was he hurt? Accident? Mind in turmoil, she hurried over to Veroniqué to answer. "Kian? What's wrong? Are you—?"

"Nothing," Kian rushed. "Sorry! I thought I said it *wasn't* urgent! I must've mistranslated."

She puffed out a breath. "Oh. I was worried."

"I don't have a lot of time and I need to give you enough notice. I'm due in a meeting like ... five minutes ago."

"Notice for what?"

"I don't know if Zariah's had a chance to gossip yet, but—"

"She and Zane are going away. Zariah's here right now," Noémie said and narrowed her eyes at Zariah's sudden gleeful look and happy bounce. Across the other side of the room, Dulcie turned her head from where she was helping a customer and smothered a grin.

"Ahh. Good. Cause, ahh, Zane said there was a mistake made in the booking and he somehow managed to score a chalet with two bedrooms and, er," Kian squeaked and cleared his throat so he could speak with a stronger voice. "He wants to know if we want to come too."

Noémie's jaw dropped. "*What did you do?*" she mouthed at Zariah.

"Say yes," Zariah prompted and clutched her arm. "C'mon, bae, it'll be a blast."

"I realize this is incredibly short notice," Kian rushed and it sounded like he was walking somewhere in a hurry. "But I was hoping you'd be free. And I would never impose on you. Zane's already paid for the chalet, and I'll pay for any extra expenses and, and he promised me a common area, so I'll sleep on the sofa."

"I ... er ..."

Noémie heard his name called in the background of where he was and then Kian swore softly. "I need to go. Look, talk to Zariah, get all the details and I'll call after the meeting, okay? Absolutely no pressure at all and I completely understand if you can't. Just think about it."

Noémie managed to squeak out an 'okay' before Kian was gone. Hanging up, she stared at Zariah.

"Skiing," Zariah prompted, grinning. "Four days, three nights. Warm fires and hot cocoa. Snow angels and snowball fights. The thrill of racing down a mountainside to get your blood charged and your heart pumping. The old cliché of bed sharing. C'mon, Noémie, what have you got to lose?"

Nothing. *Everything.* They hadn't talked about that kiss, even though they talked about the night and … things were still a little awkward and unsure and to throw them both into an overly romantic situation …

It could go very right. Or very wrong.

"We're not even there yet," Noémie murmured. Her head was reeling with possibilities. And nerves.

Dulcie directed her customer to the fitting rooms and wandered over.

Seeing she had backup, Zariah pressed, "Then this weekend is the *perfect* chance to get there."

Almost too perfect to be real.

"I already know you're not working."

Noémie tilted her head. "Yes, I am—"

Zariah's grin turned gleeful. "I bribed your girls to come in tomorrow—"

"Backstage tickets, baby!" Dulcie crowed in English. "Veroniqué and I are going to have a blast."

Zariah winked at Dulcie. "Plus Sofia said she'd come in on Saturday. You're covered."

Noémie blinked rapidly. "Covered—this is my livelihood! I can't abandon it for the weekend!"

"I can guess by your expression," Veroniqué said, the only non-English person among them, "that you're concerned. We'll be fine. I can't remember the last time you took a full day off, Noémie, let alone a holiday."

Noémie gave Veroniqué a flat look. "Sundays. I take Sundays off and—"

Hands clasped on her lap, Veroniqué smiled. "Everyone takes Sundays off."

Zariah gripped Noémie's shoulders. "They got this," she insisted. "Trust your girls."

"We got this, Noémie," Dulcie said earnestly. "We really do. I know all the procedures and Veroniqué can take care of any urgent alterations. We know what we're doing. Let us do this for you."

Noémie looked between the three women as they smiled at her. "You think of everything, don't you?"

"Looking out for my best friend, that's all," Zariah chirped. "You need to get back on the horse and, as horses go, Kian would be a spectacular r—"

"Zaz!" Noémie scolded.

Winking at her, Zariah twisted back toward the boutique. Tapping her chin, she smiled at the other two women. "We have more than enough time to find the perfect piece for her."

Noémie's eyes widened as Dulcie looked gleeful and translated for Veroniqué, who perked up.

"Train leaves at four," Zariah said, pulling Noémie behind her as she marched toward the teddies. "You'll be back in time for opening on Monday. Pinky promise."

That's how Noémie found herself escorted home to pack, with several Zariah approved lingerie pieces to choose from, then bundled into a train heading to the French Alps.

Noémie worked diligently on her laptop as it rested on the small fold-out bench in the compartment they'd booked for the train. As much as she wanted to start this weekend, she needed to get a bit of paperwork done so she wouldn't have to worry about it. Friday was normally her paperwork day, but as she'd be skiing, there were purchase orders and payments to be done today and she had to balance her books. With a five-hour train ride ahead, she had time.

She'd already sent a message to her mother, asking her

to check in on her boutique and take care of Floof over the weekend, and called Sofia, her on-call casual staff member, to make sure she was available if Dulcie or Veroniqué needed it.

Both women told her to stop fussing and enjoy the weekend. It seemed everyone had high expectations of this weekend, but it made Noémie nervous.

Sighing, she peeked up to check on the others.

Zariah sat in the chair opposite with her earbuds in as she worked on a story. Zane paced the corridor outside, talking to his manager. Kian, having already taken pictures of the train and the view through the window, was stretched out on the seat beside her, using his phone. Noticing her looking around, he smiled. "How's it going?"

"Nearly done," she replied.

"Nice period of growth, I see. Looks promising."

Blinking, she frowned at her screen, then raised her eyes to him. "Are you snooping?"

He gave her a sheepish look. "You redid those numbers three times to see if they were correct and each time you made this cute little huffy sound. I got curious."

"I see."

Ducking his head, he murmured, "I'm sorry. I overstepped. It won't happen—"

She smiled and stretched out her hand to touch his in reassurance. "No, Kian, don't be silly. It's okay. I am doing this in front of you, after all. Of course, you're curious."

He smiled in response and perked up. "Can I ask why you're upset?"

"I'm not upset," she responded. "I just ..." She glanced at him again and chewed her lip, then decided to confide in him. "I want to capitalize on this growth from the exhibit, but I ..." She scrunched her face up. "I thought an advertising campaign, like a spread in a woman's magazine, would be the best way to go. But I've never done one before. I've always relied on Internet advertising."

With regret in his voice, he said, "You might've left it a little late if you want to do a magazine spread. Celestial always has a spread coming out the week of an exhibit to keep things fresh in people's minds, but there's still time to capitalize on it."

Noémie's heart sank. "Oh … good to know." Eyes back on her laptop, she chewed her lip again. "I'll do some research."

"With your permission, I can send you a couple of contacts, fashion marketing experts who have already been proven to work. They often have a range of different marketing tools for small businesses you can choose from, so you can make the right choice of what you want for your boutique."

She looked at him in surprise. "Really? But Celestial has its own marketing team."

He nodded. "We outsource smaller jobs. And I get sent resumes all the time by people wanting to join. Some of them freelance while waiting for a position to open up and I've already vetted them so I know they're good. If you'd like their numbers, I can give it to you." His expression was tender. "You don't have to do everything on your own. There's nothing wrong with talking to experts about your options."

She puffed out a laugh. "You're right. Those contacts would be helpful."

He poked her thigh with his shoe. "You know, you're absolutely allowed to pick my brain if you like. I know it's a rule, but I don't mind if you would like to ask my opinion on things business-related. I do have expertise I'm happy to share with you."

She reached over and put her hand on his ankle and squeezed it. "Thank you. I appreciate it."

Zariah piped up, "I hope you'll do more than appreciate. Tap that brain of his. Kian knows this sort of stuff." To Kian, she said, "I swear, getting Noémie to accept help is like asking her to have teeth pulled."

Noémie rolled her eyes and pulled a face at Zariah, then looked back at her laptop.

"You know I'm right," Zariah replied with good-natured humor as she returned to her work.

Flicking a glance at Kian, Noémie said, "I won't be much longer."

"No," Kian said. "Take your time. You were rushed out with so little notice." His face lit up. "One might say you were *railroaded* into coming."

Noémie laughed. "Maybe, but at least I'm not on the wrong *track*."

Kian lifted his feet off the seat and scooted closer. "I promise, I'll *conduct* myself like a gentleman."

She grinned. "Skiing is a good way to let off some *steam*."

"That pun was *engine*-ous," he laughed.

"It made a great *one-liner*."

"Geeze," Zariah said, closing her laptop. "Listen to you two. If you're gonna flirt like that all weekend, I'm going to need to start drinking now."

"Maybe you should catch the *express* and order some wine," Noémie said.

Snorting with the effort to suppress laughter, Zariah got to her feet. "Sounds like … um … oh! just the *ticket*. I'll be right back."

Kian turned back to Noémie the moment Zariah closed the compartment door behind her. "I'm serious though. I know this was incredibly short notice and I wouldn't have minded if you said you couldn't come."

"Kian—"

He seemed concerned. "I don't want you to be uncomfortable or worried—"

"No," Noémie said, reaching up to touch his cheek. "I want to be here. With you. Promise me you won't laugh tomorrow. I haven't been skiing in years. There's probably a dozen snowdrifts up there that have my name on them. Last time I went, I managed to twist my ankle on my first slope because I was a complete klutz and crashed into a tree."

He smiled like he didn't quite believe her. "Don't worry, I can teach you. It's easy."

"Pry me out of snowdrifts, you mean. It'll be a blast, you watch."

"As long as I get to hold your hand," he said, reaching for her hand. Lifting her hand to his lips, he pressed a kiss against her knuckles, then, with closed eyes, turned her hand over so he could kiss the inside of her wrist.

Noémie's heart fluttered then took off racing as Kian opened his eyes and locked them on hers. They were alone. Together. He was making those wonderful sultry eyes at her. Now was as good a time as any. Surely she could grab him by the lapels and pull him toward her and—

The door slid open and a disgruntled Zane wandered back in, flopping on the opposite chair. "Ugh, *managers*."

Kian snorted, dropping their hands until they rested on the seat between them. "Should I take offense to that?

With a dramatic battering at the air with his hands, Zane complained, "The idea of having a holiday was so that I'd work *less*, not roam around Europe doing gigs. What doesn't he get? I need a break!"

"Must be so hard to be wanted," Noémie mock-lamented, lifting her free hand to her forehead dramatically.

"You're a hot commodity right now," Kian said. "London's golden boy."

"And you're Paris' golden boy," Zane replied, grinning. "We should combine talents. I could use a new manager."

Kian blinked at him. "What? Really?"

"Zariah is *dying* to settle down permanently," Zane said. "And honestly, while traveling Europe is awesome, we want to start putting down roots. My manager just wants to go bigger and better and all that crap. More money. More fame. I don't mind traveling for a few months a year, but I need a base. He doesn't even want to discuss it. I'm tempted to throw in the towel and return to YouTube, it's become that bad. So, if you're perfectly happy doing what you're doing, then fine. But if you're looking to switch it up a bit, I have a job waiting for you."

Kian swallowed and his hand was clammy in Noémie's. "I don't know anything about music management."

"But you know a shit-ton about managing people. You made Celestial Paris an absolute success. You're a charmer, I've seen it. Sitting in your office while I waited for you so we could go to lunch was enlightening. People just *do* things for you and it doesn't have anything to do with your father. It's you, Kian," Zane continued. "Calm and poised and an absolute people pleaser. You know people, the right people who can do what you need to be done, and if you don't know them, you find out. You want to help and you love doing it. I want that. Models are performers too, music isn't that different. You could learn."

Still looking skeptical, Kian addressed her. "What do you think, Noémie?"

She looked between them and chose her words with care. "You do go out of your way to help people and make sure things are running smoothly. Zane would be an excellent boss."

Zane sat back, smug. "Damn right I would."

"My father said working with friends is the best way to ruin a friendship," Kian said, still cautious.

"That is true, for some," Zane replied, lifting his hands to clasp them behind his head as he lounged. "But not for all. We wouldn't know until we try."

Trying to be supportive, Noémie said, "It's your choice, Kian. You partnered with Charlie and that worked out."

Kian's eyes darted from Zane to Noémie and back again. "Can I think about it?"

"Absolutely," Zane replied, grinning at him.

Zariah flung open the door and announced, "The café is open! Anyone hungry?"

CHAPTER 17

The chalet Zane rented was gorgeous. Made from pine and pink quartz, it boasted a central room, with a glass-framed built-in fireplace insert separating the living and dining spaces. Large curtain covered windows edged the room and Zane promised they would offer glorious views of the mountainside when the sun rose.

A kitchen sat against a far wall with a breakfast bar and a fridge pre-stocked with food for the next few days. Perched on top of the kitchen bench was a basket full of wines and cheese.

Two bedrooms shot off from the living space, each of them had a small en-suite and a door that led to the balcony that surrounded the apartment.

"This place is amazing," Noémie said, carrying her suitcase further into the room.

Zariah dumped her bag on the sofa. "It's even better in the sunlight. The sunsets are magnificent. We'll have to go up to the lookout tomorrow and watch it."

"How'd you find it?" Kian asked, as he and Zane began to sort out the heating. "It's so out of the way, I wouldn't have even thought to look."

"Sometimes the out of the way places are the best,"

Zariah said. "My stepdad used to bring us here for the winter holidays every year. We always stayed in the ones at the bottom though, never this one."

Noémie poked around the kitchen, plans already forming in her mind what she could cook over the weekend. Fresh bread and biscuits came to mind, seeing the flour on the pantry shelf. "You got baking supplies!"

"Of course, oh-chef's-daughter," Zane replied. "You and me, we're cooking up a storm tomorrow after skiing."

"Can't wait," she called and headed over to the bedroom she'd be using. Pausing at the threshold, she stared at the bed. A king bed, large enough to be shared and still have their own space. She glanced over her shoulder at the sofa, then back at the bed. Then, convinced she had the wrong room, she checked the other one. Nope. Both of them had king beds. Returning to the original room, she called, "Kian?"

He looked over from the heating panel. "Yeah?"

Beckoning, she tried to ignore Zane's sly wink at Zariah. She leaned her shoulder against the doorframe and waited for Kian. "This feels decidedly set up," she told him as he reached her.

Kian studied the room then did the same thing Noémie had and checked the other room before he turned his head to glare at Zane. "This is not what I was told."

"Don't look at me," Zane said, shrugging. "Not my fault."

Swinging back to Noémie, Kian insisted, "I'll stay on the sofa."

"Don't be silly. Which side do you want?" Noémie asked and walked into the room.

Kian hesitated at the door. "We don't—"

From outside the room, Zane laughed and clapped his hands. "Get it, Nomnom!"

Rolling her eyes, Noémie beckoned Kian. "Come and discuss it here where the two laughing hyenas out there can't hear."

"I heard that!" Zariah called.

"You were supposed to!" Noémie called back.

Casting a scowl out at Zane, Kian stepped into the room and half shut the door behind him.

"Which side would you like?" Noémie asked again, leaving her suitcase at the set of drawers against the wall. She removed her winter coat and draped it over the suitcase.

"We don't have to—"

She smiled at him. "We're two consenting adults. We can share a bed and, unless you sleep in the nude or snore really loudly, it shouldn't matter." With a light laugh, she teased, "Okay, so I wouldn't mind you sleeping in the nude. But if you snore, you're out."

Although he smiled at the teasing, his body language remained awkward. "I don't mind—I don't want you to be uncomfortable and I don't want you to think I invited you here under false pretenses and—"

"Kian, I love you, but you're being ridiculously chivalrous and it's not necessary," Noémie said and sat on the end of the bed, wondering at the sudden grin on Kian's face. "It's a huge bed and you're really tall. You won't be comfortable on the sofa and we both know it. Either we share, or I take the sofa. Your choice."

Still smiling, Kian relaxed, and removed his winter jacket, leaving it beside hers. "You drive a hard bargain."

Returning his smile, she flopped back on the bed and stretched her arms over her head. "This side's mine. I claim it."

Kian laughed and crossed the room to sit on the bed beside her. Lifting his hand, he rested it on her stomach. "Promise me you'll tell me if I make you uncomfortable."

Noémie touched her fingers to the back of his. "I know all about morning wood, Kian," she teased, giggling when his ears went red. "I suppose it depends on whether you're a sleep snuggler or not."

Moving his hand from her stomach, he braced it by her

shoulder as he leaned down over her. "What if I am?" he asked, his voice dropping to a purr. "It's been a while since I shared a bed. I could very well sleep snuggle and I wouldn't know."

A delicious tickle of nerves settled in her stomach. "I'm a hundred percent okay with that. Because I *am* a sleep snuggler. You're definitely going to wake up and find me plastered to your back. And probably drool on your shoulder."

He laughed. "So that's why you were asking if I slept in the nude."

She turned up her nose and pretended to be aloof. "I will neither confirm nor deny that theory."

"Begs the question what *you* sleep in."

Deliberately adjusting her sprawl so she'd appear sultrier, pushing out her chest and accenting her natural curves, she crooned, "You'll find out."

It had the effect she desired. His pupils dilated, his eyes dropped from hers to her lips and his chest expanded with a small intake of breath. Beneath his sharpened gaze, she had to fight not to lick her lips in response as she waited to see what he would do next.

A part of her wanted to toy. To play and tease and see how long it took before he broke and *had* to kiss her. Another, more vocal part, bellowed to get on with it. To *start*. Surely they'd waited long enough, teased each other long enough?

Was she going to have to issue a written invitation?

A pop from outside, followed by the sound of liquid hitting the floor and a whoop from Zariah. "Come and get it!"

Sighing, Kian sat back and looked toward the door, turning away. "Sounds like champagne is served."

No. No, this wasn't fair. They were *always* interrupted. Always something to kill a moment, destroy a mood. She wanted to start already. She'd already tried once. This time he better listen.

Catching his sleeve, she prevented him from moving away. "Kian—"

"You don't owe me anything," he said, staring at the door.

She sat up and coyly pressed her lips to his shoulder, curling her chest against his arm. "You know I meant that kiss."

He stiffened. "You were emotional. I wasn't going to take advantage of it."

"I get that." She drifted her hand across his back, then followed her hand with her body, brushing her breasts across his back. By the way he curled and lifted his chin, he *knew*. "I appreciate that." She pressed her lips to the back of his neck, to the left of his spine. Softly. Gently. A mere ghost of her lips. Moving slowly, she dusted another to the right.

Kian's breath appeared to stutter. It was empowering how fixated on her every move he was.

"But I'd been thinking about kissing you all day." Reaching the other side of him, she slid her foot along his thigh, down over the side of the bed until she could stand on it. "That's why I invited you home." The swell of her breast pressed into his upper arm now. "I knew what I was doing." A soft breath in his ear as she kissed the shell, then took the lobe between her teeth. As she did so, she ran her fingers up his inner thigh, stopping before reaching the apex, but close enough for him to understand her intention.

He leaned into her and made a strangled noise at the back of his throat.

She sidled around to stand in front of him, her hands never losing contact with him as she stroked across his chest until they were on both shoulders. Her knee pressed against the bed between his legs. His eyes, locked on her every movement, were swimming with both love and desire. Enjoying his reactions, she ran her fingernail up his throat until she reached his chin. "You already have my heart. Make some demands of your own."

The look in his eyes intensified as he took a slow, deliberate breath. He leisurely, carefully, lifted a hand to her cheek.

Lips parted and heart hammering, Noémie held still, waiting to see what he'd do. She felt open, exposed, and excited all in one. The start of something new, something equal parts thrilling and scary.

His other hand rose to toy with her bangs, drifting his fingers down to tuck a strand of hair behind her ear. Tender and gentle, he left a trail of tingles in his wake.

"Kiss me, Kian."

They slipped from her unbidden. Three words to start something new, something old, and something longed for. Three simple words and the dam broke. The gentle caress on her face became an incessant pull toward him and Kian rose to meet her in the middle.

As their lips met, he stole her breath.

A languid kiss, his mouth moved like he wanted to savor every moment, to instill her in every corner of his memory. Time slowed to the space between heartbeats. A hint of promise, a smidge of desire, and an eternity to discover. Her knees grew weak as he invaded all her senses. The softness of his mouth, the heat of his breath on her face, the scent of his cologne, the fire of his hands, all enhanced the moment her vision disappeared behind closed eyes.

When he allowed her to gasp in a ragged breath, snatched between moments and burning from the fire his mouth caused, he whispered, "I love you."

Freefalling. She knew. He knew. The words had been unsaid for so long, but hearing them, admitting them, made her head spin and her knees jelly. She locked her arms around his neck and, together, they fell upon the same idea. She pushed, his arms tightened, and the bed rose to embrace them.

Hidden beneath a curtain of hair, he worshiped her

mouth. Hands stroked and kneaded, fingers slithered beneath slips of clothing to taste bare skin at the small of her back.

This. This was the passion she'd been hoping for in their first kiss. She was being devoured, or she was doing the devouring, she didn't know. She didn't care. She wanted *more*.

"Hey, Kian! Didn't you hear me calling—*Whoops!*"

She lifted out of the kiss and, as she and Kian stared at each other, Noémie raised her foot, slipped off her shoe, and tossed it at the door. "Bugger off, Zane!"

A thump, followed by rambunctious laughter. "Sorry, Nomnom!"

"Zane!" Zariah scolded from beyond the room. "Leave them alone!"

Noémie braced her hand beside Kian's head. Her lips were tingling, her whole body buzzed with delight. "I suppose we should go see what they want."

He didn't seem to care as he kissed his way along her neck. "Stay here with me."

The huskiness in his voice pulsed fire along her spine which settled into a pooling heat in her belly. "I would," she whispered. "I want to. But your suitcase is in the other room and we'll have to do the walk of shame to get it if we go any further."

He laughed and the reverberations echoed through her body. "Or we could wait until they go to bed and go get it."

"Tempting," she said as she crawled backward. "However, there was champagne. Which means there's strawberries."

"Ahh," he breathed, understanding. "I won't stand between you and strawberries. I'll be out in a minute."

Feeling breathless, she retrieved her shoe on the way out, leaving Kian sprawled on the bed to collect himself.

"Sorry about the dumbass," Zariah called the moment Noémie exited the bedroom.

"Shut the door completely next time, babe," Zane called from his sprawl on the sofa.

"Next time, I'll aim better with my shoe," Noémie snarked at him and headed to the kitchen where Zariah was.

Her eyes shining with delight and mischief, Zariah held out a glass of champagne, with a strawberry attached, to Noémie. The look on her face told Noémie Zariah knew exactly what had happened and was waiting for intricate details, which she wasn't going to get.

"Kian!" Zane shouted as he bounced off the sofa and walked toward the kitchen. "They have a chessboard! I challenge you!"

"Yeah, yeah," Kian's voice echoed from the bedroom. "Be there in a sec."

"He needs 'a moment'," Zariah said and wiggled her eyebrows up and down. "Lucky him."

"Shuddup."

Zane squeezed Zariah's hips as he moved past her on his way to the pantry. "There's supposed to be bread too and—ah-ha! Here we go."

"Are we really going to snack now?" Noémie asked, nursing her champagne glass.

Dragging out a paper bag that contained a baguette, Zane plunked it on the counter beside the basket of cheese. "Well, you don't have to, but I am."

Noémie stretched out her hand and tore the end of the baguette off, offering half to Kian as he came out of the bedroom. He smiled at her in thanks and a heat rose up her neck caused by the eyes of her friends.

"Typical Nomnom," Zane teased. "Always goes for the tip. There's never a crust or an edge that's safe from her."

Noémie locked her eyes on Zane as she tore apart her bread. If he was going to tease like that, she'd return it full force. In French, she crooned, "The tip is the best part," then popped a piece in her mouth.

Kian choked on a piece of bread. Eyes wide, he stared

at Noémie.

Seeing Kian's reaction, Zane leaned toward her, grinning madly. "Party? What party? What'd you say? That sounded sexy. It was sexy, wasn't it? Kian, what'd she say?"

Coughing, Kian hit himself in the chest with his fist, then reached out to take a large drink of one of the champagne glasses on the bench. "That's for me to know and you to learn French."

"Uh-huh." Zane had cut a slice of the cheese as he waited for Kian to catch his breath, and used the knife to transfer the cheese to his mouth.

"Greedy guts," Zariah said, poking Zane in the side. "Tomorrow we have to go down to the town and hire ski clothes, then there's a bus at nine-thirty to the slope. Don't gorge yourself now, because you'll sleep in and we won't wake you up."

Zane pouted. Leaning sideways, he gave her puppy eyes as he plopped his head on her shoulder. "Babe, would you really leave me here?"

Zariah sighed and used her hand to bat Zane away from her shoulder. "Maybe Kian could be convinced to wake you up. But I won't."

"Not if he's eating cheese," Kian replied, grinning at Zane. "Dutch oven comes to mind. Not going anywhere near that room."

Noémie laughed. "He's got you there, Zane."

Zane left the cheese knife on the bench so he could clutch at his heart. "Betrayal!"

"Woe is you," Zariah said with a sly smile. "Maybe Noémie and I should take a bedroom for ourselves and you boys share a bed."

Kian objected, "I'm pretty sure I just said I didn't want to be in the Dutch oven room."

"Double betrayal!" Zane complained, picking up the knife again. "Don't you guys love me?" Cutting a slice of cheese, he popped it in his mouth. "Are you sure you don't want some?"

Zariah reached over and patted his back. "We might love you, but that doesn't mean we have to put up with your smell."

"I'll drink to that," Kian said and lifted his glass in a toast.

Clinking her glass to Kian's, Noémie said, "I think we all will."

"You're all horrible and mean. I am so going to thrash you in chess," Zane said with a mock scowl at Kian.

"You can try."

It didn't take long for the boys to set up their chessboard. With Kian and Zane butting heads over chess and who would go first, Zariah drew Noémie aside. "I was going to ask if you were okay with sharing a bedroom, but I guess it's pretty obvious you're fine with it."

A smile bloomed on her face. "More than fine with it."

"Finally, huh?"

"About bloody time," Noémie replied.

"Soooo …"

Noémie scrunched up her face playfully and turned up her nose. "I don't kiss and tell."

"That answers that question," Zariah replied, winking. "Next is wandering hands, Miss Sleep Snuggler. Or are you going to go with the flow and break out the lingerie?"

Noémie nudged her hip against Zariah's. "You are such an enabler."

"That's what best friends are for."

Noémie smiled lazily. "I have a plan," she said, watching Zane make a move on Kian's queen.

"Ooh, I know that look. Get it, girl," Zariah crooned with a wink. She wrapped her arms around Noémie's shoulders and squeezed. "We'll make ourselves scarce."

Noémie giggled. "Do me a favor and keep him here for a bit?"

"My pleasure. Zane can drag this match out for as long as you like." Zariah giggled and smacked a kiss on

Noémie's cheek before she released her. "Don't forget, bus leaves early, no sleep-ins, not even if you wear each other out. I've been looking forward to this for weeks and I will drag you outta bed naked if I have to!"

"Duly noted!"

It didn't take long to prepare. She snagged Kian's suitcase and headed for their bedroom. A quick shower, brushed her teeth, then she turned the lights on low and wriggled into her favorite piece of lingerie. Bright red, the baby doll was a mixture of lace, satin, and mesh, designed to both tease and enhance, with a matching thong. She'd never worn it to impress anyone else before, but wearing it now, she felt sexy. Sexy and ready to be ravished.

Lying in the middle of the bed, she took a provocative photo of herself from the nose down. Unused to doing something like this, she had to take several before she got one that was in focus and displaying enough to be tantalizing. Taking a deep, calming breath, she sent it to him.

She heard the beep as it arrived. She imagined a sharp intake of breath. Within seconds there was movement outside the door, and Zane's laughter, so she rolled onto her side and propped her head up and gave him her best sultry pose.

Kian opened the door enough so that he could slip into the room, then stopped, staring at her with wide eyes as he leaned his back against the closed door. "Wow."

Noémie smiled. "Do you like it?" she asked, trying to squash the sudden spike of nerves. He'd seen it before, twice on a mannequin and once on a model, but it was different wearing it herself and she hoped he approved.

"It's breathtaking," he breathed, his eyes skimming over her until they came to rest on her face.

She drifted her hand over her hip, pleased when his eyes were dragged away from her face and to her hand. "I thought we could spend some time together. Talk a little."

"There won't be much talking. Not while you're

wearing that."

"There'll be even less talking if I take it off," Noémie replied, pleased when Kian swallowed hard. "Besides, I did tease you with the promise of lingerie. I brought it with me, it'd be a shame to waste it."

His Adam's apple bobbed again. "It would."

He didn't seem to want to move away from the door so Noémie decided to help him out. She shifted until she was kneeling in the middle of the bed. "Come and play."

"In that order?"

She could see the effect she was having on him quite clearly and it was a wonderful feeling. "Preferably the other way around."

He groaned and thumped his head back against the door. "You're going to be the death of me." He pushed away from the door then, striding across the room to slide on the bed on his knees ahead of her.

He wasted no time connecting their lips. Moving closer, he grabbed her hips to pull her flush against him and her body molded to match his. There was no space between them, only a swelling heat. Butterflies dove into the very depths of her belly, a tingling sensation that soon encompassed her.

There was a desperation in his kiss that she met with an eagerness of her own. Teeth and tongue, mouths fused, Noémie fisted his shirt and pulled him closer still. All the sexual frustration they'd been feeling fueled the intensity of this kiss.

She slid one arm over his shoulder until her fingers spread at the nape of his neck. He pawed at her back, stroking his hands up and down her spine, unsure of how he wanted to hold her, except that it had to be everywhere at once.

He pulled back, ragged panting and glazed eyes, and rested his lips against her forehead. Gasping breath and grasping fingers, she desired more. Landing an open-mouthed kiss on his chin, she scraped her teeth on his throat and tugged at the back of his neck with her hand.

With a rasping chuckle, he ducked back down to kiss her again and the kisses turned slow. Softer. Deeper. Savoring. Warm mouth lingering on hers. Sweet-scented breaths against her face. A taste of tongue as the kiss deepened. A growing warmth against her skin from his hand. Mesh bunched beneath his touch, and then his fingers grazed against her bare behind.

Curled and cupped with both hands, Kian lifted Noémie toward him, shifting so he sat on the bed and she straddled his legs. Wrapping his arms around her, he fused their mouths together.

A plethora of kisses, excruciatingly slow and deep, before his hands flexed on her back and began to roam. A brush of fingers against her face, down her neck, stroking at the dip at the hollow of her throat. Drifting along her collarbone until they reached the spaghetti strap of her top, where he slipped his thumb beneath and pulled the strap down her arm. Breaking the kiss, his mouth followed the path of his hand with gentle, butterfly kisses.

A growing warmth and wetness caused by their shifting hips. While Kian kissed his down her neck, Noémie let her hands wander across his back and chest. As his mouth neared her shoulder, she lifted her chest, pleased when he kissed the swell of her breast instead.

Deft fingers made short work of the buttons of his shirt. Distracted by his mouth, and he equally distracted by her chest, she forgot to do the buttons at the cuffs and they tangled as she tried to pull off his shirt.

"That was suave," he laughed, bracing one hand on the bed behind him while lifting his other hand so she could concentrate on unbuttoning the cuff.

She beamed at him and tugged one of the sleeves over his wrists. "Makeshift handcuffs. You're completely at my mercy."

He laughed, and, once released, balled the shirt so he could toss it across the room. "We'll have to remember that."

Giggling, she bunched up his undershirt at the back and lifted, a request he swiftly complied with. After that was discarded too and she was able to run her hands over his wonderful chest, he went straight for the hem of her baby doll. Placing a small kiss against the hollow of her throat, he lifted the baby doll upward.

Noémie raised her arms and allowed him to unwrap her. Cloth fluttered against the bed in a discarded heap and she watched Kian drink in the sight of her with a look of reverence on his face.

"You're so beautiful," he breathed, meeting her eyes before he lowered his head to worship her.

Gentle touches, dustings of breaths, pressing kisses, and suckling skin, he touched and played and teased. Twisting them, he coaxed her onto her back on the bed so he had access to her entire body.

Boy, did he use all that access. She hadn't been aching like this, keenly waiting on his touch, for a long time. He made her breathless in so many ways and the sight of his blond hair tickling her ribs as he kissed her belly was imprinted on her mind.

Of all the things she expected during sex with Kian, taking her thong off with his teeth had not been one of them. She laughed when he rose up, wagging his eyebrows at her with her thong still in his mouth.

"That had to be the dorkiest move I have ever seen."

"Can't always be the same *thong* and dance," he told her, winking and reached for the condom she'd conveniently placed on the bedside table.

The absurdity of his pun, that he'd choose this moment to hit her with it, sent her into a spiral of hysterical giggles that didn't stop until he crawled back and settled over her.

Elbows on either side of her, supporting his weight, he waited until she caught her breath. "I think I win with that pun," he crooned.

"Definitely worth a gold medal."

"Noémie," he murmured, waiting so close and yet hesitating to move forward.

She drifted the tips of her fingers up his bare back and her toes along the back of his calves, smiling at him. "I love you."

"I love you, too," he returned, pressing a tender kiss to her jaw.

He brought the intimacy of laughter into lovemaking, something that she'd never known she'd wanted but somehow sorely missed. He teased and tickled, kissed, and licked, heightening arousal in ways she found impossible to comprehend.

Slow. So very slow. Oh to be loved like this, every stroke taking an eternity, every push with a leisurely kiss between.

He prolonged, cherishing every kiss, every thrust, meandering toward the edge, then kept them both dangling at the precipice, savoring each breathless moan, every beg, all while moving to the rhythm of imaginary music they both seemed to hear.

When she could no longer stand the feeling of being held at that precipice for so long, when the need for completion overrode her want for intimacy, she reversed their positions and took command. Rising above him, she used her whole body to work them both into a panting, moaning mess. His hands held to her breasts, her hips rolling, coaxing, she kept her eyes locked on his until the very last moment she could.

Riding the waves of pleasure that overtook her, she shattered into pieces and gave him everything, and he gave her everything in return.

CHAPTER 18

Snow *thwumped*, casting a cloud of white and cold as a Noémie-sized indent appeared in the drift gathered at the side of the beginner ski slope. She laughed, tangled in her skis and her poles, with powdered snow all around her and tried to wriggle free.

Snow kicked up as Kian slid to a stop close to the impact site. Popping his skis free of his boots with the end of the pole, he left them impaled in the ground as he hurried to help her. "Noémie! Are you okay?"

She wriggled, stuck upside down. "I'm good. Just stuck."

"That looked like it hurt."

"Nope. Well. Not much."

"You really weren't kidding, were you?" Dropping down, Kian managed to poke the clips on her boots with her pole so she could get free. "I'm beginning to think I should get a toboggan and drag you behind me."

Noémie fell out of the hole she made and onto the snow. Kneeling, she grinned at him. "*Oooooh.*"

"Oooooh, what?" he responded, eyebrows raised as he offered her his hand to help her up.

With a wink, she replied, "Perfect viewing angle."

Kian burst into laughter, pulling her to her feet and straight into a kiss.

Noémie loved that this was them now. He'd been sneaking kisses from her all day. Some lingering, some little pecks, some to the back of her hand or the corner of her mouth, some even in front of the overly excited Zariah and Zane.

Each kiss would warm her through and leave her wanting more, especially after last night. She couldn't wait to get him back to the chalet.

Breaking the kiss, Kian grinned at her. "C'mon. I'll race you to the bottom."

"You won't win," Noémie said, with a cheeky swipe at his behind. "I'm totally going to turn into one of those cartoon snowballs, rolling down the hill and demolishing everything in my path."

Laughing, he pulled her skis out of the drift for her. "You can snowball me over any time you like."

"Oh, I'll definitely sweep you off your feet."

"You'd have to catch me first."

She abandoned her skis and pounced on him instead, unbalancing them both and sending them tumbling into the snow. They wrestled and tussled, throwing the odd snowball at each other until his laughter was so carefree and infectious, she had to kiss him.

The laughter changed to a moan and he gripped her hips to pull her down to him. He crept his hands up her back, kissing her fervently, then, while she was distracted by his mouth, proceeded to dump snow down the back of her jacket.

She shrieked and curled away from the cold, thrusting her chest at his face as she rolled away from him. Scrambling to her knees, she scooped up snow and threw it back at him, and they started an all-out snow brawl, only to be caught by one of the slope instructors and scolded.

Later that day, when the cold had become too much for them and they needed to thaw, they sat opposite each other at the local ski lodge and sampled their stew and hot chocolate while watching the skiers glide by in the hopes of spotting Zariah and Zane.

Gloves resting on the table beside her, Noémie wrapped her hands around her second mug of hot chocolate and blew across the top. "Love the snow. Hate the cold."

"Great for snuggling."

"I wouldn't know," she quipped. "There's a great lack of that happening."

Kian laughed. "Poor you."

She played up the drama. "I am completely attention-starved."

Folding his arms on the table, he leaned on them as he bent toward her. "Then I'm not doing my job."

"You should get right on that."

A slow smile that drew her in and a purr in his voice. "I plan to."

She smiled at him. "It's a shame the bus doesn't go back for another four hours."

"I'm sure there's a closet around here we could borrow."

She laughed at that. "Or we could keep flirting and delay it, and it'll be sweeter for it."

A sultry smile that delighted and aroused. "I like that idea."

Trying not to flush, or drag him off to the closest closet, she said, "You know, you're so much better at skiing than I am, if you want to go do the harder slopes, I don't mind hanging out here for a while."

"I enjoy hanging out with you," he returned. "Besides, by the end of the weekend, you'll be good enough to go down them with me."

"Or I'll have broken something."

He laughed. "Hopefully not, but if it happens, I'll nurse you back to health." He studied her for a moment, then unfolded his arms. Grabbing a piece of bread, he swept the edges of his empty bowl, hunting for that last morsel of stew. "Can I ask you something?"

"Of course."

Kian turned his head to stare out the window. "I know I suggested it before, but you really should think about getting a business manager, so you can concentrate on the design aspect of your brand. What if that manager was me?"

Noémie's eyebrows shot up and she sat back, resting her mug on the table as she stared at him. "What are you saying?"

"Zane got me thinking, that's all."

Noémie studied him, waiting for him to expand his thoughts, but he continued to stare out the window at the skiers outside. "Care to share?"

Kian wrinkled his nose and pursed his lips. "Modeling and fashion are all I know. I have lots of skills and specific knowledge related to that. I could easily slip into another corporate management position somewhere else ... but music? I mean, I play piano, but I wouldn't know the first thing about putting on a concert. Or organizing a recording session."

"You said you didn't want to take over your father's companies."

"My father's, no," Kian said, turning his head to look at her. "But something I could help build that won't get snatched away the second he decides I'm unworthy? I put so much work into Celestial, and I know it can just disappear on his whim, and it's exhausting. But something I could take real pride in being a part of? That sounds exciting. And I know you don't want to be big, and I'm perfectly fine with that, but I'm sure there are things I can do to make life easier."

"Well, I suppose I could go into men's lingerie and you could model for me," she said, trying to joke. "But let's be real. I couldn't *afford* you, and you couldn't afford to work for me. I couldn't pay you even a quarter of what you earn now and there's—you'd get bored! The managing part doesn't take up much of my time and—"

"I have skills and knowledge that could help you," he said eagerly. "I could buy in as a partner and—"

"Kian," Noémie interrupted, reaching forward to put her hand over his free one. "Let me stop you there. Not that I don't appreciate you thinking about my business—I absolutely do and I'm really grateful for your advice—I don't think it's a good idea. We've only just truly gotten together. Can you imagine what your father would think if we said we were an official couple and going into business together? I mean, it appears really, *really* sketchy. "

He laughed nervously. "Yeah. You're right. That would be bad." With a heavy sigh, he turned serious. "I came on too strong, didn't I?"

"I love that you're thinking about us long term," she replied, smiling at him. "But I don't want to be seen as someone who is using you to get ahead."

He nodded. "I know."

"So maybe this is a conversation we should have in a few years. For now, we could talk about Zane's offer, if you want."

He returned his gaze to the landscape beyond the window, watching the people outside. "I don't think I'll take it."

She tried to be supportive. "You could learn about the music industry. I think Zane took you not knowing the industry into account when he offered it to you."

"Maybe. But if I took his offer, then I couldn't help you in the future."

Noémie lifted her hot chocolate and took a sip to give herself time to consider. "What do you want to do, Kian? Not me, not your father or your mother, you. You need to figure that out and then you grab hold of it with both hands and you don't let anything take it away."

Kian grabbed onto her hand with both of his. "Like that?"

Noémie burst into a smile.

Threading their fingers together, Kian lost the humor in his face. "I'm going to put some feelers out when we get back to Paris. See what the market's like, and what options I could have."

"Oh?"

"I'm … worried what'll happen when we go public. Possible backlash on you, or"—he sighed—"Father goes through with disowning me again. If I already have options in the works, it might show him how serious I am about this. About you."

"It's not like we're going to march over there and tell him straight away," she reminded him. "You said he didn't find out for about six months last time. We have time and there's still a lot we need to learn about each other." She laughed. "I mean, thirty is less than six years away."

"You want to be in a secret relationship for six years?" he questioned.

"Of course not. But if telling your father is causing you this much stress, we could at least discuss it."

He nodded and kissed her fingers again. "You're right. We should. Let's enjoy this weekend first. I just … wanted to let you know my thoughts. I didn't want you to be upset that I didn't offer my services to you first."

"What sort of services are we talking about?" Noémie asked, feeling mischievous.

He grinned. "Anything you like."

"I might take you up on that part of it," she said and squeezed his hand.

"There they are!" Zariah called from the entrance to the lodge.

Kian pulled his hands away and peered over his shoulder at the pair as Zane and Zariah separated at the door. Zane headed for the counter, presumably to order food, while Zariah bounced over toward them. "We missed you guys," she said, sliding into the seat beside Noémie. "Thought you'd still be skiing."

"Made acquaintance with one too many snowdrifts," Noémie chirped. "Needed a break before I became one myself."

Kian smiled and lifted his mug. "Pretty sure she knows them all by name and is invited to all their family reunions."

Such a wonderful day. Stealing kisses in the snow, skiing, and sledding and sitting close, sharing hot chocolates, and snuggling to get warm. Of snowmen and fireplaces and falling in the snow. Laughter and fun and even more kisses.

Noémie hadn't been this happy in such a long time.

Upon returning from skiing, she and Zane had pottered around the kitchen, baking treats and doing dinner prep, she even had bread dough rising so they could have it for dinner. Armed with treats and a thermos of hot chocolate, the four of them walked up to the lookout at the top of the mountain their chalet was on so they could watch the sunset together.

There was a set of wooden stairs that led all the way to the top and the lookout itself was wooden decking rimmed by a railing, on the edge of a cliff. Noémie peered over the edge, looking down at the drop and the trees below. They were the only ones there and the scene was just picturesque. Dusting the railing free of snow, she folded her arms along it and rested her chin on her wrists to watch the sunset.

Kian, who'd brought his professional camera, leaned over the balcony edge and snapped a photo of her, with the snow-covered trees in the background.

"Kian," she whined.

"Getting the settings right," he replied, looking at the screen. "Documenting moments. You know the drill."

"You could at least give me warning," she complained. "What if I was mid-blink?"

"You are always gorgeous," he replied, looking up from

the camera to wink at her. "From mid-blink to mid-sneeze."

Huffing, Noémie set her sights on the horizon. The sunset was turning everything a wonderful pink and orange. The valley ahead of them already was in shadow, the tops of the trees dusted pink and the clouds flowing across one of the nearby mountains was orange.

"It's so pretty," she crooned. "Serene."

"The colors are incredible," Kian echoed and lifted his camera to get a couple of snaps of it.

Curious, she asked, "Does the camera catch it all?"

"Even more so," Kian replied and took several steps back. "Stay still, I'll get a shot with you in frame."

She giggled. "Shot of my butt, you mean."

He laughed at that. "I will neither confirm nor deny that."

She cocked her hip a little more, feeling mischievous and was rewarded with Kian's slight hum of delight behind her.

"You're making this difficult," he said.

"Making things '*hard*' you mean," she quipped. She straightened and half turned toward her boyfriend. Keeping her hip cocked so her butt was pushed out, she puffed out her chest and threw him a flirty look and a kiss.

The camera buzzed. "Nice."

"Stop showing off dat ass," Zariah chirped as she sidled into frame. She spun, facing Noémie and copied her pose. "It's better with two."

"Ooooh, *yeah*," Zane crooned, materializing at Kian's shoulder. "I want copies. My dude, we are lucky men."

"We are indeed," Kian agreed and his camera continued to buzz as he took photos

Noémie giggled, unable to keep a straight face. Zariah, in full swing, pulled a duck face, then exaggerated her body through several classic pin-up poses.

"You missed your calling, Zariah," Kian called, still taking photos. "You should've been a model."

Zariah flicked her gaze to Zane and winked. "I would love to do lingerie, but I'm pretty sure Zane would buy every copy in existence to hoard them from the rest of the world."

"Damn right," Zane said. Patting Kian on the back, bounced into the middle of the girls and started his own butt enhancing pose, blowing kisses at the camera. Zariah turned toward him and began posing with him and their poses turned even more exaggerated and silly.

"Yeah, baby," Kian called, laughing. His camera was firmly planted on the trio as he snapped pictures. "Work it."

Noémie doubled over with laughter, unable to help herself, or even copy some of their poses.

Releasing Zariah, Zane turned toward Noemie, belly dancing and swinging his hips, all the while grinning madly. He reached out, taking both of Noémie's hands and dragging her into an exaggerated waltz. He spun her under his arm, then let her go halfway through the spin, and she found his hand replaced by Kian's, who then pulled her to his side.

Disoriented, she looked up at him. "What?"

"Watch," Zane said, winking at her, then turned back to the still silly-posing Zariah.

Holding his camera one-handed, Kian wrapped his arm around Noémie. "Shh," he whispered and showed her the screen on his camera and the fact that he was recording.

Noémie's breath caught in her chest as Zane moved back to Zariah and dropped to a knee. Glee bubbled up inside as she realized what was going on and she pushed her hand against her lips to keep from squealing. A rush of excitement burst inside her. It was happening. It was finally happening.

Zariah gasped as she saw him, clapping both hands over her mouth and nose. She rose on her toes and took a step backward, so her back hit the railing. The fading sunlight caught in her brown curls, lighting them to a brilliant orange.

With a squeeze, Kian released Noémie, sidestepping so he could get a better angle, with the sunset in the background and Zariah's fiery hair.

"Zariah," Zane said, smiling up at her. He reached into the pocket of his winter jacket and pulled out a small, red box. "You are my first thought when I wake up, and my last when I fall asleep. You tangle me up inside every time you smile and when you laugh, it's the most beautiful music I have ever heard. I want to spend the rest of my life with you, making music and sharing laughter and traveling all over the world. Will you marry me?"

Noémie bounced on her toes in anticipation, staring at Zariah as they all waited for her to answer.

Seemingly frozen, it took forever for Zariah to remember she needed to answer her boyfriend. Prying her hand away from her face, she extended it out to him. "Of course, I will!"

Grinning madly, Zane pulled off Zariah's glove so he could slip the ring on her finger. In a fluid motion, he rose to his feet, picked Zariah up and spun her in a circle. Planting her back on the ground, he kissed her. Deep and long and full of love.

Practically beside herself with excitement, Noémie struggled to stay as still as she could so she didn't ruin the moment for them. Bouncing up and down on the spot helped get rid of the excess energy she had from finally seeing this moment for her best friends.

Pulling away, Zane contented himself with small kisses while Zariah giggled uncontrollably and hugged him. Spotting Noémie, Zariah held her left hand out to her over Zane's shoulder, shaking it in delight. There, sparkling on Zariah's finger, was a large orange-sapphire, accented by two pear-shaped diamonds and surrounded by a halo of other diamonds.

By being acknowledged, Noémie took that as her signal she could pounce. With a squeal, she did exactly that, wrapping her arms around then both and bouncing up and down on the stop. "I'm so happy for you both! This is *amazing!*"

Chortling, Zane shifted so he could wrap an arm around Noémie and include her, while still kissing Zariah.

Happy tears, from both Noémie and Zariah. Laughter from Zane as he snuck kisses in with his fiancée.

And Kian recorded the whole thing.

Afterward, when emotions had calmed down and congratulations abounded, and Kian had taken announcement photos for the pair for them to send to family, the four of them got around to watching the now fading light of the sunset, then headed back to the chalet for dinner and to celebrate. Somewhere among the fourth bottle of wine, Zariah announced that Noémie was her maid of honor and Noémie had to design her the most fabulous wedding lingerie set, just for her, to which Noémie readily agreed.

Then, sensing she'd had enough to drink, Zane carted a giggling Zariah off to bed.

Noémie was mellow, relaxed and most of all, happy. Dressing in her silk cami, long silk pants, and socks, and wrapped up in the quilt from their bed, she waited on the balcony outside their bedroom while Kian showered.

There was a wonderful quiet outside. A stillness and a freshness to the air that wasn't in Paris. Brushing the snow away from the railing, she rested her elbows on it and stared up into the starry sky. Moonlight danced across the leaves of trees and reflected sparkles from the snow-covered ground. It was beautiful and serene and she could stare at the landscape for hours.

It wasn't long before there was a knock on the door behind her and she threw a glance over her shoulder and smiled in greeting.

Kian, wearing a long-sleeved white shirt, silk long pants, and thick socks, cracked the door open a fraction. "Hey. Can I join you?"

She lifted her arm, parting the quilt so he could slip inside and snuggle up against her back. The chilly air stole her breath away and made her shiver, but the heat from his body soon warmed the air inside the blanket again, making it toasty.

His arms wove around her stomach, his chin on the top of her head. "Love the blanket monster look."

"Blanket burrito," she chirped. "It's all the rage."

"Tasty," he said. "So why are you out here in the cold?"

"Enjoying the scenery," she replied. "It's beautiful here." She sighed wistfully and lifted her hand so she could cup her chin and rest her elbow on the banister. "I can't believe they're finally engaged. It's been such a long time coming and now it's here and I'm so excited for them both."

"Me too."

She twisted her head up. "You knew, didn't you, you sneak."

Kian laughed. "There's a reason I brought my camera."

"And here I thought it was to get sexy shots of me in lingerie."

He grinned and quipped. "Well, if you're offering."

Giggling, she lifted away from the balcony and pressed her back to his stomach and rested her head on his chest.

"Glad you came?"

"Which time?" she quipped and enjoyed the rumble of laughter he made against her back. "Yes," she continued when he'd caught his breath. "I wouldn't have missed this for anything. I had so much fun today. Plus, no broken bones or twisted ankle. A first for me."

He laughed again. "You still have two days of skiing left."

"Don't jinx me," she sulked.

"It's nice to get away from everything. Just us, no interruptions."

She laughed at that. "I still half expect the phone to ring and you to be whisked away again."

He shrugged, jostling her and then snuggled in closer. "Told Mom I was 'going away with friends' and that I was blocking her number for the weekend. She wasn't too impressed, but there's really not much she can do."

"So I have you all to myself?" No mother calling at inopportune moments? No rushing off because something came up at work? Just her and him and the bed behind them.

"You do indeed," he purred. Ducking his head down, his hands snuck up her cami at the same time he kissed her below the ear. "Whatever shall we do?"

She let her head roll, extending her neck in invitation. "I'm sure I can think of something."

"Take your time," he said, accepting the invitation by nibbling on the tender flesh. His hands tracked fire across her skin as he ran them over her. "I love that I can do this now. Kissing you, touching you, just being with you is pure bliss."

She closed her eyes and leaned into him, lifting her arm to loop it around the back of his neck, her other fisted around the blanket edge to keep it closed around them. "I do, too."

Cupping a breast, his other hand slipped down below the waistband of her pants. "*Oh*. Commando. Sexy."

She breathed out slowly, enjoying the feeling of his fingers. "Really didn't expect to be wearing clothes for this long."

He purred. "More than happy to divest you of them."

CHAPTER 19

Soft snow fell, dusting the sidewalk. Her breath steaming out ahead of her, Noémie walked out of the metro station into the frigid air. Checking her cell, she walked in the direction her map indicated in search of Kian's apartment. Zane and Zariah were going to come for dinner later, but Kian had asked her to come early so he could show her around.

Her wonderful staff hadn't burned her boutique to the ground when Noémie returned to work on Monday. Everything was clean, the shelves were bursting with stock and Dulcie had left a sticky note on the counter, "*Welcome back! Hope you had fun on your trip and the baby doll worked!*"

She'd returned to work rested and relaxed and excited about her new relationship. She'd talked to several other lingerie companies about stocking her brand in their stores, as well as several of the contacts Kian had given her about marketing and was confident that Chant de La Rose was about to undergo a nice period of growth and change.

She hadn't had a chance to see Kian since the weekend, though they talked every day. Something had been going on at Celestial that was taking up all his time. It had been a long five days, but now she'd be spending the night.

She was excited and nervous. Spending the night at his place felt like it shifted their relationship from a romantic rendezvous on a holiday and into their real lives. It was inevitable that it was going to, but it still was somehow more real. More final.

They were doing this. Trying it out and seeing if they could make it work.

Adjusting her bag on her shoulder she turned a corner and lifted her phone as it beeped at her.

Kian

Are you close?

Noémie

I think so.

Kian

I wouldn't have minded picking you up.

Noémie

It's a nice walk. I think I see your street.

Kian

I'll come down.

Noémie

Someone's excited.

He didn't reply to that. Smiling to herself, Noémie counted the numbers down until she reached the building Kian lived in. It wasn't hard to tell which one since her boyfriend was waiting on the stoop.

"When did you become a puppy?" she asked as he bounded over to her.

He swooped in to kiss her, almost knocking her off her feet. Hastily grabbing her to aid her balance, he effectively dipped her, he was so eager to kiss her. And he didn't stop there, plucking her off the ground to spin her around in a hug. "I'm so glad you're here," he said when he was sated and looped his arm around her waist. "It's been a long and stressful week, but now you're here, I know it's all over."

"Do you want to talk about it?"

"I would, but I can't." He squeezed her. "Come on, let's get out of the cold."

Kian's top floor apartment had a view of the Seine and the Eiffel Tower, which already made it impressive. Polished hardwood floors led into an open apartment. Everything shone at her and she was only in the small foyer. "Wow. I feel like I've walked into … like one of those interior design magazines," she said, slipping off her damp boots to leave by the door. "Do we need specialized shoes to walk on this floor, or are socks okay?"

Kian laughed as he hung up her coat. "Socks are fine. Cute even. Make yourself at home."

She walked farther in, her hands clutching the straps of her bag. "What are we having? It smells delicious."

"Roast lamb. You were right, I'm not a terribly good cook, but I can make a yummy roast and I know how to bake vegetables, and I figured everyone was English enough to appreciate a roast. Do you want to put your bag in my room?" he asked.

"Sure."

"Down the end of the hall and to the left. Have a look around if you like."

The hallway through the middle separated the apartment into two. One side was a large social entertainment section, with a dining table that fit eight people. Several sofas set in parallel to each other and surrounded a large coffee table, with a fireplace at the end and there was even a grand piano. The kitchen had white marble benches and was three times the size of her kitchen. The entire wall faced a breathtaking view of the Seine, with large windows or doors which lead onto the balcony which ran the entire length of the wall.

The other side of the hallway was reserved for bedrooms. Curiosity got the better of her and she poked her head into the other rooms. He had a separate den with a sofa and a huge TV screen. One of the bedrooms had been converted into a gym space, which she had to smile over, another one was an office and he still had a guest bedroom as well as his room.

Everything looked picture perfect. So perfect, she was afraid of touching anything in case she left a smudge. Blacks and whites and muted gray, the only color in the place was the fresh flowers on the table or the paintings on the wall.

His bedroom was completely different and out of place in an otherwise immaculate apartment. A large king bed covered with a bright red quilt. He had several bright, colorful throw pillows and in the middle of the bed sat a handmade teddy bear.

"No way," she breathed, recognizing the bear. Mr. Unbearable. She'd made that for Christmas when they were kids and he still had it, and its frayed appearance meant it had a lot of love over the years.

The two bedside lamps were mismatched, and one of them was covered in seashells and looked handmade, and there was a framed picture of her beneath it. The frayed rainbow mat on the floor at the foot of the bed had several cat toys on it. His bedroom had its own bathroom and walk-in robe. A large television hung on the wall opposite the bed. Several potted plants adorned the window sill.

A huge cat scratching tree sat by the window, full of colorful toys and feathers. A fabric pin board covered the entire wall by the door and the pin board was covered in pictures. Noémie put her bag at the foot of the bed and went to have a closer look.

His Instagram pictures. All his favorite moments, all in one place. Sunsets and flowers and beaches and Purrfect. Pictures of people who were important to him. A whole bunch of the Polaroids they'd taken around Paris.

He had silly selfies with his mother from throughout his life. Several pictures were of Kian in the foreground and his father standing regally in the background. He had a few shots of Mathilde too and it seemed like she'd been in the employment of the family for many years.

Noémie smiled as she spotted a bunch of photos featuring the four of them when they were younger. There were several of Kian and Zane together, as well as a few of Noémie and Zariah. There was even Noémie's school picture with a heart sticker in the corner.

There were also pictures of the four of them as they were now. There were even a few already pinned up that Kian had taken over their skiing trip, and several of the Zane and Zariah's proposal. The one they'd taken at the food market had also been printed and pinned. Their first selfie together as well. He'd gathered together several of his favorite Polaroids and bundled them together in a group. Noémie was glad that, while the one of her in the baby doll hadn't made it to the wall, the one Zariah had taken of Noémie with the baby doll on the mannequin had.

There was even a photo of them in bed together that Kian had taken on their trip, both of them smiling at the camera like complete dorks.

She spotted several class photos, tall boys standing in uniformed rows and she guessed those were from when he had returned to America, so she ran her fingers over the faces until she found Kian. Beside one of the class photos, tucked under a photo of Purrfect, was one of those old four-in-a-column photo booth pictures of Kian around sixteen with another boy who was kissing Kian's cheek. Pulling the line of photos out, she saw the last one was of the two of them kissing.

She turned it over in her hands, wondering if Kian was the sort of person to write dates or notes on the back of his photos but came up empty.

"That's Charlie," Kian said, leaning against the door frame.

Charlie, his friend and only other constant in his life. She wasn't surprised at all.

"He's cute," she said and tucked it back in its rightful place. "It didn't work out? Or did the contract break you up?"

"No. I …" he cleared his throat. "Charlie was before. I

wasn't ready to come out and he was. We … made the choice we'd be better friends."

She kept her eyes on the photos, feeling that he'd be more willing to open up to her if she wasn't looking at him. "What'd he think about your contract?"

He sighed and explained, "He thinks it's a load of trash and was justifiably angry to find out about it. Even more so that I agreed."

She nodded. "You two looked good together."

"We were good together," he agreed. "For the most part."

She smiled at him over her shoulder. "I'm glad you had one good experience with a relationship at least."

"I'm having a good one now." Kian studied her. "You knew."

"Not for certain, but"—Noémie lifted her shoulders a little in an apologetic shrug—"in your office, you said, 'Charlie and I used to'. That sentence could easily end in 'date'."

He rubbed the back of his neck. "And you don't mind?"

"It's part of who you are," she replied with sincerity. She'd heard a revelation such as this could be a deal-breaker and she needed him to know it wasn't for her. He was opening up, and she wanted him to feel safe. "Emotional connection required and out of everyone you could have, you chose me, and I chose you. That's what matters. You're bi. I am one hundred percent okay with that."

The loving smile on his face made her melt. "Even more reason to love you forever."

Happiness bubbled up inside her from his smile.

Sighing, he looked back at the wall and said, "My parents don't know. I … I'm still mostly in the closet, I guess. There's been … when I was a teenager—I mean, parties and such, people, um … kisses … Tiffany …" He paused, then rushed, "She was *really* into the sex party scene."

Noémie's eyes widened. Tiffany. That must be his ex-girlfriend. She turned to look at him. "Really?"

He nodded. "There are all sorts of sex clubs in New York and she kept expressing interest, 'all our friends were going' but I never wanted to. Not my thing, you know. I didn't find out she was going until I walked into her place one day and found one happening. All sorts of people I'd never met before, various stages of undress and she was in her bedroom with another dude."

She blinked a couple of times. "She was cheating on you?"

He shrugged. "She claimed we were in an open relationship. I couldn't be 'official' with her, and she didn't want to appear suspicious with my father."

That made her angry. "Which is proper bollocks. She was using that as an excuse to cheat."

He grinned at her for that. "Yup."

"Is that why you tried to break the contract?"

"Yeah. I thought if we could be official, she'd be happy with just me. Thought that's what she wanted. I really should've known. I struggled with it for a while, trying to keep her happy, even tried attending a sex party with her because I thought it was what she wanted. There were kisses but I bailed really quick. It's not for me and just attending it cemented that I needed an emotional attachment in my head."

"I'm sorry."

He gave her a 'meh' face. "I'm over it. She's not worth it."

She looked back at the pictures. "Thank you for telling me. Tiffany sounds … um … very selfish."

He chortled at that. "She was *awful*." He pushed away from the door and moved to join her.

"I was being polite." She smiled and caught the sleeve of his shirt between her index finger and thumb.

"I'm proud of my time with Charlie. He meant a lot to

me—still means a lot to me and our time together was good. Not so much with Tiffany. I'm seeing a trend," he continued, looking at his pictures. Stretching out his hand, his fingers lingered on the picture of Charlie. "With Charlie, I didn't act fast enough. With her, I was too fast." Dropping his hand down, he touched the corner of one of their selfies together. "I want to get it right with you."

"Well, you're doing wonderfully so far." She brushed her fingers over the wall and touched the same picture he was touching. "This is incredible, Kian. It's so you. I want to ask a million questions. About Mr. Unbearable, I can't believe you kept him. And these," she said, pointing to the sunsets, then to the class photos. "And those. And Charlie. *Everything.*"

"I'll tell you anything you want to know." Reaching out, he took her hand and pulled her toward him. "I love you," he murmured and kissed her. Taking her by the hips, he walked her backward toward his bed and coaxed her onto it. Settling over her, he kissed her in earnest and she wrapped her arms around his neck to enjoy him.

Soft padding down the hallway accompanied by a loud meow as Purrfect announced her presence. She jumped up on the bed and stuck her nose on Kian's cheek in a demand for attention.

Breaking the kiss, Kian turned to his cat, bumping his head against hers. "Here you are," he said, grinning as Purrfect rubbed her face against his. "Meet the other woman in my life."

"Were you talking to me or her?" Noémie asked as she lifted her fingers to Purrfect so she could sniff them. The hairless cat wore a little knitted white sweater that was covered in red hearts to keep her warm.

"Yes," he replied with utmost seriousness.

Noémie giggled, rolled her eyes at Kian, and scratched Purrfect behind the ear. "She's wonderful."

"Who's my pretty girl," Kian crooned at Purrfect while nuzzling her head. Purrfect mewed at him in response.

"That's right, you are."

Purrfect jumped, walking up Kian's back to his shoulder and then flopped around his neck, purring so loud Noémie could feel the reverberations.

"We're going to have to sleep around her tonight, aren't we?"

"Who said I was going to allow you to sleep?" Kian crooned. Supporting his weight on one hand, he undid the top button of her blouse. "Don't suppose I could get a sneak peek of whatever lingerie you're wearing? You didn't send a photo and I'm sad."

She stretched her arms over her head in search of Mr. Unbearable, then stuck the bear between them. "Nope," she said, peeking around the bear. "You have to wait."

He pouted at her.

"It'll be worth it."

"I know it will," Kian said, moving aside Mr. Unbearable so he could kiss her.

When Zane and Zariah arrived, Noémie was on the balcony outside looking at the incredible view of the river. There was a sense of peace and serenity in the view, the ambling river, and the people wandering the banks. A light snow fell, adding to the romance in the air.

"Holy shit," Zariah said, slipping onto the balcony. "Noémie, how can this be his place? I mean … like the place we rent in London is half this size and I thought that was luxurious. This … this is too much."

"It's daunting," Noémie said. "I'm afraid to touch anything in case I smudge it."

"Puts things into perspective." Zariah planted her elbows on the railing and whistled. "Woooooow. This view though."

"It's pretty amazing." She glanced over her shoulder at Zane and Kian as they chatted in the kitchen. "I get it, though. The house, the presentation, it's what his family wants. What's expected of him. But there are parts of this place he's made for himself. Cluttered and messy and full of color." She lowered her voice. "Have you seen his cat yet?"

"That was a cat? Looked more like some sort of hobgoblin."

"Her name is Purrfect and she really is."

Zariah smiled at her, then lost it as she clasped her hands together. "Noémie. Real talk. I can see him thriving here. But I can't see you happy in a place like this. It's … stifling."

"I don't think he's exactly thriving here either," Noémie said.

"Hmm." Zariah lifted one arm and extended it across Noémie's back, then shuffled over so she was draped all over Noémie. "It's freezing out here. Come inside."

Noémie laughed. "Okay."

Kian held two glasses of champagne out to them as she and Zariah slipped back into the indoor warmth.

"This better be the good stuff," Zariah said as she took one. "There's no point having an insanely rich friend if you don't get the benefits of it."

Kian laughed. "The 'good' stuff is overrated and mostly for one-upping everyone else. This is delicious and that's what counts."

"Excellent," Zariah said and held up her glass. "A toast," she announced. "To friendship!"

"To love," Kian said, his eyes on Noémie.

"To music," Zane said and gestured to the piano with his glass. "Does that work? Or is that ornamental?"

Kian turned and regarded it. "No, it works. It's even in tune."

Zane placed his glass down on the bench, threaded his fingers together and cracked his knuckles. "All right then. Requests?"

"Bohemian Rhapsody," Noémie responded straight away, teasing him.

Zane gave her a flat stare. "Mean. You know I like to head bash to that one. Can't play and dance."

"Piano Man," Zariah said and sat on the sofa so she could watch.

Zane laughed and headed for the piano. "Anything for you, babe."

"He plays?" Kian asked Noémie, coming to stand beside her. "I thought he played guitar only."

"Self-taught since his YouTube career began. He's decent," Noémie replied. "Enough to be able to compose. He sings beautifully."

"Yeah, he does."

Sitting on the stool, Zane cleared his throat several times and rested his fingers on the keys. Busting out a lively tune, Zane sang, "*Zazzy, my baby, Zazzy, my honey, Zazzy, my ragtime gal.*"

Zariah burst into laughter at the ridiculousness of his song and the put-on voice he used.

"I think that one might be copyrighted," Kian called.

"Don't burst my bubble," Zane called. "Right. Piano Man. Here goes."

Leaning against the kitchen bench, Kian looped his arm around Noémie's waist and pulled her to him. Her back to his stomach, he wrapped both arms around her and rested his chin on her head as they snuggled down to enjoy being serenaded by Zane.

Kian was an excellent roaster and it had been a while since Noémie had an English style roast. Rich tender meat, smothered in gravy, and roast vegetables, the kind of meal she used to get when visiting Mama Talal's place at her sleepovers with Zariah. Zariah declared it couldn't be a proper roast without Yorkshire pudding and had commandeered the kitchen to whip one up.

Once the four of them had eaten their fill and stacked the dishwasher, they retreated into the den to watch a movie, much like they used to do when they were teenagers. Zane sat on the sofa, Zariah on the floor ahead of him, while Kian and Noémie chose to snuggle up the other end.

When Zane started stroking his fingers up and down Zariah's arm and across her neck, Kian lowered his head to whisper in Noémie's ear. "It's about now that Zane's hand starts sneaking down her shirt and we squirm and pretend we don't see."

Noémie giggled. "And in a few minutes, they'll go to make 'fresh popcorn' and we won't see them again for the rest of the movie because they're snogging in the kitchen."

"So that still happens?"

"It's worse," she said. "Now they do the nasty instead of just snog and there was no handsome guy to keep me entertained." She leaned her head back so she could look up at him. "It's your home. Kick them out."

"Or," he crooned with a sly smile. "We beat them to the punch and go make 'fresh popcorn'."

Excited by that prospect, she tapped his chest. "Let's do it."

He nudged her so she'd get off him. "Anyone for popcorn?" he announced in a too-loud voice as he stood.

Noémie bounced to her feet. "Yes. Sounds great!" she chirped as they hurried to the door.

"You're not fooling anyone!" Zariah called.

"Maybe," Noémie called back. "But it's *our* turn now."

Kian didn't even allow her to get to the kitchen before he was kissing her. Hands sliding down her back, all the way down to her upper thighs, he stooped down so he could pick her up. The sharp lift broke the kiss and Noémie laughed as she looped her arms around his neck to hold on. Hooking her knees over his hips, he walked them into the kitchen and deposited her on the bench in the middle, then nudged between her legs.

Cupping her behind, he grinned at her. "This was a great idea."

"So, is it now that you try to stick your hand down my shirt?" she teased. "Or do we snog for a while?"

"We 'make out'," he joked. "And it's not your shirt where I'm putting my hand."

"So bold." She draped her arms over his shoulders and toyed with the hair at the back of his neck. "I'm intrigued."

He kissed her, hard and fast, mouth furiously moving against hers. He slid one hand from her back, under her arm then across the swell of her breast to the button on her blouse, unbuttoning just enough to free the lacy sheer bra she'd worn for the evening.

He broke from her to lean back and admire what she wore, dusting his fingers over an aching nipple. "Breathtaking," he said and attached his mouth to her neck.

Noémie placed one hand on the bench behind her to use as support, lifting her chest in invitation, one he didn't take. Instead, his hand slid up her skirt, over her inner thigh, to tease the seam of her lace panties. Gasping, she spread her legs wider.

His other hand splayed between her shoulder blades to help support her. Open-mouthed kisses against her neck and collarbone while his fingers worked beneath the lace to explore and play.

Sheer delight raged through her. She never dreamed she'd be this daring and it was thrilling and erotic and so addictive. Curtains open in a room full of glass windows. Zane and Zariah in the other room, probably doing the same sorts of things. She was experiencing why those two found it exciting to sneak away.

And she didn't care at all about how open it was. How anyone could see if they had the right angle on the penthouse apartment. All she cared about was his hand and how it made her sizzle. Then his tongue made her blaze.

She lost the strength in her arm to support herself and clutched at him instead. Moaning and rocking, she wanted more. Harder, faster, deeper. Touch him, hold him, tease him like he teased her, but all she could do was hold on and submit.

Kian nudged forward, coaxing her to sprawl on top of

the kitchen counter, then removed her underwear. Exposed and vulnerable and completely open to whatever he wanted to do, Noémie bit her lip to hide a moan as he pumped his fingers and rubbed his thumb in little circles.

She wrapped her legs around his hips and dragged him closer, trying to voice what she needed when she couldn't find the words.

Resting his weight on his elbow, he leaned over her. "Want me?" he purred.

Eyes closed, Noémie tilted her head back and breathed, "Yes."

"How much?" he asked, sounding pleased.

"You're enjoying this," she accused.

"Having you writhe like this? It's a dream come true. But if you want me that much, I'll have to stop."

"Kian," she gasped, her head tilting back and her back arching. She gripped whatever part of him she could reach, upper arm and a handful of shirt as she desperately sought release. "Kian, *please.*"

Kian fumbled one-handed with his belt buckle and she heard the distinctive noise of foil tearing and then his hand lifted away from her.

She fluttered open her eyes to watch him. "You had one in your pocket?"

"I've fantasized about you all week," he admitted with a sheepish smile. "I didn't want to have to wait or look for one."

Noémie gave a breathless giggle, which turned into a moan as he positioned himself. She crossed her ankles behind him and pulled him in. Kian leaned down, wrapping his arms around her as he started to move.

Head spinning, body focused on the feel of him inside her, Noémie clung to him. His weight fell on her, surrounding her with the scent of him. She used her legs to lock him in place and encourage him to pick up the pace. Needing passion and frenzy, she let out a breathy moan right in his ear.

This was the right thing to do, as Kian's breath went ragged. He plunged deeper inside her and picked up his pace.

Open-mouthed kisses against his neck, all the way to his mouth, and he couldn't wait until she got there, turning his head to kiss her. A hot and needy kiss further fueling the rising passion and she took his lower lip between hers and applied a little pressure. In response, he gripped her hips and thrust harder, sending ripples of pleasure pulsing through their bodies.

With a groan of his own, he intensified his movements, gifting her with the harder and faster she relentlessly chased. "You are so hot," he murmured and his movements became more focused as he drove them toward the edge. He slipped a hand between them to help her along.

She breathed reverently, "I love you so much."

"Noémie …" He curled, hunching his back so he could bite her nipple through the lace.

Noémie came undone, arching off the counter as she came, and desperately tried to keep from being too vocal. Kian swiftly followed, mouth over hers, swallowing her pleasure to intensify his own.

He slowed his actions to a gentle thrust to help them slide down from their high. Leaning on one elbow, he let his weight rest against her side to help ground her. Kissed her neck, gentle nibbles designed to soothe rather than intensify, kissed her chest, kissed the swell and then kissed the aching nipple still trapped by her bra. "Best popcorn ever."

Laughing, Noémie shoved his shoulder. "You are so corny."

Kian laughed and pulled away. Removing the condom, he dropped it in the bin and then fixed his pants, before leaning down next to her. "Having benches that matched my height was god sent. That was amazing."

Noémie licked her lips and tilted her head up. "Maybe

we shouldn't have done that here though."

"I'm certainly never going to look at this bench the same," he said.

Noémie stared at the windows, which were now glazed white. "When did that happen?"

"Oh, the windows?" Kian asked, following her gaze. His tone grew teasing. "Its automatic switch glass tied into my erection. It turns on when I do."

She laughed at that, both embarrassed and humored by his joke. "Kian," she complained.

"It's on timer. After ten, it switches to privacy mode. Did you think we were doing this in the open?"

She scrunched up her face, embarrassed to admit it. "Maybe. Just a little."

He mock-gasped. "You have a kink!"

Her blush flamed, because she hadn't realized it herself.

Kian laughed and nuzzled her cheek. "That is unbelievably hot. Let me know if you have any others we could try. We can exchange ideas."

Noémie giggled. "I may just take you up on that offer."

"We could take this to the bedroom," he suggested. "I want to peel all that clothing off you and then do this again."

It sounded incredibly tempting. "We'd have to kick out Zariah and Zane first."

"Completely okay with that." From the dining table, a phone shrilled and Kian chortled. "At least we got to finish our moment before we were interrupted."

"Ignore it," she suggested and made a playful grab at him.

With regret, he moved away. "Wish I could."

A little sad but mostly resigned, Noémie wriggled toward the end of the counter so she could use the edge to sit up.

"Oh. Shit," Kian blurted and his voice cracked.

Noémie glanced over. "Huh?"

He waved his hand, then with the phone still ringing,

he walked across the room to his office door. "I'll be right back."

She frowned at the closed door. Staying perched on the edge, she did up the buttons of her blouse. Kian would appreciate unwrapping her again. She swung her feet, glancing around the kitchen and then decided to see if she could find some actual popcorn. Scooping her underwear off the floor, she wiggled back into them.

"You're *what?*"

Hearing Kian's voice, Noémie flicked a glance at his office door, which was now open a crack, with Purrfect's rat-like tail disappearing inside. Had Purrfect opened the door?

"But that's … I've done everything you've asked!"

Something didn't sound right. There was frustration in his tone. Was he arguing with someone?

"You can't blame me for that. I took care of it!"

True anger in Kian now and Noémie curled her hands to her chest.

"I have *not* been distracted!" Without noticing her standing in the hallway, Kian shut the door with enough force to make a bang.

Zane cautiously poked his head out of the den, coming farther out as he saw Noémie. "Everything okay?" he asked, his eyes darting around. "We heard yelling."

"Kian's on the phone," Noémie said and watched in amusement as Zane puffed out a relieved breath. "And weren't you watching a movie? How'd you hear him yelling?"

Zane shrugged and looked sheepish. "No reason."

"Uh-huh."

"I can't smell any popcorn," Zane replied, his mouth slipping into a smile.

"We ate it all."

Zane laughed and winked at her. "A likely story, your flush gives you away, babe."

Noémie shooed him with her hands. "Scat. Zariah's

waiting."

Still laughing, Zane headed back into the den.

Noémie hovered in the hallway, listening but unwilling to press her ear against the door in an attempt to find out if Kian was still yelling. After a few minutes of not hearing a sound, she knocked on the door.

"You can come in."

Swallowing, Noémie poked her head through the door. Kian sat at his desk, elbows propped up on it, with his head in his hands. Purrfect perched on the desk, purring as she rubbed herself against his face and hands.

"Kian? Are you alright?"

Kian sighed and slumped back, staring at Purrfect. "Noémie," he said in a dull voice. Lifting his hand, he made a come here gesture so Noémie crossed the room to him. He turned the chair toward her as she got there, wrapped both his arms around her waist and buried his face in her chest and clutched at her. "I'm sorry," he mumbled.

"What's wrong?" she asked, stroking his back to try and comfort him. She'd never seen him like this and she didn't know how to help.

"I'm not going to be able to see you for a while," he mumbled.

"What?" she blurted. "Why?"

With regret, Kian lifted his head so he could meet her eyes. "I have to fly back to America first thing in the morning. My father wants to see me."

CHAPTER 20

Sighing heavily, Noémie tapped her tablet pen against her knee. She scrunched up her face and erased the last few lingerie selections she'd made. Another sigh and she rolled her swivel stool away from the bench just enough so she could spin a circle while staring up at the ceiling.

It was so hard to concentrate today. Puffing out a hard breath, she gave up and stood. If she couldn't choose designs, then at least she could put together some of the mock-up designs she had on pattern paper. Or even work on a commission or alteration. There were a few she could work on.

Zane and Zariah had finished their time in Paris and had returned to London. Zane had put the word out he was in the market for a new manager while Zariah had thrown herself into wedding preparations.

Noémie had been incredibly busy all week, working on marketing and liaising with the experts Kian had suggested. They'd helped her organize some magazine spreads and other advertising campaigns to compliment the growth she was experiencing. There were photoshoots scheduled for the following week which she still needed to choose designs for. She also talked to Ava Jacobs regarding her participation in an upcoming adaptive clothing event. It had been an enjoyable, yet harrowing experience, so she hadn't had much time to mope. Now, on a Friday afternoon, there was nothing to distract her while she worried about Kian in America.

After spending an amazing and bittersweet night with him, she'd seen him off at the airport in the morning. He'd given her the keys to his place and all his codes so she could feed and pat Purrfect for him while he was gone. Since he'd been in America, communication with him had been spotty. A Discord message here or there from him. Missed video calls because they had trouble matching the six-hour difference with their schedules. He only had time to himself after nine at night his time, and she was asleep by then.

She'd sent him lots of pictures. Short videos of Purrfect's antics as she'd met Noémie at the door. Longer messages about her day and what was going on. Gifs of love hearts and cat cuddles to show she was thinking of him.

At first, he'd messaged back whenever he was able. A sentence here or there, scattered throughout his day, longer love notes late in his night that she could read first thing in the morning.

The last two days she'd heard nothing from him beyond the occasional 'love you'.

She didn't know why he was in America. He wouldn't say—or couldn't say—but she theorized it was something to do with Celestial Paris. She hoped his father wasn't trying to pull him from it. Even if Kian was looking for alternative positions in Paris, she wanted it to be his choice to leave, not because he was forced to.

A week without him. Two days with no word at all.

It was ridiculous. It really was. Two months ago, he wasn't even in her life. And now she was being ridiculous and pining after him like some love-struck teenager.

She hoped he was okay.

Sighing, she shook herself. Heading to the corner, she dragged a sewing mannequin from the corner and set it up in the middle of the room. She had a mock-up pattern already done, she had to decide on which lace the prototype should be made from. That should be easy to do.

Veroniqué's chime for assistance sounded, followed by a second chime and Noémie abandoned what she was doing.

Afternoons for Noémie were set aside for designing, adapting lingerie for clients, or other business management requirements. She left the storefront for her staff with the understanding that they could call upon her if they deemed it necessary. In the beginning, she'd done everything at night after working a full day in the boutique, so it was nice to be able to rely on staff to manage the sales part for her.

A single chime signaled excess customers and was a request for additional servers. It would call whoever was in the back to the front, whether they were checking stock, having a break, or designing in Noémie's case. Three chimes were reserved for a medical emergency, something they all decided was necessary even if it hadn't been called.

A double chime was a call for the manager and Noémie arrived ready to deal with whatever waited for her.

She didn't expect that to be Celeste von Brandt.

Noémie pulled up short. "Celeste," she exclaimed. "This is unexpected." Why was she here? Had something happened to Kian? Did Celeste need another spy?

"Noémie," Celeste said and her smile felt like it was designed to be disarming. "Lovely to see you. Do you have somewhere we could talk privately?"

"Of course," Noémie said, gesturing behind her as she tried to squash the burst of nervousness that erupted in her chest. "My sewing workshop is this way. It's a little untidy, I hope you don't mind."

Celeste smiled. "Of course not." Looking at Veroniqué,

she smiled. "Nice to meet you," she said and breezed toward the back.

Noémie offered Veroniqué a wide-eyed look before she followed Celeste. "Door on your left," she called as Celeste reached it.

Opening the door, Celeste exclaimed, "Oh, how quaint. It's just like my first sewing room." She headed straight for the sewing mannequin. "What are you working on?" she asked, lifting the lace swatches to look at them.

Noémie followed Celeste inside and closed the door behind her. "Mockup designs so I can trial laces. What can I do for you? May I offer you a drink? We have tea or coffee."

"I'm sure you wouldn't be able to cater to my particular taste." Celeste perched on one of Noémie's spinning stools. "I'm here on behalf of Kian. You're aware he's in America?"

"Yes," Noémie said and pulled another stool out so she could sit down. "I'm surprised you haven't gone as well. I'm sure Monsieur von Brandt would've liked to have seen all his family at once."

Celeste laughed. "Ma biche," 'my doe' "Richard's mistress hardly wants his wife to interrupt their time together. As I'm sure you don't want Kian's wife to come while he's visiting you."

Noémie's chest seized, her brain conjuring up all sorts of old pain and anguish. "His wife?" she squeaked. "He's not married."

"No. But he will be. That is the purpose of him returning to America." Celeste tilted her head at Noémie in bewilderment. "He didn't tell you."

"He has a contract!" Noémie blurted, unwilling to believe. "He can't have a relationship. How can he get *married?*"

"Body not heart," Celeste recited and then studied Noémie. "Oh. Did you fall in love with him?"

There was a sharp twist of pain in Noémie's chest that

would've knocked her over if she'd been standing.

Celeste's expression was one she might give a young puppy falling over its own feet, sympathetic but laced with humor. "I warned you not to. You are entirely unsuitable as wife material for a von Brandt. The best you could've hoped for was a mistress, as long as you held your place. But to fall in love with him ..." Celeste sighed dramatically. "I suppose this makes it easier in the long run."

Noémie wheezed. "What?"

With an uncaring smile, Celeste lifted her satchel from the ground where she'd left it and unzipped it. "Richard and I do not want anything to upset Kian's upcoming marriage. As such, I'm contacting all his liaisons and ensuring there will not be any problems. He needs to keep his eyes on his new bride until a child is born to carry on the family name." Celeste pulled out a large wad of paper, some sort of document, and waved it at Noémie. "You have two choices, Noémie. This is a standard non-disclosure agreement, plus an adjoining contract. The offer for your silence is five hundred thousand Euro with the additional ability to stock your brand in all Celestial stores. And, because I like you, I can even include a lead designer position in Celestial's new lingerie department if you want. You can stay in Paris and be available for Kian if he ever comes back here."

"Be available?" Noémie asked, the hairs on the back of her neck rising. New lingerie department? Had ... had she been scouted? Had Kian lied? It didn't feel right. None of this felt right.

This couldn't be happening. This *couldn't* be happening.

"Of course," Celeste said, waving her hand at Noémie. "I'd rather he have proven mistresses on call who could be discreet and ... clean, than have to hire someone every time he has urges. Von Brandt men have healthy sexual appetites. It's not like you would get nothing out of the agreement, Noémie. You would be compensated for your time and, obviously, you would not be allowed to produce a child with him. That's in the contract too."

Compensated for … did Celeste honestly expect Noémie to *prostitute* her body to her son? Well, why wouldn't she? Noémie had already prostituted herself to Celeste at the dinner.

"If you don't want to, then you can take the second choice," Celeste said. She could've been discussing the weather by the blandness in her tone. "Sign the non-disclosure agreement only and never contact him again."

Never? *Never?* What should she do? What could she say?

"Silence does not become you. These are the only two choices," Celeste said, before her expression turned stormy. "Or do you think your quaint little rose song could survive the full force of Celestial, let alone the von Brandt Empire?"

She couldn't breathe. Couldn't think. Trapped, worse than before. Now her livelihood was at risk. "You're threatening my business?" she squeaked.

"I see we understand each other," Celeste said and sighed. "I'm not a monster, Noémie. I'm looking out for my son." She stood and left the document on the desk. "I'll give you twenty-four hours to come to a decision."

And with that, Celeste was gone.

Noémie stared at the door as she tried to figure out what had just occurred.

Kian was getting married? He was getting married and he hadn't told her. And he expected her to become his Parisian mistress. A kept woman, available for his sexual needs and nothing more?

That wasn't her. He knew that wasn't her. He knew what she'd been through with Jacquez. He knew and he still sent his *mother* here to tell her all that.

Everything had been a lie. All the dates, the conversations, the tender touches, the *waiting,* and the insistence she had to be *sure.*

All a lie.

Her heart screamed at her, the old hurt broke open and weeping and she didn't know if she could live through that pain again. Not again.

Why? Why had he done this? Why had he done this to her? What did she have that he wanted? That was worth all the trouble to make such an elaborate lie? Her business? It was nothing in the grand scheme. A blip on a radar, too small to worry about.

But that was what the von Brandts did. Swoop in, buy up smaller businesses, and amalgamate it into something else. They didn't care. What was another heart ruined to them?

Head hanging, she took deep, controlled breaths to try to calm herself. The document taunted her, lying discarded on the table and she wanted to rip it to shreds. She wanted to scream and rant and collapse in a heap. She wanted to go out and get drunk. She wanted to hug Zariah and never let go.

She couldn't do any of that.

"Noémie?" Veroniqué called from down the hallway. "Is everything alright? I heard raised voices."

Tears leaked down over her cheeks and dripped from her chin. She curled in on herself, hugging her arms to her chest in an effort to calm her breathing.

"Noémie?" Veroniqué's voice came closer as she wheeled herself down the corridor toward Noémie's sewing room.

Veroniqué shouldn't see her like this. There wasn't anything Veroniqué could do and she was such a kind soul. Noémie needed time to sort through what was going on. She wiped at her cheeks and cleared her throat. "Yes," she called back, trying to sound as normal as she could. "I'll be out in a minute."

It didn't make sense. None of it made any sort of sense. And yet, it made perfect sense if she looked at it from an angle she didn't want to be true.

Kian hadn't rung. He hadn't called her. He promised that he would and he hadn't. He'd gone to see his father and now his mother was offering this. But, of course, if he'd been in on this, he'd played his hand perfectly.

It all seemed too real.

And yet contrived at the same time.

Celeste was a master at manipulation. Noémie had seen that first hand. Been part of her games.

Did Kian have the same knack for manipulation? Had she seen anything to suggest he did? Any cracks?

She grabbed her phone and hit Discord to open it and tried to call him. She let it ring and ring and ring, her mind whirling, but he didn't answer. Didn't respond. Next, she resorted to an International call. No luck. That was an answer in itself.

Hanging up, she typed, '*Your mistress? Is that what you think of me? Is that all I am to you? You go back to America to get married and you didn't even have the decency to tell me? Is she even on your wall?*'

His wall.

Kian's wall of love.

Noémie dropped her hands to her lap, message unsent, and stared at her desk.

Celeste was the master manipulator. Kian … hated it with a burning passion. He hated being forced to do things by his parents. He went out of his way to protect her from that and when he couldn't, when he was in a position where he was in as much of a trap as Noémie had been, he'd tried to carry the burden and still comfort her.

Nothing Celeste claimed matched up with what she knew of Kian.

Kian, who needed an emotional attachment before he could consider sleeping with someone and since it was said during a moment of vulnerability there was no reason not to believe it. Kian, who reacted with anger at the thought she was only interested in his money.

Kian, who'd carefully cataloged everything in his life

from the time he was old enough to take photos. He'd chosen the things he loved to display in his most private place. He'd kept things from their youth, memories, and keepsakes. He'd fallen in love at sixteen and still thought of his ex fondly and was willing to share it with her. Fallen in lust and tried to break a contract and had it go badly. Found the strength to open his heart a third time and give it to her.

If the wall was a lie … then Kian had been lying to himself for years.

Something wasn't right and that something was enough to help her keep some clarity. A goal. Something to check.

Grabbing her coat, she stuffed Celeste's papers into her handbag and headed toward the door. "Veroniqué, if I'm not back before your shift ends, please close up. Put a note on the door saying there was an emergency."

"Are you okay?" Veroniqué asked, wheeling after her.

"I will be," Noémie replied and headed outside. Her mind churned, trying to sort through mismatched emotions and unreliable information.

Why, if all Kian wanted from her was sex, did he romance her for so long when he wasn't getting anything? Why did he want them both to be sure of each other? To trust each other before proceeding. Their rendezvous' wouldn't have been planned so carefully and they wouldn't have spent so much time talking about it. If all he'd wanted was a mistress, he wouldn't have gotten so angry at her on their second date, he would've just accepted.

Why include Zane in this charade? The pair of them had rekindled their friendship. It had taken time and effort of both their parts, with the added difficulty of Zane flying all over Europe. They rekindled it so much that Zane was willing to make Kian his manager, to put his career in Kian's hands. Their friendship hadn't been a lie.

Kian's actions and reactions were too intricate to be faked. But she had to see. She had to make sure.

If this offer hadn't come from Kian, then …

Something larger was at play here.

As she rode the metro, she stared out the window and tried to ignore the buzz inside her head. Thoughts kept circling, kept shouting at her, constantly at the forefront of her mind. What was she going to do? What should she trust? Pain was held at bay, lurking at the edges and waiting for the moment when she succumbed or found evidence to fight.

Purrfect met Noémie at the door to Kian's penthouse, meowing in greeting and weaving through her legs. Purrfect, the gorgeous hobgoblin of a cat. The pampered princess. A trusted secret.

"And what about you?" Noémie mused, bending down to scratch her ears. "His other favorite girl. He wouldn't have left you if he'd known he was going to be away a long time."

He would be gone a long time if his reason behind leaving was to marry. Longer if he was supposed to beget a wife with child. He'd left everything in Paris.

So he didn't know.

Or he wasn't told until he got there which might explain his silence. If her parents had sprung something like this on her, she might be too shocked to talk about it at first. But she didn't think she'd be silent about it either.

Or ... the penthouse was part of the payment. A mistress had to live somewhere, right? Have somewhere to wait until she was 'required', and have a place that matched the man she serviced.

But why a cat? The cat was the odd part out. The loose chink. A weakness in the lie Celeste spun, which means she didn't know about Purrfect.

Scooping Purrfect up, she tucked the kitty against her chest and looked at Kian's apartment. Perfect. Pristine. A representation of who his parents thought he should be.

Dismissing it, she went straight for Kian's bedroom. His private sanctum. His heart. Where he could be himself and no one else would know. No one except her and

Purrfect.

Sitting on the bed, she placed Purrfect beside her and looked at the wall. All his special memories. Sunsets and moments and people. This would've taken *years* to accumulate. There were moments from her past that she hadn't known he had photos of. The yearbook photo, for example, why would someone as rich as Kian keep an old, worn copy that looked like it was cut straight from the book. Crinkled edges and a dog ear, worn around the pinhole, parts of it were faded because it had been exposed to sunlight, while other parts had been hidden and still looked new. It had been in that position for years, even if the board had been moved.

All the pieces of his life he cherished. Slotted together, ever-expanding. Youngest in the middle, recent at the edges. And she was in there. So was Charlie. Zariah and Zane. People that mattered to Kian.

So, if this soon-to-be wife of Kian's was someone he loved, but wanted to hide because of some unfathomable reason, then there should be gaps in the wall. Missing pictures. Pictures replaced with something that didn't match the surroundings. Cracks in the lie that he'd spun around Noémie.

She stared at the wall, her eyes wandering over Kian's life searching for anything out of place. Purrfect curled in Noémie's lap, purring and Noémie stroked her fingers along Purrfect's skin. "You can lie to a person," she said, letting stray thoughts wander through her mouth. "But you can't lie to a cat. If you were just a prop in his life to lure me in, he wouldn't love you as much as he does. And you wouldn't love him as much as you do. "

Purrfect meowed, then exposed her belly for Noémie to rub.

"There's nothing there that doesn't belong," Noémie said. "Nothing was taken out. So either this soon-to-be-wife doesn't exist. Or he didn't choose her." Noémie sighed and flopped back on the bed. "He mightn't even know about her, Purrfect. An arranged marriage? That still happens, right? What am I going to do?"

She needed to talk to Kian. She needed to hear his voice and tell him what was going on. Needed to hear his side of things. Fumbling for her phone, she erased her previous message and then stared at the screen. What if he didn't know yet? What if Celeste and Richard were making a play and he hadn't been told? She couldn't blurt that out over text. That wouldn't be right. And she couldn't make him panic either, by saying it was urgent. Sighing, she decided on, '*Please call me when you get a chance, doesn't matter what time. I want to hear your voice.*'

Groaning, she covered her face with her hands. It could be ages until Kian could contact her. And her brain wouldn't stop spinning. Throwing out random thoughts and ideas, creating questions there were no answers to.

Like, if Kian knew about this wife, then perhaps that was the reason he hadn't spoken to her in the last few days. It would be hard to explain if he felt like he had to go through with it. He knew Noémie, he knew she'd never agree to be a mistress. Perhaps he was searching for a way to get out of it without ever having to worry her. After what happened last time, that thought seemed likely. He hated what she was put through and that he'd been unable to do anything about it.

Logically, Noémie thought Celeste would want everything signed and squared away before springing that on him. Give him no options. Nowhere to turn. They'd done that to him before.

Noémie sat up and latched onto that thought.

They'd done this to him before.

Not this thing. Not exactly. But they'd given him nowhere to turn but them. Kept him under their thumb.

Tiffany. Perhaps Tiffany had indeed loved Kian, but once he'd announced he was breaking his contract, what if she'd been threatened? Bought by their vast money, given a job. They hadn't even thought twice about offering money to Noémie. What would she have done at nineteen? Would she have been able to say no to a force such as the von Brandts?

Could she say no now?

Kian, on his own, running out of money because he'd never learned how to survive without it, finally figuring himself out only to be forced to return. No degree, no support system, no modeling jobs because Celeste had somehow managed to stop it? What if she'd given him no choice but to return from the youth center or she'd take that too? He'd been happy there.

God, how far did this rabbit hole go?

Celeste was paving the way to force her son into a marriage he didn't want. Silencing Noémie before any announcement was made and before she could do anything to stop this. Or even warn him it was coming.

What could she do anyway?

A non-disclosure agreement. A threat to her business. An offer of being a mistress.

Her stomach churned with anger. *How dare they.* She wasn't going to take this lying down. Not again. She wasn't going to allow them to do this to Kian. If this is what he wanted, she would hear it from *him*, not his mother.

Scrambling from the bed, and subsequently scaring Purrfect, she strode back down the hallway toward the door, pausing only to make sure Purrfect's food and water were fine.

Anger coursed through her as she made her way to Celestial Paris. She didn't have all the information, just the jagged edges of a jumbled-up puzzle, but she knew who could fill in the gaps for her.

Celeste had an office on the second floor of Celestial Paris, among the other designers working for the company. As Mathilda escorted Noémie through Celestial's design workshop, Noémie had a chance to look around. Large material racks set against the wall, plenty of sewing mannequins littered around the place, most of them wearing half-finished designs. Each designer had their own desk and space. There were cutting desks and lace departments and even a catwalk through the middle of the room.

Celeste had the only enclosed office on the floor. A polished mahogany desk for office meetings and her own design area in the corner where she could look out the window and be inspired by Paris.

There was a mannequin in the room, adorned by a gorgeous, V-necked red chiffon dress. Open back, the thin sleeves were floral lace that began at the top of the shoulder, connected at the neck then looped under the arm to the bodice at the front, ending behind a silver star of jewels sewn into the bust. From the star, the lace roped back again, across the small of the back like a belt, the silk beneath the lace falling into a long, airy skirt and left an empty v-shaped patch of fabric at the waist.

Noémie threw the dress an appreciative look before she faced Celeste.

"That didn't take long," Celeste noted, turning from her design desk. She lifted her phone and pressed a few buttons and the wall of glass between her and the workshop frosted, allowing them privacy. "There, now we can talk without gossip. What's your decision?"

Noémie rummaged through her bag and drew out the contract. In one sweeping movement, Noémie tore the document in half. "I'm not signing anything."

Celeste lifted her eyebrow at Noémie.

Noémie shook her head at Celeste in disgust. "I don't know what game you're playing but I'm not having any part of it. I'm not signing any agreements. I'm not taking any of your money. And I'm certainly not going to work for Celestial and put myself under your thumb. My business *stays* my business and I will fight you with everything I have."

"I see."

Anger churned and frothed and Noémie spoke through

gritted teeth. "Kian's not getting married, and if he is, then you're forcing him into it. Have you no regard for Kian at all? Does he even know you're doing this? You're his mother, you're supposed to love him and protect him. How can you be so horrible?"

"Horrible?" Celeste told her, affronted. She shoved away from her design desk and took several rapid steps around the desk toward Noémie. "I'm trying to protect my son!"

"From me? Seriously? What danger am I to him?"

"He loves you," Celeste said, matter-of-fact. "And that makes you the most dangerous woman in the world."

"So your idea to subdue me was to coerce me into being his mistress? You realize how that makes him sound, don't you? Kian is *nothing* like how you portrayed him."

"I'm aware of that," Celeste said with a sudden smile. She leaned against the table and crossed her ankles. "My idea was to test how strong your backbone and resolve was. I had a taste, but I needed to know more." Holding out her hand, she indicated the dress behind Noémie. "What do you think of the dress?"

The about-face was disorienting and she had trouble trying to follow Celeste's game plan. Frowning, she cast a glance behind her before she stared at Celeste. "It's pretty."

Celeste raised her eyebrows. "That's your professional opinion? I expected something more elegant from you."

"I didn't come here to give you my professional opinion on anything," Noémie snapped. "I came here to tell you to go—"

Celeste threw her hand up. "Let's not say anything we'll regret," she rushed. "Not until I've told you everything."

Noémie narrowed her eyes.

"It's one thing to say you don't want money, Noémie. It's another to turn it down when it's offered. I knew you had backbone. You have to have one if you want to deal with the von Brandt family, especially with what we're about to do."

Something wasn't right, and that made her cautious. "What are we about to do?"

Celeste sighed. "My husband has decided, in his great wisdom, to marry Kian to the daughter of his mistress. Naturally, I am appalled with the idea."

"Kian will say no," Noémie replied, absolutely sure of that.

"Kian is not being given a choice," Celeste replied. "Richard knows about you. He's using Kian's own heart against him. My wonderful son will do anything to protect the people he loves. Even sign away his life to someone else."

Noémie swallowed hard, knowing that was true.

"So," Celeste chirped, standing. "We're going to crash the engagement party."

CHAPTER 21

Smoothing down the red chiffon dress over her stomach, Noémie looked up the stairs to the ballroom. She gently touched the diamond-encrusted necklace Celeste had allowed her to borrow, then threw back her shoulders and raised her chin. She could do this. She had to do this.

Guests loitered on the stairs, talking to friends and acquaintances as they tried to take subtle glances at the new arrivals and Noémie could see in the windowed glass of the ballroom how many heads turned to follow her movements as she climbed the stairs. A few paparazzi lined the edges of the stairs, taking shots of guests as they arrived.

Steeling herself, she smiled at the man at the door and presented her invitation, who returned the smile and opened the door for her. With a polite incline of her head, Noémie stepped into elegance.

The ballroom was filled with a soft golden light. Chandeliers hung from the ceiling, illuminating polished wood flooring. The tables had been trimmed with gold and silver on brilliant white. A string orchestra sat at one end of the large room entertaining and there were several people already occupying the dance floor.

Another section had been set aside for people to mingle. Men in dinner suits and women in elegant dresses all chatted and laughed together. Uniformed waiters carried trays of wine or food to offer to their patrons and Noémie accepted a glass of champagne so she would have something to do with her hands. As she sipped it, she drifted her eyes over the crowd of people.

Kian wouldn't be here yet. Celeste had said they'd arrive late, when everyone was already in the room and make a grand entrance. Celeste also said that Kian's bride-to-be would be here, and Noémie wondered who that could be. Celeste had not been forthcoming with information when Noémie had asked about her.

There were several women around Noémie's age among the cluster of people, so one of them could've been chosen. Or perhaps she hadn't arrived yet.

Sighing, Noémie took a sip of her drink and moved through the crowd. She had to find a place to stand for when Kian arrived, one that enabled her to hide before he saw her.

It was a day of firsts for Noémie. First time on a private jet. First time in America. First time to New York. First time wearing a magnificent Celestial one-of-a-kind dress. First time wearing diamonds worth more than her business. First time to such an extravagant ballroom.

The amount of money Richard spent on this party was absolutely ridiculous. As she navigated around people, she could hear them discussing a range of things, from the decorations to the announcement Richard had planned to make. Gossip hung in the air, invigorating people's imaginations. There was speculation of a new business venture, or the von Brandts were divorcing, even Richard's father's death and Noémie didn't know why that had people excited. Didn't they *know* what it was? Didn't they know it was an engagement party?

Maybe Celeste had been wrong?

She had her instructions. She was in a situation so far

beyond her comfort zone it should've knocked her off her feet, instead, she was gliding through a crowd of people and offering a smile as she turned their heads. She had to pretend to mingle, hide among the crowd. Staying away from Richard, she had to be seen by Kian and then not, Cinderella-ing him with snatches of her appearance until she allowed herself to be caught in some sort of elaborate cat and mouse game. How Noémie was supposed to ninja vanish in these shoes, she didn't know. Nor did she know why she had to go to all this trouble instead of simply talking to him.

Finding a spot to stand at the back of the crowd, near the door to the bathroom, Noémie sipped her champagne and tried not to look awkward.

"Good evening," a deep voice purred. "That is an exquisite dress, you look divine in it."

Noémie stiffened. Squashing the urge to swear in French at him, she said in English, "Not interested."

"English accent, Asian descent, wearing a red Celestial designer dress. You wouldn't happen to be Noémie Belrose-Song, would you? Did I pronounce that right?"

Noémie's stomach dropped and she turned to look at him in shock. A tall man with a magnificent burst of red hair, dressed in a black dinner suit. Arm across his stomach, he bowed at the waist. "My name is Quinn Sterling," he said, lifting his hand to signal someone. "Celeste asked us to offer our assistance for tonight."

Shocked, all Noémie could say was, "Us?"

Quinn smiled at her. "Myself, and my husband, Charles."

Noémie's lungs locked as she turned to see Charlie approaching. Older than the picture but still undeniably the same person who'd been kissing Kian in the photo. Laughter danced in his blue eyes and his dark hair flopped against his forehead and when he smiled, Noémie could see exactly why Kian had fallen for him.

Charlie held out his hand. "Hello, little French

munchkin. Nice to finally meet you."

She took it without hesitation, so utterly relieved to have an ally in this that her knees were weak. "Hello, Charles the dumbass. I'm so glad to see you."

He laughed at the name. Cupping his other hand over hers, he squeezed it, then released her. "You look lovely."

"Thank you."

"We'll be your chaperones for the evening," Quinn said, moving from Noémie's side to stand by his husband.

"Celeste asked us to lend a hand," Charlie said, flagging down a waiter to pick up two glasses of champagne, one of which he handed to Quinn. "Since you're not acquainted with American culture and are probably not comfortable with this sort of social gathering."

"My first was an absolute disaster," Quinn said in a jovial tone. "Drank much more than was socially acceptable due to nerves, and ended up dancing on a table in my underwear."

Charlie laughed. "I knew he was a keeper after that."

Relaxing because of their easy banter, she smiled. "Definitely don't want to have that happen and I'm incredibly grateful you're here. I wasn't looking forward to doing this alone."

Charlie returned the smile. "We're aware of Richard's plans, and, if you'll pardon my French, he lives up to his name."

Quinn interrupted with a cough which held a poorly concealed insult.

With a fond smile at his husband, Charlie continued, "We want Kian to be happy. And he's not going to be if he's forced to marry that shrew. We've been trying to help Kian get out of this while he was here, and nothing we've done has worked."

Against her best intentions, she wilted. Kian hadn't allowed her to help. He had kept her in the dark about everything. However, she was glad he'd had *someone* on his side even if that someone wasn't her.

Quinn added, "We'll help out tonight. We'll run interference since the only attention you want to attract is Kian's. We'll help hide you away if needed, and when you want to finally shine, Charles is an excellent dancer."

"I would appreciate that," Noémie said, smiling and feeling at more ease. "I was afraid I'd stand out if I wall flowered."

"These sorts of events are always better if you know people and have the ability to mingle," Charlie said. "We'll introduce you, if Celeste doesn't decide to do it herself."

The mention of Celeste prompted Noémie to ask, "Celeste said it was an engagement party, but no one seems to know what this party is for."

"You know the socialites," Quinn said with a shrug. "Any excuse for a party."

"Kian doesn't know what tonight is, does he?"

Charlie exchanged a look with Quinn. "Kian hasn't said anything but *if* the engagement is announced tonight, it'll happen about halfway through. In front of so many people, Kian will have no choice but to agree or embarrass his father."

She blinked back the sudden influx of tears because it was so horrible that Kian was being put through this. Alone. How could a father do that to his son?

"It's not the worst thing Kian's had to put up with to please his father," Charlie muttered. "Probably won't be the last, either."

With a side glance at Charlie, Quinn placed his hand on Noémie's shoulder to offer comfort. "Don't worry. We'll help you."

She gave them both a watery smile. "Thank you."

Charlie and Quinn, as she learned, were very eager to gush about each other. Quinn ran an interior design business, while Charlie was an architect for one of the larger firms in New York. They'd met in college and dated for several years before getting married last year. Quinn took Charlie's last name because his parents didn't approve of his 'lifestyle'. The Sterling's, Charlie's parents, were independently rich from owning a computer software company, and were happy to include Quinn in their lives.

They were adorable together. Finishing each other's sentences. The longing looks. The smiles they shared. So in love and she was enamored.

The majority of the conversation around them died. Quinn and Charlie closed ranks around her, concealing her behind their broad bodies, while still giving her a view of the entrance.

Richard and Celeste von Brandt arrived, closely followed by Kian.

Celeste and Richard looked wonderful together, Celeste in her sparkling golden gown and Richard's suit accessories matching hers. Noémie hadn't seen Richard in a long time but she remembered his stern expression. His once blond hair now looked so pale it was almost white as it was slicked back on his head. Rectangular glasses framed his stern face, he was still as unapproachable as ever.

Nerves shot through Noémie as she once again questioned what she was doing here.

While Noémie still hadn't seen this so-called bride, she guessed it was the tall blonde woman who practically skipped over to greet Kian.

"Is that her?" Noémie asked. The woman was gorgeous in her stunning green dress, looking every bit like she belonged as she clung to Kian's arm and kissed his cheek.

"That's Tiffany," Quinn said with a nod.

"The shrew," Charlie added.

Noémie's blood ran cold. Kian looked at Tiffany and smiled, and the smile stabbed Noémie in the heart.

Tiffany the ex-girlfriend. Who'd used him, hurt him? The one who'd turned on him in a heartbeat. Had she been forced to do that by Kian's parents? Could she still love him? Tiffany, who was Kian's bride-to-be. Given another chance. He'd loved her once. He could again, couldn't he?

It hurt. It hurt so much. He hadn't told her. He hadn't said anything at all about getting married. Hadn't answered her calls last night while she tried to figure out what to do. If he'd just talked to her—

"God. His model smile," Charlie muttered. "Haven't seen that in a while. Poor Kian."

"Noémie?" Quinn asked, concerned, and he touched her on the back between her shoulders. "Are you alright?"

She swayed, her legs like jelly and her head reeling. Her eyes wouldn't leave Tiffany and Kian. Tall, regal, blond, beautiful. They were made for each other. Who was she kidding?

"I shouldn't be here." She needed to hide. She needed to catch her breath before she started hyperventilating. She didn't belong here.

Spinning, she darted for the door to the bathrooms and pushed into the hallway. Hurrying down the corridor, she followed the signs and headed into the ladies. Locking herself in a stall, she pressed her hand to her chest and concentrated on her breathing.

Why hadn't he trusted her with this information? Why hadn't he at least told her? If he was going to go through with it, the decent thing to do would have least broken it off with her before his engagement was announced so they could split amicably. It was his lack of contact that made her say yes to Celeste's plan and now she felt like this was the worst mistake of her life.

He didn't want her here. She was intruding. If he wanted her here, he would've said something.

What was she going to do? She didn't belong in his world of glitz and glamor where people played such intricate games with other people's lives. She wanted to go home, to her friends and her family and a job she loved.

Her phone vibrated and Noémie pulled it out of her garter purse to see a message from Celeste.

Celeste

> Interesting technique, but effective. By the way Kian is watching the bathroom door, I suspect he thinks he saw you. I would suggest using the kitchen entrance to get back in the ballroom.

She leaned against the wall and stared up at the ceiling. She was here. She'd come all the way to help him. She should at least talk to him before leaving. Find out what was really going on. She owed that to herself.

Sighing, she left the stall. Checking the status of her makeup in the mirror, she washed her hands and walked from the bathroom.

Charlie worried in the hallway. "Are you alright?"

The smile was watery, but at least it was there. "I wasn't ready for that."

"For what, exactly?" he queried.

"Tiffany. She's … his ex-girlfriend, right? He loved her."

Charlie frowned at her. "I suppose Kian would see her through rose-colored glasses."

"She … from what Kian said, he tried to break the no-relationship contract for her, and she turned on him. He said he doesn't have anything to do with her anymore."

"Then why are you worried?" Charlie asked, bemused.

Now that they had an outlet, someone to listen who might understand, the words and emotions rushed out of her. "Yesterday, Celeste tried to pay me off to get rid of me and today, I'm in America and Kian doesn't know I'm here, and what if this is the biggest mistake of my life? The only reason I'm here is because I trusted his wall. What if I was wrong?" Heart sore and tangled in emotions she couldn't explain, she fought the urge to cry. "What if Celeste did that to Tiffany too? What if the reason he didn't tell me was because he's with her again? He loved her once. He could do it again. I shouldn't have come, it was a mistake—"

Charlie studied her as she rambled and waited for her

to catch a breath before he interrupted, "Little munchkin, how much sleep have you gotten in the last twenty-four hours?"

She took a deep breath, released it slowly and admitted, "Not a lot."

"Trust the wall. That wall is Kian's heart and there are only a handful of people who've seen it."

"You've seen it?"

Charlie smiled. "I was there when he decided to create it. You were one of the first to go up. I remember teasing him about this pretty munchkin who went up before his parents did. The way he talked about you—I knew you were special. You were, what, thirteen? Thirteen and on his wall and now you're *still* there. Trust that."

Charlie's words warmed her heart. "Thank you."

He offered her his elbow. "Let's get you out of the hallway and back out there and I can tell you about Tiffany."

Noémie looped her hand through his elbow and held on loosely. "Celeste said I should go through the kitchens."

"We can do that," he said and headed down the hallway in the opposite direction. "Kian did love Tiffany, yes. I won't deny that. He doesn't now. After they split, after Kian managed to gain his father's favor again, he left New York and he didn't see the kind of slime that accumulated around her. She would proclaim to all who would listen she was his girlfriend. That he was off making a name for himself and he'd be back to marry her. Kian is a good man. He deserves better than that spoiled brat."

Noémie's hand tightened on Charlie's arm. "Oh."

Charlie continued, "If you ask me, I think he was coerced into that relationship to begin with. He never seemed happy with her. It's no secret that her mother, Helena, has designs on Richard and has had them for some time."

She nodded.

"Hopefully Celeste will take care of that while she's in town. Helena and Tiffany have clawed their way up the social ranks and they didn't care who they stepped on. Tiffany set her sights on Kian and never let go. He doesn't love her, Noémie. He doesn't want to marry her."

Noémie let out a slow breath through her mouth. "I know. It's been … a very long twenty-four hours. I really haven't had a chance to process what's happening." She laughed and tried to make light of the situation. "I'm sorry. I'm not making a very good first impression."

Charlie laughed. "Mine wasn't any better! You're a delightful breath of fresh air," he said. "I can see why he loves you. But be careful. There are piranhas out there who prey on any sign of weakness."

Noémie nodded. "I'll remember that." She swallowed and said in a small voice, "You used to date him."

"He told you that?" Charlie asked, surprised. He paused their walk, turning to face her.

She nodded, not really knowing why she wanted to talk about this with him.

"He didn't even tell Tiffany that," Charlie said, smiling. "See, I knew you were special."

"You're special to him, too." A shared kinship, perhaps?

"I love Kian," Charlie replied with a solemn nod. "He's a great guy, he was even my best man, you know."

That surprised her, and it shouldn't have. "I didn't."

"Yup," Charlie replied and coaxed them into a walk again. "I've never seen him happier than when he talks about you. I want to watch that grow, not watch him wither if he's with her."

"There you are," Celeste announced, as Charlie held open the door to the kitchen. Reaching for Noémie, she wove her arm around Noémie's and tugged her away from Charlie. "Kian is busy entertaining 'The Baron'," she told Charlie. "I have time to introduce Noémie. Go make sure Kian spends as much time there as possible. The Baron likes to ramble. Encourage."

"Of course," Charlie said with a smile.

Keeping her arm linked with Noémie, Celeste said, "I'll be introducing you as my protégé from Paris, who is joining us to take our new lingerie department into the new age. Now, I know it's a lie, you know it's a lie, but these people do not care. I need your name floating in their heads."

Feeling used, Noémie asked, "Why?"

"Because I want them thinking about Kian and you. Not Kian and *her*."

"She has a name. Tiffany."

Celeste gave her a sharp look. "And?"

"And warning would've been nice. She's his ex, you should've told me."

"Noémie," Celeste said, dismissing it with that infuriating flop of her hand. "You are lucky you have me. I didn't have anyone when I tried to break into the von Brandt world. I had to forge all my own alliances alone."

Noémie wasn't impressed. "Did you do the same to her as you did to me?"

"Worse," Celeste replied, pleased with herself. "I gave her no time to think. Her bitch of a mother was already hooking her claws into Richard. I wasn't going to allow her daughter to take my son."

"That wasn't very fair."

"I am not a fair person," Celeste replied. "But if it's any consolation, she made me double my initial offer and give her a job at Celestial New York. She's not even a good designer. And I didn't ask her to break his heart so dramatically."

Noémie's eyes widened. "Oh."

"So you can understand why I don't want her for Kian."

"But you want me?"

Celeste gave a long-suffering sigh. "I will be diplomatic and say I don't want anyone for Kian. No one will ever be good enough for him. But I do want him to love and be loved, and if you can do that …" she left the rest of it unsaid as they reached the first group of people. "Darlings," Celeste announced. "There's someone I'd like you to meet."

A whirlwind of introductions and a web of lies spun around Noémie. She didn't like this, not one bit, but there was little she could do about it. With no warning regarding any of Celeste's plans except that she was going to help Noémie get Kian out of this situation, there was nothing Noémie could do except go along with whatever Celeste wanted and hope that it didn't backfire.

She had no assurances that it wouldn't either. She had no assurances that all this setup for something that Celeste had planned would work. She had no assurances that these lies wouldn't bury her business in the end. The only thing she knew for certain was Celeste loved her son and didn't want him marrying Tiffany.

Celeste had told her she needed a backbone to be able to handle the von Brandts. She needed to strap more steel to her spine and get it done.

She was grateful when Quinn appeared to whisk her away from Celeste, saying that Kian had managed to excuse himself from The Baron and was heading toward them. She and Quinn hid in a corner, using a column for extra protection until Charlie joined them.

"He has definitely noticed Celeste was with someone," Charlie said as he reached them. "I'm not sure he realizes it's you, but he's definitely looking."

"I don't like all this subterfuge," Noémie said, resting her hand on the column as she looked out at the people at the party. "It's not me. Why can't I just go talk to him? It would be better if we just talked."

Charlie and Quinn exchanged a glance.

"You know, she is right," Quinn said with a slow smile. "Communication is key to any relationship. But the real question is how we divert attention so that she can get close without a certain someone seeing."

Charlie laughed and bowed at the waist, offering his hand out to his husband. "Dance with me."

Quinn placed his hand in Charlie's. "I thought you would never ask."

Noémie stayed where she was, hand on the column, and watched as Charlie led Quinn onto the dance floor. A few other couples were swaying to the music, younger people using the excuse of dancing to snatch a few intimate moments together, but the moment Charlie and Quinn stepped into each other's arms, they seemed to command attention.

Noémie didn't know what it was about them; the smiles or the way they looked at each other, the laughter on Charlie's face as he was dipped by Quinn, but there was something magical between them. And a sense of ridiculousness as well, as Quinn pulled Charlie into a mockery of a tango, even though the music was soft and sweet. They reminded her a little of Zariah and Zane.

"They're cute together, aren't they?" Kian said.

Noémie sucked in a gasp and glanced to the side.

Kian leaned his shoulder on the other side of the column, watching Charlie and Quinn. Up close, he looked wonderful in his black tailored dinner suit. Prim and proper, completely gorgeous and untouchable, and yet somehow very sad and alone at the same time. "Kian—"

"Quiet Room," he instructed, his voice low and urgent. "Ten minutes. Do you know where that is?"

She swallowed hard, anxiety keeping her frozen as she tried to gauge his reaction. Was he angry? Was he upset? Why wouldn't he look at her? "Umm … no."

"Wooden door behind us," he continued and Noémie turned her head to look. "Down the hallway, third door on the left." Kian pushed away from the column and took a step away. Lifting his hand, he fixed the cuffs on his suit and flashed her a smile as he looked at her for the first time. "You look *gorgeous*. I'm so happy to see you."

She melted into a pleased smile. "Kian—"

"I'm upset about missing the lingerie picture for that dress."

"I have one saved for you," she promised. "Garter included."

His eyes widened and flicked down for a brief second before they were back on hers. "I look forward to seeing that. Ten minutes," he repeated, the urgency in his tone reappearing. "Don't be seen."

CHAPTER 22

The Quiet Room appeared to be some sort of casual meeting room. Several sofas and small tables were scattered around the room and along the far wall were huge loveseat windows draped with red curtains that concealed most of the loveseat. It was cozy and intimate and Noémie was incredibly glad to find it empty when she got there. She suspected a room such as this could be used for sneaky rendezvous and wondered that that might be what Kian wanted to use it for. The lock on the door seemed to confirm that theory.

She crossed the room and sat on one of the loveseats, looking out into New York. She hadn't had time to appreciate the fact she was in America, in New York. So much had happened to get her here and there'd been so little time to process. The plane ride had been filled with a crash course on manners and etiquette, before being shoved at beauticians and hairdressers when they reached America and what little time she had to herself filled with worry. Even if she was only here for a short while, she hoped she had time to be a tourist and see some of the sights.

Hearing voices approaching, Noémie flicked her head

to the door. A feminine voice pierced through the closed door and Noémie held her breath.

The door opened a crack and then Kian's voice said, "I said I needed to make a phone call. Don't follow me."

Noémie bounced up on the love seat, pressing against the window frame to conceal herself behind the curtain and hoped she wasn't able to be seen. Someone had followed him and it was likely that someone was Tiffany.

"Nonsense," Tiffany said and her voice moved by Kian's and into the room. "If you wanted some alone time, all you had to do was ask."

"I *did* ask," Kian snapped. "And you followed me."

Tiffany laughed. "C'mon, Kian, you can drop the act. We're alone now. I know you want this as much as I do."

"Which is not at all," Kian said, his voice sounding from across the room from where Tiffany's was.

"Why are you being so skittish? We've barely spent any time together since you've come back. You keep running away from me. "

"There's a reason for that," Kian retorted. "We haven't spoken in years. I don't know why you're so persistent now, and playing these stupid games. It stops. All of it. Leave me alone. I'm not interested."

"You used to enjoy the games," Tiffany crooned. "We used to be so good together."

"You were toxic," Kian muttered. "And I was dumb enough to confuse love with lust."

"Pssh. Don't be silly, Kian. We're going to get married, we can—"

"I am *not* marrying you."

Tiffany's pout was evident in her voice. "Your father said you were. I waited *so* long for you to come back. Don't I get a reward for that?"

"I didn't ask you to. We broke up, Tiffany. That's the end of it."

"And who was it clawing at my door for sex?" Tiffany purred.

Noémie covered her mouth with her hand to stop herself from verbalizing a reaction. Had he? With Tiffany? While she was in Paris and desperately trying to contact him?

Tiffany continued, "How long has it been, Kian? How long since you felt the sweet touch of a woman? Remember all the fun we used to have? I bet your *aching* by now, it can be like that again."

Perhaps not, by the sounds. At least, not recently. But he had seen her purely for sex at some point. Noémie's head reeled from the turmoil her emotions were going through. From anger, to sadness, to pain, it was a lot all at once, then to add something like this on top of it.

Kian snarled, "I don't want you. I am *never* going to want you again."

Tiffany didn't sound like she cared what Kian wanted. "You won't resist when we're married."

"Oh, yes, I will. We will have the shortest, *unconsummated* marriage ever and then I'll divorce you for being unable to produce an heir. How's that sound?"

Tiffany clicked her tongue in annoyance. "Such a pouty little boy. That attitude will be the first to go when we're married."

"Get out. I have a phone call to make."

"Your loss. But if you change your mind, you know where I'll be."

The door clicked closed with the sound of a lock behind it and the room was filled with nothing but Kian's ragged breathing. "Noémie?"

Devastated and her emotions flailing out of control, Noémie slid down the window frame until she was sitting on the loveseat. She tucked her legs up to her chest and hugged them hard. Drawn by her whimper, Kian appeared at the entrance to the curtain and, as Noémie looked up at him, a tear slid down over her cheek.

"Oh, ma rose," Kian breathed, as pale as a sheet. "I'm so sorry. I didn't want you to hear that."

She sniffled and dropped her eyes from his. "Sorry," she said, angry at her own need to cry. Carefully, she flicked the tear away from her face. "It's a lot to take in."

"No, don't be sorry. This must be so confusing for you." Kian sat on the loveseat beside her, scooting as close as he could without touching her. He shuffled, reaching for her several times and retracted, as though he couldn't allow himself to touch her, before he settled on placing a hand on her ankle. "God, Noémie, I don't even know where to begin."

Noémie knew where she wanted to begin. "That's Tiffany."

Kian heaved in a sigh. Leaning back, he dug around in his pocket and pulled out a handkerchief, which he offered to her. "That's her."

She accepted and dabbed at her eyes so she didn't ruin her makeup. Because of how her last relationship ended, even though she believed otherwise, she was compelled to ask. The words would've burned her otherwise. "You haven't slept with her since you've been back, right?"

"No," he said, confused. "I'm committed to you, why would you ... oh ..." Kian's head went down and he clasped his hands together in his lap. "Right. Um ... I ... it was twice after we broke up. I ... I got lonely and scared and desperately trying to hold my life together and ... and she was there and ... at the time, I thought I could convince her to come back but I always felt used—so— um—after the second time, I didn't allow it to happen again. I left New York. It's been years since I've seen her." His head coming back up, he insisted, "Noémie, I know why you're asking. Despite what you heard, I promise you: I haven't been sleeping with her and I'm *not* marrying her."

"Why didn't you tell me?" she muttered, resentment she'd stored at his silence bubbling up. "I've been trying for days to get hold of you. Were you ghosting me?"

"No!" he blurted and his hands went for both of hers in a grab and clutch. "I would never do that to you! I didn't know how to tell you. I thought, if I could clear it all up, you'd never even need to worry! I couldn't put you through my parent's games again. I didn't expect it to drag on this long and then—"

"You should've talked to me," she scolded. "Before your mother walked into my boutique and blindsided me with the news you were getting married and offered me a fucking contract to become your mistress!"

"*What?*" The word ripped from Kian's throat and he paled.

Words spilled out of her as the dam of anger she'd stored over the last day broke. "She offered me five hundred thousand Euro, the ability to stock my brand in all Celestial stores, and a job, if I'd spread my legs for you whenever you were in town and not busy with your *wife*. It was either that or sign an agreement to *never* speak to you again. And you weren't answering your phone!"

"Oh my God. I didn't know. I would *never*—"

Noémie flinched and squeezed shut her eyes. He wasn't at fault and he didn't know and she needed to remember that. She was just so angry that he hadn't trusted her enough to tell her what was going on.

"Noémie," Kian pleaded, his voice edging toward panic. "Please. No, I wouldn't do that to you! I don't want you as a mistress, I want you as my wi—partner!" Hands touched her legs, her hands, and her shoulder to shake lightly. "Please, tell me you didn't sign anything!"

The sheer anguish in his voice forced her eyes open. "I tore it up in front of her," she said. "Told her ... well. I wasn't exactly polite."

Kian puffed out a breath and sagged. His forehead hit her knees and he slumped against her legs. "Thank God."

"I'm sorry. I wasn't going to tell you like that," she said, unhappy. "It all bubbled over."

Kian nodded and wrapped his arms around her legs to hug them.

Reaching out, she rested her hand on the back of his

head and stroked it in sympathy. "She said it was a test, to see if I had the backbone required to stand up to the von Brandts. She made it sound like some sort of cult. Her verses them kind of thing. She talked about making alliances, not friends and … like she was waging war. Richard's an alliance threatened, not her husband. They're supposed to love each other, but it feels like this giant game of who can one-up the other." Her voice threatened to crack and she cleared her throat. "Kian, I don't want that for us. I really don't."

"Me either."

"She told me about Tiffany. About Helena. About your father forcing you to marry." She told him everything she could. The conversations she could remember, the words Celeste had used. She told him about how the wall had made her realize Celeste's initial offer was *wrong* and gave her the strength to confront her.

He didn't ask questions, allowing her to talk until she'd worked through everything he needed to hear. Kian was silent when she finished, clinging to her legs and Noémie's heart was breaking for him.

"I'm so sorry," she murmured. "I didn't want to hurt you."

He shook his head, then raised it enough to meet her eyes. "You didn't. None of this is your fault. She's supposed to be on my side and it hurts that she'd do that to you."

"To you. She did it to you." Noémie touched his jacket sleeve and pinched the fabric between her finger and thumb. "I think she's done it before."

He huffed out a breath. "To Tiffany. Yeah. That would make sense."

She changed the pinch to a fistful of jacket and gave a tug. "I missed you," she murmured.

With a look of surprise, Kian lifted away from her legs. Carefully, he reached for her with both hands. Grasping her hips, he tugged her toward him and she lifted her feet so her legs went over his lap. Encircling her with his arms, he buried his face in her neck. "I missed you, too."

Noémie wrapped her arms around his shoulders and hugged him back. Stroking her fingers against the hair at his neck, she soothed, "I need to hear your side."

"I'm so sorry," Kian whispered into her neck. "I never wanted to involve you in any of this."

"I know. But I am involved. So tell me what happened. You're the only person in this place I can trust." She allowed herself a small laugh. "Besides Quinn and Charlie. I can see why you fell for him, he's sweet."

Kian pressed his lips to Noémie's neck. "I know. Charlie's amazing." One more kiss, this time on her jaw, then he pulled back. "When my father rang, he said that he was pulling me from Celestial Paris because of the whole Jacquez debacle." His leg jiggled as he spoke and Noémie wasn't sure if it was from anger or nerves. "He told me I was distracted and that was the reason Jacquez was able to do so much without getting caught." Lifting Noémie's legs from his lap, he stood and moved away from her to pace. "Which was absolute bullshit. *I* found the discrepancies, weeks before he was even told, and I worked my ass off gathering all the information before I told him. I had everything under control and the banks and the police were involved. There was no reason for him to do anything. I only told him as a courtesy."

Noémie slipped her legs off the loveseat and clasped her hands in her lap. As she watched him pace, she wondered how long he'd been holding all this in. Longer than she had been, that's for sure, and she felt bad she'd yelled at him.

"The bastard insisted I return here so we could 'discuss' it," he said, pulling a face and using quotation mark gestures. "I came here fully expecting to have to defend myself. I was armed and prepared and ready for a fight. Instead, he hits me with the fact he's been having an affair with Helena for years and he wants me to marry

Tiffany.”

“You didn’t know about Helena?”

Kian spun, pacing back across the room. “I had no fucking idea. No one bothered to tell me. I’ve been living with the delusion that he loved Mom.”

“I’m so sorry,” she told him. “That must have been horrible for you.”

Another tight spin and he was off again. “I’ve tried everything I could think of to get out of this. I even suggested that if he was so desperate to have Tiffany as part of the von Brandts, he could marry Helena and adopt her. Hell, he could write her into the will, I don’t care. No need to ruin my life in the process.”

Noémie nodded, keeping quiet so he could get these feelings out.

“But *nooo*,” he said, throwing up his hands. “He and Mom have a fucking contract which means they can’t divorce. What is it with him and these contracts?”

She echoed his sentiments. “It does seem excessive.”

“Then!” Kian declared, spinning to face Noémie and pointed at her. “Then he tells me he knows all about you. About your business and your parents and, and, and he *threatened* you! If I didn’t go through with the wedding, you’d suffer!” The anger seemed to drain from him and his arms flopped by his sides. “I can’t let him take your dreams away.”

Noémie stood and approached him. When she reached him, she lifted a hand and touched his jaw below his ear, running her finger along to his chin so she could raise his head and meet his eyes. “Don’t give away pieces of yourself because you think it’s what I want. You’re a part of my dreams too, Kian.”

His hands settled on her hips. “Really?”

He looked so lost and alone and desperate for reassurance. Noémie gripped his lapels and rose up as high as she could to place a tender kiss on his lips. “Really,” she murmured.

He chased her mouth, wrapping his arms around her to cuddle close for a more lingering kiss. "Backless," he mumbled against her lips and his hands drifted up her spine. She hummed at him in delight, loving how his hands tightened around her.

When he let her breathe again, she kept her hands looped around his shoulders. "I understand you've been through a lot this past week—"

"You have, too."

Noémie nodded and finished, "—and that you have been incredibly stressed and frustrated and didn't know where to turn. I know you were trying to protect me but I want to protect you just as much. I would've helped you. Supported you. Been here instead of in Paris."

He nodded. "I'm sorry."

She wanted to give him a moment to compose himself, but she was aware that they could be interrupted—or noticed missing—the longer they stayed holed up in here. Plus Tiffany knew where Kian was and Noémie didn't think she'd stay away. "Kian, your father plans to announce your engagement to Tiffany in a way you won't be able to say no. We need to get you out of here before—"

He met her gaze with a steady one of his own. "I'm going to publicly denounce him."

She was stunned by that admission. "Really?"

"This has been coming for a while." He lifted his shoulders to shrug. "It's one among many reasons why I didn't want to tell you. I didn't want you to feel like it was because of you. I just … I felt I had to do this on my own. It's my life, I need to take control over it." He sighed. "I want to be able to tell people about you. I want the world to know that I love you and want to be with you. I … want to rub it in Tiffany's face."

Noémie frowned.

Seeing her expression, he muttered, "Yeah, I know. Sorry. Not the right reason. Still thought about it." He sighed. "I *need* to break this contract and I've needed to do that for a while. I've already resigned myself to him reacting … like a total dick again. I'm tired of being controlled and all he really cares about is his image and his money and I have enough of my own. So why not?"

She stroked her fingers up and down Kian's lapel. "Tiffany took money to break up with you."

Kian's chest rose and fell sharply. "She did."

"Soooo," she crooned with a teasing lilt. "We should totally rub it in her face."

He smiled. "Excellent."

Noémie stared at her fingers as she brushed them across Kian's suit. Little strokes, designed to soothe and keep him calm. "Your mother has a plan."

He gently touched the diamond pendant on her borrowed necklace. "I thought she might. She dressed you up like a doll again and showed you off?"

"Yes. She's been introducing me as her protégé from Paris and saying that I'm leading up their new lingerie line. She told me to keep my distance from you tonight. Play hard to get until she signaled, then let you 'capture' me. Then I was supposed to monopolize your attention for the rest of the night."

He shook his head in disbelief. "Why did you allow her to do this to you?"

She stroked her finger along his throat. "Desperate times. I couldn't get here any other way. The earliest flight I could afford was tomorrow and that would've been too late." She shrugged. "It doesn't sit right with me. We were both pawns in whatever game she's playing against your father. All I wanted to do was talk to you, being her doll was the only way to get here."

He bumped his head against hers. "I'm so sorry."

"All this would go away if your parents just listened to you. Communicated."

"I agree. I guess Mom's idea was to keep me distracted from Tiffany," Kian mused. "To give the appearance I'm chasing someone else. Dressing you up in the part. Celestial one of a kind and von Brandt diamonds. She's marked you so when Father hits me with the marriage thing … *oooh*." His eyes widened. "Clever. Not okay, but clever." He huffed out an angry breath. "You're right. We're pawns in whatever game they're playing. And I hate it."

Noémie nodded. "Me too. What's clever?"

Kian brushed his fingers over Noémie's cheek. "Don't panic, but I think Mom wants me to walk out of here engaged to you instead of Tiffany."

Blood drained from Noémie's face and she gaped at him.

"That wouldn't be so bad, would it?" Kian asked with a hurt puppy look on his face.

"No. It wouldn't, but it's got to be *our* choice," Noémie rushed. "No one else's. I don't want to be forced into that. I want it to happen naturally when we choose."

Kian nodded and smiled. "Me too."

"I am so tired of all this fake intrigue and subterfuge," she grumbled, understanding his decision to keep all this from her so much better. "They're both playing games and you're stuck in the middle. We need to stop playing by their rules and play by our own."

"You're right."

She tilted her head at him and shuffled. "You're absolutely certain you want to publicly denounce him. Cause a scene? And rub it in Tiffany's face?"

"Absolutely." He hesitated. "Is that okay? I'd be … It'll be tough for a while. You'll stand by me, won't you?"

She knew that even if he knew in his heart, he needed to hear her say it. "Of course I will."

"Even if it takes me a while to find my feet?"

She squeezed his arm. "Even then. There's nowhere I'd rather be. I will love and support you with whatever decision you make."

Reassured, he nodded. "Then I'm done. My whole life

I've done things the way my parents wanted. I went into modeling, I got a business degree, I became a partner, and managed a large chunk of Mom's people, not just in Celestial Paris, but through all of them. I devoted my time and effort to it and now ... I'm done. I don't want to anymore. Not if they're going to continue squeezing me dry, dangling it in front of me and threatening to take it away. And I feel good about this. I can do what I want, when I want. I can be with you. No more hiding. "

"Okay," she said and smiled. "Then we're going to go out there and I'm going to ask you to dance. We can flirt and smile, but most importantly, we be *ourselves*. Oh, and you're definitely going to have the unfortunate compulsion to kiss me in front of everyone."

He grinned. "I like this plan."

"Cue dramas and yelling, or ... I don't know."

He nodded. "Leave my parents to me. They've had this coming for a while and there's a lot I need to say."

That made sense. This was his fight. "Then I will stand there and back you up all the way ... Are there pies I can throw at them?"

Kian laughed, a wonderful sound considering how horrible things were for him right now. "I wish. There's probably something in the kitchen if you're really that determined."

"Or we could grab a tray from a waiter and toss that at them."

His excitement was tangible. "I would *love* to see that. Then what?"

"Then we leave. Go somewhere else. Oh!" She shook her finger at him sternly. "I want one of those authentic New York hot dogs."

Kian's smile couldn't get any wider. "They're absolutely delicious and I did promise you one."

"Exactly," she chirped, happy. "Then ... sex. Definitely sex."

"So scandalous!" Kian declared and lifted his hand to

his forehead. "Shame on you for besmirching my innocence."

She poked him. "Oh, you love it."

"That sounds like a magnificent plan," Kian said. "There's one problem."

She frowned in confusion. Hadn't that covered everything? "What's that?"

"I seem to have forgotten how to kiss you. We need to practice."

Laughing, Noémie gripped his lapels to pull him down to her, and set about reminding him.

They couldn't tarry in the Quiet Room, not with Tiffany watching for Kian, or Quinn and Charlie waiting for Noémie. Kian left first, after telling Noémie about another way back to the ballroom. She slipped back in with what seemed like little notice and went searching for Quinn and Charlie.

The pair were among a group of men, laughing with each other and sipping champagne and Charlie spotted her first. Nudging Quinn, they excused themselves from the conversation.

"Look at that smile," Quinn said as they sauntered toward her. "You found him."

"He found me," Noémie said, beaming at them both and absolutely giddy with relief. "I wanted to say thank you."

"It was our pleasure," Quinn said with an extravagant bow.

"What happens now?" Charlie asked.

"Now," Noémie said, looking beyond Charlie to where Kian waited for her while standing beside his father, "the fun begins. You'll want front row seats. Ask your husband to dance."

Charlie laughed. "We did that already. I think Madam Montgomery needed smelling salts, she was so scandalized."

"So, do it again," Noémie said. "And I promise, she

won't need smelling salts because of you."

"*Oooh.*" Quinn offered his hand to Charlie. "This should be interesting."

Noémie smiled as she watched them walk away, then set her sights on Kian. At first, she did nothing but allow herself to hold his gaze and smile. She bit her lip, dropped her eyes demurely as she ducked her head, and then looked at him through her eyelashes. Even across the room, she could see the amusement on his face.

She wanted to have fun with this part. Sighting each other across the room. Long-distance flirts through simple smiles and held gazes. But she could already see Tiffany fast approaching Kian, so she put on her game face, squared her shoulders and prepared to take the room by storm.

She moved with purpose through the hall, swishing her hips as she walked. Her eyes never once left Kian's and his eyes never deviated from hers. She wanted to recapture the moment she'd seen him do a walk like this. Covered in glitter and wearing so little and drowning in the intensity of his gaze.

She wanted Kian to feel that same intensity directed at him. She wanted to stir a fire in his loins and make every man in the room wish she graced them with a bare glance. She wanted every woman in the room to know Kian was hers, by his choice.

She wanted him to burn.

By the way his mouth went slack, she succeeded.

Celeste materialized when Noémie was halfway across the room. "What are you doing?" she hissed.

"Going to dance with Kian," she said as though it was the simplest thing in the world.

"It's not time yet. I didn't give you the signal."

"And I don't care," Noémie chirped and continued walking. "We're done playing games. It's ridiculous. If you want to stick it to Richard for involving himself with Helena, do it without ruining Kian's life in the process."

"Don't you dare—"

Noémie tore her gaze from Kian to meet Celeste's angry expression with dignity. "You are going to lose him if you keep this up."

Celeste reeled back as though Noémie had slapped her.

Noémie moved by her and locked eyes with Kian again.

Tiffany clung to Kian's arm like a leech and Kian looked more than ready for her to rescue him. Richard spoke to an older woman in a green dress the same shade as Tiffany's and Noémie guessed that was Helena.

That made this easier.

Reaching the four, Noémie was all smiles. She didn't bother looking at anyone else. Just her Kian. Offering him her hand, she smiled and offered, "Would you like to dance?"

Interrupted from his terribly important conversation, Richard's eyes fell upon her and he frowned. Noémie felt the weight of his disapproval and didn't care.

"I don't think so," Tiffany said with a haughty sniff and her hands tightened around Kian's arm. She went as far as to press her cleavage against his arm in some sort of ownership gesture. "He's taken—"

"Absolutely," Kian said, shaking his arm free so he could bounce forward and take Noémie's hand. "I've waited all night for you."

"Kian," Tiffany whined through clenched teeth while glaring at Noémie. "You're supposed to—"

"Kian," Richard said in a voice that could strip flesh from bones and Noémie got a distinct feeling that this tone was the one that usually subdued Kian.

He didn't let it this time. "Gotta go. Can't disappoint a guest," Kian chirped and waved over his shoulder as he escorted Noémie to the dance floor. "Bye."

They stepped onto the floor beside Quinn and Charlie, who were already slow dancing together. "That was ballsy," Quinn noted. "The look on Richard's face. Man, so worth it."

"I told you coming tonight would be enjoyable," Charlie said, amused. "There might even be fireworks soon."

"Keep watching," Kian told the pair as he lifted his and Noémie's joined hands and turned toward her. Placing his hand on her waist, he pulled her into his embrace and set them in a gentle side-to-side sway. Smiling, he breathed, "That walk across had to be the sexiest thing I have ever seen."

Heat rising to her face, Noémie curled her hand around Kian's upper arm. "I had a good teacher."

Kian lifted his hand from Noémie's hip. Touching her wrist, he directed both her hands until they were looped around his neck, then slid his hands down over her body until they settled at the small of her back. "Did I tell you how much I love this open back?" he asked, his thumb stroking skin.

"I won't object if you tell me again."

"It is so sexy," he crooned. "You are gorgeous. I'm having wonderfully naughty thoughts about what I'll do with you later."

She smiled at him. "If you're a good boy, I might just let you do them."

Pulling her as close as he could in their dancing cuddle, his gaze dropped to her lips. "How long do I have to wait before I kiss you? Because that uncontrollable urge is pretty real right now."

Noémie didn't even bother glancing around to see if people were watching. "We have to out-scandal Quinn and Charlie's earlier dance."

"And make Mrs. Montgomery faint? That sounds like a challenge," Kian said and lowered his head to hers. All swaying ceased and the room around them disappeared as her eyes fluttered closed. He held her flush against him, keeping her cradled in a tight embrace. Mouth moving lazily against hers, he kissed her in a way that made her feel that she was beyond precious to him, and a way that was utterly indecent for the socialite scene.

Heat flowed down through her, pulsing down her spine to settle in her belly. Her fingers curled around his neck and she rose up on her toes to push against him. Hands tightened on her back, crushing them together, he licked her teeth and she opened her mouth for him.

Someone shrieked like a tea-kettle that had been left on the stove too long.

Kian made a noise at the back of his throat, turning them so he was between Noémie and the tea-kettle. "Here it comes," he murmured against her mouth. Pulling back, he smiled at her and gave her a gentle peck. "Love you."

Her knees were weak and her breath was ragged. All she wanted to do was keep kissing him.

"Get away from him!" Tiffany demanded. She appeared beside them and a hand grabbed Noémie's hair behind her ear and yanked.

Reacting swiftly, and relying on the self-defense classes her father asked her to take, Noémie clapped her hand over the top of Tiffany's to keep her hair from being pulled and lashed out, jabbing her fingers into the soft flesh of Tiffany's inner arm, just above the elbow.

Tiffany shrieked and released her, staggering away while clutching her arm.

"Holy shit," Kian blurted, staring at Noémie with an awed expression.

To counter Kian's awe, Tiffany glared. Her blue eyes flashed with absolute hatred as she rubbed her elbow. "You absolute filthy whore, how dare you?!"

Noémie grit her teeth in anger. Kian's face lost all expression and he stepped between them.

Tiffany burst into fat, wet tears, designed to garner sympathy. "Kian," she whined. "She hurt me."

"You grabbed me," Noémie countered in a mild tone and touched her hair to make sure none of it had come loose. "I defended myself."

"Don't you dare touch my girlfriend again," Kian

snapped at Tiffany.

The crocodile tears dried up as fast as they'd arrived as Tiffany stared at him in shock. "Your *what?*" she squeaked.

"Kian," Richard's commanding voice boomed from the edge of the dance floor and all three of them turned toward him. He beckoned, then jabbed the floor in a 'come here' gesture. "A word. In private."

Kian reached back for Noémie's hand, then pulled her forward until she stood beside him.

"Alone," Richard added.

Celeste stood offset behind Richard, her arms folded on her chest, not looking the least bit impressed. Helena, with her pathetic glare that was nowhere near as perfected as Celeste's, tried to comfort Tiffany as she made blubbery noises.

Kian's hand clasped Noémie's tightly. "How about two words?" He raised his free hand and lifted two fingers to count off the words as he said, "I quit."

CHAPTER 23

The chill from Richard's expression could've frozen the entire room, except that Kian blazed in return and his fury canceled out his father's cold. People surrounding them had stopped what they were doing to stare and whisper among themselves.

"I am not going to be manipulated anymore," Kian grated out. "I'm done. Consider this my resignation."

"Kian, petit lapin," Celeste said as she stepped forward until she was beside her husband. "Let's not do this here."

"This is exactly where I need to be," Kian returned. "So no one will misunderstand me." He raised his voice and walked a circle around Noémie while still holding her hand as he addressed the crowd. She was on show, again, but this time it was a display of pride and love, rather than a competition of who had the prettiest doll to throw at Kian. "This is Noémie Belrose-Song and she is the love of my life. In spite of what you may have heard, and in spite of what my father and his *mistress* want, I am not, nor have I ever had any intention of marrying Tiffany Farrell."

"Kian!" Tiffany shrilled her eyes darting around as she took in all the judgmental stares. "Why would you do that? You know we're meant to be together. What does this little bitch have that I—"

Kian silenced her with a look. "You're delusional." Turning back to Richard, he said, "So. The No-relationship contract is null and void. Your super-secret shenanigans are out and you know how your 'friends' love a good scandal. You have a mess you'll probably throw money at to make it go away. Noémie and I are going home. "

Celeste tried again, waving her hand as if she could fan all the scandal away. "This is a simple misunderstanding which we can rectify by you conducting yourself civilly and joining us in private conversation."

"A civil conversation," Kian responded, turning his ire on her. "Oh, this will be rich. You can't explain this away. I know what you've done."

Celeste looked taken aback that Kian would dare yell at her. "Kian—"

"*Civilly*, Mom, how much did you pay Tiffany to break up with me?"

"You did what?" Helena blurted, aghast at Celeste. Noémie could see the overly dramatic actress in her rise as she pressed her hand to her chest. "Richard, did you know about this?"

"Kian," Tiffany said with a poorly acted gasp. "I never took money—"

"Oh, shut up," Celeste said with a roll of her eyes. "Both of you."

Kian slashed a glance in Tiffany's direction. "Don't lie. You took it and then you continued to string me along."

Tiffany pleaded, "I *didn't*," she proclaimed, her voice rising to a childlike pitch. "I love you, Kian! We're good together and—"

Kian pronounced each word with controlled force, "I do not want to be with you. Not now. Not ever. I want to be with Noémie."

With a wail, Tiffany turned and clutched at her mother, who patted her on the back ineffectually and tried to scowl. Noémie didn't understand how acting like a spoiled child would help Tiffany's situation but perhaps she didn't know how else to behave. To help Kian show a united front, she held her tongue and kept her expression carefully blank. She was a watcher, not a participant.

Richard's eyes flicked from Tiffany and Helena to Kian as he scolded, "I don't like this disrespectful tone, Kian."

"I don't like how you disrespected Mom," Kian scolded right back. "Or me."

Through gritted teeth, Richard ground out, "My relationships are none of your business."

"But somehow mine is yours."

"As I told you, your mother and I—"

Ignoring his father, Kian spoke to Helena, "Did Mom make you sign some sort of 'mistress' contract? Is that why you're so hell-bent on marrying me to Tiffany? Your deluded idea of payback?"

Helena looked aghast. "How dare you speak to me that way? You impertinent, ill-mannered—"

"Helena," Richard chided and held up a palm to her, "let me handle this."

"You don't have any place sticking your nose in *my* business," Kian snapped at Helena.

Richard's hand sliced through the air as though he could chop up Kian's words. "Kian, you're being exceptionally rude—"

"Oh, I don't care," Kian proclaimed with a shrug. "I'm done being in the middle. Sort it out yourselves. I'm out."

Celeste tried a third time. "Kian, let's take this elsewhere, yes?" she pleaded, her fluster making her accent more pronounced. "This is a private conversation and—"

"What part of 'no' do you not understand?"

Noémie shifted closer to Kian and touched his upper arm to get him to look at her. "This isn't helping," she said, trying to be soothing. "Don't prolong it, it will only hurt more in the long run. If you've said everything you wanted to, we should leave."

It seemed like it took effort but he relaxed and smiled, placing his hand over hers. "You're right."

"You have not been permitted to leave," Richard snapped, his chin up. "You broke your contract by involving yourself with this *woman*"—he sneered out the word. "There will be consequences this time."

Drawn back into anger, Kian growled, "You know, if I married Tiffany, that would've broken the fucking contract too."

"Language!" Celeste scolded.

Richard clenched his hands into fists. "You are my son and you will not defy me. Tiffany is the wife I have chosen for you and you will accept that!"

Murmuring in the room increased and Noémie heard Quinn's low whistle of disbelief. Noémie spared them a glance. Quinn and Charlie stood side by side a short distance away, watching quietly and offered her a supportive smile as they saw her looking.

"Richard," Celeste scolded, moving until she was standing an equal distance from both of them instead of being beside Richard. "That is no way to speak to him. You can't force him to—"

Kian snarled, "I am not an object!"

The anger in the air had teeth and claws and it was sinking them into Kian and his father. Noémie worried what would happen if one of them took it too far. Celeste should have taken Kian's side, instead of standing in neutral ground beside the men.

Taking a step closer to Kian, she turned sideways and placed her hand on his chest to help calm him. His chest shuddered under her palm but he took a deep breath and looked at her and his expression softened. Smiling for Kian, Noémie then turned her head to address Richard. "May I ask something?"

"No," Richard said, dismissing her. "*You* have no part of this conversation. You're just a tramp after his money."

Kian bristled and Noémie slid her hand across his chest

to keep him calm. Rolling her eyes, she said, "I couldn't care less about the money. I don't want it and I don't need it. I seem to be the only one who cares about Kian's mentality in all this."

"You still have no—"

She wasn't about to let Richard interrupt her. "Why are you so determined to marry Kian to Tiffany? Why are you pushing so hard for this? You should be *listening* to your son and instead, you're alienating him."

Kian gestured Noémie, nodding emphatically. "Yes, answer that, please. I'm so sick of asking."

"I don't answer to you."

"But you answer to me," Celeste snapped, taking her first step into Kian's corner. "We had an agreement, Richard, and none of it involved signing Kian over to your whore or her daughter."

Instead of watching Richard, Noémie's eyes were drawn to Helena's sudden skittishness. She frowned and tilted her head, flicking her eyes between Richard and Helena and then over at Celeste. When what was occurring dawned on her, she couldn't help but laugh. "Oh my God."

"What?" Kian asked.

Spinning to him, Noémie rushed, "Your father threw you out the first time you were with Tiffany, right? So why is this time different? Between then and now, Helena's done something to try to force a wedding."

Kian seemed to stop breathing. Then he snorted. Then threw his head back and laughed. "Oh, that is golden," he proclaimed while people stared at him. "Of course, there's a contract, isn't there? You're so fucking fond of having everything written on paper. So, by not marrying Tiffany, I'm breaking some contract you have with Helena, right?" He waved his hand, still chortling. "I'm done. Sort yourselves out and stop involving me." With a gentle tug, he pulled her to walk beside him as he moved toward the door. "C'mon, Noémie."

"There are consequences!" Richard told him as he followed the pair in what felt like a last-ditch effort to keep him there.

"There were consequences last time," Kian said, humor still evident on his face. "I survived. I know the contract, Father. I know exactly what it entails and how to break it."

"Use your brain instead of your hormones," Richard scolded. "What are you going to do if you leave? There is no one who would take you on."

Kian smirk was evident in his voice, "You should take your own advice. Do you really think you have absolute control? You might *here*, in New York, but guess who's the power in Paris? Me. You made me a partner of Celestial or did you conveniently forget? You can't fire me. I leave and you'll have to buy me out if you want to retain control. I'm sure I can think of an outrageous sum. And then double it."

Richard's eyes flared wide.

"And now he sees," Kian said over his shoulder as they continued to walk. "I *learned* when you kicked me out. Not obedience like you wanted. I learned that I can't trust you. I learned what the world was really like. How hard people have to struggle just to get by. I learned how I can make a difference in it and I have been. I have spent the last four years securing *my* wealth and *my* name, separate from yours. You won't catch me off guard again. Disown me, I *don't* need you."

"Kian, wait!" Celeste called, her shoes clipping on the floor as she hurried after them.

"You're not even sorry this happened, are you?" Kian yelled. Releasing Noémie, he spun around to jab a finger at his mother. "You were part of it, Mom! You paid Tiffany off. You tried to get rid of Noémie!"

Noémie moved with him, taking his hand again to keep them connected.

Pulling up short, Celeste protested, "Tiffany wasn't right for you!"

"How dare you!" Helena snapped and was ignored.

"That was *my* decision!" Kian yelled. His hand clutched Noémie's as though she was the only thing keeping him grounded. She squeezed his hand and remained silent. There was little she could say or do in this extremely personal argument, except to support Kian.

Celeste reasoned, "If you had stayed with Tiffany, you would never have met Noémie. I simply showed you Tiffany's true colors before she was able to sink her claws into our fortune."

"*Our* fortune?" Kian questioned incredulously. "Is that all you care about? What about me? What about my feelings? Were they that inconsequential? You could've asked me! You could've talked to me about your concerns."

"You weren't prepared to listen," Celeste said. "You still aren't."

"Oh, so it's my fault now?" Kian yelled. "You didn't trust me enough to figure out Tiffany was not the right one for me. You tried to get Noémie to sign a fucking mistress contract, Mom. Do you know how disgusted that makes me feel? You tried and you failed. You went on and on about being discreet about my sex life, but never allowing me to fall in love. Wasn't there a point you and Father were in love? You both went through this too, why are you continuing with the tradition?"

"Kian, you're overreacting," Celeste said with a huffing sigh. "I don't understand why you're so upset about all this. If you'd just calm down and—"

"You really don't get what you've done, do you?" Noémie asked, the words bursting from her unbidden. "You have no clue."

Richard strode forward to stand ahead of his wife. "What we have done? We've protected him from gold diggers like you who would use him for his money or his fame and—"

"*You* used me!" Kian cried.

There was so much anger in the air and she wanted to shield Kian from it. He'd been through enough. Noémie raised her voice to firmly drown out the von Brandt's protest, "You have manipulated and hurt Kian way beyond his capacity to forgive or even understand. In your shortsightedness to protect your fortune, or your assets, or whatever you told yourself so you could sleep at night, you have ignored the most important thing. Your son."

Richard frowned at her.

"Would you honestly be happy *never* being a part of his life again? Never seeing him get married? Have children? You disown him, *again*, and what do you think will happen? Do you honestly believe he's going to want you to be a part of his life?"

Kian shifted closer to her and his thumb stroked against hers.

"Don't be ridiculous," Richard scoffed. "He's a von Brandt. He won't turn his back on family."

Noémie lifted her chin and her voice rang clear. "*You* have no trouble turning your back on him. Families don't have to be born, they can be found. They can be made."

"Noémie," Kian breathed, looking at her with utter reverence.

Both Celeste and Richard protested vehemently. "You don't have the right—"

"I refuse to let you hurt him anymore." Her expression hard and accusatory, Noémie demanded, "You're not sorry for any of it, are you?"

Glaring at Noémie for daring to question them, Celeste tried to spin her web of lies around Kian again. "Kian, you're emotional and you know what you're like when you get too upset. We can talk about this when you're calm and rational."

Noémie shook her head, disappointed at their behavior. "You don't get it. He *is* calm and rational. You're the ones who refuse to see what you're doing."

"Noémie, it's no good. Let's just go." Kian took a step

backward, then addressed his parents for the last time. "If either of you mess with Noémie, her family, or her business, you better be prepared to deal with me. I will be your worst nightmare," he promised.

Noémie wrapped her arm around Kian's waist, hugging into him as they walked toward the door, ignoring the calls of Kian's name behind them and Richard's demands that he cease walking away. "Are you okay?"

"No. I want to get out of here," he mumbled.

She didn't know how to make it better for him. "I'm so sorry. I never wanted this for you."

Kian shoved the door open and they left the ballroom and headed into the small foyer. "Don't be. None of this is your fault. It would've happened anyway." Signaling the lady at the coat check, he said, "What number was your coat?"

Noémie flushed. "I don't have one." At Kian's raised eyebrow, she elaborated, "I didn't have anything that would go. Celeste only let me borrow the dress and the jewelry and wearing my winter coat didn't seem right and … well …"

Kian's lips pressed into a thin line as he accepted his coat from the lady. Digging in his pocket, he passed the coat lady a tip, then threw the coat around Noémie's shoulders. Keeping his arm around her, he hurried them out of the building.

Trotting down the stairs, Kian gave a card to the valet attendant. "How did you get here?"

"Taxi," she said. Fumbling to retrieve her phone from her garter purse, she opened its leather case to get the key card for her hotel and show him the name. "I'm staying here."

He glanced at it and frowned. "Did you pick the place?"

Noémie shook her head. "Mathilde organized everything."

"And Mom paid for it, right?" Kian returned Noémie's

nod with one of his own. "Put your phone on do not disturb, or we'll get inundated. We'll get your stuff, then go to where I'm staying—"

"Kian!"

Kian tensed for a moment then relaxed and looked over his shoulder. "Charlie. Sorry, man, we have to get out of here."

Charlie waved his hand at Kian as he trotted down the steps to join them. "Not keeping you." Lacking his winter coat, Charlie tucked his hands into his pockets. "Just wanted to say if you and Noémie are still in town tomorrow night, Quinn and I would love to have you over. I'm sure Noémie would like some good memories of her time here and we'd cherish the chance to get to know her better."

"Not sure what we're doing yet," Kian said. "I'll let you know."

Charlie nodded. Extracting one of his hands, he went for his wallet and pulled out a card to give to Noémie. "My details."

Kian protested, "I would've given her them—"

"Except you didn't," Charlie admonished lightly. "I did. So there."

"I almost expected a 'neener-neener' in that," Noémie replied, accepting the card and tucked it into her phone case.

Charlie drew an exaggerated breath and Kian quickly said, "Don't tempt him."

Giggling, Noémie bounced forward to kiss both of Charlie's cheeks. "It was nice meeting you, Charles the dumbass."

As she moved back under Kian's arm, Charlie's face lit up in a grin. "She really is delightful. If I weren't a married man ... well ... Quinn would give you a run for your money."

Kian laughed dryly. "He could try." He held out his hand to Charlie to shake. "Thanks, Charlie. For everything."

Charlie grasped Kian's hand. Instead of shaking it, he pulled Kian in for a tight hug, clapping him on the back. "It'll be okay. Only good things will come from this."

One hand still on Noémie, Kian returned the hug. "I know."

"Let us know if you need anything," Charlie said. Pulling away from the hug, he gripped Kian's upper arms. "No matter what time it is."

Kian nodded.

One last pat, and Charlie turned to trot back up the stairs. Smiling at Noémie over his shoulder, he waved. "Look after him, little French munchkin."

"Always," Noémie replied and looked at Kian. His expression was torn and it was obvious he was hurting. Reaching out, she gripped the front of his dinner jacket. "Kian?"

"Ma rose," he murmured, not meeting her eyes. "I would like permission to kiss you."

Noémie swallowed. "Paparazzi?"

"Yes," he replied, his voice husky and low. "I'm sorry."

She could do this. She'd known it was coming, especially now she was in America and subject to their privacy laws. Celeste had warned her as well. She was prepared but she didn't understand why he was apologizing. "Why are you sorry?"

"We didn't have a chance to discuss this and I know you're not prepared. I'm asking for a lot. I want the media focused on us and our relationship and not what happened in there, and to do that, we need to announce that we're together. It's not the way I wanted to do it—"

With a smile, she lifted her chin. "Permission granted."

"Are you sure?"

She tugged on his jacket. "Just kiss me, Kian."

Turning toward her, he cupped her cheek with one hand and leaned down to kiss her. Nothing like the kiss he'd bestowed upon her on the dance floor. Short and sweet, and while still caring, it held a sense of professionalism as well. A display kiss. Enough romance to be pleasing to the eye, without being blatantly sexual.

Pulling back, his thumb stroked her cheek. "It's official now," he said, sounding regretful.

Gazing into his eyes, she smiled. "Kiss me again," she suggested. "The way you want to, not like you're performing."

"I will," he promised and dropped his hand. "But if I start, I won't ever stop. And we need to get out of here."

A gorgeous and sleek silver Aston Martin pulled up and the valet Kian had spoken to hopped out to offer Kian the keys and receive his tip.

Shocked, Noémie stared at the car. "No way."

Humored, Kian opened the passenger door for her. "Yes, way."

"This is amazing!" Sliding into the passenger seat, she waited until he slipped into the driver's seat before she said, "You didn't have one in Paris." She let her eyes skip all over how fancy the dashboard was, and how sleek the interior felt, before she focused on Kian.

He slipped the car into gear and entered traffic. "Paris, I don't need to be showy like I have to here. People are more impressed by an expensive bottle of wine, a nice dinner, and a good quality suit than they are with a car."

"True," Noémie said with a nod. "Is it yours?"

"Yeah. Birthday present. Don't know why, since it's here and not where I'm living." He shrugged. "I think my father was trying to use it as an incentive to visit, but I'm not a car person." Stopping at a set of traffic lights, he reached into his pocket and pulled out his phone, putting it in the dock on the dashboard. "Hey Siri, call Amanda Fitzgerald."

Noémie raised her eyebrows at him in silent question.

"My publicist here in America," he elaborated. "Things are going to snowball now and I don't know what's going to—"

"Good evening, Kian," Amanda chirped as she answered. "I must say, that was quite a show you put on this evening. Although, I would've loved some warning Noémie was going to be here."

"Thank you. And I didn't know about Noémie. She was a surprise for me, too."

"She was there?" Noémie blurted, her eyes darting from the phone to Kian's face.

"Good evening, Noémie," Amanda said. "And yes, I am. You looked beautiful and regal, darling. That will come in handy."

The traffic lights turned green and Kian continued to drive. "What's the mood now?"

"Your parents haven't stopped arguing since you left, but they have taken it behind closed doors. Everyone's gossiping, so we need to move on this as fast as possible. I'll have something ready for you in a few hours since it's apparent you want to make the deadlines tonight."

"Yes."

"Also I have a few photos which I can leak to gossip mags, I think that kiss on the dance floor will trump the performance you gave outside on the steps and I have exclusivity."

Kian released a slow breath. "Yeah."

"Tone of voice preferred?" Amanda asked.

"Matter-of-fact," Kian replied, in the same voice he would use if ordering a cup of coffee. "With sympathy slanted toward Noémie. I don't want any blame on her at all."

"I would recommend we stick to fluff pieces at the moment to bolster Noémie's public opinion. She's unknown in America and that makes her a wildcard. Plus, I am certain that your parents will want to put a hush order on tonight. Richard's PR rep is already talking to people."

"Do you think that will hold?"

"Depends on how fast his PR moves. I can prepare several possible pieces, but until we know their reaction, and you have all your legal pieces in place, we can't move on them. However, we can get ahead with public opinion if we release the fact that Noémie's your romantic partner."

Staring straight ahead, Kian said, "Agreed."

"If the media gets hold of the argument tonight, we can spin it to be more sympathetic toward you and Noémie. Forbidden love, political marriage, that kind of thing. It depends on how bad you want to make your parents look."

He swallowed. "Right."

"I won't do anything without your permission. I'm heading to my office now. I'll liaise with Florian so he can work on the French releases. Talk soon," Amanda said and hung up.

Silence filled the car.

Having listened to the conversation, Noémie was certain of one thing. "You … you were *really* prepared for tonight."

Kian nodded and Noémie's heart sank to her toes.

"I'm so sorry," she rushed, upset. "I feel like I came and stomped all over the plan you had. I shouldn't have come."

Glancing her way, he reached over and took her hand, dragging it back to his knee. "No," he soothed. "It's not like that. I'm glad you're here. You're the only thing keeping me sane right now."

She wasn't sure she believed him, especially when everything felt like it would've gone better for him if she hadn't been here. "Will the media get hold of what happened?" she asked in a small voice.

"Maybe," he replied, squeezing her hand before he put his back on the steering wheel. "Mainstream won't care. Business will care more about the implication of a von Brandt split than who I am with. The tabloids will clamor over the kiss for a while until we're ready with the rest, but, Noémie, even if I have everything prepared, it doesn't mean *anything* will happen. There might be a single report and that's it."

"Oh." Was he sugar coating to spare her feelings? She didn't know how any of this worked. "You made it sound … um… urgent. Scary."

"It could be if we're not ready with a response. I suspect Tiffany will sob to anyone who will listen, but that's what Amanda's for. To prevent it."

"Oh," she said again, feeling inadequate.

Kian swallowed. "My father … is not a good man to anger. I suspect there'll be rumors and whispers, but nothing until he's ready. I'm prepared for the worst-case scenario and everything in between."

"What's the worst-case scenario?" Noémie asked, not sure if she wanted to know.

"That he fights me on this," he said and lifted his chin in determination and rested his hand on hers. "He'll lose." With a soft look and a gentle smile, he said, "I'm yours, for as long as you'll have me. There's nothing that he can do to stop that."

CHAPTER 24

Kian drove through the streets of New York and Noémie plastered herself to the window to take in all the nighttime sights and sounds. She hadn't had much of a chance to see the sights so it was nice to take a moment. Besides, she didn't know what to say to Kian at the moment and he seemed to prefer the silence.

It didn't take long to empty her tiny hotel room of the small carry-on luggage she had and hand over her keycard to the reception. She hadn't had time to do anything in the room itself except for shower, before hairdressers and makeup artists arrived to make her presentable for tonight, though the evidence of their presence had vanished.

Kian stood in the doorway to the room, watching her rush to collect her gear and said little. She didn't know why he didn't wait in the car while she did this but she guessed he didn't want to be alone with his thoughts.

The silence continued in the drive to his hotel. Noémie rested her hand on his knee as she looked out at New York. She didn't know what to say to make things better for Kian, if there was anything she could say to help. Kian seemed to be holding together, if barely.

They turned a corner and carefully placed lights lit up a

multitude of trees. Pathways and secret places, she knew of only one place in New York like that, but she still felt compelled to check. "Is that Central Park?"

"Yes."

She plastered herself to the window again, trying to see everything. "Wow. It's so pretty!"

"We can go for a walk tomorrow, if you want?"

She bounced in her seat in excitement. "Do they have hotdogs?"

With a sad sounding laugh, he said, "Yes. Absolutely they do."

The hotel he pulled into was huge. Glamorous. Carpets at the doorway, their valet and luggage attendants waiting at the door, and a spectacular view of Central Park. He had a hotel on the street surrounding Central Park. She didn't even want to think about how much this cost him per night. "You didn't stay with your father?"

He turned the car up the valet driveway. "*She* was staying there with him. The second I found that out, I got a room elsewhere and didn't tell them where it was. I got some alone time at least. It's nice. You'll love the view."

"I'm sure I will." As they pulled to a stop, she asked, "So they won't know where we are?"

"No." Kian hit the button to pop the trunk. "This place prides itself on discretion. If word got out they leaked a guest name, no one would trust them," he said, then exited the driver's door.

Noémie watched him sadly, turning her head as the valet opened Noémie's car door. She smiled at the valet, stepping from the vehicle. "Thank you."

Kian pulled Noémie's suitcase from the trunk, handing it over to a porter before returning to Noémie to offer her his elbow. She wove her arm through and hugged his to her chest, pressing herself against him as she took in the hotel. A five-star hotel, the best of the best. Prestige oozed out of every surface, even the doorman was immaculately dressed and poised as he greeted Kian by name.

Someplace she'd never have dreamed staying, unless it was for something really special, like a honeymoon and she'd been saving for years as a treat. Kian had been living here all week.

Noémie twisted her head as she tried to take in the immense gold and crystal themed foyer as well as keep up with Kian's stride. "Wow," she said, tilting her head back to view the huge circular lighting in the ceiling.

A woman in a manager's uniform approached Kian with a bright smile. "Mister von Brandt, welcome back. Can we be of any assistance this evening?"

Placing his hand on Noémie's wrist to drag her attention away from the foyer, Kian presented her. "This is Noémie Belrose-Song, my girlfriend. She is to be given absolutely anything she desires while she is here. Treat her as you would me."

Noémie wasn't sure about that. With a slight frown, she started to protest, "Kian—"

"Let me spoil you," he replied, sparing her a tight smile. "Please."

She didn't like his smile. It felt wrong. Sad.

"It would be our pleasure," the woman said, still smiling. "Welcome, Miss Belrose-Song."

"Thank you," she replied, her eyes fixed on Kian.

Kian continued, "We'd appreciate it if we were not disturbed."

"Of course."

"Thank you," Kian said and escorted Noémie to the elevators where the porter was waiting with Noémie's suitcase.

She was getting the *Pretty Woman* vibe from all the luxury, but, glancing at Kian, she thought the joke would fall flat if she said anything. It was clear now they were almost alone, now they were almost somewhere he didn't have to pretend, cracks were forming in the carefully crafted facade. She had to be ready to pick up the pieces when he fell apart.

When they reached Kian's room, Noémie spent a few seconds glancing around. Very large and spacious, it was bigger than her apartment. The front door opened into a living area. A corner room, with two views of Central Park. A round table with a bouquet of fresh flowers stood near the door. One wall was filled with a huge TV and a circular sofa faced it. Kian's laptop was set up on the desk by the window, with several large folders stacked beside it. The gray winter coat she was fond of hung on the back of a chair.

The king bed was contained in its own room, with double doors leading into it, and it was made with little mint chocolates on the pillow. There was a picture of her on the bedside table, but no other personal touches. It didn't feel like he'd spent much time here at all. Considering how much he'd had organized tonight, she wondered if he'd even had time to sleep.

The breathtaking nighttime view of the New York skyline over the top of Central Park drew her in and she wandered over to the window to stare. Since the room was warm, she slipped out of Kian's jacket and left it beside his gray coat, then slipped off her shoes.

"Anything else, Mister von Brandt?"

"Have you eaten, Noémie?"

She turned back toward him and smiled. "Ahh, no. Not yet. I was too nervous."

"There's a restaurant here," he suggested.

"It closes at eleven," the porter said helpfully.

She didn't think he could handle dining in his current state. "Maybe we should order room service?" she suggested, which was met by a nod of agreement from Kian. "In a little while."

After receiving his tip, the porter showed himself out, leaving Noémie and Kian alone.

Kian kicked off his shoes, threw his dinner jacket at the lounge suite, and loosened his tie. "Make yourself at home. I'll be a minute, I need to—"

The sadness in him was oppressive. It leaked out of him and filled the room. "Kian," she breathed and held out her hand toward him, inviting him to join her.

Kian froze, one hand clutching his tie. He was tense as he stared at her, like he was being torn in two. The need to pull away, and the want to stay. "I'm not ready to talk."

"That's okay," she said, stepping toward him with her arms open. "I hug, too. I'm soft and squishy and nice to cuddle. No talking required."

Slowly, he pulled his tie away from his collar and wound it around his hand. "My father said never show weakness," he mumbled, his eyes fixed on his hand.

"Maman always said take the good with the bad," she replied and moved toward him. She took her time, letting him know she was coming so he could decide if he wanted to stay or go. "No one can be strong all the time. Trust your partner to be a source of strength when you can't."

"I don't … I don't know how to …" So lost. So sad and alone. He was having trouble keeping it together.

Reaching him, she sidled as close as she could without touching him. Lifting up on her toes, she stretched out a hand and brushed the back of her fingers against Kian's cheek. "I'm here to help. Any way I can."

He melted. Folding into her, chin on her shoulder, he surrounded her. Arms fitted completely around her back, clutching the opposite side as he lifted her into his chest. Wrapping her arms around his neck, she held on. She hummed under her breath and stroked the hair at the back of his neck.

He didn't hug for long, the bare back and the view over her shoulder getting the better of him. Lips pressed to her jaw before he placed her feet back on the carpet. Clearing his throat, he pulled back and his hands drifted across her skin to the lace straps of her dress. Lace slid from her shoulder and she lowered her arms so that he could peel the dress from her. With a soft rustle, red chiffon fell and puddled on the floor at her feet. Swallowing hard, he touched the red lace at her hip, then the garter purse on her leg. Raising his eyes to hers, he said, "Stunning."

She kept her eyes on his, tilting her head and smiling. "Thank you."

"If I'd known, we'd never have made it out of the Quiet Room."

"That's why I didn't tell you," she purred and reached for him.

He retreated, taking a sharp step back. "I need to shower."

Noémie blinked at the sudden change in tone. It was a switch that had been flicked, from aroused to scared.

"I feel … I can't … I need to—" his voice cracked, broke, shattered, and she watched as tears filled his eyes.

He wanted to hide in the water. He felt unclean from what happened. He didn't want her to see. Any number of possibilities could be true but one thing she felt was certain. He was running away from her.

It brought tears to her eyes. "Kian—"

He retreated further, walking backward toward the door she guessed was to the bathroom. His hand fumbled behind him for the handle. The door opened behind him, and he hesitated in the doorway. "Join me?" he asked, looking everywhere else but her.

She wasn't sure if it was shyness or resistance in his tone. "Okay," she said and touched the necklace. "Let me just put this away."

He nodded, disappearing into the bathroom and leaving the door open as an invitation.

With a heavy heart, she stooped down to pick up the dress from the floor, raising her eyes to the bathroom door as she heard the shower start. He wouldn't have had time to even undress so …

He was using the noise of the water to hide his distress.

She wasn't going to let him go through this alone, so she stripped off as fast as she could, packing away both the dress and the borrowed jewelry so she could return them.

Multitasking, she took down her hair and swiped her face a few times to wipe off most of the makeup.

Kian, when Noémie entered the bathroom, was beneath the too-hot water, head hanging. Hunched at the waist, his arms extended so his hands could brace on the side of the shower.

With his head under the water, he didn't hear Noémie until she slipped into the shower behind him. He startled, glanced back at her under his arm then leaned into her. "Hi," he said, his voice sodden with unshed grief and turmoil.

Wrapping her hands around his torso, she pressed herself against his back. "Hey." Noémie turned her head, resting her cheek on his back so she didn't drown under the spray of the water. "I'm here."

"I'm sorry," he croaked. "I'm not dealing with this well."

"Don't be," Noémie soothed and pressed her lips to his back. "I don't expect you to deal with it. I'm just here. Whatever you need."

He made a strangled noise and hunched his shoulders more. He seemed to be concentrating intently on his breathing. Too fast and unsteady to calm him. "There was no other choice. Nothing else I could have done."

Nothing she could do except be here for him. "I'm so sorry. I'm here."

The dam broke. Body shuddering, Kian lurched forward and pressed the top of his head against the tiles. She moved with him, holding on tight and stroking her hands along his torso to soothe him.

She didn't speak, beyond a few croons and while he didn't turn around to cuddle her and take what comfort he could, he let himself have that release of emotion he so desperately needed. He gave all the pain, desperation, and frustration of the last few days to the water and let it be washed away.

He let her witness him at his weakest, and while her

heart hurt for him, his trust meant the world to her.

He slowly relaxed under her soothing hands. Shifting his weight, he braced against the wall with one hand and used the other to cover hers. Then he curled against her, leaning into her embrace, and finally turned to cuddle her. He sank down, sitting on the tiled floor, and tucked her onto his lap so he could bury his face in her neck. "Thanks for being here."

They stayed there for a time, curled around each other, holding tight and loose all at once. Water trickled down their bodies and pooled in the places where their bodies aligned. He studied her hands, weaving his fingers through hers, then releasing them again, only to stroke her palm again. A kiss against her skin, another returned to him, an intimacy that filled them both and soothed aching hearts.

Eventually, he sighed, lifting his face to the water to wash it. "We should get out before we wrinkle."

She hummed. Her hair was probably a tangled mess of sodden product and that needed to be rectified. She picked up a strand to study it and pulled a face. "May I borrow your shampoo?"

Eyes red, he looked raw as he smiled. "Sure."

His large hands held her by the waist as he hoisted her to her feet, then kissed her belly as he stood too. Kissing her neck, then cheek, Kian reversed their positions, allowing Noémie to wash all the hairspray and shine out of her hair while he left the shower. She washed as fast as she could, and Kian wrapped himself in a towel and watched her with an unreadable expression on his face.

While she washed, a plan formed in her mind, something that might take his mind off things, or if it didn't, gave him a safe space to talk.

Stepping from the shower, she grabbed one of the towels. After drying herself and her hair as much as she could, Noémie took Kian's hand. "I want to do something," she said and led him out into the bedroom.

"What's that?"

She pulled the covers back on the bed and then went to her suitcase for her moisturizing cream. "Lie face down."

He lifted an eyebrow at her, baffled.

"Please."

Climbing onto the bed, he followed her instructions and, when he was comfortable, Noémie straddled his back.

"Really?" Kian asked, skeptically.

"Really." Lathering her hands with cream, Noémie ran her fingers down his back until she reached the small of it, where she spread them out to massage across his hips. Digging her fingers in slightly, she applied pressure with them up his back until she reached his shoulders, then used her thumbs to gently manipulate the muscles there. "Ahh, Monsieur von Brandt, you carry a lot of tension in your shoulders."

Kian snorted. "You don't say."

"It's a good thing I'm into fashion," she said. "I heard massage therapists need a touch of style."

"There's wood you can touch if you want."

With a giggle, Noémie said, "That degraded quickly."

"You *are* naked and sitting on my ass."

"It has that perk."

"If you like, I can roll over and we can talk about the first thing that comes up."

Noémie snorted. "Down boy." Dipping down, she kissed his shoulder. "Relax and enjoy it."

Kian sighed and rested his cheek on the pillow.

"I just realized you've probably had a lot of these," she said, hesitating.

He hummed noncommittally.

That embarrassed her. "So," she said in a small voice. "Um … you can probably tell I don't know what I'm doing."

"It's different when you do it," he assured her. "I can totally tell you're touching me because you want to, and you want to make me feel better and I love it. Don't stop."

Smiling, Noémie continued her gentle administration

on his back.

With a chortle, Kian said, "If you want to turn it into a sexy massage with a happy ending, I am absolutely okay with that."

She worked on his shoulders again, gentle rubs and circular pressure from her fingers to keep him talking. "Now, that makes me wonder if you've had one before," she teased.

"No, but I am very intrigued. I feel nakedness against my butt and I want to explore it."

Noémie laughed. "Soon. Just wait."

He hummed, low in his throat and she felt his muscles tense. "I did the right thing, didn't I?"

Noémie breathed out slowly. She hadn't been sure if this would help relax him or coax him to talk, or lead into sex, but it seemed Kian didn't want to bottle any more. "I think you did. Things couldn't have continued that way anymore and they weren't listening."

"I don't know what to say. I don't know where to even start to process what happened today."

"We don't need to talk," she assured him. "But, if you wanted, you could start with how you're feeling."

"I feel … hopeful. I think."

Noémie blinked, pausing for a moment. "Okay," she said and ran her fingers along his spine.

"I don't have to play their stupid games or sign any contracts. I don't even have to talk to them. I don't have to care what they do anymore."

Without saying anything, she continued to stroke and soothe.

"But I do, don't I?" Kian asked in a small voice. "I still care about them."

She used the ball of her palm to rub a tight spot. "They're your parents, Kian. That isn't going to change. You're not going to magically stop loving them."

Kian lifted up, tucking his elbows underneath him to prop himself up. "I don't want to forgive him. Or Mom. I still can't believe she did that to you."

"I didn't say you had to," Noémie soothed. She lay down against his back, hooking her hands over his arms to hug him from behind. "You don't have to do anything. You've said everything you need to say to them. The ball is in their court. Let's just enjoy this time together."

"That sounds like an excellent idea." In a quick move, he flipped them so that she was on her back and he could snuggle into her chest. "How long can you stay?"

"I have an appointment with Ava Jacobs on Monday I can't miss. She's only in Paris for the day and seeing a lot of other people too, so I can't reschedule." She hesitated and then said, "I hope you don't mind, but I gave your code to my mother. She'll take care of Purrfect for you. I'm sorry, I couldn't think of what else to do and I didn't know what other arrangements you usually made for her."

"That's fine. Thank you." He sighed and circled her nipple with the tips of his fingers. "Seeing you there tonight was a shock. Wonderful and amazing, but I was so scared too."

"So was I," she admitted softly. "I'm really glad Charlie and Quinn were there to help."

"I wanted to be the one there for you," he muttered, morose. "I was going to ease you into that world, not throw you in the deep end and expect you to survive. One wrong move changes everything. You don't know the panic I felt when I saw you."

"Kian, it's not—"

"But also pride," he continued, his voice soft and sincere. "So many things could've gone wrong tonight. Watching you dancing to my mother's tune, *again*, all I wanted to do was race across the room and rescue you. Keep you from seeing what I was going to be forced to do. But you didn't need rescuing. You were confident. Regal." He trailed his fingers along her skin. "So beautiful. You took the place by storm, it was amazing to watch. I'm so lucky to have you in my life."

She pressed a kiss to his still-damp hair.

"If I asked you to marry me … what would you say?"

Her heartbeat took off racing at a pace she knew he could hear, especially with his head on her chest, but his fingers didn't stop their gentle circles. He was emotionally compromised and she needed to be careful with her answer. "Kian … I'm not sure that—"

"Hypothetically, of course," he soothed. "And not a 'let's elope to stick one to my father' way."

"Oh. Good. Cause Zariah would kill me."

He snorted. "She'd kill both of us."

"Hypothetically," she said, speaking slowly. "I would say that I can see it in our future as much as you can, and that there's no rush. We've only just started and there is plenty of time to get there at our own pace. There's still so much we don't know about each other. Basic, everyday things. Mundane stuff like cleaning, or shopping. Waking up together. Finding out what your favorite book is, or fave movie. What makes you feel better when you're sick. Moving in together and figuring out how that would work. Learning all your unique idiosyncrasies, showing you mine. We need to do all that first. Then talk marriage."

He nodded, accepting that answer. "Things are going to be uncertain for a while. We need to stick together."

She brushed her hands along his shoulders. "So, come home to Paris with me."

"Home," he breathed in a weary and heart sore tone. "Never really had one."

"You have one with me. We can build it together."

"I want that," he said, lifting away from her chest so he could cup her face and gaze into her eyes. "Oh, I want that so much. No more rules. No more contracts. Just you and me, my precious rose."

He kissed her and it echoed the kiss he'd bestowed on her while dancing. She was completely and utterly treasured by him and there was no other way for him to tell her other than through his lips and his body.

He worshiped her and showed her in so many ways. The gentle kiss against her mouth, the fluttering of lips dancing across her skin, the delicate suck against her neck. Tender touches and soft grasps as he filled her. Holding her gaze as he whispered promises of love and adoration before he kissed her.

She returned everything, repaid his love with her own. Legs and arms enveloping him to cradle him close, to hold on tight, to make him feel like he deserved to be loved. Bittersweet lovemaking, she took his tears and his pain as well, distracting him from the feeling of abandonment by his family and gave him one of his own, a family he made by choice, to hold fast and uplift.

CHAPTER 25

The bell to Chant de La Rose's door rang again and Noémie raised her head from her sewing machine. The bell had been unusually noisy today. Lots of customers, but Veroniqué hadn't asked for assistance, so she assumed it wasn't anything she couldn't handle.

She lifted her arms above her head to stretch, then secured the adaptive commission she'd been working on before she rose. Veroniqué needed a croissant break soon and by the sound of that bell, needed a hand.

Customers today seemed to be younger women. Mid-twenties to late teens, some of them in pairs as they looked through stock.

Veroniqué rang up sales, with two people waiting in the queue and several milling around as they looked at items. Stepping up behind her, Noémie rested her hand on Veroniqué's shoulder. "Let's get these sorted so you can have a break," she said.

Veroniqué puffed out a breath. "Thank you."

Standing beside Veroniqué, Noémie beckoned to the next lady in line. "Bonjour, Madame. How may I help you today?"

The woman stared at her for a long moment, glanced

down, then back up. "You're her. Noémie Belrose-Song, right?" the woman gushed in English with an American accent, breaking into a grin as she shoved a magazine at Noémie. "You kissed Kian von Brandt! Are you together?"

Noémie tried to focus on the waving magazine. It seemed to be a gossip focused one, probably the one she'd been warned was coming out today. A full two-page spread and the largest picture was one of Noémie being completely and utterly kissed by Kian at the party.

A sinking feeling burrowed deep into her belly as several other women in the boutique turned their heads to study her.

So far, there had only been fluff pieces about her and Kian released. Acknowledgments that she and Kian were seeing each other and had attended a von Brandt party in America. General information about her and how they met, enough to whet the public's appetite for gossip. There had been no word from Celestial, or the von Brandt's reaction to Kian dating, but neither had they gone public with the split between Kian and his parents.

The von Brandts had been silent on all fronts and Noémie didn't understand how that was possible. In this age of free media and instant access to Twitter and other media platforms, there should be rumors galore, but while Noémie had heard that the socialite community in New York were lapping up the gossip, the media weren't reporting anything.

She'd googled and found a lot of pictures of her and Kian taken by paparazzi in America, especially when they'd ventured out to grab some hotdogs and see the sights, and not much else. No mention of the fight at all. When she asked Kian about it, he sighed and told her money bought a lot of things, including silence.

The gossip hadn't followed her back to Paris. In America, they hadn't been able to move without being snapped by paparazzi, but the attention had died when returning to Paris. Here, Kian was a model and the face of

Celestial, he wasn't Richard von Brandt's son, and Paris was reacting accordingly. There had been a few paparazzi waiting at the airport when they'd arrived home—her first time in first-class which was an experience—who had requested permission to take some shots. There'd been a few requests for interviews appearing in her business email, complete with cash incentives, but they were easy to turn down.

"Is this how you landed him?" the woman asked, holding up a negligee. "That's pretty sneaky. What's his favorite set? I'd love to have one!"

Noémie's eyes narrowed at being called 'sneaky'. It wasn't any of the woman's business. Trying to remember what Florian, Kian's French publicist, had told her, she smiled and said, "Kian and I were friends when we were teenagers and we recently reconnected."

"Ahh. I see," the woman said with a shrewd look in her eyes that reminded Noémie of Zariah looking for a story. "So the fact that he's the face of Celestial and you own a lingerie boutique had nothing to do with it?"

Noémie shook her head, not liking what the woman was implying. "I design exclusively for women."

"But you *are* a designer," the woman continued, looking like she'd sprung Noémie.

If the woman was going to grill her like a reporter, Noémie would treat her like one. "Yes," Noémie replied and lifted her hand to try to receive the garment the lady was holding. "Would you like to purchase that?"

"I'd like to purchase whatever Kian von Brandt fancies," the woman said. "Which one is his favorite?"

"I'm afraid you'll be disappointed. I would never disclose that information. Would you still like to buy that, or shall I return it to the rack for you?"

The woman made a huffy noise. "I'll buy it."

Noémie smiled and set about organizing the woman's purchase.

She encountered several customers, mostly American

tourists, who only wanted information on Kian, either asking about what lingerie he liked or what he was like as a person, one lady even asking if he ever came into her boutique and if she stayed, would she meet him. Some wanted Kian's autograph. Some wanted to see if she could get pictures of him. Some wanted to know if she had a secret sex dungeon out the back and if that was how she met Kian.

Some were polite, some were incredibly rude. There were several of them whose language degraded to name calling because she dared date him. While she'd been warned that some people would take Kian dating as a personal insult and to expect some backlash, it still hurt.

"I don't know how you do it," Veroniqué said as she opened a box so they could restock at the end of the day. "You politely denied them all, doesn't it make you angry that they ask?"

"It'll die down," Noémie said as she hung lingerie. "It's initial excitement, that's all. The same thing happened when people figured out I knew Zane."

"You're a hot commodity."

Noémie smiled. "Absolutely."

"It's good for business, I suppose," Veroniqué mentioned.

Noémie stilled and lowered her hands.

Veroniqué didn't seem to notice as she continued, "Imagine if you told them which one he liked. You could make hundreds of sales."

"We're not doing that," Noémie said more sharply than she intended.

Veroniqué jolted and swung to look at Noémie. "I'm sorry, I didn't mean—"

"No." Noémie cringed and rubbed her fingers on her forehead. "No, Veroniqué, I'm sorry. I shouldn't have snapped. It's …"

"A touchy subject."

"Yeah." Noémie touched Veroniqué's arm in apology.

"I couldn't do that to him. It's not why I entered a relationship with him and I don't like knowing that people think I'm using him."

"They don't know you like we do," Veroniqué said, remorseful. "I'm sorry, it was a joke in poor taste."

"Don't worry about it," Noémie replied and then gestured to the box. "Finish hanging these up then you can go home. Thank you for your hard work today."

Noémie waited until Veroniqué had left before she started tallying the numbers for the last few days. Normally, she did this on Friday, among all the other paperwork and orders, but today she needed to check.

There had been another hike in sales. It seemed to start with online sales on Sunday, the day after Kian's break from the family when the first media release occurred. It didn't seem to be any particular piece that was selling well, more like a general increase in sales. Not uncommon in the grand scheme of the way business worked, but she hadn't run any advertising beyond her normal internet banners and the exhibit, and her magazine spread wasn't due to be released for another week.

She took comfort in the fact that this new hike seemed to be a smaller hike than the one she'd had when she'd run the exhibit. It would probably continue to grow as more articles were released about their now-public relationship. She didn't like the feeling that her increased business was a result of him, as inevitable as it was and she hoped she spoke the truth about it to Veroniqué. It would die down as interest dwindled. She didn't want to be yet another person who used him to get ahead.

Even though he'd probably known that was going to happen anyway, she needed to talk to him about it.

Glancing at the time displayed on her phone, she sighed.

Kian would still be working at Celestial and putting in another late night and she wondered if she'd see him tonight or whether he'd wait until the weekend. He had to get things in order, and neither of his parents had spoken to him yet, so he worked under the assumption he was leaving. Life never stopped and let someone breathe when disasters happened, it kept moving along swiftly and people either followed or perished.

She gathered up the designs she was supposed to be working on during the day, packing them away so she could take them home with her. Gathering the little cash they kept on-site, she stowed it away in the hidden safe and locked up for the evening.

The air was brisk as she stepped out into it, and Noémie clutched her coat a little tighter, wondering if it would snow again.

"Mademoiselle Belrose?" a voice called in French, a heavy American accent prevalent. "Do you have a moment?"

Noémie sighed, watching her breath steam out ahead of her. A tall man in a business suit, she didn't get a read on him. Reporter? She didn't respond more than looking at the man.

"My name is Randall Farrell," he said and held out a business card. "I work for 'Silk to Pine for Lingerie' and we're expanding into Paris and looking for reputable lingerie boutiques to join our association. Chant de La Rose is a rising star in Paris and we are interested in purchasing the business."

Taking the card from him, Noémie's eyes widened in recognition. Randall Farrell. The person who supposedly sent those silk people to spy on Celeste. Silk to Pine for Lingerie? The name was in English and it was a mouthful. Did they have anything to do with Pineford silk? Probably. And if that was the case, she wanted nothing to do with him. "No."

Randall paused, then pressed, "I don't think you understand what we could offer you. If you would join me for dinner, we can discuss—"

"Chant de La Rose is not for sale," Noémie replied.

"This is highly rude. I do not know how it is done in America, but here, business hours are closed. It is time for rest and relaxation." She inclined her head and moved away. "Bonsoir."

"Miss Belrose, I apologize for not knowing the local customs. Please, if you could spare a moment—"

"Chant de La Rose is not for sale," she repeated.

"Would you at least look at the proposal?"

"Business hours begin at nine tomorrow." She pretended she didn't hear anything else as she walked away. If he was going to be rude and corner her, she was going to return that and leave. If he was serious, he'd return in the morning, during business hours.

The first thing she did when she got home was to kick off her heels and give Floof a chance to stretch his wings and clean out his cage. After sending Kian a text message saying she was home—and receiving an emoji heart in return—she made herself a sandwich and set up her laptop and tablet so she could get some work done.

Not much online about 'Silk to Pine for Lingerie'. A single branch in New York that seemed to be doing okay, according to the star ratings, but they seemed to be a new business. They were linked to Pineford Silks, no surprise there. Other than that, there wasn't much information. Non-entity. She wasn't interested.

She set that aside and opened a design sketchbook.

An hour or so later, she had half a dozen sketches of the new 'Zazzy' line she'd been imagining for a while and now had an incentive to create. The theme was bold stripes of color nestled within black, something she knew Zariah would adore. Orange, pinks, reds, and a striking royal purple. One set of Zariah's choice would be exclusive to her as a wedding present, but the rest she'd be free to sell in her store.

Smiling to herself, she sent Zariah a screenshot of what she was working on and received a lot of button mashing and gifs of cartoon characters with heart eyes and a '*gurl you know me so well! I want all of them'* message in return.

Stretching her arms above her head, she checked the time and went to refill her water bottle. She pulled out her sewing mannequin, selecting the first pattern she wanted to work on and set up her paper patterns.

Kian called close to nine, sounding exhausted. "It's going well," he told her and she could hear the noise of his car in the background. "My lawyer got back to me today and we have a couple of things prepared, whether that be a buyout or a partnership annulment … it depends on what my parents decide to do."

Putting her phone on speaker so she could continue to work, she said, "They still haven't reached out to you?"

"They probably assume that this will blow over. A temper tantrum. Mom will be in for a shock when she gets back."

"Just your mother? Not your father, too?"

"As far as I know, although it could be both of them. I can't wait for all this to be over, and things go back to … well, not normal. Better."

"I'm sorry."

"Don't worry, Noémie. I'm ready for it."

"I feel like I'm watching from the sidelines," she lamented. "I wish I could help more."

"You *are* helping," Kian insisted. "I wouldn't be doing this if it weren't for you."

She gave up all pretense of working while talking to him. "That's what I'm worried about."

"No, I mean, I wouldn't be doing it this way. I'd still do this, but it would be hard and fast and I wouldn't care who it hurt. With your support, I'm being sensible. I'm trying to do things in a way that doesn't bring any ire onto us in the long run. Plus, I'm looking for other jobs. You're helping me to do this the right way."

"Oh."

"I fucked up my communication twice with you. And maybe I'm overcompensating by telling you absolutely everything."

"Don't stop," Noémie said. "I like it."

He puffed out a breath. "Okay. Good. Oh, while I remember, I'm also updating my will. Rather than everything I have returning to my parents, I'm …" he snorted, "leaving it all to Purrfect. I was hoping I could put you down as her power of attorney."

Noémie's eyebrows shot up. "My boyfriend, the cat lady."

Kian laughed. "I like the sound of that."

"What? Cat lady?"

"Boyfriend," he purred. "You can do whatever you like with it, Noémie. Donate the lot if you want. But I want her looked after. It's just in case."

She didn't like to think about that but she understood why he felt he had to. "I would've made sure she was. But, yes, you have my permission."

"Thank you."

"I'll use the money to buy Purrfect a boyfriend, and call him Purrecious."

Kian snickered. "I see."

"And they can have babies; Purrincess, Empurrer, Shakespurr and … Spot."

"I love it. *Purrfect* names. I approve. I may even have to do it."

Noémie giggled. "What are you doing now?"

"Sooooo," Kian drawled and she could hear the humor in his voice. "I'm currently driving to my girlfriend's place. I'm hoping she'll come home with me for a night of sordid snuggling."

She smiled. "I see."

"Pretty please? I feel like I haven't seen you in years."

"Why don't you stay here?" she offered.

"I don't have anything and Purrfect has been alone all day. I'm probably going to come back to a bathroom full of shredded toilet paper again. "

Noémie laughed. "Have you eaten?"

"There would be a very slim chance of getting a table anywhere this late."

"I have fresh bread and frozen stew in the freezer. I'll bring it with me."

"Sounds delicious."

"How far away are you? I need a chance to clean this mess up and pack a bag."

"Are you designing?"

"I did that already, but now I'm assembling," she said and sighed. "And doing a poor job of it tonight. Need a handsome man to distract me."

"I'm so on that. Ten minutes away."

"Plenty of time. See you soon."

Noémie stared up at the ceiling, lying as still as she could while Kian curled against her. She wasn't sure the way Kian clung to her in his sleep was a good thing in the long run. It didn't feel the same as being snuggled back at the cabin, back before all this started. This was a clutch, as though he couldn't bear to let her go. In his fitful sleep, he roused every time she moved.

She didn't mind. His life was in turmoil right now, because she'd come into it. She was a catalyst for change, and maybe the change would be good and necessary, but right now, all Kian could feel was the bad.

It was okay for tonight. Or even the next week. The next few weeks would be hard for him and she would do everything in her power to make it easier. She needed to talk to someone about this and get some input on how to help him through. She wondered how asking him to see a therapist would go, or if it was even necessary at this point.

One thing she did know, she couldn't allow him to become too dependent on her for support. He needed a larger group than just her. That's where Zane would be able to make a difference. Charlie too.

All they had to do was wait to see what the von Brandt's retaliation would be.

CHAPTER 26

Standing in Kian's kitchen, wearing a silk slip nightgown, Noémie idly watched the bacon sizzle on the stove and fed Purrfect little bits of bacon rind. There was still some fresh bread from last night's stew which she could toast when the bacon and eggs were almost ready. She didn't often have bacon and eggs, preferring fruit or a croissant for breakfast, but she knew Kian liked them.

"Really not sure if you're allowed on the counter, Purrfect," Noémie said as she leaned on the counter and scratched the kitty behind her ears. "Our secret if he gets you in trouble."

Purrfect meowed at her and rubbed her face into Noémie's hand.

Scratching Purrfect under the chin, she said, "If this becomes a regular thing, we're going to have to discuss rules."

Purrfect flopped, exposing her belly and wriggled as she invited pats.

Noémie complied, lifting out of her lean to drink some of her coffee while she petted the cat. Carting her coffee cup over to the bacon to check it, she said, "Do you think he'd notice if I stole his coffee machine?"

"I'd definitely notice that," Kian said from the hallway. "But at least I know what to get you for a present."

Noémie threw a smile over her shoulder at him. "Good morning!"

Walking into the kitchen in his silk boxers and nothing else, Kian dropped a kiss on Noémie's temple and then headed for the coffee machine. "Morning. Want another one?"

"Still going on this one, thanks. How do you like your bacon?"

"Crispy."

Noémie wandered back to continue feeding bacon rind to Purrfect while Kian made himself a coffee.

"I think I could get used to this."

Noémie looked over at him. "Get used to what?"

Kian leaned his back against the bench and crossed his ankles. "Us. Snuggling all night. Waking up to the sound of you and Purrfect. Spending time together in our underwear in the kitchen. The simple things."

She laughed. "Don't get used to it."

"Why not?"

"I don't walk around in this at home. If I get comfortable, it'll be sweatpants and one of your shirts."

Kian's eyes widened, then he smiled with a dopey looking expression on his face. "You'd still look amazing. Even more so."

Shaking her head at him, she headed for the eggs so she could start cooking them. "So, what are your plans for today? And how many eggs?"

"Two, please. Let's see … hmm … meeting with my lawyer at ten for final checks, then I have one with my publicist at eleven-thirty … then that's it. There's nothing more I can do until I know what my parents decide. Maybe I'll come bother you."

Noémie cringed. "Bad idea."

"Why's that?" he asked, then straightened out of his lean. "Are you being harassed?"

She moved around the kitchen to fetch the bread so she could toast it. "If you call women asking which lingerie is your favorite, or whether I have a secret sex dungeon out the back, then yes, I'm being harassed. I mean, not all of them are polite."

He winked at her. "Tell them the red baby doll."

"I'm not telling them anything. I'm not going to use you for sales, Kian," she said, more sharply than she intended. Forcing her tone softer she continued, "It's mostly fans of yours. People who wanted to see if I could get an autograph, or check me out to see if I'm good enough, or accuse me of trying to use you. I went through the same thing when Zane wrote that song about Zariah and me."

He sounded woeful, "I'm sorry."

She waved her hand at him to indicate she wasn't sorry. "Florian really helped. I can handle the attention."

"I know you can. It's … probably going to get worse when people find out I'm going to quit modeling completely."

"What?" Noémie squeaked. "You are?"

"I'm twenty-four," he said. "I've already cut back on a lot of modeling and have moved on to focus on the business side of things. I just did it to help out Mom." His smile slipped into a smug grin. "And to seduce you."

"It worked."

"I know," he crooned, then lightened his tone. "I can still do photoshoots if I want, but the walks? Not for me anymore. But!" he chirped. "Here's the thing. I bet I could start my own modeling agency if I wanted to. I have all the interpersonal and management skills and I've already networked with all the fashion houses through Celestial."

Noémie tilted her head at him and sipped her coffee. "Would you be happy doing that?"

"I don't know," he said, grinning. "But I'm excited to think about the possibilities."

She smiled, happy that he was excited. It was a good

start.

"I thought I might take a class in photography too," Kian continued, his eyes shining. "Do some formal training. There's a couple of photographers I know that I could easily hire to give me some private lessons. I want something just for me."

Happiness bubbled in her chest. Making plans for the future, thinking about himself, all good signs. "That sounds like a good idea. Let me know before you announce you're quitting modeling, though. I'd like to be prepared for the lynch mob."

"I was thinking more like fading, rather than an official retirement." Kian scratched the stubble on his chin. "You said you went through this before. With Zane?"

Noémie nodded. "To a degree. I mean, I wasn't his girlfriend, just a friend. But the sentiment's there. My fifteen minutes of fame, so to speak."

"I think it'll be longer than fifteen minutes this time." Kian went to the cupboard to fetch some plates for their breakfast. "I wonder if he'd be willing to do a media piece with us. If we can remind the media you've rubbed shoulders with famous people before, they might be less likely to think you're some sort of gold digger."

Noémie turned from the toaster, putting the toast on the plates Kian had left for her. "Do we care what other people think?"

"For a while, we do," Kian said as he opened the fridge. "Juice?"

"Please. Then Zane probably won't mind."

Working together, they busied themselves with the final preparations of their breakfast. It was nice moving around each other as they cooked. An easy shift in their relationship, just being together. Kian was right, she could get used to this. As they sat at the table, Kian's doorbell rang.

With a putout expression, Kian rose again and headed for the panel beside the front door. Pressing a button on the intercom, he said, "Bonjour."

Celeste's voice was clear as it echoed through the speaker. "Petit lapin, this is degrading. Why did you change your codes?"

Noémie froze, her slice of bacon halfway to her mouth.

Kian shot Noémie a panicked glance, then pressed the button to speak. "What do you want, Mom?"

"I brought baguettes and ham."

Kian frowned. He shuffled his weight from side to side then said, "I thought you were in New York."

"I just got back. We can have breakfast together. Let me up."

Shaking his head in bewilderment, Kian said, "We *never* have breakfast here. You like to be waited on and—"

"First time for everything. Hurry up. People are looking."

Releasing the button, Kian turned toward Noémie and hurried, "There's a dressing gown in my bathroom you can wear if you want to. Can you lock Purrfect in my bedroom and grab a shirt for me, please?"

She rose, scooping Purrfect off the counter, who protested loudly at being torn away from bacon scraps. "Should I get dressed?"

"No," Kian said and pressed the button to let his mother up. "Let her see she's disturbing us."

Noémie hurried to do what he asked. Putting Purrfect on her cat scratching tree, she rushed into the bathroom, grabbed the blue plaid dressing gown and the first t-shirt she could find and closed the door on the way out to keep Purrfect inside.

Tossing the shirt to Kian, she followed his gesture to sit back at the table. Tying the rope of the dressing gown, she sat down and waited.

Kian slipped on his shirt, opened his front door enough that Celeste could get in, and returned to sit by Noémie. "This should be interesting," he muttered and reached for his knife and fork.

Too nervous to eat, Noémie picked up her coffee and tried to appear like she belonged. "We should've stayed at my place."

"Yeah. We should've."

"Kian," Celeste declared as she breezed into the room. She stopped at the threshold to the dining area and raised her eyebrows. "Noémie."

Noémie inclined her head in greeting.

Kian stabbed a piece of bacon with his fork. "What do you want, Mom?" he asked and shoved it into his mouth, chewing while he stared at her.

"Don't worry about your little temper tantrum." She flopped her hand and walked into the room. Placing the baguette she brought with her on the table, she sat opposite Kian. "All is forgiven, your father and I are—"

"No, it really isn't."

She didn't appear to hear him. "Everything's worked out. You don't have to marry Tiffany, and you get to be with Noémie. We can forget all this nonsense and move on with our lives."

With an exasperated noise, Kian said, "Mom, in case you didn't get the memo, I quit."

She dismissed that with a wave of her hand. "Don't be silly. Kian, fetch me a plate."

Kian didn't move from his chair. "Still no apology," he muttered. "I don't know why I expected one."

"I don't have anything to apologize for."

Noémie lowered her coffee to the table. "Calling what happened Saturday a 'temper tantrum', when it was clearly the result of years of accumulated anger and pain, diminishes your sense of responsibility and continues to hurt his feelings."

"Exactly," Kian said. Dropping his eyes to his food, he sliced an egg in half. "If you're not prepared to even acknowledge that then there's nothing more to say. You can see yourself out."

Celeste sat back in her chair and drummed her fingers

on the table. "I beg your pardon?"

Kian slapped the egg on a piece of toast, then lifted both morsels of food to his mouth to take a bite. Chewing, he stared at his mother.

Following Kian's cues, Noémie picked up a piece of toast and bit into it. The piece felt like it stuck in her throat and she washed it down with her juice.

Swallowing, Kian asked, "Ma chérie, would you like a ride to work this morning? I can drop you off on the way to see my lawyer."

Nodding, Noémie said, "Would you mind if we stopped at my place first, I'd like to check on Floof and—"

Sitting forward, Celeste interrupted, "Your lawyer? Why are you seeing your lawyer?"

Kian huffed. "Oscar has the partnership buyout papers. I expect you'll be served today since you're back in Paris."

Celeste's eyes widened and she paled. "You had papers drawn up?"

"When are you and Father going to start taking me seriously?" Kian snapped. His knife and fork clattered against his plate. "Ma rose, it's delicious," he said as he pushed away from the table. Dropping a kiss on the top of Noémie's head, he carried his plate toward the kitchen. "But I've lost my appetite."

Noémie nodded. "That's okay. I under—"

Celeste declared, "You can't go through with this."

"Too late," Kian replied, loudly scraping his food into the trash. "It's all drawn up."

Tossing her mane of blonde hair, Celeste announced, "Your father and I are getting a divorce."

"And somehow she makes it about her," Kian muttered and his plate clanged against the bench. He jerked open the dishwasher. "So, guess that means Helena will get what she wants. Yay."

Celeste shrugged. "Don't know and I really don't care. Petit lapin, as part of the settlement, I get Celestial. All of them. They're mine, to do with as I please. I want you to be the new CEO."

"No."

Noémie glanced over her shoulder at him. Kian had braced his hands against the island bench in the middle of the kitchen as he glared at his mother.

"Kian," Celeste chided. "I'm offering you the responsibility you always wanted. Don't be ungrateful."

Kian laughed bitterly. "No. You want me to choose between you and Father and I'm not going to do that."

Her hand to her chest in disbelief that her son would dare speak back to her, Celeste looked the very picture of a hurt, betrayed mother.

Unfazed, Kian pressed, "I'm sorry you and Father are divorcing but I'm not surprised. I meant what I said. I'm done. Please leave."

Celeste's gaze darted between Noémie and Kian, unable to believe. "How are you going to survive?" she asked. "You can't afford to live without—"

Kian snarled, "You have no idea what I can afford. What business investments I've made. All the charities I've donated to in an attempt to do something *good* with this completely unnecessary shitload of money you throw at me so I don't 'embarrass the family' again. Did you really think I'd take him cutting me off lying down? That I'd just rest on my laurels and take what he gave me? You have no clue what I'm worth without you. I *own* this apartment, Mom. This and a dozen others like it around the world. And I don't even like it. It's all for show, because I'm a von Brandt and it's expected. I have a cat that I have to hide every time you come around because it's too *domestic* for you. Maybe I'll sell this and buy something I can be myself in. A garden for Purrfect. Somewhere Noémie will feel at home too."

During Kian's speech, Celeste's eyes had been growing wider and her face had been losing color. At the mention of Noémie, Celeste's eyes snapped to her and she snarled,

"So, you got what you wanted."

"Yes," Noémie replied, not allowing Celeste's verbal swipe at her connect. Unlike Celeste, she'd been watching Kian with a sense of pride and now she smiled at him. "I got Kian's love. That's all I ever wanted."

Celeste abruptly stood, the chair she sat on squeaking against the floor. "I can tell when I'm not wanted." She grabbed her bag and threw it over her shoulder. "After everything I've done for you."

Kian made a noise of disgust. "Here we go."

"I raised you, I sacrificed for you—"

"Celeste," Noémie said, interrupting her as she rose from her chair as well. "I don't doubt that you love your son. He knows that you do. He just wanted that love to be unconditional."

Celeste gave her a haughty, offended look. "How dare you—"

"How we feel about someone is a very personal experience," Noémie said, walking to the door. "For parents. For lovers. For friends. If you *feel* something, in your bones, it's hard to look beyond that even when logic says something else. He feels like your love has conditions and expectations he can't possibly live up to." Noémie opened the front door and looked at Celeste expectantly as she waited. "Maybe you should prove him wrong."

Celeste swung to appeal to Kian, who simply gestured for the door. With a loud, overly-exaggerated huff, Celeste stalked toward the door. "Fine. I can take a hint. Don't come crying to me when it goes bad for you."

"I won't," Kian called.

With one last glare at Noémie, Celeste stalked through the door and Noémie closed it behind her.

Turning away from the door, Noémie was smothered by Kian's embrace. Arms over the top of hers, he picked her up and squashed her to his chest. "I love you so much."

Noémie laughed. "I love you too."

"I've never seen her so stunned," Kian said. "That was amazing." Plopping her back on the ground, he changed his grip on her. Arms beneath hers, stooping down to grab the back of her thighs, he picked her up and wrapped her legs around his waist. "I'm the luckiest guy in the world."

Noémie looped her arms across his shoulders. "We've got time before I need to be at work if you want to have dessert."

Kian spun on his heels and carried her toward the bedroom. "I like the way you think."

CHAPTER 27

Humming to herself, Noémie studied the mannequin torsos. She'd asked Veroniqué to put together a display for the front window in the hope of increasing Veroniqué's fashion confidence and it looked like it was working. "Nice choices," she said, nodding in approval.

Veroniqué beamed with pride. "Thank you."

"Bold, complementary colors, with a variety of styles. We should switch one of them for an adaptive piece."

Adjusting the turn of her chair, Veroniqué said, "I thought maybe Lucy could wear the adaptive piece this week."

Most of the mannequins Noémie had in her store were torso ones, easy to move and dress, but Lucy, their one realistic mannequin, lived in the window and was difficult to relocate so she was redressed there.

Veroniqué wheeled over to the table and presented her idea; an orange lace teddy. "What do you think?"

Noémie flicked a glance at Veroniqué's other pieces, then broke into a smile. "Rainbow!" she said, delighted. "It's perfect."

Veroniqué and Noémie spent a few minutes taking photos of the torsos against the blue curtain so that

Noémie could update the boutique's Instagram page. After that, Noémie threw the orange teddy over her shoulder, picked up the first torso and hauled it out into the boutique.

Dulcie spoke to Randall Farrell, who smiled as he saw her. "Mademoiselle Belrose," he said in greeting, speaking French.

Noémie placed the torso on the floor behind the front counter, out of the way of the hallway. Pulling the orange teddy from her shoulder, she let it hang over the torso. "Dulcie," she said and nodded to a customer by the baby dolls. "They need assistance. I'll handle this."

Wide-eyed, Dulcie took the hint and excused herself.

She stepped up to the counter and clasped her hands together. "It's Mademoiselle Belrose-Song, Monsieur Farrell."

"My apologies," he said with a sheepish smile. He placed a briefcase on the counter beside her and clicked the two locks on the side. "We seem to have started on the wrong foot. I'm here on behalf of—"

"I have no interest in selling my boutique," she told him. "I thought I made that clear."

"We have a unique opportunity," Randall said, beginning his sales pitch with no regard for the fact she said no. He reached into his briefcase and pulled out a folder. "A mutually beneficial partnership. Silk to Pine For has a large boutique in New York, you have a rapidly growing clientele here and we feel with our guidance, we can grow this business into something that can rival the great fashion houses. We also have a world-renowned silk supplier, Pineford Silks, who are willing to fund designs and provide silk. As outlined, we would be willing to keep you on as a manager, as well as any staff you have. It's a lucrative deal for both parties." He placed the folder on the counter and pushed it toward her. "All we ask is that you look through our offer."

"Monsieur Farrell," she said, steepling her fingers on

the folder and pushing it back. "You're not hearing me. We're not for sale. And I'll be honest. I've had dealings with Pineford Silk before and I'm not interested."

"It's a very lucrative deal," he repeated as if that could make a difference. "It could set you up for life."

The bell on the door tolled. Noémie and Dulcie called, "Bonjour!" in greeting.

"Ugh," the person who entered complained in English. "Uncle Randy, it's so tacky. I can't believe you'd think this one was suitable."

A shiver ran through Noémie. She knew that voice, it was etched into her brain. Turning her eyes to the door, her eyes widened as she saw Tiffany standing there.

Uncle Randy. *Uncle.*

Tiffany's eyes were glazed as she looked around the shop, passing over Noémie as if she wasn't there. She huffed, then lifted her hand to check her nails. "It's too small. I need to impress him, not bore him to bits."

Tiffany. Here in Paris. Obviously looking for a way to win Kian back. She wasn't going to let him go without turning everything into a dramatic fight. She also didn't appear to recognize Noémie. To her, Noémie was just another retail worker. Some Eurasian woman that didn't mean anything, because she wasn't glamoured up to high heaven.

Randall sighed and answered her in English. "You need a foothold in Paris. We want the designs and clientele, not the shop itself. Amalgamated with the other small boutiques, we'll have a larger base."

Noémie narrowed her eyes at the conversation. Clearly, Randall didn't know she spoke English. He hadn't done his research. He didn't even seem to know who *she* was. How could he not know that?

"But Uncle Randy—"

"Beggars can't be choosers, Tiffany," Randall scolded.

"Whatever. Just get on with it."

Dulcie turned and gave Noémie a significant look, but

Noémie shook her head and gave her a subtle signal to ignore it. No point causing a scene.

Randall picked up his briefcase and left the folder. "Thank you for your time, Miss Belrose-Song," he said in French. "Please, if you decide to change your mind, the offer is still on the table."

Noémie pressed her lips together and refused to answer, less Tiffany recognize her voice.

Tiffany looked at Noémie at the mention of her name, but did nothing but pout.

Why didn't Randall know who she was? She and Kian were all over gossip magazines at the moment. Perhaps that was egotistical of her. Maybe Randall didn't know what had occurred in New York. Maybe Tiffany lied to him. She had no idea, but she was more than relieved when the pair left the boutique.

"What was that about?" Dulcie called.

Noémie shrugged, not knowing how to explain it.

Dulcie stared at the door in disbelief. "She was so rude."

"Yes. She was. I'll be right back." Reaching under the counter for her phone, Noémie walked toward the back room for a little privacy. She couldn't believe Tiffany was actually here, in Paris, and still under the notion that Kian would want to see her. Kian needed to know she was here before she started causing trouble.

Noémie tried calling him, but the call went straight to voicemail, something not uncommon given the week he'd had. Rather than leave a voicemail, which might get lost among many, she sent him a quick text about Tiffany. He'd get back to her when he got off the phone.

Then she called Milo as a courtesy and asked him to inform Celeste about Tiffany and Randall's visit and what was said. She wasn't quite sure why she did that, but a part of her felt she owed Celeste a heads up at least.

Once that was done, there wasn't anything else she could do unless one of them got back to her, so she got back to work and picked up the torso again.

"We're going to switch out the window," she told Dulcie, seeing that she was free of customers. "Veroniqué has the rest ready, I'll get started on Lucy."

"Sounds good," Dulcie replied and disappeared down the hallway to help Veroniqué.

Kicking off her shoes, Noémie climbed into the window display and took a few minutes to shift all the old torsos out of the way so they could get Veroniqué's picks in the window, then started on Lucy.

Undressing the mannequin, she passed the old lingerie piece to Veroniqué as she arrived. "Do you want her in the middle?"

Veroniqué beamed. "Lucy should always be the center of attention."

"That she should," Noémie said and undid the studs at the bottom of the teddy in preparation for dressing Lucy.

"*You stupid bitch!*"

Something crashed into the window and cracked the glass. Time seemed to slow as Noémie turned her head, trying to figure out what was going on.

"I knew it was you!" Tiffany slammed her hand on the glass, a tabloid magazine with Noémie and Kian's picture displayed. "Did you think I wouldn't figure you out?" Her face red with rage, she swung her handbag like a club in a second assault on Noémie's window. It hit with a bang, slamming into an already weakened plane of glass.

It shattered and glass flew and Noémie instinctively cowered.

Veroniqué shrieked. Dulcie, farther back in the boutique, cried out.

"You're dead!" Tiffany shrieked, scrambling through the hole she made in the window. Calling Noémie several horrible names, she swung her handbag again and it connected with Noémie's upper arm.

The blow hurt like hell. It felt like the bag was full of bricks. Noémie staggered, trying to scramble away from the insane woman. Shards of glass cracked beneath her stockinged feet, cutting into her skin. Desperate to protect herself, she grabbed the stand of one of the torsos and interposed it between them to act as a shield.

She hunkered behind the torso and moved it side to side to intercept Tiffany's handbag strikes. Noémie tried to think, tried to act, but there was only time to react. So loud, so scary, glass everywhere, and a banshee screaming at her. Tiffany wasn't the only one shrieking. Dulcie bellowed, Veroniqué yelled, customers in the shop cried out, and people in the street beyond were beginning to shout warnings.

She threw a wild glance to the side, backing away as much as she could. She stumbled down from the raised floor by the window, trying to step between the gaps of shattered glass while keeping Tiffany at bay. "Dulcie! Call the police!"

Still ranting and screaming, Tiffany continued to swing her bag wildly as she tried to attack Noémie. She was like a rabid bear, she didn't care what damage she was doing, all she thought about was hurting Noémie.

Terror filled her. So much glass, it was impossible to navigate while trying to ward off the flying handbag. Her feet stung, she stood mostly on her toes trying to lessen the amount of damage she was doing to them. Her arm ached from that first blow and a dozen places on her tweaked. She had to stay on her feet, if she fell …

Tiffany's bag slammed against one of the racks and sent it flying toward Veroniqué. Stuck in her wheelchair, there was no way for her to dodge.

Noémie saw red as the rack's engulfed Veroniqué. "Hey!" she bellowed. She hoisted up the torso so she could grip the metal stand. Swinging the torso toward Tiffany like a club, it connected with Tiffany's arm, knocking her back.

Tiffany staggered and Noémie planted the top of the torso on Tiffany's chest and shoved her back. Using this technique, she managed to force Tiffany against a wall. Bracing her legs, she formed a wedge to hold her there. "What the hell is your problem?!" Noémie shouted and peered over her shoulder. "Dulcie?!"

"You can't have him," Tiffany snarled, trying to wriggle out from beneath the pressure Noémie was exerting on her chest.

"That's not up to you!" Noémie yelled back.

"You complete slag! You seduced him!"

Noémie rolled her eyes. She glanced over her shoulder, trying to see what was happening behind her.

Tiffany grabbed the torso and tried to shove it away from her chest. "He'll come back to me! I can offer him so much more than you can!"

She couldn't offer him acceptance, compassion, and love, but Noémie wasn't going to engage with this. Let Tiffany sprout whatever lies she needed to tell herself. "Dulcie?"

Veroniqué let out a small, pained cry. "I need help."

"You're a fucking retail worker," Tiffany declared like it was a bad thing. "You're not even a designer!"

"They're coming!" Dulcie yelled, racing around the front desk to get to Veroniqué. "V, hang on!"

People started appearing in the shop, passersby came to offer aid, and Chant de La Rose was inundated with a whirlwind of activity. One of the bakers from across the street took it upon himself to restrain Tiffany, who was now openly weeping and still calling Noémie names. A woman wearing the uniform of the men's tailor several doors down helped Dulcie untangle Veroniqué from the rack of lingerie.

Randall appeared in the crowd, face pale, brow dotted with sweat as he tried to get the baker to release his niece and was mostly ignored. People swapped stories or helped move the remaining racks of lingerie to the corner so it was out of the way. People milled curiously outside.

Police officers arrived to take control of the situation,

as well as a medical team to assess the physical damage. There was a yell as one of the police officers attending upended Tiffany's bag. Among the clutter was a torn copy of the latest gossip magazine and a brick. The banshee started screaming again after that, claiming the brick was planted.

The adrenaline she'd had coursing through her veins drained, leaving Noémie feeling weak-kneed and light-headed. If Tiffany had connected that with her head, she could have killed Noémie.

One of the medical team members helped Noémie over to sit in a chair by the changing rooms. Veroniqué was already there, being treated for several cuts to her hands, with Dulcie fretting nearby.

"Dulcie," Noémie said, catching the distraught woman's hand. She needed to be practical. Get things done. "I need you to lock the back rooms and get the police our security camera footage."

Dulcie sniffled and wiped her nose. "Do you want me to bank everything?"

"Please," Noémie said. They didn't have much cash on site, most people preferred to pay by card, but it was better to remove all cash from the premises as the window would be compromised. She winced as the technician cut her stockings so he could get to her feet. "Can you get my phone too, please?"

Dulcie nodded, hurrying away.

Noémie rested her hand on Veroniqué's shoulder. "Are you okay? Do you want me to call your mother?"

Tearfully, she nodded, her wide eyes fixed on the ranting Tiffany. "Who is that woman? What's she saying?"

"A lot of garbage," Noémie replied, hissing in pain as her foot was turned. "I'm so sorry you were caught up in this."

One of the neighboring stores brought in a large board to secure the window for the night, and the police said they would help install it once they'd finished taking photos and statements for their investigation.

Noémie hurt and she didn't want to look to see the damage. Her feet were the worst, having to dance around and evade attacks over glass. Her arm ached from where the bag first hit and it would probably bruise. Keeping her eyes firmly on her phone and not her feet, Noémie set about doing the harder tasks.

Noémie made several phone calls. First, she called her building's agent to inform them what had happened and start the process of getting the windows replaced. Second was to Veroniqué's mother to explain there'd been an incident and Veroniqué had been injured and needed help getting home. After that, she called the insurance company to let them know she'd be logging a claim and get the forms necessary emailed. Then, after all that, she called Kian.

"Hey," he said, answering on the second ring. "Got your message, I'm—"

Noémie nearly burst into tears at hearing his voice. Everything was suddenly too much for her to cope with. When she tried to speak, her words came out a muffled sob.

"Noémie?"

She gulped in a breath. "She attacked me."

"*What?*"

"The police are here," she mumbled. "There's glass everywhere and my feet…"

Feet thumped against the pavement. "I'm coming. Hang on, I'm not far."

She hung up and stared at the phone in her hands.

Tiffany sat in the corner, sobbing loudly, with Randall arguing her case with the officer questioning her. Several other officers were collecting witness reports and other evidence, including the footage from the cameras.

Noémie sat and gazed blankly at the window and poor Lucy as the hustle and bustle occurred around her. The technician finished with her feet and moved away to report to the police.

Dulcie, having finished her tasks, came to sit beside Veroniqué. "What happens now?" she asked, worrying her thumbnail with her teeth.

Noémie tried to smile and it came out a grimace. "You two go home. Full pay until the boutique is fixed and restocked. Don't worry about a thing."

"Noémie, we're not concerned about that," Dulcie soothed. "Just let us know what you need. We're here."

She swallowed hard and nodded. "Thank you. I think everything should be sorted. The agency knows, they'll send someone soon and—"

Her attention was drawn to the door as Kian arrived at a run and her heart sang at the sight of him. He was here, everything would be okay.

After a brief word to the officer outside, he was allowed in. He entered slowly, his eyes darting from the broken windows, to the blood on the floor, to Noémie, Veroniqué, and Dulcie.

From her corner, Tiffany gasped dramatically. "Kian!" she shouted and tried to get past the officer questioning her.

Kian completely ignored Tiffany as he moved through the room, heading straight for Noémie.

Randall, oblivious to where Kian was looking, stood in his way. "There you are," he said in English.

"Randall," Kian muttered. "Why am I not surprised?" He sidestepped and moved around the man. "You really don't want to be here right now."

"This is all a misunderstanding," Randall said, trying to be soothing as he followed Kian. "It's a simple lover's tiff. A cry for attention. You know Tiffany is prone to theatrics."

"I don't care," Kian said.

Grabbing Kian's arm, Randall pressed, "I'm sure we can work something out, I need you to help me with that girl."

Kian pulled up short and turned to Randall. "*That girl?*" he asked, anger biting his tone.

Randall didn't appear to notice as he waved his hand in Noémie's direction. "Charm her, bribe her. Do your thing."

"My *thing?*" Kian spluttered, affronted.

"Convince her this was a misunderstanding. We can pay for her silence and the damage done to her shop."

"You can't be serious."

"Tiffany's your girlfriend," Randall's voice turned scolding. "It's your duty to make this go away. You've clearly been away too long and have forgotten where your loyalties lie—"

Noémie piped up, speaking English. "You can't bribe your way out of this, Monsieur Farrell," she said, pleased when Randall looked her way and paled. "I will be making a complaint."

"And I'll be backing *my girlfriend* all the way," Kian snarled, shaking his arm out of Randall's grip. "The girlfriend your niece attacked. In broad daylight, with a multitude of witnesses. I don't know what lies Tiffany's been spinning or why you'd be stupid enough to believe her delusions. Let me spell it out for you; we aren't dating. I haven't seen her in years."

Randall seemed flabbergasted. "But—"

"She can't talk her way out this time. Tiffany's *done*. Take off your fucking blinders and look at the news once in a while," he continued, turning back to Noémie. "Are you okay?"

Noémie crossed her ankles and tucked her feet beneath the chair and held out both her hands to him. "I'm okay."

Reaching her, he took her hands in one of his and hunkered down so he could wrap an arm around her. She curled her hands under his arms to the back of his shoulders to hug him back. Still cuddling, he dropped down to one knee beside her. Pulling back, he looked her over, getting paler and paler as he did and in spite of her hiding her feet, he saw the bandages she had. "Your feet?"

"Glass cuts," she replied, ignoring the fact that Tiffany had started calling Kian's name, moaning it like she was being hurt. "I'm glad you're here."

"Kian," Tiffany pleaded. "Please, I need to talk to you!"

Ignoring her, Kian kept his gaze on Noémie. "Noémie, sweetheart, I'm so sorry." He stretched out a hand and touched below a small bruise that was forming on her cheek. "I never thought she'd go this far."

Nodding, Noémie squeezed his hand. She let out a shaky breath and said, "I need to go see a doctor and get a report done for the police. Some cuts require more attention than the technician could give."

Kian swallowed hard. "My car isn't far, I'll drive you," he said, then looked at Dulcie and Veroniqué. "Did you get hurt?" he asked, switching to French. "I can drive you to a hospital, or home, whichever you prefer."

Both Dulcie and Veroniqué started talking together, telling Kian what happened. Kian, listening intently, gently touched the back of Veroniqué's hands to inspect the bandage. He extended his hand further to squeeze Dulcie's hand to show solidarity, then returned to Noémie.

Noémie didn't know how he managed to follow Dulcie's and Veroniqué's story, but he nodded along, allowing them to speak, offering sympathy at Veroniqué's injuries.

Tiffany let out a banshee cry as one of the officers snapped handcuffs over her wrists. She proceeded to weep, complain, and call Kian's name as she was escorted to the door. It wasn't until she kicked one of the officers and tried to make a break for it that Kian turned to watch.

"Well. Now she's done it," he muttered, then turned back to Noémie. "What do you need?"

"I just want my boutique back," she said. "Some peace and quiet. And a hug."

Wrapping his arms around her again, he stroked her back. "I'll see what I can do about the rest of it."

CHAPTER 28

By the time they'd finished gathering all reports for the police, as well as having Noémie's feet tended to, it was late in the evening and Noémie was exhausted. Kian had been more than attentive during the day, barely leaving her side and insisting on carrying her everywhere rather than allow her to walk.

While they'd been at the hospital, Kian had received an email from Amanda, letting him know that Tiffany had released her 'version' of events early that morning in America. Tiffany claimed that she was Kian's longtime secret fiancé until Noémie had seduced him away with her wicked French wiles. She painted Noémie as nothing but a whore after Kian's money. She said that her mother had been in the longtime employment of Richard von Brandt, who used his position of power to coerce sex from Helena. Tiffany even went as far as to accuse Celestial of bribing both Tiffany and her mother to keep them silent about the whole affair. It also claimed that Tiffany was coming to Paris, determined to 'rescue' Kian.

Unfortunate timing for Tiffany. Because of her actions, the attack on Noémie was already in the news in Paris. Kian called Amanda and explained the situation and

Amanda said she'd liaise with Florian to form a response with emphasis on the fact that Noémie had been injured during an altercation initiated by Tiffany.

Tired, sore, and ready for some quiet time, Noémie snuggled into Kian's chest as he carried her up the stairs to her apartment.

"I could probably find a pizza place or Chinese for takeout," Kian said.

"There's a coupon on my fridge," she said, getting her keys out of her handbag. "We can get pizza delivered."

"Sounds perfect."

A wonderful smell wafted down from the landing near her door and Noémie's mouth watered as they drew closer. "Or," she said, excited. "We could have Maman's soup!"

"Is that what the smell is?" Kian asked, eager.

As she unlocked the door, she heard Floor and her mother whistling inside. "Hello!" she called, giving the door a shove so they could get inside.

"Noémie!" Roxanne rushed, slipping Floof back into his cage so she could hurry over. "How are you? Oh my goodness, your feet!"

"I'm okay," she said as Kian nudged the door closed with his foot. "Looks worse than it is!"

"Jin!" Roxanne scolded, rushing across to bat at her husband's feet. "Off the sofa! Kian needs to put Noémie down."

Jin, from his comfy position on the sofa, snorted and blinked blearily at them. "Oh!" he said, snapping awake.

For a few minutes Noémie was fussed over. Cushions placed beneath her feet, her jacket taken by Kian, and long hugs from her anxious parents.

"We were worried." Roxanne leaned back from her hug.

Jin, overprotective, fluffed her pillows. "Are you comfortable?"

"I'm fine, Papa," Noémie soothed and touched his hand. "Stop fussing."

"We have dinner for you both," Roxanne said, pointing to the kitchen. "I didn't think you'd want to cook tonight."

"Thanks, Maman."

Roxanne followed Kian as he moved to hang their coats. "Good to see you, Kian. Thank you for keeping us updated."

"Great to see you, too." He smiled, and then was smothered in a hug from Noémie's mother. Looking at Noémie with wide eyes, Kian returned Roxanne's hug.

Roxanne pulled back and patted Kian's chest. "How are you holding up?"

"I've been better," Kian said.

"Go and sit with Noémie," Roxanne instructed, walking into the kitchen. "I'll serve dinner."

Partway across the room toward Noémie, Kian's phone beeped and he lifted it. Eyes widening, he said, "I need to make a call, may I use your bedroom?"

Noémie smiled and nodded. "Go ahead. Soup?" she asked Roxanne. "It smells delicious. We could smell it all the way up the stairs."

Happily preparing bowls, Roxanne chirped, "Not too extravagant because we didn't know how long you'd be. There's fresh bread to go with it and a treat for both of you. Jin, can you come help, please?"

Jin hurried to the kitchen, returning with fresh-cut bread and a bowl of soup which he placed on the coffee table in front of Noémie. She scooted to the edge of the sofa and picked up her spoon.

"Shall I serve one for Kian?" Roxanne asked, looking toward the bedroom as if he could answer through the walls.

"Wait until he's off the phone," Noémie said, blowing across the top of her spoon to cool her soup. "He's been on and off it for ages, trying to get things organized." Having a mouthful of soup, she licked her lips. "This is delicious, Maman!"

Roxanne smiled as she carried over her and Jin's bowls.

"Thank you."

"What kind of things?" Jin asked.

Noémie ripped up a piece of bread to soak up the soup. "He's been organizing a few things. Making sure Veroniqué's okay. Talking to his publicists here and in America. He's organizing a cleanup crew to help with the glass tomorrow and is getting unbreakable glass for my windows so this doesn't happen again." Seeing her parents place their soups on the opposite side of the coffee table, she passed over two cushions for them to sit on.

"Unbreakable glass?" Jin asked. "Will your landlord cover that?"

"Kian said he'll pay the excess," she said, glancing toward the bedroom. "He feels responsible, even though he's not. But it's important for him to feel like he's got some control over the situation, he has so little control over everything else right now, so I'm letting him do that."

Concerned, Roxanne stirred her soup and said, "Does he expect more jilted ex-lovers to come out of the woodwork?"

Noémie shook her head and lifted a spoon to her mouth, blowing across the top of it. "Tiffany's the only one who has a problem with us."

Roxanne and Jin exchanged worried glances, then Roxanne leaned forward. "How's he really doing?"

Considering her words, Noémie dunked a piece of bread and ate it. "Sad and trying to hide it. But he's also hopeful and energetic and looking forward to having options."

A sense of relief from Roxanne and she smiled. "That's good to hear."

"I can't imagine what he's going through," Jin added.

Roxanne stretched her hand across the table and took Noémie's. "Noémie, we're worried about you. Both of you. This sort of thing … You're in the news and … I've been having customers asking if we're related! Now you've been attacked!"

"I know, Maman," Noémie said with a nod to acknowledge her mother's worries. "I never expected this either, and neither did Kian. We know the media interest will die down eventually. Kian and I went out together for weeks before people were told. I'm a hot commodity right now, that's all. Zane doesn't get accosted in the street and neither does Kian."

"But they do," Roxanne insisted. "Maybe not on the street, but they do on the internet. Emails. Instagram. All of those places. Living in a fishbowl is not what we imagined for you."

"It won't be like this all the time," Noémie promised. "Yeah, he's famous, but he's not international movie star famous. Take off the makeup and hair gel and he's just Kian. People recognize the name, especially in the fashion world or America, but the average person won't. We go out in public together all the time and no one has said anything. Plus," she continued, getting riled. "Zariah said she hasn't seen anything in London in the normal papers, only the fashion ones. This will die down."

"Still, you're at the mercy of public opinion," Jin said. "There's really no choice but to ride out both its approval and scorn. That doesn't mean we have to like it. We'd be remiss as parents if we didn't talk to you about it."

Roxanne added, "Kian is wonderful, he really is. But he comes with a lot more baggage than we anticipated."

With a nod at his wife, Jin agreed, "Most people do, once you get to know them."

"I appreciate the concern," she said smiling at her parents. "I understand where you're coming from. I'm really *happy* with Kian. Regardless of what's happening right now, I'm still happy and I want to be with him."

"We can see that," Roxanne said and leaned forward. "But, ma fée, what are people going to do when Kian announces he's breaking from his parents? Or leaving Celestial? Don't you think some of them will blame you?"

There had been no official word about the divorce, not

yet, and out of respect for his mother, Kian had delivered his resignation and partnership buyout papers to Celeste and left it at that. Noémie would be lying if she said she wasn't worried. "Which is why we're doing this carefully."

"We're worried," Jin said, resting his hand over the top of his wife's.

Noémie nodded. "Me too."

"If there ever becomes a point where it's too much, we hope you know that it's okay to take a step back."

She blinked at him, and then her look of surprise morphed to a frown.

"Not from Kian!" Jin rushed. "From the media circus. Don't be surprised if he asks the same sort of thing, or pulls away from you. A loved one getting hurt is incredibly hard. Even though it's not his fault, I bet he blames himself."

Closing her eyes, Noémie nodded. "He does." Opening them back up, she concentrated on eating her food.

Roxanne asked, "Can we help with the store tomorrow? Your feet are in no condition to be moving around. Jin and I can fetch and carry. We'll be happy to—"

"I'm not sure what's happening yet." She looked at her feet, wondering how bad they would be tomorrow. Most of them were minor cuts which hurt if she tried to walk on them, but two gashes had to be glued and she suspected her feet would swell overnight. "It depends on how I'm feeling."

"We could bring a picnic lunch," Roxanne said and wiggled her eyebrows. "Hot chocolates and sandwiches."

Noémie laughed. "That would be appreciated. Thanks."

The three of them had finished eating and were sitting around the coffee table enjoying hot chocolates by the time Kian was done on the phone.

Roxanne made to rise. "Are you hungry, Kian? Come sit down, I can—"

"Thanks, I'll get it," he said, moving into the kitchen.

"Everything okay?" Noémie asked.

"Yeah," he said, and stooped down to get himself a bowl from the cupboard. "Everything's fine. This smells delicious, Roxanne."

Roxanne beamed. "Thank you."

Within the hour, Roxanne and Jin had cleaned up the kitchen, done the dishes, and bid them farewell to head home.

Tired, Noémie sighed. Folding sideways, she lay down on the sofa and propped her feet up. "Ahh."

"How's the pain?" Kian asked as he locked the front door.

"Manageable," she replied.

Reaching into the pocket of his winter coat hanging by the front door, he pulled out the painkillers the doctor had prescribed. "Have some now, it'll kick in by the time you're ready to sleep."

"Good idea."

He filled a glass of water for her and brought it and the painkillers over. "Do you need help having a shower?"

She scooted over so he could sit down on the sofa by her hips. "You just want to see me naked."

He flashed her a grin and held out the glass. "That's a given."

After taking the painkillers, she fixed her eyes on him. "How are you?"

He dismissed that with a wave of his hand and a smile. "Don't worry about me." He leaned across her, resting his elbow on the back of the sofa. "I'm more concerned with you."

"We've been looking after me all day," she said and rested her hand on his chest. "Your feelings are just as important."

He balled his hand and propped his elbow on the sofa, using his fist as a headrest. "What do you want to know?"

She chewed her lip. "You didn't yell. You didn't even look at her."

"I walked in there, all I saw was you."

She poked him in the belly. "Flirt."

"It's true." He rested his free hand on her stomach and tucked a finger between the buttons on her blouse so he could touch bare skin. "I never thought she'd come here, but I really should've expected. Tiffany thrives on attention, negative or positive. If I engaged, that would've been seen as a win and given her incentive to keep going." He sighed. "Florian—that's who was on the phone before—said Mom responded to Tiffany's media release."

Noémie's eyes widened. "Really?"

His finger made little circles on her belly. "She responded by firing Tiffany and launching legal actions against her for breaching a non-disclosure agreement."

"Holy shit," she breathed, unable to believe Celeste went there. "Wait, so Tiffany was still working for Celestial as well as this … Piney Silk thing?"

"Seems like it, which wouldn't have worked in her favor either. It's more than enough reason to fire her." He hummed. "The speed at which it happened suggests that Mom's been poised to strike for a while. Though, I'm really surprised that's all she did, if I'm honest."

She adjusted her head on her pillow. "What do you mean?"

"Mom's very much a fan of killing two birds with one stone, but she didn't even take a swing at Father. There was no media release. No mudslinging. She acted and didn't make a big deal out of it."

Noémie considered. "Maybe that's coming."

He wrinkled his nose. "Maybe."

"Or maybe she's listening to you."

He nodded. "That's what I'm hoping for. Florian made some discreet inquiries and said the non-disclosure agreement Tiffany broke involved some sort of bribery on her part. Florian implied Tiffany had some sort of intimate details about me that Tiffany told Mom she would release to the media, but he couldn't tell me more than that."

"Intimate details?" she asked and swallowed. "That sounds pretty scary."

Kian shrugged. "It's news to me. Naked photos, perhaps? I mean, it was in the middle of my modeling career. Nineteen, yeah, that would've been devastating. Now … well … there are already some shots out there of me with body paint on. And in men's underwear. Not a big deal."

Noémie smiled and bit her bottom lip.

"What?" he asked with a tilted head.

"Making a mental note to look that up."

Kian laughed. "You've seen me naked, ma rose."

"And?" she asked, then teased. "If I said there were pictures of me in lingerie I hadn't shared, you'd want them."

He blinked and, with a slow smile, leaned closer. "*Are* there pictures of you in lingerie you haven't shared?"

She giggled and sang, "Maybe."

"*Oh*, here's an idea. Maybe we should take some."

She laughed. "Maybe." Losing the teasing mood, she placed her hand over his. "Do you think she ever recorded you at the sex parties? You said you went to one or two, even if you didn't participate."

The smile on his face dimmed. "Ehhh … maybe? Probably, knowing her." He pulled a face. "But recording devices weren't allowed, for that very reason, and if she did record, it definitely wasn't consensual and that's a crime in New York."

"It is?"

Kian nodded, then sighed. He adjusted his lean against the sofa and turned his eyes to watch Floof preen himself in his cage. "The fact that Mom's already begun legal proceedings means whatever Tiffany has, it was enough to prompt a non-disclosure agreement. Which she's now broken and that's going to cost her. I'll talk to Mom."

"Won't this cause problems?" Noémie asked. "I mean, people can put two and two together and assume Tiffany had something on you."

"Maybe," he mumbled and lifted a shoulder to shrug. "But the way Mom's media release was worded, it was for something else and her 'lies' were an attempt to circumvent the firing."

"I see. What are we going to do?"

"I was advised to ignore it."

Advised to, but would he? "Are you going to?"

He reached over to touch her face and brushed some hair back over her ear. "I can't ignore her attack on you."

She tapped her lips, then reached out to drift her fingers up and down the placket of his shirt. "You said before that if you respond to her, she wins. So maybe we *should* ignore it."

He narrowed his eyes in thought. "I don't know that I can."

"The way I see it, she's in a foreign country, she's alienated you, she's alienated her mother, because if Helena really loves your father"—she patted Kian's chest as he pulled a face—"Helena won't let the implication she was forced slide. And if she doesn't, then she still needs to distance herself from Tiffany because of what she's done. Randall was just embarrassed pretty badly, he mightn't want to help her either and—Kian, I still don't get how he didn't know who I was."

Kian pulled a face. "I only met the guy a few times, but it always seemed like Tiffany had him wrapped around her finger. He did whatever she wanted. Like the sun shined out of her ass or something. She could tell him the sky was green and he would believe it. From what I know, he recently managed to land a job at Pineford Silks and I suspect he used his connection to Helena, and therefore my father and the promise of a lucrative silk deal to secure it."

"Which hasn't been panning out because the silk tender isn't being renewed."

"Exactly. I think Father may have known, which is why

the marketing team was sent to Mom. That way she could refuse, and he could save face with Helena. It's not *his* fault."

Noémie sighed.

He rubbed her belly and continued, "This 'Silk to Pine for' place popped up in New York about a month or two ago, making a lot of noise, and wouldn't you know it, it gets its silk exclusively from Pineford Silks."

"And Tiffany supplies the designs, since she worked as a designer at Celestial, she must be good. So, they do what Celestial does, come in, buy up smaller business and make a new one."

He smiled at her and nodded. "You got it."

"She's really something," she said, shaking her head in dismay. "You shouldn't have anything else to do with her."

He considered that. "Cause she'll take it to mean I still care."

"Let the police deal with it. The best thing we can do is show everyone just how in love with each other we are. This hasn't rattled us. Show her that she's nothing to us. And even though she attacked us, she didn't hurt how we feel about each other."

He smiled at her in that tender, sweet way that made her heart race and turned her insides to goo. "We should get you to bed," he said, standing.

"Are you staying?" she asked as he scooped down to pick her up. "I know my bed isn't very big, but I don't want to be alone."

Settling her in his arms, he smiled. "I am not going anywhere."

CHAPTER 29

With a sigh, Noémie dropped a mesh teddy into the box to be written off. She picked up the tablet resting on a chair beside her and marked the teddy off as to be destroyed for insurance purposes. Some of the meshes were fragile, especially when hit with flying glass. While she could sell them at a discount if they had small snags, some of them were too far gone that the cost and time dedicated to repairing them was greater than the cost of replacing them.

While she hated the idea of throwing away good pieces, she could also use this opportunity to do a stock take and then reorder. The store would remain closed tomorrow so she could make sure all the glass was cleaned out of every crack and all the lingerie was clean.

Kian chatted with the window repairman, helping out as he replaced all of Noémie's glass with unbreakable glass panels. He'd set her up with everything she needed within reach, so she wouldn't have to walk anywhere, and constantly checked in on her. While it was sweet of him, she kept forgetting that she shouldn't be walking, and got scolded a few times.

Lifting another piece from the rack, she inspected it. Tiny snag, barely noticeable, and not in a place that would detract from the rest of the outfit, so she put it in the discounted rack and moved onto the next.

Her phone rang and Noémie took a small break to answer it.

"Hey, babe," Zariah chirped. "How are you today?"

"Tired. Sore. Grumpy."

"Poor baby. I hope Kian's looking after you."

Noémie glanced out the front window at her boyfriend and smiled. "He's fussing. Just like everyone else."

"Can you blame us?" Zariah replied. "It's not every day that our best girl gets targeted. Zane is ready to fly over and bust heads."

Noémie laughed. "As long as he brings you with him."

"That's guaranteed. We're so ready just to buy overnight flights so we can hug you to bits."

"I wouldn't say no," she replied.

"Zane! She didn't say no!" Zariah called. "Pack your bags!"

Noémie laughed again as she heard Zane bellow in the background, but couldn't make out what he wanted to say.

"So, did Tif-fanny make bail?"

"Tif-fanny!" Noémie giggled. "I like that one!"

"Zane thought up a bunch more, not all of them are as … polite as that one, but it's my fave."

"I'll tell Kian, he'll die laughing." Her eyes drifted to him through the window, watching as he laughed with the repairman. "No. As far as I know, she's still incarcerated, but we haven't really checked."

"Good. She deserves to rot in there. How much stock did you lose?"

Noémie sighed. "One complete rack is almost all a write-off. She smacked it and it fell on Veroniqué. Between all the glass on the floor and the people we had trampling around yesterday, I can't sell any of it. The rest of the stock is okay, but I'm checking it all anyway. It's surprising how far that glass flew."

"Ouch. And V's okay?"

"Cuts to her hands and she and Dulcie are pretty spooked."

Zariah sucked in a breath.

Noémie rushed, "—I checked in with her this morning and she's fine. Said it was a case of 'looks worse than it is'."

"Well, good, that poor girl. Give her my love."

"Of course."

"We saw Tif-fanny's release, bunch of garbage that it was. But we also saw Celestial's response. Sooooo," Zariah crooned in a sing-song voice. "What was the non-disclosure agreement for?"

Noémie laughed. "Oh, listen to you. After the gossip. Are you sure your calling was a travel blogger and not a big shot tabloid reporter?"

"Completely off-the-record. C'mon, curiosity abounds. What's she got? Something naughty on Kian?"

"How is that the first thing you jump to?" Noémie complained.

"What else could it be? People are gossiping that Tif-fanny received hush money and now she's come out and said she's Kian's fiancé, there's rumors everywhere!"

"People? Or just you?" Sighing, Noémie dropped the teasing. "We don't actually know. I think Kian's calling his mom later to find out."

"Ugg," Zariah complained, sounding put out.

"If it's something juicy," Noémie chirped. "I'll be sure to keep it from you."

Zariah laughed. "Speaking of juicy, is Kian helping you stock take, or is he imagining you in all of those sexy lingerie items?"

Noémie feigned outrage and embarrassment. "Zaz!"

"Inquiring minds, Noémie! Zane reckons by the end of today, Kian will have a pile of clothes ready to take home for a 'test run'."

Noémie rolled her eyes at the phone. "How do you know he doesn't prefer me naked?"

"I'm sure he does," Zariah proclaimed. "But they love unwrapping too!"

Withholding a giggle, Noémie said, "It's a shame you and Zane aren't here then. All this good product, going to waste. This one is even in your color. Such a shame."

"Oh, ha. Point taken. I'll leave you to your stock take then. Zane's got a couple of interviews today regarding a new manager, he'll be glad to hear you're okay. But don't be surprised if we take the midnight flight!"

"Thanks, Zaz," Noémie said. "I'm fine, really. I'm being looked after. Tell Zane good luck, I hope he finds what he's looking for."

"Anyone other than Scummanager. Let us know if there's anything we can do to help."

"Will do! Love you!"

Smiling to herself, she selected her favorite playlist on her phone to play and then picked up the next piece for examination.

"All fixed!" Kian announced, walking back inside. He dusted his hands together, then wiped them on his jeans. "We can turn the heating up without it all escaping."

"It looks great," Noémie replied, returning an undamaged mesh back to its hanger, and then waved at the window repairman as he packed up his gear. "Thank you."

"How's it going in here?" Kissing her cheek on the way by, Kian headed for the back where he knew the heating controls were.

"Pretty good, I think I'm nearly ready for the next batch," she said as she glanced at the wall and then licked her lips. "Do you know anyone handsome who could put the kettle on? It's in my workshop. I'd like a tea."

With a teasing smile, he said, "So English of you."

"Blame Zariah. And Papa."

"Sure, I can do that."

Zane's song about her and Zariah came on the playlist and Noémie started singing along with the words and bopping along with the music. Zane knew them both well, the song was lively and catchy, and talked about their crazy friendship and how he could never compete with 'My girl's best friend', but why would he want to when his girl was happy to have them both.

"Is that one of Zane's songs?" Kian asked, walking back into the boutique area. "Catchy tune … Oh! This is yours!"

"It is!" she said happily. "Zaz and I usually dance up a storm to this one." With a wistful sigh, she hung the baby doll she'd been inspecting up on the rack.

"I see," Kian said. Reaching her he bent down and spun her chair until she faced him. "We never did finish our dance."

She blinked at him, then down at her feet. "But—"

He scooped her up, wrapped her legs around his waist, and then placed his hands beneath her thighs to hold her weight, cuddling her against his chest.

"Kian," Noémie laughed. "What—?"

The song was too cheerful for a slow dance, it required movement and laughter and revolving around each other. Kian did all the work, waltzing her around, spinning them both, and even exaggeratedly dipping her, all without allowing her feet to touch the ground.

The spinning made her giggle uncontrollably and caused a belly-laughter to bubble up in her boyfriend. Her face hurt from the too-wide smile and her heart pounded from his closeness. Such freedom in his smile, in his movements and she wondered if he'd ever had a chance to dance like this before.

The song ended and the next one on her playlist started, a slower, more romantic song and the mood in Kian shifted too. Aligning their bodies better, he settled into a gentle, side to side motion. Noémie moved her hands from gripping his shoulders to hold on, to playing with the tufts of hair at the nape of his neck.

He hummed. "This is nice."

"It is. I could certainly get used to being this tall."

He laughed at her and kissed her jaw. "Remember how I asked you if anyone's gotten frisky in the change rooms?"

Noémie smiled, knowing exactly where this was going. "Of course."

He grinned at her and wiggled his eyebrows in what she guessed was supposed to be seductive, but really made him look like a rabbit, which in a sense was fitting. "Do you wanna?"

Laughing, Noémie shook her head. "That would be completely unprofessional," she said. "And I don't think my feet could handle it."

Kian pouted at her.

"I will, however, allow you to choose one item to take home."

He burst into an excited smile. "Really?"

Noémie nodded. "Absolutely."

"Awesome," he said, eyeing off the racks of clothing. "Do you have a favorite?"

"Of course."

Eagerness laced his tone. "Which one?"

"That would be telling," Noémie teased. "And it'll be fun to see if you can guess." She lifted her finger and booped his nose. "You get one guess a week, and whatever your guess is, I'll wear it."

"Well, now I'm torn between wanting to know what it is and never finding out."

"It'll be fun searching for it though." Especially since her favorite piece was the baby doll she'd worn for their first time.

Eyes on the lingerie, Kian pressed his lips to her forehead. "That it will. Which ones are the magnetic ones?"

Noémie grinned. "Planning on ripping them off me?"

"Absolutely." He hunkered down to deposit her back on the seat.

"Go on, Monsieur von Brandt," she said, pointing to the section he needed to look at, then tapped him on the rump as he moved toward it. "Make your selection."

"You really should consider going into men's lingerie," he quipped. "I could wear some for you then."

Noémie smiled and let her eyes stroke over him. "All you need is a bit of glitter and I'm good. Or your ass in those jeans. *Mmmm.*"

Kian laughed. "That's why you wanted me in jeans!"

"I will neither confirm nor deny that."

A polite knock at the door turned both their heads to see who it was since it was too early for it to be her parents.

Her eyes widening, Noémie swallowed hard as she looked at Kian, "Did you …?"

Staring at the door, Kian shook his head. "I was going to call her later about the media release, but I haven't spoken to her yet."

She bit her bottom lip. "Are you ready for this?"

"I guess I have to be," he replied and reached for her phone to turn the music off. He walked to the door and opened it just enough to talk to her. "Mom."

"I heard about what happened," Celeste said from the doorway. "I wanted to make sure Noémie was okay."

Kian blocked the door. "She's fine, Mom."

She gave him a watery look. "Kian, may I have a moment of your time?"

Kian stepped away and pulled the door open more.

Celeste entered but stayed close to the exit. "Noémie, how are you?"

"I'm okay," she replied, crossing her ankles beneath the seat. "I can't walk very well at the moment, but it's healing."

"I was appalled to discover what happened," Celeste said, glancing at the glass piles on the floor, waiting for the cleaners to come later that day. "Was anyone else—"

Kian folded his arms on his chest and kept his face emotionless. "How did you know we were here?"

His bluntness didn't seem to affect Celeste. "A hunch,

nothing more. You weren't at home and I knew Noémie had been hurt and her store had been damaged, so I thought I'd take my chances here first. My next stop was the chocolate shop, since Roxanne said she and Jin lived above and I didn't know where Noémie lived. I needed to talk to you regarding a couple of things and you haven't been answering your phone."

Kian narrowed his eyes at her. Thrusting his hands into his pockets, he said, "Alright. Talk away."

"Did you see Tiffany's media release?"

Kian nodded. "And your response. What'd she have?"

Celeste cast a significant look at Noémie. "I don't think—"

"So it *is* sexual in nature," Kian concluded, his mouth twisting in distaste. "You do realize if it was a sex tape, without my consent, we could've reported her to the police."

Nervous, Celeste fiddled with her handbag and shook her head. "It wasn't a sex tape."

"Then what was it?" Kian asked and frowned as Celeste made another not so subtle look at Noémie. "I have no secrets from her, you know."

With an exasperated noise, Celeste complained, "I was *trying* to be discreet. Everyone has secrets and I'm pretty sure there are things you don't want her to know. "

Kian rolled his eyes. "Not everyone. And while I might have things I haven't told her, it's a 'yet' not a 'never'."

Showing a united front, Noémie clasped her hands in her lap and watched Celeste as she waited.

Celeste sighed. "Fine," she announced in a blasé tone, as though it didn't matter. "Tiffany came back to me after accepting the bribe to break up with you, and because I was furious by the way she'd hurt you, I wasn't going to give her a job at all. She could take the money and get out. She said you'd been scratching at her door to satisfy an … 'itch', and that she could string you along as long as she wanted and no amount of money would keep her from doing that. I saw an out, saying that she hadn't broken up with you and that I wasn't paying her anything." With a third glance at Noémie, Celeste said, "She had evidence you were … erm … 'experimenting'."

"Experimenting?" Kian asked with a frown.

Celeste nodded. "Tiffany claimed that if she wanted, she could scare you off women for life. I offered to pay her a stipend and give her the job and then bound everything under a non-disclosure agreement."

Kian stared at his mother in disbelief. "And you believed her?"

"She had evidence."

Noémie chewed on her bottom lip as she watched this play out, not sure if she wanted to include herself in the conversation.

"And it never even occurred to you to talk to me about it?" Kian continued, then laughed. Taking his hands out of his pocket, he shoved them through his hair and half turned away from his mother. "No, of course not, you and Father had disowned me." He laughed again. "I'm bisexual, Mom. I wasn't 'experimenting' with anything." To Noémie, he said, "Remember how I told you about Tiffany's parties?"

Noémie nodded and guessed the rest. "Some of the kisses?"

"Yeah. There was one that was, erm, overly attentive and dramatic. I bet she recorded."

With a watery voice, Celeste gurgled, "Why didn't you tell me?"

Kian raised his eyebrows. "Tell you what? That I'm bi? You haven't exactly been approachable, Mom. Why would I want to?"

"I'm your mother!" Celeste complained.

"You never thought to tell me that my father was having an affair with a woman who I thought was his assistant for God knows how long. Don't act all high and mighty, Mom. Communication has never been great. If you'd talked to me, Tiffany could've been avoided."

"I was trying to protect you," Celeste proclaimed, her voice rising.

Kian huffed and rolled his eyes. "It was for my own good, right? Just like being disowned was in my best interest. What else did you come here for?"

Celeste's brow creased at being dismissed. "Kian, I don't like this tone," she scolded. "You should've told me."

"What would it have changed?" Kian asked, getting angrier with every word. "You didn't trust me to figure out Tiffany wasn't right for me. You paid her off. Then, you tried to do the same thing to Noémie. Not only that, but you also spent years paying off someone to hide the fact that I could be 'experimenting' with the same sex like it was some sort of dirty secret. Do you really want to keep going with this conversation?"

Kian's expression dared her to try, but Noémie hoped Celeste would take the out Kian offered her and let it go. If she pushed now, Celeste could break everything beyond the point of return.

After a tense moment, Celeste dropped her eyes and Noémie allowed herself a small sigh of relief.

With a huffy breath, Kian forced away his anger. "So, what else did you come here for?"

Taking one of the straps of her bag off her shoulder, she rummaged through and pulled out a large envelope. Holding it out to Kian, she said, "The payout for the partnership, as per your request."

Kian's jaw dropped. Reaching out slowly, he took the envelope from Celeste and stepped away from her. With a startled look at Noémie, he opened the envelope and pulled out the papers to read it. After a few moments, he said, "You're … you're not going to fight me on this?"

Celeste lifted an eyebrow at him. "Did you want me to?" she asked, then looked down and allowed regret into her tone. "If I'm honest, I believe the divorce could go bad, even more so because Randall is in town digging up dirt. And whatever dirt he finds, you can bet that's getting back to Helena."

"Is there any dirt to find?" Kian asked, concerned.

Celeste studied him, then shook her head. "I don't want you entangled in our mess. You were right about a good many things and I think striking out on your own will be a good thing for you. You've been in our shadows for too long."

With a torn expression, Kian reached for her, then dropped his hands back to his side. "Mom …"

Celeste squared her shoulders. "Has he spoken to you at all?"

Kian shook his head. "No. I suspect he's waiting for me to make the first move and I'm not going to this time."

Celeste sighed. "So stubborn. He won't be happy when he finds out I allowed you to break the partnership agreement without speaking to him."

Tilting his head, he shrugged. "That's his problem."

"You're a von Brandt, Kian. You were born and raised to live the kind of life your father's money would provide," Celeste said then looked at Noémie. "You, on the other hand, are not suited for that way of life."

Kian bristled and Noémie frowned.

"The von Brandt way of life will eat you up and spit you out and leave you nothing but a husk. That wonderful passion you have, that fire inside, they would extinguish it and the world will be poorer for it. You are never going to be comfortable with the kind of life Kian's father wants him to have." Celeste's eyes were compassionate and full of grief and Noémie wondered if she was speaking about herself.

Kian's tone was slashing. "Neither will I."

"No. You won't," Celeste said and smiled. "You fit into her way of life perfectly."

Frowning, Kian said cautiously, "What are you saying?"

"Don't let your father drag you away from the life you

want to build. I spent years listening to your father complain about your grandfather's rules and restrictions and then he turned around to put those same restrictions on you. And, to my shame, I didn't protect you from that." Her expression turned melancholy as she looked at Kian. "Sometimes I am amazed by how sweet and considerate you turned out, especially when I consider how I raised you. You came back from being disowned a changed person, for the better. Don't lose that." Celeste looked into her bag again. "Ahh. Here," she said and pulled out a brightly colored feather on a stick, which she handed to Kian. "For your cat."

While Kian was staring at the present, Celeste turned and walked for the door. "All the best, petit lapin. You as well, Noémie. Be good to each other."

When the door closed behind her, Noémie prompted, "Kian, go after her."

Lifting his eyes from the cat toy, Kian blinked at her. "Huh?"

"That had to be the most honest conversation you've ever had with her."

"She's probably trying to manipulate the situation," he muttered.

"That's entirely possible," Noémie admitted. "However, even if she's being manipulative, she gave you what you wanted. She let you go. She's *trying,* probably the only way she knows how. Baby steps, but she is. You're in control now, you don't have to let her back in, but if you want to … set the boundaries. Give her a reason to keep trying. A little hope she hasn't lost you completely."

"Oh." Kian blinked again and his expression cleared. "You're right. I'll be back."

She smiled to herself as Kian charged from Chant de La Rose and raced after his mother, Even if his father didn't want to try to salvage a relationship with Kian, Noémie was glad his mother was making an effort.

CHAPTER 30

Smiling brightly, Noémie turned to the next person waiting on her.

"Hello, I'm Mila Bisset," the tall woman said. "I run a community blog for families of people with special needs and my question is two parts."

Noémie nodded. "Absolutely, how may I help you?"

The Paris Adaptive Clothing Exhibition was in full swing. Designers who excelled in adaptive wear gathered to exchange information and present their clothing in a fashion walk or attended presentations by other designers regarding innovations.

Noémie had just completed her presentation about her clothing line and the design choices she'd made. She'd had several models with disabilities demonstrate the ease at which her products could be worn and was now answering specific questions from people after the presentation.

Mila beamed. "First, I'd love to know who your supplier for your magnets is. I was playing with your corset at your exhibit before and they're ingeniously placed and practically invisible, but seem super easy to unhook, and then I was looking at the bra and pantie set, and those magnets are wonderful."

Noémie nodded. "That particular corset isn't designed to be worn for long, it's more of a tease and a temptress look specifically for playtime. I have other corsets with stronger magnets to be used for shapewear; it depends on what the client wants."

Comprehension dawned on Mila's face. "Ooh, I didn't think of that."

Smiling, Noémie continued, "The bra and pantie set are everyday wear, so I needed something that would ensure people they weren't going to be let down at an inopportune moment."

"And what about those customers with pacemakers?" Mila asked.

"I always warn clients, and all magnet lingerie also comes with a press stud counterpart, or can be modified to accommodate a client's particular needs. May I have your business card? I will email you through the company I use for my magnets, I'm sure they'd be delighted to help you."

Mila scrambled through her bag and produced a card. "Excellent. I would appreciate it."

Noémie flipped the card over and wrote on the back to remind herself to send an email.

Mila said, "My second question is regarding affiliation. I would love to include a link to your underwear on my site and I was hoping to get a return link."

"We can certainly discuss that," Noémie replied and added the request to the back of Mila's card as well, and then offered Mila her business card. "If you don't hear from me in a few days, please don't hesitate to send a reminder. I've been a little inundated with requests."

"I'm not surprised. It's quite a venture, I've not seen many people offer anything as wide of a variety as you do. It makes a change from the plain whites and simple studs."

"Oh, there's a few of us around. Every woman deserves to feel beautiful," Noémie said. "It's ever-expanding as more and more people become aware. Thank you for coming!"

The next people to approach Noémie's exhibit was a young preteen in a wheelchair and her mother. One glance over the wheelchair and all the equipment strapped to it gave Noémie a lot of information on why they might be here.

Nervous, the woman asked, "We were wondering if you sold training bras? All her friends at school have already started wearing them and the only ones I could find were over the head or back hooking."

Noémie smiled. "Absolutely," she said and handed the woman a business card, then addressed the girl. "I have an assortment of bras online in a variety of patterns. There are a few available in my boutique, if you'd like to drop in. If nothing suits, I have private fittings so you can commission exactly what you want, down to fabric pattern and clasps." Flicking her eyes back up to the mother, Noémie noted, "While the private fittings can be a little more expensive, we also make sure every need is taken into account. In certain cases, there are grants available with some charity organizations."

The mother gave a relieved smile and relaxed her shoulders as though a weight was taken off them.

Noémie addressed the girl again. "I'm certain we'll find or make something you'll love." Glancing at the Sailor Moon sticker on the girl's chair, she said, "I bet we could even find a star and moon fabric for you."

The girl gave Noémie the brightest of smiles.

Chant de La Rose's business had boomed. The boom had started in January, as a result of all the effort she had put into the lingerie exhibit, and consistently gotten stronger. There had been a hike of interest when her relationship with Kian had become public, but that had soon dwindled and while Noémie was no longer a hot commodity in the media, her merchandise was. Now, in late April, the growth was constant.

The online store was getting orders from all around the world, and it wasn't a single piece that was outshining the others. Everything was selling well. She was getting requests and sending stock from Australia to Argentina, there were even a few shops in London and New York who'd gotten official reseller contracts from her.

She'd even had several organizations contact her about her adaptive lingerie, with specific needs in mind to aid people with limited mobility, including offers for funding to produce lines slanted toward particular disabilities.

It was thrilling, and the long-term contracts coming in meant she needed to hire extra staff so she could devote all her time to designing and creating. She barely spent any time in the boutique itself anymore, spending most of her time in her design workshop in the back. Dulcie had expressed interest in taking on a larger role, supervising the new staff and training them up, as well as working out the staff schedules, so Noémie sent her on a few professional development courses. Now, Dulcie had three new staff members working under her, while Veroniqué worked more as a seamstress/junior designer with Noémie in the workshop modifying or creating apparel.

If business continued like this, and it had no signs that the growth would stop anytime soon, expanding her boutique to include a larger design/sewing area was now a certainty and not a possibility. With Veroniqué a few months away from her degree, Noémie would even be able to employ her as a full-time junior designer if that's what Veroniqué wanted.

It was all so exciting. And a little frightening by how fast it was happening. Her initial figures predicted five to ten years before she could expand to a full workshop. Not two.

She was a hundred percent ready to throw everything she had into her business and help it continue growing. She didn't want to expand faster than she could handle it, but she didn't want to sit on her laurels either. With Kian's help, Noémie had modified her business plan to accommodate the accelerated growth. His support and advice as her business boomed had been invaluable.

News of the von Brandt divorce broke in America the day after Celeste visited Noémie's boutique and the stock market had held its breath. Within hours, Kian was fielding calls from reporters and stock agents to see what involvement he would have in the divorce.

Since Noémie knew little about the stock market itself, she took Kian at his word when he said share prices dropped dramatically when people discovered he'd already left Celestial. He said that a lot of other businesses Richard had his tendrils in also had a similar drop in share prices when the rumor that Richard had tried to force Kian into an arranged marriage emerged.

The American rumor mill had worked overtime, each rumor seemed more outrageous than the last, and while Noémie's name was dragged through the mud on occasion, most of the American media had portrayed her as standing by Kian's side, offering him support while his parents went through a messy divorce. The French media gave the whole debacle no more than a passing glance, but then Richard von Brandt wasn't the von Brandt Paris paid attention to.

Kian gave her complete access to Florian, his publicist in France, who coached her in how to react to the media. What to say, what not to say. How to stand, how to say everything and nothing in something as simple as a smile. Florian was a great boon to the whole situation and helped Noémie feel secure when she talked to the media.

And to everyone else too. Noémie's confidence in public speaking soared. She was more confident talking to clients, event organizers, charities, and other adaptive wear creators. Doors of opportunity were opening and Noémie was going to do everything she could to keep them open.

People like the young girl in the wheelchair and her smile made it worth it.

The whole experience at this exhibition had been extraordinary.

Once question time was over and Noémie had thanked her models, she packed up her equipment from the presentation and walked through the exhibition back to her exhibit to find Veroniqué and see how she was doing.

Veroniqué beamed at Noémie as she approached. "We've had so many inquiries!" she announced, wheeling toward Noémie. "Plenty of orders as well. It's going to keep you busy for weeks."

Bending down, Noémie flicked through all the notes Veroniqué had made on the laptop. "Woah."

"It's been amazing. You're going to need to hire a secretary to help sort through all this."

"Great work, Veroniqué," she said and laughed. "Maybe I should hire Kian after all."

"Might not be a bad idea," Veroniqué said, giggling behind her hand. "Oh, also, Ava left the tickets for tonight."

Noémie nodded. Ava was Noémie's contact within the event organizational circle. The tickets were for the after-party gala. "Ahh, excellent. Do you need a break?"

"I'm good," Veroniqué said. "Dulcie was here earlier to deliver some business cards so she took over for a while."

Noémie nodded and joked, "We never seem to bring enough of them to these sorts of things, do we?"

"To be fair, I don't think anyone anticipated this sort of reception."

Noémie laughed. "That is very true. Okay," she said. "Why don't you head home so you can get ready for tonight? The front doors were closed when I walked past so they've stopped letting people in. I can finish up."

Veroniqué nodded. "Thank you."

Leaving Veroniqué, Noémie sat at the desk and added to the database Veroniqué had started, listing all the requests for information she'd gotten during her presentation. Most of the questions were for information about her suppliers, or requests for fitting appointments, but Veroniqué was right, she'd have a lot of work to get done over the next few weeks.

Noémie smiled.

Standing in her bathroom, Noémie checked her makeup one last time and put on the earrings that had been a gift from her parents for her twenty-first birthday. Patting her hair, she gave it one more spray and slid her flower comb into place above the bun.

Slipping out of her bathroom, she went to her bedroom to dress. She'd opted for something she felt both comfortable and amazing in. A black, v-line dress with a trumpet skirt, the dress had striking golden sequins sewn into the bottom of the skirt. The same bold leafy sequin pattern was copied along the straps of the otherwise open back and across the belt with larger embellishment at the small of her back.

A polite tap at the front door, before Kian slid his key into the lock. "I'm here. Noémie?"

She called, "I'll be right out!"

"Are you naked? Can I watch?"

Noémie laughed. "Nope. Not naked. You missed out."

"Dang it."

Slipping her feet into her stilettos, she grabbed her clutch from her new, king-sized bed, courtesy of Kian and his insatiable need to spread out and the fact he'd been too tall to be comfortable in her other bed. She figured if he was going to be spending the night here a lot, since he seemed to prefer being at her place than his, they may as well be comfortable.

Purrfect had even come for a sleepover once or twice, a fact that had bewildered Floof. The cat and the bird had been very interested in each other but Noémie hadn't been willing to let Floof out to greet Purrfect just yet.

Kian hadn't decided what he wanted to do with his life, but there was no rush to make a decision either. He was taking private photography lessons with one of his favorite photographers and seemed to be enjoying that. Every time he talked about it, he lit up with excitement, explaining the different filters he'd learned, or talking about lighting. With the increase of content on his photography Instagram as he tried out new filters, angles, and locations around Paris, his followers had begun to increase too, without anyone realizing who he was and he was enjoying the anonymity of that. With spring in full swing and the flower gardens gorgeous, he was getting excellent shots. On Sundays, they'd started traveling out to the countryside around Paris scouting for locations and enjoyed visiting the smaller towns.

When Noémie suggested he open an online store for his photographs, selling prints and postcards or even framed enlargements for the wall, Kian had thrown himself into researching that, then had commissioned a website so he could sell them. He earned a small profit and even began looking at selling his photos to galleries. It was nothing when compared how much he earned with his investments, but Kian seemed to appreciate the fact that this was his money, earned purely on his own.

"Wow," Kian said as he caught sight of her. Smiling, he gave her an appreciative once-over. "You look amazing."

A smile lit up her face. "Thank you." Stepping closer to him, she rested her hand on his black jacket and tweaked his tie. "You look handsome as well."

"Who's the designer?" he asked, still looking at her dress. "You look so fierce in that."

"It's my design."

Kian's eyes widened, not from disbelief, but appreciation. "No way, really?"

She nodded. "Final project for ESMOD."

"You are full of surprises."

"Just don't tell your mother," she said.

He ran his fingers over the sequined stitching. "She will want to poach you." He followed the sequined belt around to the back. "Oh my god. Open back. How am I supposed to be a good boy and keep my hands to myself tonight?"

Noémie laughed and gripped his lapels to pull him down so she could kiss him. "Who said I wanted you to be a good boy?"

"Duly noted."

While Noémie had been to fashion galas before, this one had a different look and feel to it from the moment she walked in. There were so many models with disabilities acting as display statues and many of the guests were in wheelchairs, all of whom had been catered to. There were tables wheelchair height scattered around so people could leave empty champagne glasses on them. A lot more sofas had been hired so people could sit, and chairs could be positioned in the gaps in the seating. There was a stage up one end of the hall with a long table near the microphone, with a ramp leading up to the stage.

Ava met them at the door. "Mademoiselle Belrose-Song!" she exclaimed in English with a London accent as she adjusted her wheelchair so she could face them. "Wonderful to see you. I'm so glad you could attend."

"I wouldn't miss it," Noémie said. "It's been a wonderful exhibition. This is my partner, Kian von—"

"I'm Kian," he interrupted with childlike eagerness. "I'm her plus one!"

Noémie blinked at him, wondering when he got replaced by a puppy.

"Pleased to meet you," Ava said, with an unsure but amused smile. "I hope you enjoy tonight." Looking back at Noémie, she said, "We've had a lot of wonderful feedback about your presentations. I've seen magnetic underwear like yours before, but never on such imaginative and provocative pieces. Your invisible magnets and hidden stitch pocket were brilliantly combined and I know there are a lot of adaptive wear designers eager to incorporate your ideas into their clothing line."

Noémie beamed. "So I've heard. I've had a lot of people approaching me about my suppliers and my stitching and I'm more than happy to share."

"I'm so glad you agreed to join the exhibit," Ava said. "I know it was short notice but I do hope you'll join us again in the future."

"I would love to."

Ava beamed. "There's refreshments and champagne on offer. Please enjoy your evening."

"Thank you," Noémie replied and looped her arm through Kian's elbow as they walked away. "What was that about?"

"I've never been a plus one before. It's a unique opportunity for me. Did you see her face?" he continued. "She didn't even know who I was. I can be just Kian, Noémie Belrose-Song's plus one. No one expects anything for me, and all attention is on you. It's *fantastic.*"

Giggling, Noémie hugged his arm. "You are such a dork."

"But I'm *your* dork."

Noémie laughed at his dopey expression. "Okay, Monsieur von *Song.*"

"Von Song!" he crowed and chortled. "I love it! I'm so gonna use that." He leaned over and kissed her temple. "You are amazing."

"Thank you. Would you like wine?"

"I'll get us some," Kian chirped and his excitement was infectious. "I'm the plus one!"

She laughed. "That doesn't mean you need to wait on me."

"What if I want to?" he crooned at her. "What if I want to worship the ground you walk on?"

"You'll get a chance to later tonight."

"Excellent. Can't wait." Another kiss, this time on her head, and a sneaky hand across her back, and he went to search for drinks for them while Noémie looked for Veroniqué.

She didn't make more than ten steps before someone was introducing themselves. She recognized the man before her as one of her exhibit neighbors so was pleased to have a name to go along with the face. He specialized with shoes and wanted to talk about the various hidden stitching she used and whether or not they could work with leather as well, and Noémie suspected the reason he asked was because lingerie was so closely tied with bondage gear.

She had tried her stitch with leather before and was able to give him a little insight into how it could work, although, as she told him, she suspected Velcro would continue to work better on shoes and while he agreed, he looked forward to experimenting with her stitch.

Someone included themselves in the conversation, asking why she didn't use Velcro for her creations and Noémie replied that she did, but it depended on the material she was using. Some meshes and lace tended to get damaged by Velcro.

Kian returned, maneuvering into the circle of people and passing Noémie her champagne glass. Noémie barely had time to thank him and smile before someone else dragged her back into the conversation.

More people began to include themselves in the conversation as someone asked about the magnets and the hidden stitching. Noémie explained that magnets also damaged washing machines or clothing if they weren't removed before washing, which resulted in her creation of a hidden compartment to store the magnets while the apparel was being worn and remove it while it was being washed, without the client having to fiddle with stitching. The idea of using magnets wasn't unique to her, but she managed to find a way to make a client comfortable and secure with magnet placement around such a personal area.

Kian, silent and steadfast, held her hand as the group of designers exchanged plans and various ideas. They talked about the problems in their industry and possible solutions. They talked about politics. They talked about stitches and patterns, hemlines and hosiery, pleating, and plaids.

It was invigorating. She was bursting with ideas, all she wanted to do was go home and sketch. Little words, an idea, a spark, something someone had done that she could grow something else from.

"I know that look in your eye," Kian murmured, low enough that she could hear. "You're inspired."

She curled her fingers around his and stroked his thumb with hers. "Can you blame me? I want to get this all down, there are so many good ideas and designs that will help people that I can modify. It's invigorating to have so many like-minded people in the same place." She turned toward him. "Just warning you, I need at least thirty minutes of alone time when we get home. I need to get this all down."

"Absolutely. I'll make you a cup of tea and keep Floof distracted so you can work."

She beamed at him. "You're amazing."

"You're the amazing one," he said, glancing around, then locked eyes on her. "I've been coming to these sorts of things with Mom for years. For her, it's always about being first. Setting a trend. Lording it over everyone else. Being seen as a powerful figure and having people scrape and scratch for your attention. Watching you here, now … you're in your element. Talking nonstop, sharing your ideas, and listening to others voice theirs, encouraging people, it's … incredible. You're inspiring." He lifted their joined hands and kissed the back. "You don't hide who you are and you make me want to be a better person, just so I'll be worthy of you."

"Kian," Noémie breathed, not sure what to say.

He laughed at himself. "Sorry. That came out a lot sappier than I intended it to be." Releasing her hand, he plucked her empty glass from her hand. "It seems I have erred in my duties as a plus one and allowed your drink to empty. Would you like another one?"

"That would be wonderful."

CHAPTER 31

After a long week, it was nice to be able to leave Chant de La Rose early and head home. Bidding goodbye to Dulcie, Noémie tucked her hands into her pockets and headed for the metro. She had a few hours before Kian would come to take her to dinner with her parents for her birthday.

Arriving home, she kicked off her shoes at the door and let Floof out of the cage so he could get some exercise and fly around her apartment. He chirped at her and burst into song as he happily flew from stand to light fixture to kitchen bench and then landed on her head. Lifting her hand, she invited him to perch on her finger so she could give him scratches.

Knowing that she'd be spending the night at Kian's after dinner with her parents, she cleaned out Floof's cage, left him fresh vegetables, and went to pack a small bag. A shower and a change of clothes and she redid her usual crown hairstyle before sitting down to play with Floof for a while.

Before seven, Kian knocked on her door. Peppering Floof with kisses, she put her precious boy back in his cage.

"Happy birthday!" Kian said, swooping in to kiss her

soundly. She melted into his embrace and the kiss lasted long enough to send a warm heat rippling through her.

Kian chuckled and pecked her nose as he released her. "I got to kiss an older woman. You naughty cougar, you."

Noémie laughed at his silliness. "This is going to be a thing, isn't it?"

"Until September, absolutely." With a silly grin stuck on his handsome face, Kian picked up the bag by the door. "Are you ready?"

She nodded and switched off her lights. Closing the door behind her, she made sure it was locked before she looped her arm through his. "Where are we going for dinner?"

"It's a surprise," he said with a grin and a wink. "Your parents are meeting us there."

"Do I get my present now?"

"Demanding in your old age," he cheeked. "You want your new walking stick now?"

"So mean." Abandoning his arm, she paused her walk down the stairs, waiting until Kian took a step so he was below her, then jumped on his back. "Now you have to carry poor little ancient me."

He laughed and hooked one hand behind her to support her weight. "My pleasure."

Pressing her lips to the back of his neck, she murmured, "And my present?"

"When we get there, impatient old lady."

"*Hrumph*," she grunted playfully. "Watch it, young whippersnapper. You wait until you're my age!"

The two of them talked non-stop as Kian navigated the streets of Paris in his car. She didn't know where he was taking her for dinner, but it was fun to guess, throwing a name of a random restaurant in the direction they were heading at him every now and then to see if she was right.

"I have a confession to make," he said, as he pulled into a street. "We're not going to a restaurant."

"We're not?"

"I have to make a stop first."

"Okay." She frowned at him as he parked the car outside an apartment complex. One that she recognized. "Wait, didn't we come here a few weeks ago?" she asked.

A suspicious and sly grin developed on Kian's face as he snapped off his seatbelt. "Yup. We did."

A feeling of anticipation filled her. "It had that apartment you liked."

Kian had been apartment hunting to downsize from his penthouse apartment to somewhere he could feel comfortable in and he had asked her to accompany him to check out his shortlist so he could get her opinion. They'd all been wonderful homes and she deliberately not asked how much they would cost him.

By far, her favorite had been the gardened apartment. Not in Paris itself, the apartment was in the suburbs, hence its ability to have a garden. The living room opened into the walled garden, with huge windows which meant that even in the winter, the living room could view the garden. There was an outdoor terrace for entertaining that doubled the size of the living room when the doors were opened. The kitchen had been twice the size of her little one, with plenty of storage space. Separate dining area, a laundry, and three good sized bedrooms upstairs, two of them had a balcony that faced the garden, a large bathroom, and the master bedroom had an en-suite and a walk-in wardrobe.

The apartment had been so open and sunny, Noémie had loved it. She knew Purrfect would love having access to a garden to sun herself. The master bedroom also had the perfect wall for Kian's photographs and she could see him being happy there.

Opening his door, he said, "The one that you gushed over."

Pulling a mock-affronted expression, she exited the car. "I did not."

"You so did. I can tell when you gush, right down to the 'I love this place' bounce you had when we left."

Trying to contain her excitement, she blurted, "Did you decide to rent it?"

"No," he said as he strode around the car to her. "I bought it. I'm that extra."

Noémie lifted her eyebrows at him, then giggled. "Yes, you are."

Reaching her, he took her hand. "Let's go look at my new home."

His excitement was contagious and she bounce-stepped behind him. "Did you bring me here so we could 'christen' each room?"

"Now, *there's* an idea," he said, spinning to walk backward so he could wink at her. "Make sure you hold that thought." Opening the front door, he gave her a gentle yank and scooted her inside the apartment first.

The smothered giggle was the only warning she got before Zariah leaped out at the end of the small entrance hallway and blasted her with a party horn. "Surprise!"

Noémie shrieked in delight and pounced on her. "Zaz!" Wrapping her arms around her best friend's neck, she hung on. "What are you doing here?"

Zariah hugged her back hard and bounced on the spot. "I couldn't let my best girl celebrate without me!"

"You were supposed to wait in the living room," Kian scolded playfully.

"Sorry, man," Zane called. "Can't contain her when she's like this."

Peeking over Zariah's shoulder, Noémie was stunned by what she saw.

Kian had already completely furnished the place and had set up for a birthday party. Bright furnishings, yellows, and reds, to match her favorite sunset picture of Kian's blown up and framed as a feature for the wall. Deck chairs on the decking matched colors with the armchairs and sofas in the lounge. Colorful balloons and party streamers were tacked up around the walls, the doors to the garden were open to give everyone more room.

So many people milled around. Friends she hadn't seen in years, and some she'd seen mere hours ago. She spotted Charlie and Quinn grinning at her, her parents and both sets of grandparents chatting in the garden with Mama Talal and Celeste. Veroniqué, Dulcie and her husband and several ESMOD friends were also clumped together in groups, chatting. All the people who were important to her, even—

"Lexi?" she blurted, spotting her. She grabbed Zariah's arm and shook it, certain her eyes were playing tricks on her. Lexi rarely traveled as it was hard for her to move all her specialized equipment. "Lexi's here?"

Zariah giggled. "Yup. Ya boy chartered a plane for her, her carer and everyone else who came from London all special. I tell you what, that was an experience."

Twisting, she gaped at Kian. "You did? Kian, that would've cost a fortune."

Kian shrugged and smiled sheepishly. "With all the drama I've put you through, I wanted to say thank you. Thank you for putting up with everything and being there for me. This was the best way I could think of."

"Before you get mad at him: Me and Zane covered some of the cost too," Zariah said with a smile. "We had planned to do something similar, but Kian's way is so much better."

"*Someone* has to be able to spoil you," Zane said with a mock pout. "You won't let us."

Noémie tackled Zariah in a hug, then spun and pounced on Kian. Looping her arms around his chest, she hugged him hard. "Thank you, Kian. This is the best gift ever."

With a timid laugh, he hugged her back as he walked her farther into the room, then pecked her forehead. "It's not over yet. Go say hello."

"Don't I get a hug, too?" Zane's pout deepened and Noémie released Kian so she could tackle hug him as well. People noticed her arrival and cheered and then she was surrounded by friends and family wishing her a happy birthday and getting hugs in return.

This was her sort of party. A home full of people she knew and loved who were pleased to see her. Who laughed and told stories and enjoyed each other's company. Music down low, spirits high and free-flowing wine. Noémie mingled, spending time with everyone who'd come to celebrate her birthday with her.

Noémie, Lexi, and Zariah hadn't been together like this in such a long time and the three women spent a good part of the evening catching up with each other. Zariah's upcoming wedding monopolized most of the conversation, with all three of them excited to be a part of it.

Noémie chatted with Charlie and Quinn, who had come over to Paris for a holiday and so Quinn could design the interior of Kian's new home. Zane got along with them like a house on fire, the three men became fast friends who seemed to relish teasing Kian. Every time she approached the four of them, they were telling dirty jokes or talking about music or design and having fun.

Celeste being at her party had been a welcome surprise, as was seeing how well she seemed to be getting along with Roxanne and Mama Talal. Noémie had watched Kian and Celeste rebuild their relationship slowly over the last few months and the three of them had gone out to dinner on occasion. Although the divorce wasn't final yet as Richard lived up to his name, Celeste seemed to be in high spirits.

Richard had not yet contacted Kian and Kian was adamant he wouldn't make the first move this time. Noémie didn't know what to do about that situation, but she also knew that not every situation had a solution. If Richard ever wanted to mend the bridges he'd destroyed, that was up to him.

Toward the end of the night, she managed to snatch a moment alone with Kian in the kitchen.

"You look happy," he said, pressing his lips to her forehead. "Enjoying tonight?"

She hugged his arm to her chest. "It's been incredible. Thank you."

He glanced around the room, then locked his eyes on her. "Can I steal you away for a moment?"

Eager to snatch some alone time with him, and perhaps a couple of kisses, Noémie nodded.

Putting his wine glass on the kitchen bench, he looped his arm around her and herded her off to the master bedroom as fast as he could.

It didn't work. Zariah caught them sneaking up the stairs to the bedrooms with a knowing smile. "Don't be long," she warned. "There's cake soon."

"We won't," Kian promised.

Purrfect lay in the middle of Kian's bed curled up in a ball. The blinds had been drawn for privacy and Noémie was pleased to see most of Kian's wall already in place. She flopped on the bed with a sigh and stretched out her hand to scratch Purrfect's chin. "This place is amazing. I'm really glad you decided on it. Bit sneaky, I could've helped you move."

"Nah, I think having it as a surprise was so much better. I wanted somewhere we could both be comfortable," he said, walking into the walk-in wardrobe. "And I think this place suited us best."

"I agree," she said. "It feels so much more like you."

Kian walked back out of the robe. "I have your real birthday present. If you want it."

Noémie sat up. "Real?" she questioned and shook her head. "Kian, this party was enough for me, it's amazing!"

"I firmly believe I should be allowed to spoil you on your birthday," he said, then hastily amended, "And our anniversary, Christmas, Valentine's Day and Chinese New Year."

She laughed.

Sitting beside her on the bed, he passed her a small

paper box. "Happy birthday."

It didn't look like a jewelry box and she could feel something sliding inside it as the box tilted. Hoping he didn't splurge too much on her, especially since he'd already spent a lot of money, she kissed Kian's cheek in thanks and opened it. Frowning at the contents, she tipped it onto the palm of her hand.

It was a small keychain with a little silver rose on it, with a key already attached to the loop. A key on a loop and a ring hanging on the clip at the top. Rose gold, the ring was shaped into a rose and accented with diamonds along the petals, and leaves engraved into the band of the ring. Beautiful and delicate, but it didn't look like an expensive, over-the-top engagement ring she'd thought Kian 'Extra' von Brandt would have gone for. Swallowing, Noémie looked at Kian for an explanation.

"I love you," he said, gazing at her with an adoring smile. "Every day I fall more in love. It's amazing and wonderful and I honestly never believed I would be allowed to be this happy." He rested his hand on her knee. "I want to build a life with you, that's why I bought this place. We walked in and I felt like we both belonged. It was the only place we both felt in sync with, so I knew I had to get it." He reached over and picked up the key itself. "This key is to the front door," he said. "Which you were obviously going to get anyway, but it comes with an offer. When you're ready, and not before, I would love it if you'd move in here with me."

Swallowing again, Noémie touched her finger to the rose ring. "And that?"

"It's a promise ring," he said and laughed at the way Noémie relaxed. "I know, it's silly, corny and completely American of me, but … well … For a while, it felt like all I brought into your life was my family drama. There was nothing you had to hold onto to prove that I loved you."

Noémie looked pointedly at his unfinished wall.

He chuckled. "That's not something you can carry

around with you."

"I beg to differ," she said. "It's very important to me."

"I just … I wanted something concrete to signify us. That we are together. That we chose each other." He unclipped the ring from the keychain and rested it in the palm of his hand. "One day I do plan on asking you to marry me and this is a promise until that day."

Noémie's heart took off racing and her head span in delight. If this was her reaction to him saying it, what was going to be her response when it actually happened?

He studied her. "You don't have to accept it."

She wasn't about to let him take it back. Picking it up, she said, "I'm not up-to-date on which finger it goes on."

His face burst into a bright smile. "Whatever one you like."

After a moment's consideration, she slipped it on the ring finger of her right hand. It was a little loose, so she knew she'd have to get it resized, but that didn't matter.

"It's gorgeous, Kian. Thank you," she said and kissed him. Pouring all her love into the kiss, she tried to tell him everything she felt by using her mouth and her body. All the love she had, all the happiness that they were together, all that joy and lust and love meshed together. She treasured him and she wanted him to know that too. To feel it and believe it as much as she believed in him.

As she buried her fingers in his hair, Kian moaned into the kiss and his hands wrapped around her hips to pull her flush against him. The kiss became heated, Noémie ran her tongue across his teeth and he opened his mouth.

While keeping her mouth firmly attached to his, she shifted so she was standing and pushed against him, coaxing him to lie down so she could straddle his hips. His hands worked their way inside her top to cup her breasts as he grew as carried away as she was.

A burst of laughter from downstairs and Kian pulled away. "We should head back to the party," he said with regret. "They'll miss you soon and I really don't want them to come looking."

Noémie huffed and wriggled her hips. "No fair. We were getting warmed up."

Kian snorted. "We can probably distract them with cake."

"Can't we kick them out?"

"Yeah, that would go down well. 'Everyone get out, Noémie wants to start christening all the rooms'."

"It's my present to me," she declared.

Kian laughed and sat up. Cupping her face tenderly, he said, "Let's go spend time with your family."

Smiling, Noémie rested her hand over his. "Our family, Kian."

His smile lit up the room and etched itself eternally on her heart. "Our family. After that, we have all the time in the world."

THE END

ABOUT THE AUTHOR

Rikkaine Thompson lives in the Northern Territory of Australia with her wonderful husband, one boisterous child, and two grumpy teenagers, and a puppers named Toby.

Eldest of three, she was born and raised in Darwin to teacher parents who fostered a love of reading. Her early years were filled with love, light, and the written word, a love that has followed her all through life.

In high school, her family moved to Katherine, where she met her now-husband and they fell in love. At band camp. Before the movie was popular.

After graduating from high school, she and her husband moved back to Darwin. Having children put a dampener on writing for a time, but as they started school, she found herself with a lot more free time to pursue the things she loved which didn't run away on stubby little legs giggling like crazy when she caught them.

Her parents taught her how to read, then how to turn the written word into pictures in her head, and she taught herself how to put them on paper. Or a post-it note. Or on the inside of her wrist in permanent marker at two in the morning.

Heart of the Rose is her fourth novel.

THE FACELESS SERIES

- Shift
- Twist
- Tangle
- Flare – coming soon

CONNECT WITH RIKKAINE

Follow me on Facebook
   https://www.facebook.com/rikkainethompson/
Follow me on twitter
   https://twitter.com/rikkaine
Visit my website
   https://rikkainethompson.com